# Praise for *In Too Deep*

"*In Too Deep*, by newcomer Ronica Black, is emotional, hot, gripping, raw, and a real turn-on from start to finish, with characters you will fall in love with, root for, and never forget. A truly five star novel, you will not want to miss…"—*Midwest Book Review*

"Ronica Black's debut novel *In Too Deep* has everything from non-stop action and intriguing well-developed characters to steamy erotic love scenes. From the opening scenes where Black plunges the reader headfirst into the story to the explosive unexpected ending, *In Too Deep* has what it takes to rise to the top. Black has a winner with *In Too Deep*, one that will keep the reader turning the pages until the very last one."—*Independent Gay Writer*

"…an exciting, page turning read, full of mystery, sex, and suspense."—*MegaScene*

"…a challenging murder mystery—sections of this mixed-genre novel are hot, hot, hot. Black juggles the assorted elements of her first book with assured pacing and estimable panache."—*Q Syndicate*

"Black's characterization is skillful, and the sexual chemistry surrounding the three major characters is palpable and definitely hot-hot-hot…if you're looking for a solid read with ample amounts of eroticism and a red herring or two you're sure to find *In Too Deep* a satisfying read."—*L Word Literature*

## By the Author

In Too Deep

Wild Abandon

Hearts Aflame

Deeper

Flesh and Bone

The Seeker

**Visit us at www.boldstrokesbooks.com**

# THE SEEKER

*by*

Ronica Black

2009

**THE SEEKER**
© 2009 By Ronica Black. All Rights Reserved.

ISBN 10: 1-60282-128-3
ISBN 13: 978-1-60282-128-6

This Trade Paperback Original Is Published By
Bold Strokes Books, Inc.
P.O. Box 249
Valley Falls, NY 12185

First Edition: December 2009

**Credits**
Editors: Cindy Cresap and Stacia Seaman
Production Design: Stacia Seaman
Cover Design by Sheri (graphicartist2020@hotmail.com)

# Acknowledgments

This book would not have been possible without the help of friends and beta readers. For those who read the early version, I thank you! You kept me going.

Kathi, for your valuable insights early on.

Cait, for your valuable support and insights throughout.

Cindy, my editor, it's always a pleasure.

Stacia, for editing and making sure all my ducks were in a row. I thank you for your always careful eye.

To my publisher, Bold Strokes Books, and everyone involved in this process. Thanks for everything. A million times over.

# Dedication

For Doris Opal Bumgarner

# PROLOGUE

*Seattle, Washington*

Keri Scott-Boudreaux hugged herself on the couch, curling her legs beneath her as the fingers of the tree branches outside clawed hungrily at the windowpane. Heavy blots of rain splattered the glass with every strong exhale of the wind. She stared beyond it, into the inky blackness of night, watching one lone silver cloud drift over the small moon. Below, Puget Sound surged and churned with the storm.

She inhaled deeply, catching the far-off tingling scent of swirling salt water and rain. Normally, she loved a good storm. But tonight was different. Tonight it was more unsettling than elemental.

She rested her hands on her protruding belly and tried to relax. The baby had been kicking throughout the day and she hoped it would now, to help ease her qualms. As if sensing the new life inside her, Jaxx, their large golden retriever, stood to nudge her hand. She patted his head and gave a small smile, always thankful for his calm, protective presence.

The house was quiet, the children asleep. The television played the highlights of her husband's football season in silence. She should be happy and relieved that Tom had played so well and his position was secure ahead of the upcoming draft. She should turn on the lamp next to the couch and flip through the baby catalogues, eager to choose the décor for the new nursery for the house in Lafayette, Louisiana, their hometown. But instead she sat in darkness, calmed by none of it, uneasy.

The phone sat on the end table next to her and she knew she could call her sister and tell her what was going on, but she didn't want to concern her. Kennedy was a behavioral profiler, a former agent with the FBI. Just talking with her always eased her anxiety. But Kennedy was arriving the next day. There was no need to cause her to worry now. Keri was sure to get an earful either way, so she decided to put off telling her until tomorrow.

Just as she was imagining what Kennedy's words would be, a powerful gust of wind dragged the tree branches along the side of the house. Long, loud scrapes seemed to shoot straight up her spine. She jerked and Jaxx pulled away from her, ears back and on alert. She rose quickly and padded across the room to the hallway, where she flicked on the light. She checked in on her boys and found them sound asleep, one strewn across the top bunk with a pajama leg shoved up above his shin, the other curled onto his side on the bottom bunk.

After closing their door behind her, she switched off the hall light and crossed to the other side of the house. Jaxx followed, his head at her hip, claws clicking on the wood floor. She maneuvered through the darkness, fearing that turning on a light would illuminate the house like a giant fishbowl.

She found her way to the kitchen, which glowed under a soft night-light. She opened the fridge for her evening bottle of water and then eyed the control panel to the house alarm. During the day she kept it on "chime," which let her know with a single beep if a door or window was opened. The boys were forever running in and out the back door, setting off the big alarm, so she had been keeping it on "chime" as an effective compromise. And lately she had been keeping everything locked during the day as well, as an additional precaution. So far, things had been calm, and she armed the security system fully at night when she was ready for bed.

She was just about to do so when Jaxx pawed at the back door. Letting him out, she registered the single chime and then shut and locked the door behind him. The assault of cold and rain and salt caused her to shiver. When Jaxx scratched at the door, she let him back inside and secured the locks. Her finger hovered over the alarm panel when she heard it.

Another chime.

She froze.

Blood pounded in her ears.

She focused on the tiny green panel light that indicated the master bathroom door to the backyard was ajar.

A single chime sounded again, rooting her terror completely. The green panel light extinguished. The master bathroom door had been opened and then closed.

A door that she knew for certain was locked.

She stood as still as the black of night, staring at the doorway to the master bedroom. She couldn't move, could barely breathe. Terror seized her entire being. All that separated her from the master bedroom was the dimly lit hallway.

She knew she should grab a knife, a bat, something, anything. But the figure stepped into view before she could move. The presence jolted her and she shrieked, her hand flying up to cover her mouth. Hot tears ran down her face. Jaxx barked, pitched high in fear, and lowered his head.

The figure appeared to be male, covered head to toe in black. A dark ski mask covered the head. He seemed to see her and instead of fleeing, he stepped slowly into the hallway. Next to his thigh a sharp hunting knife reflected the light from the bedroom. He moved carefully, one slow, deliberate step at a time, twisting the knife almost all the way around again and again with the methodical turn of his wrist.

Hot blood flooded her face and chest. Her heart thudded so loudly and thickly it nearly deafened her. She knew she should move. Run, flee, attack. But she was rooted to the spot, sheer, pure, unadulterated fear anchoring her to the floor.

Her breath shook as she whimpered into her hand. She couldn't scream, she couldn't risk waking the boys. But even if she'd been able to, her breath seemed to be rushing too quickly from her body. She thought again of her children.

Her boys. Her angels.

The heat in her face nearly sizzled through to bubble on her skin. The man halted in his approach as Jaxx barked and then whined with fear.

The sound jolted her. Shook her thoughts. Broke through the growing wall of fear. Suddenly, she stood straighter. Her boys. She had to protect them. At any cost.

She grabbed the phone off the kitchen counter. A weapon she hadn't realized she had.

She lifted it and dialed.

"Nine-one-one, what is your emergency?"

"Someone is in my house!" she whispered hurriedly.

"There's an intruder in your house?"

"Yes! He's standing right in front of me." Quickly, she rounded the kitchen island, putting it between her and the intruder but still enabling her a full view of him as he stood at the entrance to the kitchen. Jaxx stuck to her side.

"I've got someone on the way, ma'am, stay calm. Stay on the phone with me. Can you get to safety?"

"No. I can't. Not right now."

"Try to get out of the house."

"I can't!" She couldn't leave the boys, but she wasn't about to share that information.

The masked intruder remained still, angling his head slightly as she spoke to the operator, as if amused. The knife rose slowly and he turned it over as if mesmerized by its glinting.

He wasn't afraid and he wasn't retreating. She knew he could hear her. Did he think she was bluffing?

"Ma'am? Ma'am, are you still there?"

"Yes, I'm here."

The intruder took another slow step.

"I'm on the phone, you motherfucker! Can you hear me? They're coming for you!" Her voice cracked with strain as she shouted. Her body trembled and Jaxx barked shrilly.

She began to cry but she wasn't afraid for herself. Jaxx barked again and she shushed him, glancing hurriedly toward the other wing of the house, terrified her boys had been awakened. The man followed her gaze curiously.

What was this? Why wasn't he running? It was like this was a game, one full of curious amusements and obstacles. Almost as if he enjoyed everything she said and did.

A game. Power. Control. Suddenly her sister's words sounded in her mind. What fed people like this was the fear and control of their victims.

She decided she would give him neither.

Sucking in a deep shaky breath, she spoke to the 911 operator.

"There's a man in my house." She spoke loudly and with complete control. "He came in through the master bedroom door and he's standing in the bedroom hallway in front of me. On the east side of the house."

The man took another step closer to her but she didn't budge. "He's about five foot eight, a hundred and forty pounds. He's dressed in all black with a mask, but I can tell you that he has blue eyes."

The man took another step and raised the knife higher. She clenched the phone as well as her teeth and took a step toward him. Challenging him. It was fight or flight, and she was ready to fight. If she stood any chance at all, she had to trust her instincts and the knowledge of her sister. "He has a knife, he's white." She glanced down at his feet. "He's wearing blue and dark gray Nike runners, about a size eight." She met and held his icy gaze, glaring at him, almost daring him to lunge.

*You will not hurt my children.*

The man stared at her. She could feel the strange energy coming from him. Intense, chaotic, and sinister. The unease in the air caused Jaxx to yip and whine.

From the other side of the house she heard the voice of her son Landon. "Mommy?"

Her body reacted at once. She took another step toward him.

"Leave. Now." Her voice was low and deadly serious. "Or I swear to God I will get my own knife and shred you to pieces."

He turned to look toward the voice as Landon called out again.

Sirens screamed right behind the cry, approaching quickly.

Her rage had grown and now it drowned her fear ferociously, holding it down until it clawed for the surface, bubbles surging upward from its chest. She pulled a knife from the butcher block behind her and then stomped toward the intruder. She screamed at him.

"You sick, twisted fuck!" She threw the phone at him and nearly grinned when it smacked into his forehead. She lunged toward him, knife held high. Catlike, he turned and fled before she could reach him. But she kept on, sprinting and screaming like a madwoman, chasing him out into the stormy black night.

The door to the master bath hung open, the rain and wind pummeling it. Darkness loomed just beyond, having swallowed the intruder whole. Terror gripped her once again and, breathing hard, she yanked the door shut and held it tightly.

"Mommy?" Landon stood at the bathroom's entrance, face contorted with worry.

"Come here," she said, sinking down to the floor. She enveloped him hurriedly, kissing him and holding him tight. Then, as she heard the sirens and the shouts of responding officers, she carried him to the bed, lifted the phone, and dialed. It only rang twice before her sister answered.

"Kennedy? It's me—it's Keri." She fought back burning tears. Kennedy seemed to know at once that something was wrong.

"What is it? What's going on?"

"Someone broke into the house." Sobs overtook her. "He had a knife—mask—I'm so scared, Kennedy. I'm so scared."

Then Kennedy said the words she needed to hear. "I'll be right there."

Keri ended the call, then buried her face in her son's hair and cried.

# CHAPTER ONE

*Four months later*
*New York City at dusk*

She watched and waited. Waited and watched. She was getting good at waiting. Even better at watching.

They would be arriving any minute now. Any minute now she would show her true love that she meant business. She shoved her hands down deep into the pockets of her thick coat. Cold tingles of rain fell upon her face as she looked up into the graying sky. The muted pewter color made her think of her blood. The way it had slowly deadened over the years, feeling as if it had grown darker and heavier, running black inside her, turning her skin gray just like that sky.

Willing her sludge-like blood to do its job, she pushed her way into the gathering crowd, needing to get closer. She had to find the perfect spot. And she had to be close.

The man in front of her was larger, heavyset. Yes, he would be perfect to hide behind. She swayed from foot to foot, the irritation and anxiety of standing and waiting for over an hour settling in. She ran her fingers over the cold steel of the gun she had hidden in her coat pocket. She held it close, warming it with her hand. It wouldn't be long now.

Shoves came from behind her as a couple of kids pushed their way to the front of the crowd just behind the police barrier. They had homemade signs, the words lettered in glitter. They giggled and bounced with excitement. Couldn't be any older than eleven.

She looked away, her skin suddenly on fire. Her stomach clenched as the giggles turned to shrieks of glee. She grimaced. They were in the way.

Briefly and oh so sharply, she thought about killing them. To kill that part that reminded her of herself. The thought clawed at her brain, fighting to stay as it was forced out. Killing them wasn't an option. Too messy. But she would think about it later that night. Mull it over in her mind, play out each possible scenario again and again. Relish it all, mentally roll around in the warm blood and laugh at the brutal screams.

But reality came barreling back. She had to do something. Quietly, she moved to the other side of the large man. Now. That was better. She tried to focus but still the girls giggled and shrieked with excitement.

"Shut the fuck up already," she mumbled.

The large man glanced at her.

Immediately, she looked away from him and tugged on the bill of her ball cap. She couldn't afford to call attention to herself.

Closing her eyes, she forced herself to block everything out and concentrate.

As she shifted her weight she wondered if her true love had read her letters. She had sent dozens of them, wanting and needing the attention of the woman she would die for. But there had been nothing in response. Only an autographed eight-by-ten photo of Veronica Ryan. And that had angered her. She and Veronica were in love. But others were keeping them apart. Well, not anymore. She would find a way. Didn't anyone understand what she was trying to do? Couldn't anyone see that she was incredibly intelligent and one hundred percent devoted to the one who meant the most in the world to her? The one person she knew would understand her if she would only open her eyes and pay attention? Veronica needed her, needed her help. They needed to be together. Forever. She shoved her hands down deeper into her coat pockets. No one had paid her any mind, and now it had led to this.

But it was better off this way. She would take care of things once and for all.

As the first of many limousines pulled up, she eased closer to the big man and gripped her gun harder.

It was time.

❖

Cold-looking rain streaked across the window of the Lincoln limousine as the car splashed through the streets, hurrying to a Manhattan destination. It was dusk in the city and the weather was quickly cooling off as the black of night crept in daylight's door. Shawn Ryan sighed and rubbed her temples. Nervousness and agitation pumped through her blood.

"I told you I don't want to go. I hate these damn things," she said to her wife, Veronica.

"You're going," Veronica replied, not really wanting to talk about it. Shawn was never happy when it came to public appearances, and it was evident in her voice and always evident in her attitude.

"Rory has a fever; I should be at home with her and Kiley. *We* should be at home with our kids." Frustration strained Shawn's throat as she watched the buildings go by, gray and dreary with the New York rain. She was desperate for Veronica to hear her, but she knew she wouldn't listen. She never had before.

Veronica sat in silence as she stared out the vast window of their stretch limousine. Shawn watched her with growing anger, hating that her own wants and wishes were never put first. Veronica met her stern gaze.

"It's one little benefit, Shawn. I think you can handle doing this for me for just a couple of hours." Her voice was patronizing, her look blank and unconcerned.

"A couple of hours?" Shawn asked with excitement, but careful not to yell. She never yelled and she wasn't about to start now. She prided herself on always being the calm and levelheaded one. Veronica was the one who walked the wide range of emotions, not her.

God, she hated these kinds of engagements, and they were never just a couple of hours. The benefits, the people, the fans, they always required more than your time. They demanded your life.

"I don't want to hear this," Veronica said shaking her head, as if Shawn's words were annoying. "We're obligated, you know that."

"When's it going to be enough, V?" Shawn clenched her hands together in her lap, so tired, so frustrated, so damn fed up. "When the kids are moved out and married? Then will it be enough?" She sighed, her voice wavering with emotion. Veronica had a demanding career, and lately she had been spending much of her time away from home.

It seemed she saw more of Veronica in the magazines than she did in their home.

"It's work. It's my job. It's what pays for our home, our vehicles, our life." Veronica glared at her, the look that always was a warning. Then, just as quickly as it had spawned, the look was gone, replaced by surprise as her cell phone rang. She dug it out of her expensive tailored suit pocket. "It's Clair, I'll call her back. She put these new hair extensions in, what do you think?"

"Don't do that, V," Shawn said, swallowing back her tears of fury.

"Do what?" Veronica fingered her hair.

"Change the subject, like what I say doesn't matter."

Veronica sighed, dropping her hand away from her hair. "What were you saying?"

Shawn wrung her hands and spoke, trying her best to remain calm. "Don't act like you have to do this. Like we're living paycheck to paycheck. You've made millions of dollars in the span of your fifteen-year career. We're set for life and you know it." She knew it wasn't about the money and she hated when Veronica pretended like it was. The plain and simple fact was that she craved the attention, craved the limelight. She couldn't live without it. And she had sacrificed her marriage and family in order to keep it.

"Jesus, Shawn," Veronica whispered with anger. "What the hell do you want from me?" Her emotions were quickly getting the better of her, as they always did, and Shawn braced herself for the wrath of her temper.

"Don't yell." Shawn kept her voice low, not wanting the driver to hear. The last thing she wanted was to read about this squabble in a tabloid magazine.

They sat in silence and both acknowledged the presence of the driver. The divider was up but they both knew from unfortunate past experiences that he could still hear if they raised their voices.

Shawn eased the tension in her hands and watched Veronica's profile. Her skin was like cream, her sculpted cheekbones brushed with the crimson of her harnessed temper. Shawn sighed again, calming her shaky breaths. She hated it when Veronica yelled and she didn't want to fight with her right now. She didn't want to fight with her ever. But fighting was one thing they did well, and lately they had been doing a lot of it. She met Veronica's dark eyes and spoke calmly. "I want you to tell me that this will all stop soon. That you'll come home and stay home." *Please tell me you will. Tell me there's hope for us after all.*

Veronica stared out the window at the many faces on the street blurring with the rain. The limousine slowed and they passed a line of police officers who directed the vehicle up alongside the red carpet.

"I can't promise that. You know I can't."

Shawn bit her lower lip and tried to fight back the tears that were biting at her throat. *So there it is. This is how things are going to be.* She stared at her hands, her body burning with the need to lash out in hurt and anger. Why couldn't Veronica just walk away from all the glitz and glamour? Why couldn't they just turn around and go home? She didn't understand. She never would.

"I won't do any more of these benefits," Shawn said as the door opened directly next to her. If Veronica wouldn't give for her, then she would stop giving as well. But inside she held little hope, knowing that little would faze Veronica. Nothing would stop her. Not even the loss of Shawn's support.

"Fine," Veronica replied, her voice stern.

Shawn climbed from the vehicle, fists clenched at her side. Veronica ran one last practiced hand through her hair before stepping out into the cold drizzle after Shawn.

Bright flashes assaulted her as the dozens of photographers began snapping photos. She and Shawn were America's famous lesbian couple. Veronica the successful actress, Shawn the beautiful, doting wife.

That was an image Veronica wasn't about to let slip away. She waved at the crowd as her large bodyguard Monty approached from the car behind. He was flanked by two more security personnel she'd not taken the trouble to get to know. Monty shut the limousine door behind her and opened a black umbrella but she shook her head, refusing it. She wanted nothing impeding her grand entrance.

"Veronica, over here!" photographers yelled immediately, drawing her into their world, snapping photo after photo. She stood proudly, posing from side to side.

"You look great! Who are you wearing?" Their flashbulbs lit them up in a startling lightning storm. She moved further along, smiling and waving, leading Shawn gently by the hand. Her security moved with them, keeping their immediate path clear. Her public relations person wasn't there to guide her, so she began readying herself for the quick interview stops up ahead. She smiled again, enjoying the fact that she would be able to pick and choose which networks she spoke to and which she would snub.

The enormous cluster of fans began to scream as she neared. "I love you, Veronica!" Young girls screamed, waving their arms, holding up homemade signs lettered in glitter.

"I love you too!" she yelled back, blowing a kiss. The crowd laughed and cheered, thrilled at her attention. She left the carpet, touched by the young fans, and approached a few kids who stood behind the police barrier. They squealed with delight and jumped up and down as she shook their hands. Their hands felt small, cold and damp from the rain. She smiled once more and pulled away. The shouts continued to come from every angle as she waved at the crowd.

The noise filled her ears as the excited faces of the fans filled her mind. Adrenaline surged through her pleasurably, causing a warm rush through her veins. This was her mantra, her drug, her addiction. And she would be damned if she was going to give it up. These people needed her almost as much as she needed them. It was her calling, it was who she was.

Glowing from her high, she looked to Shawn, who stood waiting for her graciously on the carpet as she always did. She met her gaze briefly and knew that Shawn was silently reminding her that they were not done talking. Shawn was still upset. But she stood smiling, a plastic yet dazzling smile. Veronica smiled back and by all appearances they looked like the happiest, most beautiful couple on the planet. Veronica blew another kiss to the crowd and took a step toward Shawn. She grabbed her hand, ready to accompany her inside.

As they turned to walk down the red carpet together, a loud pop rang out. Instantly, Veronica felt Monty slam into her, tackling her to the ground, knocking the wind completely out of her. The crowd screamed as people panicked and tried to run. She looked to her empty hand where only seconds before Shawn's had been.

Frantic, she searched and found Shawn on the ground next to her, her blond head contrasting sharply with the lush red of the carpet. Her sparkling eyes were wide and frightened, focused on Veronica like a trapped animal. A spot of dark red pooled on her shoulder, drowning more and more of the sequins of her dress with every passing second.

Veronica cried out for security to cover Shawn, but the other guards were surrounding her solely, completely focused on her rather than Shawn. Monty was yelling, trying desperately to shield both Shawn and Veronica with his body as he tried to direct the other two guards. In seconds that seemed like an eternity, several more security guards rushed to them and Monty moved to Shawn.

Screams continued to come from the crowd as people tried to run for cover. Chaos erupted around Veronica and her heart thudded madly in her chest. She watched as men and women tripped over one another in order to get away. Helpless and trapped by the bodies of the security guards, Veronica reached out and grabbed Shawn's hand. It felt cool, bringing a sob to her throat. Now it meant something more than her apparent indifference. Now it meant something dangerous. More men arrived, surrounding them in a protective tight circle as they yelled, fingers pressed to their earpieces.

Veronica breathlessly tried to reassure Shawn. "It's okay, Shawn. It's okay." She held Shawn's gaze, shuddering at the terrified look on her face. Shawn looked scared to death, her lower lip trembling. Monty pressed on her shoulder, trying to control the bleeding, screaming for an ambulance.

"It's okay. It's okay," Veronica said again.

As she repeated the words over and over, she thought back to Shawn's simple request. If she would've listened to her, this wouldn't have happened. If they had stayed home, everything would be okay. But she hadn't listened. Instead, she had put her family in danger by exposing them to the public. And now Shawn had been shot.

She clenched her eyes shut as one of the security guards repositioned himself atop her, still determined to keep her down.

She looked back at Shawn, helpless.

She had paid the ultimate price for fame. She had paid with her family.

Why couldn't she stop?

# CHAPTER TWO

*Lafayette, Louisiana*

"Ninety-nine, one hundred!" Kennedy Scott declared as she crept through the lush green of the Louisiana lawn. She grinned as she heard the giggles of her young nephews coming from behind a tree.

"I see you!" she shouted as the boys sprang from behind the large trunk. She dove dramatically, purposely missing them as they shrieked by her with glee.

"Auntie Kenny, come get me!" Luke shouted, running as fast as he could in his denim overalls.

"Yeah, come get us, slowpoke!" Landon mocked, a playful grin on his face. Luke stopped running ahead of him, and the two collided. Both boys tumbled and then crawled their way back to a stand, full of excited giggles.

Kennedy stalked toward them, back hunched, fingers out like claws. "I'm going to get both of you and when I do, Poppy's going to cook you with the crabs!"

"Agh!" the boys shrieked and then giggled as she ran along after them, picking them up and slinging them over her shoulders in victory.

"Instead of a crab boil we're going to have a Landon and Luke boil!" She carried them toward the barbecue in the backyard where the large boiler sat.

"No, Auntie Kenny, don't cook us!"

"Don't cook you? Why not?"

"'Cuz we're yumans, that's why!"

"Yumans?"

"Yeah!"

"Well, yumans are good!"

"No!"

Laughing harder, she flipped them over and eased them to the ground.

"Then how about if I just tickle you!"

"Yeah!"

She couldn't help but laugh, their hearty giggles contagious. They were rolling on the lawn when the back door to the house opened up.

"Kennedy!" Keri stood holding the phone.

Landon and Luke saw their advantage and jumped on her upper body, smothering her with tickles and mock elbow jabs in return.

"What is it?" she called out as best she could from beneath the boys.

"It's the phone for you." Keri approached and held out the phone. Kennedy looked up in surprise and the boys stopped their roughhousing, sensing the change in her.

"It can't be for me, I'm on vacation." She frowned, resting her arms along her knees, catching her breath. It was why her cell phone was switched off and her apartment was empty and gathering dust. She was needed here.

"He said it's urgent."

Kennedy pushed herself up, noting that Keri appeared equally concerned. Kennedy took the phone carefully as if it were fragile.

"Scott."

"Kennedy, it's Allen."

She tensed, knowing immediately it was very serious, something that would be impossible to ignore. "I'm on vacation, Allen." He was her longtime friend and mentor and she knew he wouldn't call unless it was urgent. Still, she hoped for some reason he had made a mistake. That maybe her reminding him of her much-needed time off would somehow change his mind.

"I know and I'm sorry. Sorry for having to call you at your sister's. But this, I think you should hear me out on this one."

She sighed. "Go ahead."

"Have you seen the news? It's all over the news."

"Why don't you just tell me? I'd rather hear it from you," she said, her anxiety growing.

"It's Veronica Ryan."

"The actress?" She turned away from her nephews, who swung happily on their swing set. Her trained mind immediately raced to possible scenarios.

"Yes," Allen said. "Her lover was shot yesterday evening."

"And?" It was terrible news, but she knew he wasn't yet to his point. And all she wanted to do was to return to her nephews, to pretend like he'd never called.

"She's received threats."

"The threats came before the shooting?" Where was her security? Why was she even out in public?

"The threats had been coming by mail," Allen explained. "But they weren't discovered until this morning."

Suddenly, her mind whirled and her mouth grew dry. *Letters. Unwelcome and strange. An attempt on a life.* The situation in Seattle came rushing back. She had almost lost her family to an obsessed fan. And now it was happening again, to some other family. It always would. It would never end. As long as there was fame, there would be the possibility of trouble, a fan with nothing else to live for.

"What's this have to do with me?" She knew, but she held out hope that maybe Allen only wanted a phone consult from her. She'd left the FBI over a year ago to go out on her own. But even that had seemed to be too much. "You know I'm not working right now. I just can't do it. Not now."

"She wants the best."

"I'm on vacation." Another scenario came to her mind. *Children taken from their beds, stripped from their bicycles, their tiny bodies found in ditches.*

She thought of Luke and Landon. *I can't do it. Not now. I can't leave them.*

"I know, but damn it, Kennedy, her wife was shot. She's scared for her kids."

Kennedy gazed at her nephews. They swung happily on their swing set, cheeks red and cherubic from the rough play, grass staining their knees, purple Kool-Aid marking their upper lips. God, how she loved them.

"Find someone else. There are plenty of others who—"

"She's asked around, Kennedy. Everyone tells her you're the best. The Bureau is in on this, but she wants you too."

Kennedy shoved her hand deep into her jeans pocket. She looked to her sister, who was listening intently, a look of anguish on her face.

"Listen, Kennedy, this is big, huge. After this you can really name your own price, make more money—"

"It's not about money, Allen. It's about…" *Family, protecting them, keeping the evil in the world away from them.* Evil that she knew all too well. Evil that would forever haunt her dreams "My time," she finally finished, unable and unwilling to explain further.

"Kennedy, they're terrified. I know you and your family know how that feels. All they want is an evaluation. A simple profile and your suggestions."

"Where?"

"New York."

"I'll think about it." As she said the words, Keri turned and walked silently back into the house, leaving the door open behind her.

"Veronica Ryan has already sent her jet to Lafayette Regional. So whenever you're ready."

"I said I'll think about."

But Allen knew her too well. Her empathy continuously beat out her reason.

"And, Kennedy? You're doing the right thing by helping her."

She heard the click as the call disconnected, then, whispering, "Tell that to my family," headed inside after Keri.

"I didn't say I would go," Kennedy offered softly. But Keri kept wiping the kitchen counter, taking out her frustration on the dish rag.

"It's not fair, Kennedy," she finally said. "Up until…recently… you've never taken any time for yourself. You've been a slave to the Bureau, working case after case. I mean, I know it's your job and God knows you've got a gift for it. But I'm glad you quit. It was too much. The things you've seen, it was getting to you. I thought you going out on your own would make things easier on you, but…nothing's changed. You're still alone and distant, a shell of who you once were."

Keri tossed the dish rag in the sink and sighed, her lower lip trembling. "And I'm still…" She looked away, her voice strained and weak. "Scared."

Kennedy knew about Keri's nightmares, the constant anxiety that seemed to plague her. She knew because she'd been experiencing the same things for months. She wished more than anything that she could take on Keri's suffering herself, but she couldn't. All she could do was be there for her, give her some comfort with her presence.

"I know," Kennedy whispered. What happened in Seattle still haunted them all. Even though Keri had acted courageously and intelligently, they both still thought about all the different things that could've happened. Kennedy tried to talk to her about it, but Keri often refused, holding the darkness within, jumping at every sound, pacing the house at all hours of the night. They had always been close, but now they were twins. Twins trudging through the darkness of fear.

A heavy dread washed over her. The pain and suffering she continued to endure were hazards of her job. Something she knew she'd have to deal with. But Keri's suffering was unfair and undeserved.

Kennedy needed to be there for her. To try to make it better. Which was why the thought of leaving her family now seemed unimaginable. She had been with Keri and the boys since immediately after the intrusion, refusing to leave their side. She should've been there sooner. But the kidnapping and child murder cases that had haunted her career and nightmares for years had needed her attention once more. They'd found another body and were nearly convinced it was related to the previous cases. But the subsequent investigation had proved otherwise, and her longtime case was still unsolved.

Shadows from the past walked through her mind as she thought of the thirteen children: six girls, seven boys. All of them taken, some from their beds, others from the back lawn. She could still see little Tyler Hobbs's bicycle lying on its side in the grass, a red-tinted Popsicle stick consumed by ants under the handlebars. He had been pedaling around the backyard, eating a Popsicle the last time his mother saw him.

That bicycle stuck in her mind. Midnight blue with bright yellow lettering and matching seat. Dozens of Pokémon stickers clinging to the frame. She could hear his laughter, see his smiling face as he dug up the sand in his sandbox. She'd watched the home video of the boy dozens of times.

So when she got the call it nearly killed her. Little Tyler Hobbs had been sexually assaulted and strangled, his body dumped in a ditch on an abandoned road, five days after he went missing.

The other cases had similar endings. They'd never caught the perpetrator. Her one unsolved case. Until Keri's intruder. Now she had two.

Frustrated, she ran her hands through her hair. The baby monitor on the counter lit up. She listened as her infant niece cooed from her crib. Keri disappeared down the hallway, already calling to her.

Guilt and fear washed over Kennedy once again. How could she leave them now? Even if Tom was home, the thought still made her uncomfortable. And he would be leaving soon to start the season. Plus the fact that he didn't know the first thing about the obsessive criminal mind. But what she knew terrified her. The intruder had known too much. He had watched and studied for an extended amount of time. He had known that house, known Keri's routine, when and where she was at all times. He had wanted Keri. To possess her, control her, own her. And most likely…to kill her.

Kennedy knew he was probably still obsessing, carefully waiting, planning his next move. His fantasies would never go into remission. Keri would always be on his mind. Kennedy thought of the letters. The ones Keri hadn't told her about until it was too late. Four of them. Sent directly to the house. Praising Tom on his abilities and praising Keri on her beauty and motherhood. They were handwritten on plain white paper. Dark blue ink, and simple enough in content. But they were intrusive and unwelcome. And seemingly scrawled with certainty and done quickly, as if the writer wasn't concerned with errors and appearances. This troubled Kennedy. It made him look rash and impulsive, ruled by his emotions. And arrogantly confident. Just like the break-in. So bold and fearless. And yet so carefully planned. He could've slashed Keri to bits but he hadn't. No, the offender was organized, but his control was wearing thin. He would soon become more bold, more careless. And much more dangerous.

The thoughts weighed her down. She walked to the stove and stirred the pot of seasoned beans. Of course there was no guarantee that the letters had come from the intruder, but Kennedy was willing to bet they were. Keri had also told her about a man in the stands at the home games who had sat nearly sideways in his seat to stare at her. The first time she saw him he got up and left. The second game she had gotten up and left. By the third game, she had requested him removed and security had escorted him out. And then the letters had started arriving.

Keri described the staring fan as a small-framed white male in his early thirties.

A needle in a haystack.

Keri returned to the kitchen carrying Natalie, Kennedy's bright-eyed niece. Her dark hair was pinned up in a tuft, while a reflective pool of drool glistened on her chin. Kennedy smiled at the sight of mother and daughter settling down at the kitchen table. Instinctively, she moved to the stainless steel fridge and retrieved a bottle of breast milk. She heated it in the microwave for exactly twenty seconds, shook it to make sure the heat was even, then promptly handed it over to Keri, who tested it on her wrist.

Natalie took it eagerly and closed her eyes.

Kennedy watched in silence, touched somewhere down deep every time she saw the two together. She smiled inwardly as warmth spread through her, replacing the blackness of fear. She stirred the beans again and moved to sit at the counter. As she got comfortable on the stool, she cleared her throat, knowing she still needed to discuss matters with Keri.

The Ryan case called to her, as many cases did. Perhaps it was because of Seattle, because there was a family in fear involved. Victims, like Keri. Maybe she could help to catch their assailant. Then maybe at least one family could sleep in peace at night.

Natalie suckled her bottle noisily and Keri spoke, sounding nowhere near ready to discuss Kennedy's leaving. "The new Adidas catalogue came." She motioned with her head, letting Kennedy know where it sat on the table. "Go ahead and pick out what you want now so I can place the order."

Kennedy rose from the stool, not missing the fact that Keri didn't want to discuss anything serious. She sat across from them and began mindlessly flipping through the catalogue. Tom had a contract with Adidas and received ten thousand dollars a year in free merchandise from the company.

"I'm not sure what I should do here," Kennedy said softly, glancing up from the catalogue. She thought of their past. They had been raised by a young single mother, which had forced them to grow up quicker than they should have. Kennedy had been more of a mother to Keri than anyone else. Especially when their mother had to be away for seventeen hours at a time, leaving them alone in the small house to go out and work multiple low-paying jobs just to survive.

Keri met her gaze from across the table. She wanted to beg Kennedy to stay, but she knew she shouldn't and wouldn't. Kennedy had a gift for reading people, especially criminals, and if she could help Veronica Ryan's family, then she had to let her go. She had to let Kennedy go be who she was. She glanced at the new life she held in her arms. Tom was home, and with Kennedy's help, they had hired a security team to watch the house and property and go with them wherever they went. She had to trust that things would be okay. With a weak smile, she swallowed and said, "Go. They need you."

"Keri…"

"Go, Kennedy. This address is unlisted, the property is gated off and guarded." She rocked Natalie and kissed her lightly on the forehead. "Go help that family. We'll be fine."

❖

*Scarsdale, New York*

She sat in her little car and watched. The street was moist from a recent cold drizzle, some dead leaves blowing in the slight wind. She stared at the wet pavement, watching the dry leaves weave patterns as they blew in circles across the ground. It had been roughly forty-eight hours since the shooting, and the urge to see her work had been too great to resist. She had to see her true love, to know what she was doing, to see if she had understood the message.

A car passed by and she hunkered down into her thick hooded sweatshirt. She squeezed her arms tighter across her chest as the bite from the cold wind penetrated her vehicle. She was close now, so close she could feel her true love nearby. Every time she got this close her body hummed with powerful excitement. Just knowing her love could be near, knowing they were breathing the same air, experiencing the same weather, the same sights, the same smells, sent thrills right through her.

She could still recall the cold drizzle pelting her hat and shoulders, the tips of her ears. She could see Veronica's dazzling smile, the twinkle in her brown eyes, the two veins under the delicate skin of her neck… and then her scent had come as she shook hands with the girls. Light and dizzying and truly blood slamming. It had coursed through her as quick and as hot as lightning, stirring an animal yearning in her she'd never known. And then Veronica moved away, grabbing hold of her wife's hand. Shawn. The smiling blonde. The thief of hearts in a silver dress.

She cranked her car and put it in drive. She pulled her sunglasses down from her crooked hanging visor and eased them on. Her blood pumped heavily as she drove down the street and made a left turn. She was getting closer now and the feel of her true love was growing stronger, pulling her like a magnet. But she fought the force of it and turned when she reached the entrance to the gate, taking in all she could as she drove away.

A dark Lincoln sat at the gate awaiting entry. She swallowed hard and stepped on the gas.

Who was in the car? Veronica? A friend? Family?

Fury sizzled like static as the frustration of not knowing rushed through her. A gust of wind blew more stiff leaves across the street. Someday. Someday soon the person walking through the gate would be her. Someday soon she would be the one who was needed.

❖

Kennedy leaned back against the seat of the Lincoln Town Car. They had been driving for the better part of an hour, heading away from the city to one of New York's suburban towns. Even though her feet were firmly on the ground, she still felt a bit nauseous from the flight so she'd inched down the window for some fresh air.

As she breathed deeply, she glanced at her surroundings. The clouds were gray, wispy, and thick, but not quite ready to shed more rain. The neighborhood was upper class, large Tudor-style homes nestled in thick, abundant acres of lawn. Most of the homes had private entrances, the properties walled off. She eased forward in her seat to look through the windshield. They'd stopped at a gate and she could see the rear of the mansion through the bars. This house was like its neighbors, private gate and walled-off property. She hadn't expected anything less.

The driver lowered his window and spoke into the call box. The response was clouded with static and difficult to understand. Frustrated, the driver leaned out the window and shouted, but only more static came back.

Kennedy looked around quickly, searching for a Bureau presence. But there was no one guarding the gate, no camera eyeing the cars that drove up or drove by. She saw only two vehicles inside the gate, a Range Rover and a minivan, both parked inside a garage flanking the house. No one was walking the property. And no one was coming in clear on the call box.

Hurriedly, she climbed out of the car.

The air felt cool and misty against her skin. She didn't bother retrieving her coat but instead moved to the front of the car. The driver ceased shouting and eyed her.

"I'll be right back," she said calmly, giving him a small wave, silently asking him to wait. Carefully, she stepped up onto the hood of the car and turned toward the gate.

"Hey, what the hell," the driver called out and she could hear his door opening.

"Shh." She glanced over her shoulder at him and waved him back. And before he could argue any more she hoisted herself up onto the gate. Slowly and with care, she eased herself over and jumped to the ground. Her feet stung as she straightened. Walking out the pain, she gave one last comforting look to the confused but silent driver.

Heart beginning to leap with excitement, she jogged toward the back entrance of the house. As she came to the end of the lawn and reached a driveway, two big black dogs came barreling toward her. A spark of fear tried to catch aflame inside her, but she wasn't afraid of dogs and she knew she had to show calm assertiveness. Their barks were pitched high in excitement and she stopped her run to greet them.

"Hey, puppies." She held out her hands in welcome. She relaxed a little when she saw that they were young black Labradors. Their fur felt like moist satin, their tongues heavy and light pink as they panted.

"Good, guys," she cooed, patting them on the head. "Come on, let's go."

They followed her eagerly as she picked up her pace again.

She glanced at her watch. Two minutes in and she had penetrated the second barrier: the dogs.

She slowed her pace as she came upon one of the back entrances. A Mercedes sedan she couldn't see from the gate sat on the far left of the house, an M.D. tag on the plate. A physician was at the house, but still no sign of any FBI agents. She thought for sure based on what Allen had said that the place would be crawling with them.

She reached one of the back doors and caught her breath. The dogs were still by her side and she scratched them pleasantly along their backs. They weren't trained to attack, they were only there for appearances. She glanced back the way she had come, noting the beautiful and secluded property the house sat on. She ventured it was at least five acres of land. Five acres of unsupervised land. Determined and unwilling to let up, she turned and clutched the door handle.

It was unlocked. Softly, she opened it. A soft beep sounded and she saw a light illuminate on a security control pad. She stiffened, waiting. But no one came. She closed the door behind her and noted another sound, the repetitive plunk of piano keys. The same notes, again and again.

*Do re mi fa sol la.*

*Do re mi fa sol.*

Mirroring the sound from the piano keys was the pitter-patter of quick-moving feet on the upper level. A child was running and laughing. She headed in farther, noting the warmth and comfort of the house and the smell of fresh-baked cookies. She walked quietly on the polished wood floors, the dogs at her side. The walls were a deep beige and covered in expensive-looking painted canvases. Fresh flowers bursting with color sat in vases on nearly every end table.

She found her way into the kitchen.

"Hello!" she called out. No one seemed to hear her. She glanced at her watch. Four minutes in and she was inside the house. Her stomach lurched at the lack of security. She leaned on the counter and the dogs sat at attention on the tile floor, waiting for her command.

Her ears pricked as a surge of static sounded from behind. The intercom box to the gate was mounted on the kitchen wall. She pressed the button and tried to communicate with the driver but had no luck. Only more static. She was just about to press the button to open the gate when a stern voice spoke.

"Excuse me? What the fuck do you think you're doing?" The voice was strong and female and very unhappy.

Kennedy turned slowly, knowing at once to whom the voice belonged. Veronica Ryan.

Meeting Veronica's dark brooding stare, Kennedy said, "I'm Kennedy Scott."

Veronica was silent for a moment and Kennedy wasn't sure if her name had signaled recognition or not.

"Who let you in?"

"I let myself in."

Veronica scoffed and moved to the large stainless steel refrigerator for a bottle of Vitaminwater.

"You're the hotshot FBI agent," she said before taking a couple of small sips.

"I'm no longer with the Bureau."

She twisted the cap back on. "Mmm. Right."

Kennedy studied her. The first thing that struck her was that Veronica didn't seemed pleased, much less grateful, to see her. Allen had relayed just how badly Veronica had wanted her, so she was a little surprised at Veronica's apathy and almost irritated tone. The second thing that turned her stomach was the fact that Veronica didn't seem the least bit concerned with how she had come to be in the house.

"Aren't you interested in how I gained entry?"

Veronica returned the bottle to the fridge and smoothed down her zip-up Valor jacket and matching athletic pants. When she met Kennedy's gaze again, her eyes flashed with intensity.

"I just assumed you had no manners."

Kennedy straightened, a bit stung. "Your intercom at the gate doesn't work. So I climbed the gate and came in through the unlocked door."

Veronica didn't speak, just listened. One of the dogs yawned and lay down next to Kennedy's foot.

"The attack dogs are vicious, aren't they?" Veronica said.

Kennedy wasn't amused. "It took only four minutes for me to get from your gate to inside your front door."

"Four minutes, is that all?" For a brief instant she appeared a little concerned. But it passed just as quickly. "I'm glad you're here, then." She gave a thousand-watt smile that had surely blinded millions of fans.

It didn't shine so bright with Kennedy. "What if I had been someone else? Would you be concerned then?"

"Oh, I'm concerned. I'm just not going to have a meltdown. We obviously have some security issues, which is why you were called in the first place. So again, I'm glad you're here."

Again the smile.

Kennedy didn't return it. It was superficial and well practiced and it made her uncomfortable. Veronica was incredibly beautiful in a porcelain doll kind of way. Flawless pale skin, dark hair and eyes, full, soft-looking lips. But her beauty was marred by her words, a crack in a beautiful, priceless vase.

"V?" A woman entered the kitchen from the other side. She stopped when she saw Kennedy.

Veronica stepped up to place a kiss on the woman's cheek in a move that suggested it was somewhat forced and false, Veronica merely staking her claim in Kennedy's presence.

"This is the woman the FBI told us about."

"Kennedy Scott," Kennedy offered.

"Shawn Ryan," the woman said, reaching out for Kennedy's hand.

Her hand was slight but warm, her other arm in a tight sling. She gave Kennedy a small smile but Kennedy could tell it was genuine by the ease in which it spread. Shawn was somewhat shorter than Veronica, with a slight but strong build and delicate features. Her hair was cut short and bleached blond, accenting her face. But what really drew Kennedy in were her eyes. Sparkling blue-green sapphires looked out at her, luring her in. Kennedy found herself staring and the realization caused patches of heat to rise to her face. She cleared her throat and forced herself to glance back at Veronica.

Kennedy didn't understand her reaction and felt more than embarrassment. Straightening her spine, she forced the confusion to the back of her mind and focused on doing her job.

"You wanted her, and I got her," Veronica said, puffing out her chest as if she were indeed very proud of this feat. "Your very own FBI agent."

Kennedy corrected her. "Former agent."

"Oh," Shawn said softly to Veronica. When she looked back at Kennedy she smiled again, searching Kennedy with silent questions. But there was an immediate difference in how the two women looked at her. In Shawn there was no need for dominance, no flash of hungry ego.

"You're very welcome here," Shawn said. "I hope you'll be able to help."

There was only warmth and sincerity.

Kennedy nodded, grateful, and watched as Shawn leaned a bit on Veronica. It wasn't an affectionate gesture, but one of necessity. It was evident in the way she grasped at Veronica's jacket and winced. And as Kennedy saw her hand begin to tremble, she almost took a step to go to her, to help her into a chair.

"She's still weak," Veronica said, wrapping a protective arm around Shawn.

Kennedy took a closer look and saw, for the first time, the dark shadows under her eyes. She also noted the paleness of her skin, the weakness in the way she moved.

"I'm so sorry," Kennedy said, feeling a fool. "I didn't realize you were still—"

"I'm not," Shawn said. "I mean, I'm not as bad as I look." She laughed a little and touched her temple. "I just got a little dizzy is all."

Kennedy still had the strange urge to help her, to take her gently by the hand and lead her to a couch or even a bed. She blushed again profusely as the thought of Shawn and a bed played around in her mind.

"You look a little warm," Shawn said, this time looking directly at Kennedy. "Should I turn off the heat?"

Again Kennedy cleared her throat. "No, that's not necessary." She touched her eyebrow with the tip of her index finger just as she had done for years, trying to get hold of herself. She had never reacted to anyone this way before. Why now? And why the wife of a famous actress, a client in need, no less?

Kennedy felt her entire head rush with heat as her mind wandered to what Shawn would look like if filled with want and passion, the heated desire for another. Emotions she herself had never felt.

She pressed harder on her eyebrow and looked to the floor. *Focus, focus.*

"Agent Scott?" she heard Shawn ask.

Kennedy raised her head and dropped her hand. "Please, call me Kennedy." She could literally feel her skin burning. And at that moment she hated the total loss of control she was feeling. Maybe it had been too long. Maybe she should've come back to work sooner. Or maybe not at all.

"Kennedy, okay. Are you sure you're all right?"

"Yes, thank you." Suddenly she was very thirsty. Maybe some ice water would do her good. "Could I have some water, please?"

"Of course," Shawn said, turning to walk to the fridge. Kennedy went to go after her but Veronica saw her and beat her to it, halting Shawn with a hand on her elbow.

"I'll get it, honey."

"Thanks." She turned back to Kennedy just as a man carrying a leather satchel walked in from the neighboring room. He had a cell phone pressed to his ear as he voiced a good-bye. Flipping it closed, he eyed them all and gave Shawn a concerned smile.

"You should be resting, Shawn, remember what I said."

"I'll make sure she does," Veronica said, wrapping a possessive arm around Shawn's waist after handing Kennedy a cold bottle of water.

"Make sure you do," he said, noticing Kennedy.

Shawn immediately voiced an introduction. "Kennedy Scott, this is Dr. Cornwall."

"Ms. Scott," he said with another nod, one which Kennedy returned. He returned his phone to the holder on his belt and then tugged on his navy blue and yellow striped tie. His face lit up as he looked toward the stove. "I will leave you ladies to it, then, as soon as I get one of those cookies."

"How 'bout three or four?" Shawn asked. Veronica grabbed the plate full of freshly baked cookies and offered it to him. Dr. Cornwall grinned and took three. He took a generous bite from one and tipped it graciously at Shawn. "Take care, now."

"I will."

He nodded politely at Kennedy and headed for the door.

The dogs trotted eagerly after him, on major cookie alert.

"V," Shawn said, seemingly noticing the dogs for the first time. "Why are they in the house? They're supposed to be outside, watching the grounds." She called them away from the door and affectionately patted their heads when they returned to the kitchen.

Kennedy watched her, completely captivated, and noticed that despite her weakness and injury, she was in very good spirits. It only further impressed her.

"I'm assuming they came in with Agent Starling," Veronica said, her sarcasm going far from unnoticed.

"Yes, they did," Kennedy said. *If I'm Starling, who does that make you? Hannibal Lecter?*

Shawn seemed puzzled.

"They followed me in," Kennedy explained, finding her arms crossed over her chest. She knew it was a subconscious gesture on her part and she knew it was for protection from these two women. But for very different reasons.

"I wanted to see how difficult it was to gain entry into your house." She looked from Shawn to Veronica, and where before she saw a hint of egotistical hunger, now she saw a cold, jealous stare, chilling Kennedy to the bone.

"And apparently it wasn't very hard, right, Agent...er, Kennedy?" Veronica asked, her voice laced with sharp ice.

Kennedy tried to regain her composure. They were both causing such dramatic swings within her, shaking her up, causing her to question her own ability to remain detached. Something she absolutely had to do to effectively work a case. Clearing her throat, she eyed her watch. "I made it inside in less than four minutes."

"Oh my God," Shawn whispered, swaying a little at the harsh realization.

Veronica squeezed her tighter, steadying her. A look of anger creased her brow. "Kennedy, if you don't mind, my wife needs her rest." After a rude glare, she focused her attention back to Shawn. "Come on, honey, go lie back down on the couch—"

"If you don't mind," Kennedy interjected, her own anger surfacing, "I need to talk to both of you." *I need to do something, anything to get me refocused on why it is that I'm here.*

Veronica straightened at the firm request, a rod of anger erecting her back. She shot daggers her way, obviously not used to people countering her directions.

"It just so happens I do mind. My wife has just been shot, practically killed, and——"

Kennedy's heart rate kicked up, Veronica's words igniting something within. She didn't understand why, but the actress was seriously rubbing her the wrong way when hundreds of criminals had tried but failed to do so.

Kennedy decided to be blunt. "It will happen again."

"What!" Veronica whispered with anger, while still trying her best to lead Shawn back to the couch.

"I said, it will most likely happen again."

"And just how the hell do you know that?"

"It's my job to know." Kennedy at once felt relief at the focus of the case returning to her mind. "I haven't read the threats yet, but from what I do know, this wasn't an accident, Ms. Ryan." She glanced from the angry face of Veronica to the striking yet soft face of Shawn. "The shooter was aiming to kill. He won't miss twice. The killer only shot once, not at the entire crowd, which says a lot about his motive. From what we do know about the trajectory of the bullet and where it originated from, the shooter could've shot you point-blank in the head, Ms. Ryan." She looked to Veronica. "When you approached some fans at the police barrier, the shooter was right there, on that side of the crowd. So it's safe to assume that your wife was the target, not you. He nearly succeeded in shooting her through the heart."

Her own heart pained at the fear she saw wash over Shawn's face. She continued, needing to drive her point home. "He has to be more than a little upset that he missed."

"Are you sure?" Shawn asked, obviously afraid.

Veronica looked to Shawn and her face reddened at Kennedy's words. "Shawn is trying to heal, she doesn't need to hear this—"

Kennedy countered, her voice lowering with intensity. "You asked for me and you got me. I left my family to come help you." Her throat tightened at her own words. She spoke sternly and with conviction, doing her best to keep her anger somewhat harbored. She knew if she was going to work this case, she needed Veronica to hear and respect her. "I'm here to help you. I need to be honest and straightforward with the *both* of you. Not just you." Her gaze traveled over their faces before she continued. "Shawn is a part of this just as much as you are, if not more."

There was a brief silence, the clinking of the distant piano keys long faded.

Eventually, Shawn nodded in understanding. She glanced at Veronica, who stood staring Kennedy down with obvious defiance.

Kennedy noted the look from Veronica and felt her anger try to surface again. "And another thing. For all you know, I could be the shooter. You haven't asked for any ID and yet I'm the one who penetrated your *security* and walked right in."

The blood drained from both their faces and Veronica removed her hand from around Shawn. She took a step toward Kennedy and then halted, fear showing itself for the first time on her face.

Relief washed through Kennedy at finally having reached her. Now she could get down to business, and quickly, because she had a feeling this more reasonable side of Veronica wouldn't last for very long. "Who's running your security?"

"Monty," Veronica replied.

"Get him in here. I want to talk to all of you before nightfall. That is," she paused, wondering herself, "if you still want me here?" She aimed the question first at Shawn and then at Veronica. Veronica nodded reluctantly while her hand returned possessively to the small of Shawn's back.

Veronica spoke, softer but with determination. "We'll talk in the living room so Shawn can lie down."

Kennedy agreed, worried for Shawn herself. She'd grown very quiet and she trembled ever so slightly. They both jerked in surprise as a loud clamor came from the staircase in the foyer. The patter of feet meeting wood floor soon followed as two little girls came running into the kitchen.

"Mommy, look!" The taller one threw herself against Shawn's leg and looked up at her with a huge grin. "I did my makeup and Kiley's too!" The shorter one eyed Kennedy and stopped to put a finger in her mouth and twist her foot in a bashful gesture. She lowered her head and then tilted it to the side, lipstick smeared around her mouth and blue eye shadow caked along her eyelids, with some glitter mixed in for good measure.

Kennedy smiled faintly as thoughts of her nephews filled her mind.

The girls seemed to be about the same age as the boys. Both were blond and under the age of six.

"Yes, look at you," Shawn said with a forced strength that caused her voice to tremble. She ran her hand through the older one's hair. "Good job."

"I was gonna do yours, Mommy, but Kiley ate the rest of the lipstick."

"Oh, no. Good thing it was safe for little kids, huh?"

The older one nodded firmly. "Uh-huh. 'Cuz Kiley's a little kid and she doesn't know any better."

Kennedy smiled.

Shawn saw her and smiled as well. Veronica, on the other hand, stood still, staring her down with a cold, brick-wall kind of look. Impenetrable.

"Girls, turn around, there's someone here I want you to meet," Shawn said. "This is Kennedy."

The girls looked up at her with curious gazes. Then, to her surprise, the taller one approached. She held out her hand and in a practiced, confident voice she said, "I'm Rory Ryan, nice to meet you."

Kennedy couldn't help but chuckle as she took her tiny hand.

"Nice to meet you, Rory, I'm Kennedy Scott."

"That's my sister, Kiley," Rory said, turning to point at the smaller girl, who now stood clinging to Shawn's leg. "She's shy."

Kennedy waved and Kiley waved back, but then she quickly turned and shoved her face into Shawn's pant leg. If Shawn was worried about makeup getting on her pants, she didn't show it.

Rory continued with introductions, pointing to the dogs who panted next to her. "This is Noche and that's Día."

"Night and day, very cool. Who named them?" Kennedy asked.

"I did!" she said proudly. "But Mommy helped."

She placed her hands on her hips and Kennedy noticed her one missing sock and painted toenails. A frilly princess dress was tugged over a T-shirt and purple corduroy pants, as if they'd been playing dress-up. "Noche is a good boy 'cept when Mommy makes a turkey. He tries to pull it off the counter and eat it. Oh, and Día, you have to be careful because she eats crayons and then poops different colors." A strange look came over her for a moment and she tilted her head and looked back toward the stove. Then, just as quickly as the conversation had started, it ended.

RONICA BLACK

"The cookies are done!" she shouted. Racing to the stove, she licked her lips and bounced on the balls of her feet. "Yummy, yummy, yummy."

Kiley quickly joined her, trying her best to peer over the stove. Veronica held out the plate for them.

"Not too many," Shawn said. "They haven't had dinner yet."

"Oh, they'll be fine," Veronica said.

Shawn started to protest but then seemed to remember Kennedy and she let the argument go.

"Excuse me, Ms. Ryan?" a male voice called out from near the front door, causing them all to turn. "There's an FBI agent at the gate wanting entry." A large man entered, and Kennedy took in his giant muscular frame and sharp crew cut.

"I'm already here," she interjected, curious to interact with the Ryan family's source of security. "That's former agent, to be exact." She held out her hand and offered a smile. "I'm Kennedy Scott."

He took it a bit hesitantly but then tightened his grip. His smile was crooked and forced and she could sense that his uneasiness outweighed his curiosity. She couldn't blame him, of course. This was his turf, after all.

"I'm here to help," she said, hoping it would ease the building tension. He dropped his hand and scratched his scalp. Kennedy noted the lack of an earpiece, visible firearm, or radio.

She hoped he'd just arrived to work and hadn't yet armed himself for security, but she knew it was probably wishful thinking.

Seeming to sense the growing tension in the air, Shawn spoke up. "Girls, why don't you go back upstairs and continue playing. We have some grown-up stuff to do down here."

Rory chomped noisily on her cookie, as did Kiley.

"Okay, Mommy." Rory took Kiley's hand and led her out of the kitchen. "Nice to meet you, Kennedy Scott." She grinned a chocolate chip smile.

Kennedy returned it. "You too."

"Kennedy, this is Monty. Our head of security," Veronica said.

"You have a last name?" Kennedy asked.

"Hessinger. Why is your driver still at the gate?"

At least he was somewhat perceptive.

"I came in on my own," Kennedy said. "To see how easy it would be to get in."

His face fell and then reddened.

"And I'm sad to say it took me less than four minutes to gain entry to the house."

A vein stood out on his forehead. "I'm sure had we known you were here, that could've been prevented."

"Well, whoever is threatening this family won't just walk up and announce themselves. Nor will they sit out there and wait. They will move in just like I did." She held his gaze, driving the point home right away. "How long has the call box been out of service?"

"Since Sunday, when all your people started showing up."

"Why hasn't it been fixed?"

He clenched his jaw.

"I told him it could wait," Veronica said. "There were other pressing matters at the time and I told him it could wait until later in the week. The gate still worked and—"

"I can't imagine what could be more pressing than your safety," Kennedy said. She held up a hand when Veronica started to tell her just what was more important. "Never mind. It's later in the week now. Have you called to have it repaired or replaced?"

Monty answered. "I called this morning."

"I hope you also requested some cameras for the property as well."

"I have."

She sighed. "Good. Who works with you?"

He hesitated, clearly not enjoying having to answer her. "Two other guys."

"They have names?"

"Yes."

"Write them down for me along with their training and backgrounds and then call them in later for a meeting."

"What for?"

"For the sake of your jobs." Her voice was strong, thick with the seriousness of the situation. Security at the Ryan household was far worse than she could've imagined. Especially since her main job here was to profile the attacker, not to play bodyguard. But if she was going to help, she was going to help in every way she could. And help, it seemed, was something this family desperately needed in order to be safe.

"Monty, it's all right," Veronica said.

"She's threatening my job," he said.

"No, it won't come to that, I promise. I sign your paycheck, not her." She shot daggers at Kennedy. "Monty listens to me. He does what *I* tell him."

*Great. So your happiness is his main goal, rather than your safety.*

"Then you better tell him to listen to me. If you want to live through this."

Veronica walked away, her distaste for Kennedy evident.

The road ahead of them grew longer by the minute.

"When is Special Agent Douglas arriving?" Kennedy asked, suddenly anxious for the levelheadedness of her mentor. "Why aren't there agents here?"

"He should be here any time now," Veronica called from the living room. Shawn smiled weakly at Kennedy and led her into a large room furnished with two couches, a love seat, and two additional matching chairs.

Shawn offered Kennedy a seat and then sat slowly on the couch outfitted with a bed pillow and a blanket. Veronica sat next to her and Monty made himself comfortable on the ottoman of one of the chairs.

"As for the other agents," Veronica said, "I told them all to go home. The house was too crowded and they were making Shawn nervous."

"I told you I was fine," Shawn interjected.

"No, you weren't. They were scaring you with all their talk and running about."

Kennedy felt the blood drain from her face.

"Ms. Ryan, if you are going to refuse our help, then why am I here?"

Veronica glanced at her quickly, turning from Shawn. Her eyes glinted with a rising temper. "Your help is exactly what I'm asking for. And that's exactly what I expect. Not the changing and rearranging of our lives. I still run the show here, not you."

Kennedy fought the urge to lash out at her. Veronica was stubborn and arrogant, refusing to listen, refusing the help, placing her family at greater risk with every move she made. Kennedy could take no more. She would go back home, where she was wanted and needed.

"I think there's been a mistake," she said. "I can't help you under these circumstances." She stood to walk out, her blood pounding in her ears. Nausea closed her throat as she thought of the two little girls so close to the age of her nephews. They needed to be safe. And she could only hope someone with more patience than she had would be able to help them.

"Wait," Shawn called out. "Please."

Kennedy stopped and stood very still. An elaborate clock chime sounded from a neighboring room in the house, letting her know the time. She studied the large professional photos on the living room wall. Photos of the Ryan family, denim clad with white blouses, taken in the dark sand with the gray surf behind them. They looked happy and loved, the girls laughing and cuddling with their mothers. Sighing, she turned slowly and met Shawn's pleading gaze.

"Won't you please at least wait for Special Agent Douglas? We desperately need your help, and I promise we will listen."

Veronica tried to protest but Shawn wouldn't have it.

"No, V, please. Think of the girls. Let these people help us."

"But they want to change everything."

"I'm scared, V," Shawn said softly. "Look at how easily she got in the house. That terrifies me."

"I know, and you don't need to be scared like that. Which is why—"

Shawn shook her head in defiance. "No. I'm more frightened of doing nothing. Of letting this monster get us." She wiped away a tear and took in a shaky breath. "Please, V. Listen to them."

Veronica sat in silence. She studied Kennedy for a long moment.

"For me. For the girls," Shawn added. Veronica's face softened and she nodded her agreement.

"Okay," Kennedy whispered, knowing she was still on shaky ground. But Shawn was right. They had to think about the girls. "I'll just go get my bags from the driver." With their lack of security, she knew there was no way she was leaving tonight.

"You're staying here?" Veronica asked, surprised.

"Yes. For tonight. I have a lot of work to do. And I think you need me."

"I don't remember discussing that. We don't need you to stay here. We only need you to find out who is behind this. We have security. Monty—"

"You *still* haven't asked for my ID, Ms. Ryan," she said. "From what I've seen in just the last twenty minutes, you desperately need me here. Your family needs me here."

Veronica started to speak but stopped herself. Instead she closed her mouth and shook her head, then turned and tended to Shawn.

❖

"Kennedy." Special Agent Allen Douglas greeted her with a warm smile and a hearty handshake.

"Allen, good to see you. Sorry I was so gruff on the phone."

"No need for apologies, I understand. And it's always nice to see you. Wish it was under better circumstances, of course," he said as they made their way into the living room where Shawn and Veronica waited.

"Seems like the only time I see you is under dire circumstances," she said. Allen had been one of her instructors in behavioral sciences at the FBI Academy in Quantico. Now he worked out of the National Center for Analysis of Violent Crime. Allen, along with Kennedy, was one of the best in the field. They had worked together on dozens of other cases and she respected him like no other.

"If you don't need me, I'm going to go back outside and walk the property with my team," Monty said after showing Allen in.

"I'd like for you to stay," Kennedy said. She saw the tiredness in Monty's eyes and she knew, despite his bravado, that the shooting had probably seriously affected him. "You can fill the others in later."

"Thank you, Monty," Shawn said, with a smile from the couch. The big man returned to his seat with a long sigh.

"I see you've already made quite an impression," Allen said, winking at Kennedy.

"Don't I always?"

"Can we get started please? Shawn really needs her rest." Veronica's patience was once again wearing thin.

"Yes, of course." Allen sat next to Kennedy and opened his briefcase to remove several files stored in large three-ring notebooks. "No one other than Bureau has seen these. Not even the local police. Not yet."

Shawn held Veronica's hand, both of them taking deep breaths. The letters would most likely cause quite a reaction. Kennedy had seen it before. When someone threatens your life and your loved ones, a deep-rooted fear you didn't even know you had suddenly bursts through your soul and spreads like a wicked vine, twisting itself around your heart, your lungs, your mind. She felt for them at that moment. Especially for Shawn. This wouldn't be easy.

Allen placed the notebooks on the coffee table before them.

"This is the UNSUB's latest letter. Postmarked two days before the shooting."

"UNSUB stands for 'unknown subject,'" Kennedy said.

Allen opened the first binder and removed a letter inside a clear plastic protector. "These are copies. The originals are at our lab for forensic analysis." He passed it over to Kennedy. Immediately, she noted the block magazine lettering. Allen spoke again.

"The UNSUB took the time to find every word in a magazine, cut it out, and paste it on a piece of thick white paper."

At once Kennedy knew the UNSUB was higher functioning and organized. This was not at all random or spur of the moment. Not in any way.

"What does it say?" Shawn asked, trying to see.

"No, honey, you shouldn't read it," Veronica countered.

"Yes, she should. You both need to," Kennedy said.

Veronica eyed Allen.

"Kennedy's right."

"Here." Kennedy handed the letter to Veronica. "See if you recognize the wording or anything at all about it."

"I'm not stupid, Agent Starling."

Allen shot a look at Kennedy. She knew what he was thinking. And she knew he would apologize for Veronica's behavior later, feeling guilty and responsible for bringing her into this case. Allen was a smoother-over. The calm, strong glue that held most investigations together. It was the reason he was made field supervisor of so many cases.

Still, it was too bad that no one was going to hold Veronica Ryan accountable for her behavior.

Allen refocused on the letters. "After the shooting, we went through Ms. Ryan's fan mail and discovered three letters. As you can see, they escalate rather quickly." He handed them one at a time to Kennedy.

She arranged them appropriately, wanting to go in chronological order. She read the first one.

*Hey Veronica Ryan. Ry-guy.*

> *Can you see me now? Because I see you. I see us together. Why can't you see that? You will soon.*
> *My love for you will not die. I love you. I love you. I LOVE YOU.*

She handed the letter to Veronica. She heard Shawn take in a quick hushed breath as she viewed the content for the first time.

"Do we really have to do this right now?" Veronica asked.

"The sooner the better," Allen explained.

"It's okay," Shawn said, wiping her tears. "I need to know. We need to know."

Kennedy read the next note.

*Hey Veronica. My Ry-guy.*

> *I miss you. I need you. I see your sadness. I know you need me.*
> *I will die for you. I will do anything for you.*
> *I love you. I want you. Why don't you want me?*

*Soon, my Ry-guy, soon.*

"What are you thinking?" Allen asked, running his hand over his lightly stubbled jaw.

"A lot of things," Kennedy said, still examining the letter.

"Like what?" Veronica asked, skeptical.

"For one thing, our UNSUB is a woman."

"A woman?" Allen asked. She understood his surprise. Women weren't as likely to develop such strong sexual obsessions, let alone act on them with violence.

"Yes," Kennedy said. "She's in love with you." She looked back at Veronica. "Or she sure thinks she is."

"How can you be sure it's a woman?" Shawn asked.

"You see here?" She held up the third letter.

*Hey Ryan. Roni Ryan. Ry-guy*

*Miss me? I know you do. I love you. Nothing will change that. Your bitch wife cheats on you. I saw her with my own eyes.*

*She's not good enough for you.*

*I am. Take me. I'm yours. Nothing will ever change that.*

*NOTHING. I LOVE YOU.*

"See how personal she gets with her feelings? And how she's jealous of you?" Kennedy directed the question toward Shawn. "And she doesn't start off with violence. Not right away. She eases into it. She feels connected with Veronica. See the use of the nicknames? She's trying to reach out. She's got it in her head that she knows you personally. She wants your attention."

"But I didn't even get the letters in time to respond to her," Veronica said, rubbing Shawn's hand.

"She's written before," Kennedy said. "Before these magazine letters, there were handwritten letters. I'd bet my life on that." She looked to Allen, who was going through his notes.

"I thought the same thing. I would guess that there's probably close to a dozen or so, written before these."

She filed through the magazine letters, eyeing them all closely.

"She wrote a lot by hand. Maybe ten to twenty. I'd say well beyond a dozen. And when she didn't get the response she wanted, she started in with these. The more she felt ignored, the more threatening the letters became."

"So ten to twenty handwritten letters from a female," he repeated as he wrote.

"Yes. And look for them to be relatively normal and unassuming. They will contain personal questions aimed at Ms. Ryan, requests to meet up, maybe an expression of her feelings toward Ms. Ryan, but nothing violent. She didn't want to scare Ms. Ryan off. Not right away, anyway." She looked to Monty. "You want to come have a look?"

He stood and approached with caution, as if the letters might strike. He held each one carefully and swallowed hard as he did so. Kennedy could see the fear on his face.

"Seen anything like that before?" she asked him. "In the mailbox or on the property?"

He nodded. Shawn leaned forward. "You have?"

"Last week, there was some graffiti on the front wall."

"Well, that could've been anyone," Veronica said.

"No, it was like these. It said, 'Soon, my Ry-guy.'"

"Oh my God," Shawn let out, covering her mouth.

"I didn't know what it was. I mean, I didn't think it had anything to do with Ms. Ryan."

"I'm glad you told us," Kennedy said. Some would've never mentioned it, preferring to save face. "Thank you."

He returned to his seat looking ashen.

"This is crazy," Veronica said, shaking her head. "I'm good to my fans, I don't understand this."

"She's not a fan, Ms. Ryan," Allen said softly. "She's obsessed with you. Feels that you owe her something because she's convinced you're meant to be together. This goes way beyond fandom."

"Do you have poor boundaries with people, Ms. Ryan?" Kennedy asked, already knowing the answer.

"How do you mean?"

"Yes, she does," Shawn interjected.

"I don't understand," Veronica said, looking first to Shawn and then to Kennedy and Allen.

"I noticed how casual you are with Monty," Kennedy said. "He's head of your security, yet you are as casual with him as you would be your brother."

"I treat him like one of the family," she stated proudly.

"I think what Kennedy's trying to say is that—" Allen started.

"That I'm too nice."

"In a matter of speaking, yes. You have an ability to make people feel like they know you on a personal level," Kennedy explained. She knew the actress was known for her close relationships. She let people in, some of them before she even knew them well at all, and it had, in some cases, led to very public disagreements and hurts.

"And that's a bad thing?"

"In this situation, yes."

"This is my fault?"

"No, of course not. It's just a good idea to distance yourself a little from here on out. This woman, for whatever reason, feels that she's in love with you. That you two are meant to be together. And if neither you nor Shawn have had any extramarital affairs, it's safe to assume that she's unstable and that her fantasies are unfounded."

They sat in silence as the word *affairs* lingered in the air. She hated to even suggest it, but she had to know. And she could only hope that Shawn and Veronica would be honest with her.

"There have been no affairs, have there?" she asked into the stifling silence.

"No, none," Veronica answered, squeezing Shawn's hand.

"Shawn?" Kennedy asked, needing to hear it from her as well.

"No," she said softly.

"Then I would like to suggest that you and your family get away for a while while the FBI hunts this UNSUB down."

"Don't you mean lunatic?" Veronica asked with a scoff.

"No. No, not at all. She's not crazy, Ms. Ryan. She's organized and very justified by her own means. Believe me, it would be easier if she were crazy."

"I see," she said, shuddering at the words.

"What do you mean by organized?" Shawn asked.

"Her actions are premeditated and well planned. She's manipulative, cunning, and narcissistic. Her actions are deliberate and methodical and she lacks empathy and remorse."

"It's all about control for her," Allen added. "She feels powerless in life, therefore she strikes out and tries to control her victim."

Kennedy studied the letters and shook her head. "I don't know, Allen. I think our UNSUB may skew into the disorganized arena as well." She met his gaze. "She's very intense in the way she's obsessing over Ms. Ryan…it would take up a lot of her time. Leading me to believe she's a loner, with few social skills. She can't relate to other people or form relationships. I would say she's unemployed, lives alone, rarely ventures out, and she may be unkempt in appearance. And if she's coming here and leaving her mark on the walls, I'd say she's very bold and even fearless."

"So what does that mean? If she's disorganized as well?" Shawn asked.

Allen cleared his throat. "It means she's also likely to act spontaneously. That her violent behavior could be acted out on impulse."

"And that's dangerous," Veronica added softly.

"It's very dangerous, Ms. Ryan. It means we will not be able to predict some of her behavior. Increased stress in her life will set her off. Something probably happened just before these magazine letters and the shooting itself. And now that she's had a taste of the violence, she might want it again, to achieve her high or sexual thrill. I would say our UNSUB has some extremely dangerous qualities about her. Which is all the more reason you and your family should leave for a while."

"I can't, I'm shooting a new film next week."

The words were spoken sternly, letting everyone know that putting the movie on hold was out of the question.

"Then perhaps, at the very least, Shawn and the kids should go away somewhere," Kennedy suggested.

"I don't want them to. They can just go with me."

"Your presence on the set of the movie would be well known. It wouldn't be safe for them there. Or safe for you either," Kennedy countered.

"It's better for them to go away someplace less exposed, Ms. Ryan," Allen added.

"It's not safe here," Kennedy said. "I'm betting the UNSUB already has this house staked out and mapped. And remember how easy it was for me to get in today?"

Shawn grew paler, then spoke. "What about security? If we're apart, then—"

"We will help you get new security," Allen said.

"No," Veronica said, shaking away her far-off look. "I want Monty with Shawn and the girls."

Kennedy sighed. "I'm afraid he's not trained—"

"Now just a second," Monty said, standing. "I may not be some fancy FBI agent, but I've been doing this for fifteen years."

"I'm not attacking you personally, Mr. Hessinger. I'm just concerned you're in way over your head here. Your security team is small and probably unqualified in a lot of ways. The security here at the house is terrible. Things need to change. Help is needed."

"Then hire some new people and train Monty and the guys," Veronica said. "Do whatever you have to do, but he stays. He's tried to make a bunch of unnecessary changes that I wouldn't allow. That's not his fault."

Monty's face reddened and his jaw flexed. Kennedy knew it was a useless fight.

"You teach him, Agent Starling," Veronica said, holding her gaze. "You go with my family and you show him how."

Kennedy felt floored, like her feet were nailed to the ground and the walls were closing in on her. She had to get back home, to her family, to watch after them. "I couldn't possibly—"

"If you go, then I'll know they're safe." Veronica looked completely serious and her voice had softened considerably. "I'll feel better if I know you're with them."

Kennedy didn't know what to say. A few moments earlier Veronica was throwing daggers her way and doing her best to claim Shawn and her "property." Now she wanted Kennedy in their life.

"I need to work on the case," Kennedy said. But Veronica was quick to come back, aiming her question at Allen.

"Can she work this case from a different location? I'm sure you've done it before."

"Ms. Ryan—" Kennedy started.

"Look, out of the dozen or so agents who have been here the past couple of days, you're the only one who told me like it is. You know what you're doing and you're honest and forthright. I want you with my family."

Kennedy didn't respond but merely shared a glance with Allen. She knew what he would say. He would tell her to go. This was a famous family and the Bureau was doing all that it could to help them. But Kennedy was still hesitant. She was a trained behavioral profiler, not a bodyguard.

Even so, she knew the ropes, and most of it was common sense. And hadn't she been playing bodyguard to Keri and the kids?

Allen cleared his throat. "This is something we'll have to discuss."

"What's to discuss?"

He held up a palm. "There's a lot to consider here, and I'm not saying no."

Kennedy started to protest, but he looked at her and silently asked her to refrain.

"My guys and I, we know what we're doing," Monty said.

Allen pegged him quickly. "You need some help and you will get it. Regardless of Kennedy's whereabouts."

"It will be fine, Monty," Veronica added.

Kennedy stood. "I need some air."

Allen followed her, gathering his things. "Good idea."

❖

*Yonkers, New York*

She had missed. That knowledge sent her mind into a fit of pandemonium. All the practice in the world meant nothing if you couldn't perform when the time came. She would have to work harder. Think about it some more.

If there was one thing she was good at, it was thinking about things.

How had she missed?

She grimaced at her reflection in the mirror. "Stupid bitch." She leaned across the bathroom sink and fingered a thick strand of hair. Satisfied with the color, she dunked her head and rinsed out the bleach. The scent of it burned her nose. She liked it. And she liked it even more as she rose and studied her reflection. With a half grin, she began to towel dry her hair.

Veronica liked short, bleached hair. So short, bleached hair was what she got. She looked better than Shawn Ryan if she did say so herself. She thought of her and grew angry.

It had been seven days since her failed attempt to kill her.

Maybe the little bitch didn't have a heart. Maybe that's why she'd missed.

Yes, wasn't that what he'd always said? *"The blond ones are toys. They don't think or feel. They are just there for amusement."*

She wrapped her bleached head in a towel and headed into the dining room of her tiny apartment. She eyed the table covered in magazines but decided to check the windows first. With the blinds pulled, she checked the small yard and the face of the neighboring building. No one was watching. No one was there.

Relieved, though only temporarily, she crossed back to the table and sat down to examine her latest letter. She was only missing one word now. The word "again." Latex gloves on, she grabbed a magazine and began flipping through it.

For the most part, things had been running smoothly. No one had questioned her or even suspected that she might somehow be involved. She really didn't think anyone ever would because she'd been so careful. The disguise she'd worn, the big man she'd hidden behind, all of it had been carefully executed. She'd also made sure the cameras had been parallel to her rather than facing her.

The cops were probably still analyzing each bit of footage, searching for her, the silent assassin.

Part of her was sure they would never get her. But another part feared being found. And yet another part…dared them. Again, she rose and went to the blinds. Again she checked to make sure no one was watching. She lived in a corner apartment; that way she had access to each angle of view. It was the only way she felt safe.

The sun was setting and that was good. Soon she would venture out for some food and more magazines.

She went back to the table and caught the television news about the shooting. Shawn Ryan had been released from the hospital after an overnight stay and was expected to recover fully. The police, at this point, had no suspects.

She smiled a little and looked back down to the word she held with her tweezers. Then, licking her lips with excitement, she pasted the word in its place.

She held up the newest letter to the light. Heart racing, she grinned as she read it.

*I won't miss again.*

❖

*Scarsdale, New York*

Kennedy couldn't sleep. After her talk with Allen, she'd known she wouldn't be able to. Instead, she sat on the queen-sized bed in one of the many guest bedrooms, going over the files on their UNSUB. The threatening letters were so intense, so personal and angry. She shuddered as she thought of the mysterious woman behind them.

She scribbled words in her notebook. *Loner, paranoid, obsessive. Obsessions escalating to violence. Possibly a late bed wetter, raised in poverty level, broken home. Raised by an overly controlling or violent guardian. Unemployed. Ruled by fantasy.*

She chewed on the tip of her pen as she paused in thought. Their shooter was driven by fantasy, no doubt thinking and obsessing about her actions before she executed them. And now that she had attempted the shooting, the UNSUB was left hanging, just waiting to reenact the fantasy once again. This time perfecting it.

Yawning, she glanced at her watch.

Two a.m.

A soft knock came from her door. She jumped up at once, ready to draw her weapon if need be. She'd made sure the house was locked up and she knew that Monty was downstairs, keeping guard. But nevertheless, she was uneasy.

"Agent uh, Kennedy?" It was Veronica but Kennedy didn't relax even a little as she pushed open the bedroom door.

"I need to talk to you."

Kennedy motioned toward the bed, offering her a seat. She noted that her face was red and puffy. She had been crying, and recently.

Veronica sat slowly.

"There's something you should know."

Kennedy waited in silence. She knew that whatever it was, it wasn't good.

"When you asked us earlier about an affair…"

Kennedy swallowed hard with surprise. While the thought had crossed her mind, her heart now raced at what she was about to hear.

"I didn't tell you the truth."

"How so?"

"I've had an affair." The words hung in the air like thick, stifling smoke. Finding it hard to breathe, Kennedy did the only thing she could think of. She asked questions.

"Just one?"

"Yes."

"How long ago?"

"I ended things a couple of months ago."

*Jesus*, Kennedy thought. *This complicates things.* She couldn't believe what she was hearing. Her thoughts went immediately to Shawn. Did she know?

"How long did the affair go on?"

"About six weeks."

"Does Shawn know?"

"Yes, I just told her."

Poor Shawn. Kennedy couldn't imagine how she was feeling.

"Was it a woman?"

Veronica clouded, obviously stung by the suggestion she might've been with a man. "Yes."

"Do you think this woman could be responsible for the shooting?"

There was another long silence.

"I don't know. She didn't take the breakup well at all. She yelled and screamed at me, even followed me for a while."

*Shit.*

"Who is she?" Kennedy needed to know, but a part of her was curious as to just whom she would choose over Shawn.

Veronica took in a shaky breath. "Sloan Savage."

Her brain searched for an image to accompany the familiar name. It didn't take long. "The rock star?"

"Yes."

Kennedy tried to picture Veronica having an affair with the punked-out lead singer of a widely popular rock band. She couldn't understand it. What had driven Veronica into the arms of a wild rock star? There was obviously more to Veronica Ryan, different layers, deeper behavior.

"This changes everything. We'll have to investigate Sloan fully."

"Yes, I understand." Veronica looked at her with watery eyes. "I'm sorry. I never meant for it to happen." She swallowed back a sob.

It left Kennedy feeling uneasy. As if it was almost…forced.

Kennedy fought for something comforting to say, but there were no words. Only the obvious.

"Ms. Ryan, we're going to do all we can in regard to your family's safety." She hesitated but then placed a comforting hand on her shoulder. "Okay?"

Veronica nodded and began to weep. Her body shook with uncontrollable sobs and she wiped at her tears as if she were angry at herself for crying. "I can't believe what I've done. I knew I shouldn't have, but I just couldn't help it. Do you ever feel like that?"

Kennedy watched her helplessly. She didn't answer, she wasn't sure how.

"No, of course not," Veronica continued, looking away. "You're one of those people who has total control over everything in their lives." She laughed. "You're one of those perfect people, aren't you?"

Kennedy cleared her throat as her uneasiness grew. Veronica was upset and distraught and focusing on Kennedy, her own pain and guilt far too great to face all alone.

Kennedy understood her pain, but she also couldn't help but wonder how Shawn was feeling. She glanced up at the door, her ears straining to hear her cries across the large house.

"How's Shawn?" she asked, unable to resist. Veronica fidgeted and sucked in a quick breath. Kennedy saw the hint of anger once again.

"I-I don't know. If she's hurting nearly as bad as me…"

"Is she still in the house?" Suddenly, she was alarmed and fearful that Shawn had left, alone.

Veronica looked at her in surprise and confusion. "Well, yes."

"Is she okay?"

Veronica rose quickly, as if she were completely offended by Kennedy's concern for Shawn.

"She's fine. I mean—I'm sorry. I'm just hurting so bad." Her stare locked with Kennedy's, pleading for empathy. "Shawn is safe. She's in the house, in our bedroom. I, on the other hand, am here crying in front of you."

Why didn't she want to talk about how Shawn was feeling? Was it because she felt too guilty or because she was too focused on herself? Whatever the reason, it was being made clear that Shawn was off-limits for the time being.

Kennedy sat very still, knowing that Veronica wanted her sympathy. Even if she had known what to say, she wasn't sure if she would have offered it.

Veronica studied her for a long, painfully drawn-out moment. Then, taking a quick step back, she wiped her face and propped her hands on her hips.

"What now?" she asked. "What do we do now?"

"We stick to the plan. We move your family to safe ground while we investigate this fully."

"Where to?" Veronica asked, all business now, her sadness replaced by cold indifference. It was like night and day, an emotional light switch simply turned on then off.

"Someplace secluded. Someplace Sloan or anyone else would never think to look."

Veronica began to pace.

"We vacation in California. Shawn's parents live there," she offered, thinking aloud.

"No. It needs to be somewhere you've never been before."

Veronica looked down as she walked. "Shawn's always wanted a house on Hilton Head."

"Does anyone else know that?"

"I don't think so. She just confessed it to me a couple of weeks ago."

Kennedy was vaguely familiar with the wealthy resort island located just off the South Carolina coast.

Kennedy stood. "I'll have to talk to Shawn to make sure no one else knows. If all is clear, then it sounds perfect to me." They would have to make arrangements right away and leave as soon as possible.

"I'll have my assistant find a house," Veronica said, ready to leave the room to go make the phone call.

"No," Kennedy said firmly, halting her. "Let me do it. I don't want your name attached to this in any way."

Veronica stood still for a moment. Her nostrils flared and Kennedy could tell she was debating whether or not she should fight her on this.

She wrung her hands and fingered the large diamond on her left hand. After glancing at it, she looked back up, wounded. "Okay," she finally whispered.

"Are you still going to go film your movie?" There was a chance she might cancel the shoot to salvage her family. Some people would. But somehow Kennedy didn't see Veronica doing that.

"Yes," Veronica answered, raising her chin a little as she spoke. "Shawn and I think it best if we go our separate ways for now."

Even though Kennedy hadn't known Shawn for more than a few hours, she knew that Shawn valued her family immensely. The news of the betrayal must've shaken her tremendously. Kennedy could only imagine.

"Will you go with them?" Veronica asked, searching Kennedy's face, once again pleading with her sad eyes. "With the affair and everything..." She paused as she took a deep breath. "Shawn's really upset and I would just feel better knowing you're there with them."

"I understand," Kennedy offered quietly. The thought of Shawn and the girls virtually alone and heartbroken on the tiny island left her feeling anxious and uneasy. Something in her drove her to want to protect them, to care for them. She'd already discussed it with Allen and they'd both agreed that she should go, at least for a little while, to help with the security at the very least. Sighing, she eased her hands in her pockets and spoke. "I'll go. But only for a couple of weeks or until we catch the UNSUB. Whichever comes first."

"Whatever you need to do," Veronica said, offering a weak smile of gratitude. She walked slowly to the door and then turned. "Please, take care of them for me."

Kennedy held her gaze. "I will."

❖

*The grass was green, so thick and green it reflected silver in the shining sun. Somewhere nearby a lawn had recently been cut, the scent of it sharp and heavy in the hot air.*

*Lying in the thick grass was a small boy's bicycle, blue with Pokémon stickers stuck here and there along the frame.*

*People moved around it, hurriedly walking, talking, writing on*

*small pads of paper, snapping photos. Many of them wore sheriffs'*
*uniforms or lightweight FBI vests.*

*She moved among them like a ghost, floating through the crime*
*scene tape. As she knelt to examine the bike, the world around her*
*blurred and slowed, the bicycle and its immediate surroundings the*
*only thing she could see.*

*In the distance, she heard a wind chime and the back wheel of*
*the bike began to spin. There was a Popsicle stick lying beneath the*
*handlebars, still stained red. Ants feasted on the remaining sugar. The*
*wind chime sounded again and suddenly she could see the bicycle*
*upright with a child pedaling it around and around the long driveway.*
*He steered with one hand while the other held the Popsicle up to his*
*mouth. His blond hair blew up from his scalp in the breeze. His cheeks*
*were bright and his feet bare.*

*As he continued to pedal, something caught his attention. A car*
*at the end of the driveway. A man stood next to it, holding a balloon. It*
*was bright yellow and shiny. It was a Pokémon.*

*The man walked toward him, balloon bouncing in the breeze. He*
*came closer and then headed off the driveway and into the side grass,*
*smiling, welcoming him to follow. The child did so, having to pedal*
*harder in the grass.*

*"Do you like it?" the man asked, kneeling down to face him.*

*The child nodded, fixated on the balloon. It was Pikachu. He loved*
*Pikachu.*

*"Would you like to hold it?"*

*Again the child nodded.*

*"Here, go ahead. But hold it tight, don't let it get away."*

*The child dropped his Popsicle and climbed off his bike, letting*
*it fall to the ground. He took the string in his sticky little hand and*
*grinned as the balloon bobbed over him, glimmering in the sun.*

*The man laughed and touched his nose in a playful manner. "That*
*balloon was made just for you." He smiled. "Would you like to see*
*some more?"*

*The child looked at him.*

*"There's a lot more over at the park. There's Charmander and*
*Squirtle and even a Blastoise. And you can have as many as you*
*want."*

*The child looked hesitantly back at the house.*

*The man did not falter.*

*"Your mom said it was okay. She's the one who told me Pikachu was your favorite. Would you like to go see all the others and show off your balloon?"*

*The child stared up at the dancing Pikachu. He nodded.*

*"Okay, then." The man smiled and took his hand. "Let's get going. We'll even get some ice cream on the way back home."*

*They walked hand in hand through the grass to the car. The man opened the passenger door and helped the boy inside with his balloon. Then he rounded the car, crawled in behind the wheel, and drove away.*

*She stood watching as the car disappeared. Then, suddenly, she was back at the scene staring at the bicycle. The wheel had stopped spinning and the Popsicle stick began to run over with blood. Suddenly, she was standing in a ditch along the side of the road, just out of town. There was more crime scene tape, more law enforcement milling about. Again she seemed to float through the tape. The sharp scent in her nose was no longer grass. And there was no bicycle.*

*She clenched her jaw and forced herself not to look away. There, nestled in the thick knee-high weeds, was the little boy, face down, arms out at his sides, nude from the waist down. In his hand he clutched a string with a nearly flat yellow balloon connected to it. Flies swarmed around him. On the back of his shirt a message was written in longhand and pinned to the fabric.*

Seek and ye shall find.

*The words played over and over in her mind. And then, to her horror, the boy's head turned all the way around and he opened his dead cold eyes and looked at her.*

*"Why didn't you save me? Why?"*

Kennedy bolted awake, throwing the covers off. She was covered in sweat and struggling for breath. The image of little Tyler Hobbs still swirled in her mind, his head twisted around gruesomely. His words sang in her ears and she choked back a sob.

The nightmare wasn't a new one. Tyler had haunted her dreams for years. He'd been the first one taken, the first one killed. His captor had held him for five days before finally strangling him. Then he'd dumped his body along a popular road near the outskirts of town.

Kennedy hated to think about what all had happened to him during those five days. Unfortunately her imagination was cruel, played out on the stage of her nightmare. Standing, she steadied herself and then walked to face the mirror on the bureau. She stared into her pale face and haunted gaze. She thought of the balloon string clutched in his little hand. She thought of his face and the horrible cries of his mother when they told her they'd found him.

"I'm so sorry," she whispered into the air, hoping somewhere, somehow, he could hear.

Then she opened her eyes and sighed. She glanced at her watch and saw that it was just after six. She'd only slept for a couple of hours.

Deciding to start her day, she quickly showered and dressed and headed toward the kitchen, the strong smell of fresh coffee leading the way.

Outside, dawn stretched its sleepy arms and yawned, casting a cool blue-gray haze in through the windows of the mansion. Silvery dew had been breathed gently upon the lawn, coating it in a light white mist. She poured herself a steaming mug full of coffee and stared out at the property. Absently, she placed her palm against the glass, just as she had done the day before on the plane. It felt heavy and cool against her skin, contrasting sharply with the hot mug she held in her other hand.

Yawning, she cupped the cool hand over her mouth. She hadn't slept well, too uncomfortable in a virtually unguarded house. And then, after Veronica's confession, she had been on the phone most of the night making the travel arrangements with the help of Allen and the FBI. She had seen Shawn only briefly, to ask her if anyone else knew about her desire to go to Hilton Head. She'd said no but nothing more.

Kennedy had worried for her, but she knew there wasn't much she could do other than make the travel arrangements and hire the Ryans some new security. Veronica had insisted that her remaining two bodyguards go with her to her movie shoot, while Monty and the new guys went to Hilton Head with Shawn and the girls. Kennedy and Allen had both insisted Veronica take on additional personnel as well, someone with better training, and after a while she agreed. The new men were ex–Secret Service and they knew their stuff.

She took another sip of her coffee as she thought about Sloan Savage.

She had asked for any information on Sloan Savage to be copied and sent to her in Hilton Head as well as through e-mail. Agents would be questioning the rock star later today and she wished she could be there. More than that, though, she wished for the singer to be solely responsible for the shooting and the threats. If she was, then the family would be out of immediate danger. But that was wishful thinking at best. She didn't know much about Sloan, but what she did know didn't fit the profile.

She glanced at her watch and noted the time. She needed to meet with Monty to go over some things. She needed to probe into his background and get more information on his training. More than likely, Veronica was right and what hindered him from doing a better job was the boss herself. That could be fixed.

"Good morning," Shawn said in a strained and exhausted voice.

Kennedy straightened at her presence and watched as she poured herself some coffee. She still had on her flannel pajamas and her short blond hair was tousled and unruly.

"Morning."

"I don't know about you, but I didn't get much sleep." She laughed a little at her statement.

Kennedy examined her silently, noting her pale and drawn face, the dark shadows still lingering under her eyes. Now they were accompanied by a puffy redness from hours of crying.

"I stayed up making the arrangements," she confessed.

"Hilton Head?"

"Yes. We leave in a few hours."

"I've always wanted a house there," she whispered, sipping her coffee, a far-off look on her face.

"For what it's worth," Kennedy started, unsure of the words she was searching for, "I'm sorry for all that you're going through." Shawn had a startled look. Her coffee mug shook as the pain traveled through her, consuming her once again. Kennedy took a step toward her, desperately wanting to just reach out and hold her, to shield her from the hurt and betrayal. But she stopped, halted by reason and professionalism.

"Thank you." She set down her mug and her hand rose to lightly stroke her throat, as if it would somehow give her the strength to speak. "But don't feel too bad for me." She held her gaze. "I knew it all along deep down. I just didn't ever do anything about it." A sob choked her and she covered her mouth and forced it down. "Sometimes…sometimes denial can be a blessing, you know?"

Kennedy swallowed hard. "Yes. I do."

"You know what the real kicker is?" She looked away from Kennedy and laughed. "When she said she'd been unfaithful, I thought okay, this I know. Tell me about her. I've been waiting for you to. But then she said her name and I died. I knew about one, yes. But it wasn't Sloan." She sucked in a quick painful breath, picked up her coffee mug, and turned to walk away.

Tired and strung out, Shawn hoped she would make it to Hilton Head before she collapsed from exhaustion. Her shoulder ached and her body cried out for rest, but her battered heart and mind wouldn't allow it. Veronica's confession, while not a complete surprise, had been a walking nightmare nonetheless, shocking in its details and the revelation that it was yet another woman besides the one she'd been sure of. She still couldn't quite believe it to be true. It seemed like a dream, so sickening and surreal. Was it real? Was any of this really happening? She swallowed down more tears, knowing it was, but wishing like hell it wasn't.

They'd grown more and more apart the last two years but she'd preferred to deny any thoughts of infidelity. Veronica flirted, yes, and she loved and sought attention, but the thought of her actually having sex with another had just been too much to bear. And when she had tried to talk to Veronica about their floundering relationship, Veronica didn't want to listen, even flat-out refused to talk about it.

They had always said they would talk about it if either one of them felt the urge to be intimate with someone else. They were supposed to talk about it *before* it happened. Shawn realized now that she'd really counted on Veronica to do that. But it seemed that Veronica hadn't been able or willing to. Claiming that it had been uncontrollable, something that had happened so quickly that afterward she'd hurt over it, knowing it was a mistake, and she just hadn't been able to bring herself to tell her.

But that was with Sloan. Who knew what the story was with the other one. And any of the possible others.

Her stomach flipped. How many were there? Did she really want to know? Could she handle it? And why had she been so goddamned stupid?

The cold hard truth was that Veronica had serviced herself. Had put her own needs ahead of Shawn and everyone else. She had done it for years. First with the fame and its demands, and now with the affair. It was time Shawn faced it.

She walked zombielike back to her bedroom. Veronica stood next to the bed packing in silence, readying for her departure. Unable to handle the sight of her, Shawn turned and headed instead into the children's bedroom. After placing her nearly empty mug on the chest of drawers, she sat carefully on the foot of Kiley's bed, tucking the covers in around her sleeping form. The girls shared a room, too scared to sleep alone in the dark at night. She wiped away a tear as she thought of her close-knit little family. Sadness threatened to overwhelm her. Her little girls slept on, oblivious to their mother's anguish. She hoped they would never have to experience the heartache she was feeling. And she hoped they never would have to know about the betrayal.

She kissed Kiley's warm forehead and rose from the bed. Then, while wiping away another tear, she approached a softly snoring Rory and kissed her as well. She watched her girls dream their sweet innocent dreams a little longer.

Dreams she no longer had.

## CHAPTER THREE

*FBI Field Office, New York City*

"Ms. Savage, are you comfortable?" Special Agent Allen Douglas asked, staring at her blond and black–streaked hair.

"No. But does it really matter?" she responded, sucking deep on her cigarette while fingering her eyebrow piercing.

He wished for the third time that Kennedy was there to help interview Sloan Savage. While he knew he could handle her, Kennedy had a way of reading people that rivaled all his other colleagues. It was something innate and went beyond what he could teach. But Kennedy had agreed to go with Shawn Ryan and look after her. She'd e-mailed him questions and was awaiting Sloan's answers.

The fact that Kennedy was no longer a sworn agent also could cause potential problems. Some would complain. Not all, but some. So he had to include her carefully.

Allen crossed his legs and smiled pleasantly. Sloan's painted red lips were full and beautiful and he watched as she pulled the cigarette from her mouth and expertly released delicate rings of smoke into the air. He studied her brown eyes and noted her striking face and slightly snub-tipped nose. It seemed to express her mood and hold it in place. She was a beautiful woman but hid it well behind her punk-girl attitude and ensemble.

He reviewed what he knew about her, having gone over her personal background earlier that morning.

Melissa Ann Bradley, a.k.a. Sloan Savage, was twenty-eight years old, never married, and employed as an entertainer. She lived alone, preferred cats to dogs, ate only raw food, had seven tattoos, and left high school her junior year to pursue her music career.

As she was growing up, she lived with her maternal grandmother after a sexual attack by her mother's boyfriend. She was hardheaded and verbally aggressive, and she'd had several small scrapes with the law while a teenager. An infamous story told of her stealing a ring in a home burglary to pawn for her first guitar.

Currently, she made millions, had two homes and twelve vehicles, had dozens of famous friends, and partied nearly every night at posh nightclubs after sleeping the day away. She did plenty of recreational drugs, mainly marijuana, ecstasy, and cocaine, and she loved to grin and give the paparazzi the finger. A self-professed bisexual, she'd mainly stuck with females the past five years. Veronica Ryan had been one of a dozen.

Sloan fingered her cigarette and stared at the star tattoo on her inner wrist.

Allen hated the smoke, but he was allowing it, hoping it would help her to open up.

They'd already spent two hours with her, asking her easy "get to know you" questions, ones he knew the answers to. He used them to gauge her truth-telling reactions and behaviors. She seemed pleasant and cooperative for the most part, amused by her surroundings. She'd willingly come with them after they dropped in on her at home. She most likely would've gone anywhere with them in order to get them away from her property.

"Can I go now?" she asked, sounding bored and tired. "I could be at home, you know. Doing absolutely nothing."

She rubbed her face and smeared her heavy eyeliner. She didn't seem to care.

They were in an interrogation room, small and poorly ventilated. Cameras stared at them from every tall corner and a rectangular mirrored window hid those who were listening in.

"Are you high right now, Ms. Savage?"

She seemed to be having trouble holding open her eyes.

"No." It was a sharp answer. "Is it against the law to be tired? I was out all night and you people showed up before I could get to bed."

"Veronica Ryan," he said quickly. He watched her carefully, trying to catch her off guard.

She stared at him.

"Oh, right. V." The cigarette returned to her mouth. "What is it that you want to know, detective?"

"It's Special Agent Douglas," he corrected her. "And we want to know about your relationship with her."

"You think we're together or something?"

"We know you've been intimate," he said. "We know about the affair."

"So what's to say?" Her body tensed a bit.

"Tell me about her. Tell me about the affair."

"We fucked. So what?" She took another drag and blew the smoke out of the side of her mouth.

"How long did you fuck?"

"At a time? I don't know, two, three hours. Then we'd get high, rest, and go again."

She was growing agitated but her posture was still open. She wasn't crossing her arms, rubbing her face, or fidgeting.

"How long did the affair last?"

"A few months."

Veronica had said six weeks. Who was telling the truth?

"Why did it stop?"

Her brow creased and she leaned forward. Confrontational. "She said she didn't want to anymore."

"And that was it?"

"Yeah."

"How did you feel about that?"

"I didn't care. No biggie."

"You weren't in love with her?" he asked.

She laughed at the question. "I'm not Cinder-fucking-ella here. It was just fucking."

Again the story differed. Veronica claimed that Sloan hadn't taken the breakup well at all. That she'd been in love with her. Obsessed, even.

"What about these?" He shoved copies of the threatening letters across the table to her. She glanced at them and then sat straighter in her chair. The anger fell from her face along with the color. Her shoulders relaxed but she was obviously piqued with interest as she spread the letters out, reading each one.

"What is this?" she asked, dousing her cigarette in the ashtray to focus.

"Recognize them?" he asked. "Because I happen to know that the breakup wasn't what you wanted. Ms. Ryan told us you were very upset. That you even followed her for a while."

"What *are* these?" she asked again, acting baffled and seemingly ignoring his accusation.

"They're the threatening letters Ms. Ryan's been receiving."

"And you think I did this?" She looked up.

"You've got a reason to."

"No." She shook her head. "I'm not into this sort of thing. This is…" She held up one of the letters, studying it. "Way weird. And frankly, they're too nice. I told V to her face how I felt, and even if I had wanted to, I wouldn't have been able to find those words in a printed magazine. That must've taken hours."

"Did you threaten to kill her?"

"Fuck, yes. I was angry. I threw some shit at her too, some of the gifts she'd given me, and I told her to get the fuck out."

"I thought you said it was 'no biggie'? The breakup."

She quickly licked her lips. Anxious. "I got upset, okay? I felt like she was just dumping me, like a piece of trash. The way she did it…it wasn't cool."

"Will you take a polygraph?"

"If it means you'll believe me and let me go home, then yes."

He was surprised at her willingness.

"Will you grant us permission to search your home?"

"Oh hell." She chuckled all deep and throaty. "You're a pushy bastard, aren't you? I'd have to call my lawyer on that one."

"Why? Something to hide?"

"Yes. But it has nothing to do with this."

"Illegal substances?"

She didn't respond. She fished out another cigarette and lit it. After a long drag she said, "Get a warrant and I'll welcome you with open arms. But I'm telling you, you're wasting your time. V and I are finished. She ended it and I got upset. But I finally wised up and accepted it for what it was. Fucking. That's it."

Allen sat back in his chair. His gut told him that Sloan Savage was not involved. The rock star with the bad-girl looks was just what she appeared to be. A rebel without a cause. She was too careless to be their UNSUB. And probably too drugged up most of the time to be able to actually do most anything. He couldn't see her taking the time to find each word in a magazine, carefully gluing it onto a page. He couldn't see her standing in that crowd waiting with a gun. She was right, she was too emotional. She flew by the seat of her pants and said whatever was on her mind whenever it was on her mind.

No, their UNSUB was more intense, more cunning, and inwardly focused.

But he hoped he was wrong. He hoped Sloan was involved and that she acted alone and the case would be closed. But if he was right and Sloan was innocent, then they had a long road ahead of them. It would mean long hours, more threats, and possibly another attempt.

"You want my advice?" Sloan asked. "She's pissed someone off. Not me, but someone. And trust me, there are plenty of other bitches out there that she's probably screwed over. Find them and ask them."

With his hands in his pockets, he stood to walk out of the tiny interrogation room. Another agent entered to continue the more intense questioning. As Allen went to ready his team for the polygraph, only one thought replayed through his mind.

He always hated being right.

❖

*Hilton Head, South Carolina*

Kennedy set the last of the bags down at the foot of the stairs. Her head ached as her mind spun sharply, as if wrapped in barbed wire and turning over and over. She could feel each stab, each squeeze of the wire. For hours she'd thought of nothing but the letters and the shooting, trying to place their UNSUB, get inside her head. She still wasn't positive it was a woman, but her gut told her it was. Profiling was still very much an art, and law enforcement wasn't supposed to count on it as fact. It was only a tool to help aid them in identifying a suspect. Nothing was set in stone.

Behind her the girls squealed with laughter as they maneuvered through the bags to run up the stairs.

"Sorry," Shawn offered softly, attempting to lift one of the suitcases herself. "They're excited."

"They should be. A big house on the beach…every kid's dream. Every adult's dream, for that matter." She placed her hand over Shawn's and took the bag, then secured the handle herself.

"No lifting."

"I'm capable of helping."

"No, you're not. And there's no need." The new security guys had arrived, and there was always Monty.

Kennedy smiled at her reassuringly. But Shawn didn't buy it.

"You look as pale as I do."

Kennedy was a bit taken back at her frankness. "Yes, but I haven't been shot recently."

She reached for another bag and swung it over her shoulder. Then she grabbed another matching suitcase and started the ascent. Shawn followed.

"You really didn't have to come. I know that you'd rather be at home."

"I said I would come. I never go back on my word."

"Never?"

"No, never."

"That must be tiring."

"Exhausting."

Shawn laughed a little. "I'm grateful. Truly I am. Thank you."

They reached the top of the stairs and Kennedy followed the sounds of the girls. She found them in a room painted the color of a fresh peach with white bed tables and a matching chest of drawers. They were jumping on the beds and singing, "Ten little monkeys jumping on the bed. One fell down and bumped his head…"

Shawn took immediate control. "Girls, you know better. Get down."

"Look, Mommy. Look how high I can get!" Rory said.

Kennedy set down the luggage and fought off the growing lump in her throat, thinking of Landon and Luke and how much they would love the house and love playing with the girls.

"Girls, you know better. Get down."

"Ahh, Mom, please? We promise we won't bump our heads." They giggled.

"No, now get down. It's not our house and we need to show some respect." She helped them both down and straightened the homemade-looking quilts on the beds.

Kennedy left them and found Monty ascending the stairs with three more pieces of luggage in tow.

"Where to?" he asked. The bags were Shawn's.

"There's a master suite over here," Kennedy said. Monty followed as Kennedy led. Just down the hall from the girls' room, double doors opened into a large space with polished hardwood floors, a thick rug with cream and white squares, and a fireplace. To the left stood an old-fashioned maple dresser, and next to that was a sitting area with wicker chairs and cream-colored cushions. A coffee table matched the maple dresser and held thick round candles and two issues of *Southern Living*. To the right a king-sized bed backed up to the wall, and just beyond it French doors led out onto a terrace for an incredible ocean view.

Monty looked around and nodded as if she'd asked him a question. They'd already walked through the house together before Shawn and the girls set foot inside.

"Some pad."

"Yes, it is. Hopefully it will be a safe pad as well."

At that moment, Larry and Phil, the new security guys, were out walking the immediate grounds and the beach. For the first time since she'd stepped off that private jet in New York, Kennedy felt somewhat safe.

Monty cleared his throat and rubbed at the hair and freckles on his thick forearms. She knew he wanted to say something. She waited.

"I just wanted to say…uh…thank you for agreeing to keep me on."

He looked at her briefly. It must've been difficult for him to say thanks, considering she'd shown up and turned his turf upside down.

"No need to thank me, Monty. Ms. Ryan insisted on it, and given your background and record with the family, it's safe to assume you're a good man and a very fine bodyguard. We'll rely on both of those qualities in the near future."

He nodded and again cleared his throat. He seemed uncomfortable.

"Monty, I'm not here to step on your toes. We only want the family safe."

His brow creased and he pivoted to walk from the room. "I'm going to get the rest of the luggage."

Kennedy watched him go and the silence he left in his wake bore down on her. She turned to look at herself in the mirror above the dresser. Her face was strong but pale, which was emphasized wtih her thick hair pulled back in a tight ponytail. Her brown eyes seemed sunken and devoid of life. No wonder Shawn had said something. She didn't look well.

The tiny cross on her neck glinted in the lamp light and she ran a finger over it. It had seen much, that cross. Too much. She approached the bed and traced her fingers along the cream bedspread. She scanned the fireplace and settled on a door to the right of it. It led into a large bathroom. She flicked on the light and stared at the white marbled floors and counters. There was a huge claw-foot tub next to a good-sized standing shower. Beige and cream towels were folded on shelves and hung on racks.

"Some room, huh?"

Kennedy turned and found Shawn a short distance away near the bed. She looked very frail standing in the big room.

"Yes. Very nice. Do you think you'll be comfortable in here?"

"Me?"

"Yes. We're putting you in here. It's the largest room in the house." The house was nearly four thousand square feet, with six bedrooms and four baths. Three bedrooms were on each floor, and she and the others had decided that the guys would sleep and guard in shifts downstairs while Kennedy took the upstairs with Shawn and the girls.

"I realize that, but I don't need to be the one in it. I can take the room next to the girls."

Kennedy explained. "I was planning on taking that one simply because it's near the stairs. If someone were to get in downstairs and they tried to come up…" She didn't finish, unwilling to go into great detail. "If you needed to, you and the girls could escape through the terrace."

"Do you really think that'll be necessary?" Shawn gently touched her throat and glanced out the French doors.

The gesture slammed into Kennedy's bloodstream, causing it to surge, and hotly. The tenderness of her hand, the delicateness of her neck... "No." She forced herself to focus. "But you should have a plan. To be safe."

"You're really worried about your family, aren't you?"

Kennedy met her gaze. Where had that come from? "Yes."

"There's more to the story, isn't there?" Shawn's gaze weighed her down. She wanted to flee but couldn't. Shawn knew that Kennedy's family had been threatened. But she didn't yet know the details. The only reason Kennedy had shared that information was so that Veronica would listen and follow orders.

Kennedy didn't answer. She didn't need to. Her body grew rigid at the thought of her family, and heat rushed to her face.

"I'm sorry. I'm being nosy."

"No." Kennedy cleared her throat. "It's just...intense. And overwhelming."

"I know how that feels," Shawn said softly, laying her fingers on the bedspread where Kennedy's had rested moments before.

More heat came but it wasn't fanned from fear. Kennedy imagined their fingertips touching, the soft pressure, the warmth, the spark...the glittering desire she'd hopefully see in her eyes.

A sharp buzzing came from her pants pockets. Kennedy fumbled for the cell phone and quickly opened it.

"Scott."

"Kennedy, it's Allen. I'm afraid I have bad news."

"What is it?"

"It's the Ryans. They've received another letter. I think you better have a look at this."

Kennedy looked to Shawn and then back to the floor. Allen sighed and she knew he was worked up. "I've scanned the letter. Check your e-mail and call me back."

Shawn looked like a deer in headlights.

Kennedy closed the phone and slipped it into her pocket.

"What's wrong?" Shawn walked with her to the door and finally, to halt her, she placed her hand on Kennedy's shoulder.

Meeting her gaze, Kennedy said, "Everything."

❖

*Scarsdale, New York*

Something was wrong. Where was the big man who always walked the property? Where were the kids? She shifted in her seat and turned the focus on the binoculars. The yard beyond the gate came into view and she slowly panned from left to right. The vehicles were all there but the house seemed quiet. Way too quiet. And where were all those FBI suits she'd seen mulling about? Where was everyone?

Angry, she tossed the binoculars aside and opened the car door. The door squeaked as it was shoved closed. The air felt cool and crisp and she pulled up her hood, slid on her sunglasses, and walked toward the property. Her heart tripled its pace just as it always did when she got near her love. She inhaled deeply, hoping to once again catch the scent of Veronica's perfume. But only moist air came to her, tinged with the scent of dead leaves. Fall had started earlier this year and she hated it. There was nothing worse than skinny black trees, branches looking like claws as they blew in the wind. When she was little she used to fear that they would grab her if she came too close.

But now nothing scared her. Not even getting caught. While she tried like hell not to, it was the game that really interested her. Cat and mouse. It was thrilling and dangerous and wonderful. But the game was starting to not be enough. Her highs were coming quicker, falling shorter, and not feeling nearly as satisfying as they once did. She didn't know what that meant. Only that she'd do anything for her high, for the game.

She stopped about ten feet from the gate. Normally, she'd walk up and press the call button on the box. It didn't work, and sometimes she could hear Veronica or Shawn or even the girls come through on the static. Oh, the thrill of hearing Veronica. Right there. On the other side of the gate. Talking to *her.* Answering *her.*

Anxious to do just that, she took a step and then halted. Her heart pounded and her brain sizzled with its own panicked static. The call box wasn't the same. A new one had taken its place. She looked hurriedly around. Two cameras were mounted on the gate, shifting toward her, the lenses spinning for focus.

"No," she breathed, backing up. "No." Nearly tripping over herself, she turned and sprinted back to the car. Once inside she cranked it and revved the engine, staring at the gate.

They had done this to her. Against her. Trying to keep her away. She hated them. Hated them all. How could they? And how could she not have known?

Foot forced against the accelerator, she slammed the gearshift into drive and the car surged ahead, wheels spinning and smoking. She flew down the street, gripping the wheel hard, stare trained on the gate. Her mind went to Shawn and the shot that should've killed her. She should've died. Died. Damn it. She just should've shot the whole fucking crowd, leaving no one to bear witness.

But she hadn't. The gate loomed closer. And now here she was. Nearly right in front of her. She'd show them.

She closed her eyes and braced for impact.

# CHAPTER FOUR

*Hilton Head, South Carolina*

Shawn sat in the sand and watched as Rory and Kiley ran toward the sea. They screeched with delight as the churning silver water rushed over their tiny feet. Frothy foam ringed their ankles as the water drew back and a breeze came, strong with the scent of salt and sand. It was heady but comforting. She rubbed her injured arm, attempting to warm herself, the early evening air slightly cool for August. She was glad she made the girls wear their hoodies.

Taking in the breeze she looked up and down the beach. To her right about a hundred yards away stood Phil, and to her left at about the same distance stood Larry. Both had yet to change into shorts and they looked odd standing and staring out at the sea in their pressed slacks and button-down shirts. Every once in a while one would look around and push in on his earpiece and say something.

Their presence, while comforting, also left her feeling strange and exposed. And somewhat closed in. She was used to security. Monty and the boys, as they'd called them, went everywhere. The girls even referred to Monty as Uncle Monty. She couldn't imagine life without him. But this new team, the new rules, they were strictly business and far from casual. More than anything, it unnerved her to know just how serious and dangerous her situation was to need such measures. What had happened to their life?

Her stomach caved in on itself, collapsing from the unknown darkness created by the shooter and Veronica's extramarital affairs.

Panic and fear and detrimental grief stirred in that darkness and she fought back the biting tears.

None of it was all right. None of it was okay. And she wondered if it ever would be again.

A chill crept through her and she tried to blame it on the breeze.

"Mama, look!" She was forced back in to reality by Kiley. She was running at her, holding up a long, dripping piece of seaweed.

Rory followed, nearly out of breath. "We found a lot of it," she said. "What is it?"

Shawn smiled though weakly. "It's seaweed." Rory and Kiley were so young, so innocent, maybe they wouldn't remember any of this. Maybe they would only remember happy times.

"Seaweed?" Kiley asked.

"What the heck is seaweed?" Rory added.

"It grows in the ocean. It's a plant."

"Oh," the girls said in unison.

Then Rory said, "Let's go find some more!"

"Yeah," Kiley said, jumping up and down. "Maybe we'll find some sea flowers."

Shawn watched them go and then she dipped her hand in the cool thick sand, letting it filter through her fingers. She looked out at the sea and saw someone riding Sea-Doos and she could smell the smoky scent of a barbecue as someone prepared dinner at one of the large homes nearby. Beyond Phil she could see specks of people here and there, running, walking, some lying in lounge chairs. But overall the beach was relatively quiet for as many homes as there were. With summer ending, most had headed home for the off-season. It would be nice to have some privacy. And the girls would love having the beach to themselves.

She watched as the sun got ready for bed. It smiled down at Rory and Kiley with rays of deep orange. They shrieked as the water chased them up the shore, several strands of seaweed dragging behind them. Under different circumstances this would have been a very happy time for her. But she was weak and overwhelmingly tired. It took all the strength she had to just keep her eyes open.

"Hey."

Shawn turned slightly at the voice and wrapped her arm around her knees, holding them tight against her injured arm and chest. "Hi." She tried not to stare at Kennedy in the light of the setting sun. It played off her skin and hair beautifully. She could also tell that she bore bad news and this unsettled her even more.

"Thought you could use some hot cocoa and a sweater." She held out both and offered a smile.

"Thank you." Taken aback, she could only look up and smile. "You read my mind. I can't believe how chilly it is."

Kennedy handed her the mug and then placed the cardigan over her shoulders. Shawn couldn't remember the last time someone had done something so thoughtful without anyone else around to notice and impress. Veronica always had to put on airs.

"It's the clouds, I think. Usually they make it muggier, but today they made it cooler. Mind if I sit?"

"Please do." Physically, she welcomed her kindness and company. But mentally, she had no desire to hear what Kennedy was about to say. She was becoming quite a dichotomy to Shawn. Warm and sincere and attractive, yet the bearer of horrible news and knowledge. Things she couldn't probably ever even imagine. She watched as Kennedy eased down and stared after the girls. Her jaw muscles worked overtime and Shawn knew she was troubled.

"It's bad, isn't it?"

Kennedy looked at her and then looked back out toward the sea. "I'm afraid so."

Shawn sighed. How much worse could it get?

"I don't want to know, but I know you have to tell me. So please, just do."

Kennedy drew up her knees and interlocked her fingers. "Another letter arrived this morning at the house in Scarsdale."

When she didn't respond, Kennedy continued. "It said, 'I won't miss again.' But that wasn't the worst of it."

"It wasn't?"

"No." Her eyes were rich in depth and sensitivity as they held Shawn's. "There was a photo included. One of you and Ms. Ryan and the girls."

Shawn sucked in a panicked breath.

"It was taken from a magazine and Xs had been drawn in marker over all the eyes."

"Oh my God." Shawn tried to stand. Kennedy reached for her and held her shoulder softly.

"It's okay. Please sit."

Reluctantly, Shawn eased back down.

"Something else has happened as well."

"I don't think I can take much more." She trembled, her gaze fixed on the girls.

"About two hours ago a car rammed into the back gate of the house in Scarsdale."

"What?"

"It came at it nearly full speed. The gate opened partway but mostly stayed intact. The driver then reversed and sped off."

"They didn't catch him?"

"No. But the new cameras did. Unfortunately, they only showed a hooded driver and a stolen tag number. I've asked them to review the tapes completely, hoping whoever it is came around before."

"So he's still free."

"Yes. However, I think this is the same suspect from before. And I still think it's a woman. Her behavior is escalating and she's becoming more and more willing to take risks. Given these circumstances, I think we made the right decision in coming here."

"But your family—"

"My family is okay for the time being. They want me here, helping you."

"They do?"

"Yes."

Shawn teared up, unable to stop it this time. "I don't know what's happened to my life. It all seems so out of control and circuslike. As if none of it's real. I'm so scared."

Kennedy hesitated for a split second and then placed her arm around Shawn's shoulders, careful not to hurt her wound.

"It's okay," she whispered.

"No. No, it's not." She wiped her tears.

"It soon will be."

Kennedy's gaze was strong yet soft. And Shawn found herself believing her. "It will?"

"Yes."

"How do you know?"

"Because I'm getting to know you, and you will make it all okay. You will get through this. And you will keep your head held high and you will raise your girls and someday soon you'll feel happiness again."

"But what about love? Will I ever feel that again?"

Kennedy looked away and slowly removed her arm.

"What? What is it?" Shawn watched her closely.

"I'm afraid I can't help you there."

"Why not?"

Kennedy began shoving her hand deep into the sand. She didn't respond. And suddenly Shawn understood. All that knowledge, all the traveling, the caseloads she must've carried—it was very possible that Kennedy had never had anyone in her life.

"I know you're not married, or at least I assume you aren't. But do you have someone?"

"No."

"Have you...ever?"

Kennedy looked at her and her irises churned like the sea, full of fire and sadness. "I better go call Allen." She stood but backed away before she brushed herself off.

"I'm sorry, I shouldn't have asked."

"It's okay. It's just...not something I like talking about."

Shawn stood as well, placing her hot cocoa on the sand. She didn't want Kennedy to leave but she knew she must let her go.

"Can I ask one more thing? It's not about you."

"Sure."

"Did they talk to Sloan Savage?"

"Yes."

"Does she have anything to do with this?"

Kennedy sank a hand into her pocket. "They don't yet know for certain, but so far, no, they haven't got anything on her that says she does."

"What do you think? Do you think she's involved?"

"Honestly? No. I think it's someone else."

"Another lover?" Her throat clenched around the painful word.

"It's difficult to say. My instinct says no, but I've been wrong before."

The wind whipped at their hair and faces and beat around in her ears.

Shawn wished it would take her away and deafen out everything. Crying, she turned away from Kennedy and hugged herself. When she turned back a few moments later, Kennedy was gone.

❖

*New York City*

The popular nightclub was throbbing from the inside out. Throbbing so fierce and so loud Veronica Ryan almost always could imagine the mortar shaking loose from between the old bricks. Tonight she actually did see some falling loose like sand as she was hurriedly escorted through the back door.

Up the back stairs, she went straight to the VIP room. The area was dimly lit and somewhat crowded with a few celebrities and their friends. She smiled and nodded at a few, pleased that she was by far the most recognizable. The room was cool and free from the stench of cigarettes and sweat from down below. She made her way toward the back, where six large booths lined the wall. Candles flickered at the center of each table, set alongside bottles of Cristal on ice.

She was almost happy save for the painful pressure in the small of her back and the hot breath on her neck. Her new security was worse than a leech. And what was worse was that her two regular guys up and quit. These new jerks had chased them off.

"This isn't wise, Ms. Ryan," he said in her ear. "You should be at home where you are safe."

She frowned at him and twisted away from his hand. Why did she have to get stuck with the Terminator? He was as bossy as he was buff, all wrapped up in a nice suit. His pal, RoboCop, who walked like a corncob was up his ass, was ahead of them scoping out the room.

"Safe? Ha! At home? Right. We all saw the car smash into the gate and we all read the latest letter." Finding her favorite booth, politely reserved for her as always, she eased into it and tossed her light sweater to the Terminator. He had the gall to look shocked and offended.

"I'm not your errand boy, Ms. Ryan."

Ignoring him, she straightened her pin-striped button-down shirt and smoothed her hands over her worn jeans.

"Look at how drop-dead gorgeous you are!"

Veronica turned and shrieked with excitement as two familiar people approached. She rose and greeted both the man and the woman, holding the woman for a few seconds longer.

As they sat at her table, she realized she could only remember the woman's name. Jill Reichart, a well-known, luscious soap star. But she'd forgotten her young beau's. Just as well, though, because it wasn't him she was interested in.

"Ms. Ryan?" the Terminator asked.

She wanted to ignore him but she knew he wouldn't go away. "Yes?"

He was still holding her sweater and his face was flushed red. "I have to insist that we leave at once. We don't have the manpower to properly—"

She smiled. First at her guests and then at him. "What's your name again, honey?"

"Kyle."

"Kyle, right. Listen, Kyle, why don't you go find somewhere else to stand and do your job? And give me a little privacy with my friends?"

He blinked in surprise.

"Go on now. I won't stay long, I promise."

He straightened and looked for a moment just like his pal RoboCop.

"That's it. Shoo." She made a little motion with her hand, encouraging him to leave.

When he finally did so she sighed. "This new security is killing me."

"No pun intended," Jill's young stud said, laughing.

*What an idiot.*

She played it up. "I've been trapped in my house like a prisoner."

"I can't believe what happened," Jill said. "How's Shawn? We've all been so worried."

"She's okay. She's a tough one." Her stomach pained at the mention of her. They had not parted on good terms. And now she was in Hilton Head with that woman dripping in righteousness and all things pure, Agent Starling.

"What a fucking psycho," the man said. "To actually try and kill you."

"It's the fans," Jill said. "I get it all the time. Some just don't know when to stop. They think they know everything about you and that you're the best of buddies, when really they don't have a clue. I once had a woman follow me into the dressing room at Neiman Marcus. Just walked right in behind me and started talking."

Gino, the club's owner, walked up and bowed his silent hellos. Ever the gentleman, he opened the champagne and filled a flute for each of them.

"Thanks, Gino." Veronica gave him a winning smile.

"No, thank you. You make my club famous."

Touched, she rose and hugged him. Then she kissed him on the mouth, which drew several whistles.

He walked away pumping his fists in the air, loving the applause. She smiled and said, "That's my number one man."

Laughing, she sat back down as a popular pop song began to play.

She loved this song and thought briefly about going to one of the platforms to dance. But she'd only do it if Jill went with her. And if Jill went with her, she'd prefer to dance in private.

"So have I told you, V? That the writers are toying with me going lesbian?"

"Really?" She raised an eyebrow.

"I told her to go for it," the man said. "Turns me on just thinking about it."

Veronica studied his faux mohawk and his Hollister clothes. He was youngish, probably mid to late twenties, with nice muscles and pretty-boy good looks.

She had to get rid of him.

Jill smiled coyly at her. "I was wondering what you thought of it. And if you'd help me. I've never played a gay character before. I'm afraid I'd go about it all wrong."

"Not you, babe. You'd be great," he said, kissing her on the cheek and then flashing a bright smile.

"Say, uh, sweetie," Veronica said to him. "Would you do me a favor?"

"Anything."

"Would you go down to the deejay and request a few songs for me?"

"Sure." He rose like a man on a mission.

"Anything from the eighties. Prince, especially Prince," she said.

After giving Jill a quick peck, he left quickly and Veronica slid next to her, resting her arm along the back of the seat. She looked deep into Jill's blue eyes for a long moment before she spoke.

"Yes, I think you should do it," she said slowly. "And, yes, I'd be glad to help."

"Really?" Veronica watched as the pulse jumped in her neck. Then she watched as she slowly and carefully licked her lips.

"Definitely," Veronica whispered.

"I think I might like that."

They were only inches apart and white flames shot through Veronica's body.

"I know I will."

She placed her hand on Jill's denim-covered thigh and felt her react. Then, very slowly, she traced her fingertips upward.

"What about Shawn?"

Veronica stopped her hand. "What about her?"

"Would she be okay with this?"

Veronica removed her hand.

"With her just being shot and all—"

Veronica pulled away. She rose and downed her glass of champagne. She was refilling another as Jill tried to apologize and urged her to return. But there would be no returning. Jill was out.

Why did she have to bring up Shawn? At a time like this? When she just wanted to get out and away from the house and all the madness and just have fun? She was leaving for her shoot in a day, so she only had tonight. And the house was so goddamned lonely and empty and she missed the girls and she missed Shawn but she couldn't stand that look on her face. It was better when Shawn merely suspected and they could go about their lives pretending. Now that she knew, things had changed. And Veronica hated it.

Turning to escape from Jill, Veronica crossed the room to the back corner toward the restroom. Just as she pushed in on the door, she heard shouting and clamoring. A glass broke somewhere and she saw the Terminator sprinting across the room toward her. Then, just as quickly, a hooded stranger ran right into her and shoved her into the restroom. They slammed against one of the stalls and the stranger hurriedly shoved the door closed and locked it. Then the person turned and lowered her hood and removed her sunglasses. It was Sloan.

Breath knocked from her lungs, Veronica struggled to speak. "Sloan?"

Though breathless as well she seemed to have little trouble speaking. "What the fuck do you think you're doing, V?"

Her pupils were large and she wasn't wearing any makeup. Veronica had never seen her out in public like this.

"Telling those motherfuckers that I could be the one who shot at you? Fuck you, V." She shoved her finger painfully into Veronica's sternum.

Instantly, banging came from outside the door.

"Open the door! FBI!"

*FBI? What the hell?*

Veronica didn't have time to ask before a terrified woman exited from one of the stalls. She had on stiletto heels and some semblance of a top. Her large breasts heaved as she breathed in panic.

Sloan yelled at her. "Stay right there and keep your mouth shut! And as for you," she looked to Veronica. "I want answers."

More banging and more yelling. Someone said to get the manager to open the door.

"I didn't tell them I thought it was you," Veronica said. "They just assumed because—"

"Because we fucked?"

"Because you got crazy after I ended things." Veronica spoke softly and gently.

Sloan looked frayed and wired. Clearly she wasn't well and clearly she was causing a scene. Veronica had to think quickly to get out of it. She was afraid of Sloan. Afraid of her unstableness and temper. Whether she was the shooter or not, Veronica didn't want to be alone with her.

"*I* got crazy?" Sloan shouted. "Me? Who was the one who said we should run off and get married? Who was the one who said Shawn mistreated you? Who was the one that said I was the best fuck she'd ever have?"

Veronica flinched as more banging ensued. "I may have said those things—"

"May have?" She laughed loudly and then banged the stall wall with her fist. "Remember that last night we were together and you were between my legs and you said you had your two favorite things right there? Remember? And then you snorted a line off my clit and then—"

"That's enough, Sloan."

"You lied to me, V." She looked like a child. A lost child. "That's what got to me." She grabbed her head and clenched her fingers in her hair. "And now these fuckers won't leave me alone. They fucking follow me everywhere!" She pounded on the bathroom door in return as they banged again. "Tell them to stop, V. I can't take it anymore."

"I will," Veronica said quickly. "I'll tell them."

Keys jangled from outside the door and Sloan sank to the floor. Strange whines rose from her almost like a dying animal. Veronica watched her, her own heart pounding loudly. She looked to the woman in the stilettos, who stood ramrod still, her face truly shocked. The door was pushed open quickly and several angry men bombarded the bathroom. Sloan was tackled and held on the floor as the Terminator and RoboCop shoved Veronica outside, asking if she was okay. They spoke hurriedly into microphones all the while.

Cameras began to flash as they maneuvered her back through the VIP room. Fellow celebrities and their friends had now become blood-hungry sharks, eager for a photo.

"Did she hurt you?"

"Are you okay?" All of these were being thrown at her from agents and citizens alike.

"Yes," she said, only to be told not to speak.

The men escorted her outside and helped her into her limousine. Again she assured them that she was okay.

"Can we just go, please?" she asked. She was suddenly tired and embarrassed and angry at Sloan for causing such a scene.

"Special Agent Douglas wants to speak to you first," said the Terminator. He barely got the words out before the door was opened and the agent slid inside.

"Ms. Ryan," Special Agent Douglas said. "We weren't expecting you here this evening." Obviously he and his colleagues had been tailing Sloan.

"I didn't know I had to inform you."

He grimaced but chose not to argue. "Did Sloan hurt you in any way?"

"No."

"What happened, then?"

"She just wanted to talk. She's upset that you guys are all over her."

"There's a reason we are all over her."

"She doesn't see it that way. Can I go home now? I've had enough of everyone's so-called security for one evening."

"Why are you here, Ms. Ryan?"

She glared at him. The nerve. "My social life is none of your damn business."

"Oh, but isn't it? You're the one who asked for our help."

"Yeah, and look at all the good it's done me."

The special agent didn't back down. "Sloan said there have been other women, Ms. Ryan. Is this true?"

She clenched her teeth. "Get the hell out of my car. I'm going home."

He stared at her hard for a few moments and then climbed from the car. When the door slammed shut, she yelled up to the driver.

"Get me the fuck out of here."

❖

*Hilton Head, South Carolina*

*Cold, rain-slicked street. High weeds off to the right, blowing and bending sharply when the wind came.*

*"Goddamn baby killer." The words rang through her ears as she passed a group of huddled detectives. She could hear the rain thumping off their fedora hats. The sharp scent of manure was in the air. It hung heavy in the rain.*

*"This makes number four," someone said. "What's it gonna take to get this guy?"*

*"Goddamn baby killer," a detective said again. "She was only nine."*

She was nine and it was her time. *Kennedy didn't know where the words came from, but they kept on.* She was nine and it was her time.

*She came up on the crime scene tape vibrating in the wind. She ducked underneath and saw for the first time the pale white flesh against the brown of the weeds. She wanted to look away but couldn't. She wanted to reach down and shake the little girl awake, but she couldn't.*

*She stared at her tiny nude body. At the bruises on her back. At the purple marbling that ringed her neck.*

She was nine and it was her time.

*The sentence played around in her head like a twisted nursery rhyme. Then she saw the note taped to the little girl's back.*

Seek and Ye Shall Find.

*The wind picked up again, teasing the locks of the little girl's hair.*

*Madison. Her name was Madison. She was a daughter, a sister, a student. She collected scented stickers and Beanie Babies. Her favorite movie was* Annie *and she knew almost every line by heart. She was someone. Someone special.*

*She stood and stared and wondered what horrors Madison had endured. How was she taken? Where was she kept? What all had this monster said and done to her?*

*And then it happened. What she knew in her gut would happen the second she felt the wind and dipped under the crime scene tape. It was what happened in every dream. And even though she was aware it was just a dream, she was helpless to stop it.*

*The cold and rain began to slow down, warping into a slow moving tunnel. Movement came from the weeds. Madison.*

*Deliberately, her head started to turn, twisting and popping until her cold lifeless eyes were fixed on Kennedy. Heart pounding and gut aching, Kennedy was frozen to the spot as Madison spoke.*

*"I was nine and it was my time." She sang it, light and hearty, again and again.*

*Then she laughed but stopped just as soon as she started. Her eyes rolled back in her head as she said her final words.*

*"You didn't find me. You didn't find me before it was my time."*

"No!" Kennedy sat straight up, struggling for breath. She was surrounded by darkness, unsure of her whereabouts. Hurriedly, she felt around and discovered a window next to the bed. Desperate for light and air, she tugged on the string of the blinds and they slid upward noisily. She was about to open the window when she caught sight of the silver sea in the distance.

Hilton Head.

Shawn Ryan.

Taking a deep breath, she began to relax.

"Everything okay?"

Kennedy turned toward the door, which she could now make out. "Yes." She rose from the bed and turned on the light. Shawn was standing in the doorway wearing a lightweight satin robe. It looked like a pale blue.

"Nightmare?"

Kennedy cleared her throat. "Yes. I'm sorry if I woke you." She was a bit embarrassed, knowing that she was supposed to be the one on constant alert watching the house, not Shawn.

"It's okay. I wasn't asleep anyhow."

"No?"

Shawn's eyes looked very clear. Like the Caribbean Sea.

"Nope." She chuckled at herself.

Kennedy sank down on the bed and checked the time on her wristwatch. Two thirty-five.

The walkie-talkie on the night table crackled to life. Obviously they'd heard them from downstairs. A good sign.

"Herring one to Herring three."

Kennedy swapped her wristwatch out for the walkie talkie.

"Herring three."

"Give status, please."

Kennedy stood and walked past Shawn to look in on the girls. Both were sound asleep with stuffed animals held securely. She checked their window and then went into Shawn's room to do the same. All looked secure.

"Code four. Nest and eggs secure up here."

"Ten-four."

She returned the walkie-talkie to her nightstand. Shawn was still watching her as she shook out a pair of soft jeans.

"You wear boxers." It was more of a statement than a question.

Kennedy glanced down at her white Hanes T-shirt and matching boxer shorts. Suddenly she felt self-conscious. What must this woman think of her in her silly sleeping attire? More importantly, why did it matter to her what Shawn thought?

"Yes, to sleep in."

Shawn looked her up and down. "It's nice."

Kennedy pulled up her jeans and looked at her, unsure what to say. She hesitated in buttoning her jeans.

Shawn blinked back into reality. "I'm sorry. I'm being rude." She palmed her forehead. "It's just…it's been a long time since I've seen a woman…a woman other than V…"

"No need to explain." Kennedy could sense her confusion and embarrassment. She was still a little embarrassed herself. Sitting on the bed, she tugged on a pair of socks and then rose to pull on another shirt over the white one. Then she crossed back to the nightstand, stepped into her sneakers, and attached her firearm to her waistband. She also slid her phone into its normal place on the waistband of her jeans.

Shawn watched from the doorway. When Kennedy finally met her eyes again she smiled and said, "Would you like a cup of coffee?"

Kennedy nodded, knowing that sleep wouldn't be returning to her for a long while. "I'd love one."

Downstairs, after checking in with Monty and sending him to bed, Kennedy gathered her laptop and the copies she'd printed of the latest threatening letter. In the kitchen, she heard Shawn making the coffee and for an instant something fluttered in her chest as she imagined the two of them together, sharing a home and sharing an intimate morning similar to this.

But just as instantly, she shoved the thought away. Her feelings toward Shawn were growing more and more concerning. She didn't understand them, nor could she seem to control them. She'd never felt this way about anyone before. Not since her first year of college had she even considered having feelings toward someone else. She'd always been focused on her education and then her job and then case after case after case.

She didn't know how other agents in the BSU were able to have families and a private life. With all the traveling and the disturbing things they dealt with on a daily basis, it was miraculous that any were in any steady relationships at all.

Shawn hummed as she retrieved mugs from the cabinet. Despite it all she was somehow managing to keep her chin up.

Kennedy watched her and wondered if she was really alone because of the demands of the job. Or was it simply because she'd never met anyone like Shawn before? Someone who stirred her insides, seemed to see into her soul. Someone she would give anything to protect and make happy.

Where was all this coming from?

She thought of Keri and what she would say. "You're alone because you choose to be alone. You don't let anyone in because it's safer that way."

Kennedy examined the pages in her hands. Keri was right. That was part of it. Whatever the reasons were, none of them were simple.

Shawn Ryan definitely was not simple.

This wasn't just another case.

"Cream or sugar?" Shawn asked from the nearby kitchen.

Kennedy rose and rounded the counter. She retrieved the milk and stirred it in herself. She thanked Shawn, who smiled.

"Thank you. It's nice to have someone to talk to. Nights are the worst."

Kennedy offered to pour for Shawn, who nodded and slid her mug over. Kennedy understood. More than she would've liked to. As she poured, she said, "The darkest part of the night can be the most frightening. Heavy blackness like that, it can hold all sorts of things just out of your sight. Your fears, your problems, your secrets. And there they sit and wait and watch. Hiding in that darkness. It makes it difficult to sleep and it makes it difficult to be awake."

Kennedy took a sip of the hot coffee and then lowered her mug to find Shawn staring at her.

"Who are you, Kennedy Scott?"

Kennedy laughed, surprised. "What do you mean?"

Shawn laughed as well. "You're something else, you know?"

Kennedy returned the milk to the refrigerator and they both carried their mugs into the living room, where they sat comfortably on the couch, Shawn on one end, Kennedy on the other.

"Why don't you have someone special in your life?"

Kennedy took another sip and hesitated before answering. "For many reasons, I suppose." She left out the part about how she'd just pondered the same question herself.

"Such as?"

"My job, for one. I get called away on weekends, holidays, in the middle of the night, in the middle of family get-togethers, in the middle of soccer games. And they aren't calls to report just down the street, either. They are calls requesting my presence in Michigan, the Midwest, Georgia, Hawaii, the U.K. Instances where I'll be gone anywhere from a couple of days to a couple of weeks. It's very difficult for my family, and I can't imagine what it would be like for my partner."

Shawn considered this for a moment, holding her mug snugly in her lap with both hands. "But I thought you were working on your own now? Doesn't that put you in control?"

Kennedy nodded. She had a point. "You would think. But the calls still come. Take this situation, for instance."

"I know, I feel so bad. You shouldn't have to be here."

"That's not what I mean. I just meant that the call came, regardless of what was going on in my life. And when the call comes, you go. But it is somewhat nicer now that I get to pick and choose what to take on."

"Have you had to turn anyone down yet?"

Kennedy smiled. Shawn was quick and right on her. "Not yet."

"No one?"

"No."

Shawn laughed. "Why not?"

"I can't seem to say no."

"Is that what happened in our case?"

"Yes."

"Now I really feel bad."

"Don't. You really need the help and you and your girls deserve it."

Shawn's eyes sparkled. "Thank you."

"You're welcome."

Again she appeared thoughtful. "You said 'partner.'"

"Yes."

"You are gay, then?"

Kennedy stood, uncomfortable.

Shawn clutched her forehead. "I'm sorry." She sighed. "I keep crossing the line with you. I don't know why I can't just shut up. I'm just so thrilled to actually have someone to talk to. And you just seem to be such a mystery…" She shook her head. "I'm just pathetic, aren't I?"

"No, you're fine. I just, I'm not sure how to answer that." *Should I answer? Would she see right through me? Would she know that I think about her like that? Can I answer? Do I even know what the hell is going on? No. I don't.*

She cleared her throat. "There hasn't ever been anyone in my life like that. Male or female."

Shawn was silent for a moment. "Because of your work?"

Kennedy stared into her coffee, willing ripples to form into some kind of repetitive pattern. Something she could get lost in. When they didn't, she leaned on the kitchen counter for some much-needed physical and mental support. "Because I didn't have the time or the need for it."

Shawn seemed to contemplate. "What about now? Or the future? Are you ever going to want or need it?"

Kennedy looked at her. She was staring right into her. "I don't know."

Normally Kennedy wouldn't even have this discussion with Keri, much less a woman she'd met just a few days ago.

"Sometimes love comes when you least expect it. It's not something you can control. It just happens. Much like your calls."

Kennedy didn't say anything. But she understood exactly what Shawn meant. A week ago she would've disagreed. She could always control her feelings. But not now.

"I think, if the time comes, you should give someone a chance," Shawn said softly. "You deserve happiness just like anyone else. Regardless of your job. I just hope you don't continue to push the world away."

*If the someone were you, I would.*

A heavy silence fell between them. Kennedy's feelings were swirling so out of control inside her. She had to focus on the case, on anything else. This woman was speaking to her. Playing the strings of her long-forgotten heart. She continued to stare right into her.

"That nightmare—"

Kennedy panicked. "Please, don't."

"It happens a lot?"

"Yes."

"It was about a case, wasn't it?"

"I don't want to talk about it."

"It might help."

"It won't."

"How do you know? No one should have to—"

"I don't need any help." She'd raised her voice and Shawn fell silent. Kennedy immediately regretted it. "I'm sorry."

"Don't be." Shawn looked sad. "It's my fault. I pushed you. Butted into your business—"

"It's not you. It's me. I-I can't talk about it. It's very difficult."

"I understand."

Kennedy sighed. "No, you don't. It's bad. Very bad."

"The case? Or the nightmare?"

"Both."

Shawn stared at her. "I'm sorry."

Kennedy's throat tightened. "Missing children. Kidnapped children."

Shawn was silent. Waiting.

"Taken. Some of them right from their homes. Thirteen of them."

"Were they ever found?" Shawn asked softly.

Kennedy forced her burning throat to open. "Yes. Twelve bodies. Murdered."

"Was it the same person?"

"Yes. Forensics confirmed it."

Shawn looked away. Covered her mouth. "That's terrible. I couldn't even imagine. If anyone ever took the girls..."

Kennedy blinked back her brimming emotions. She couldn't continue to speak about it. Not right now.

Shawn seemed to sense it. She changed the topic.

"When I first met Veronica, I thought she was the most incredible human being I'd ever seen." She smiled. "And then she spoke."

They both laughed softly. Kennedy was grateful for the subject change. Her heart seemed to beat again as she returned to the sofa to sit. Shawn continued.

"We were young. Single. Struggling artists in New York. It was all terribly romantic."

"You were an artist?"

Shawn sipped her coffee. "Mmm. I was a dancer."

"Really?"

Shawn's entire being came to life. "Ballet."

Kennedy suddenly wished for all that background information from the Bureau. It would be nice to know more about Shawn.

"You gave it up?"

Shawn nodded. "I had met Veronica and her career started taking off. We were in love and in lust. Slowly, I started to pull away from it. I grew tired of always trying to find shows, the constant injuries. I was getting old."

"Do you miss it?"

"Yeah. Sometimes I do." She looked lost in thought. "But what I really miss are those early times with Veronica. She was so passionate and thoughtful. She was wild but she was completely enamored with me. It was the two of us versus the world. I thought it would last forever." She took another slow sip and stared through the coffee table. "But then she got a movie. And another one. Soon her name and face were on the magazines. Offers came pouring in, along with the money. We bought a place uptown. I started seeing less and less of her. I complained. She asked me to marry her. I agreed. We grew further apart. I complained again. She suggested children. I agreed. On the surface, we had the life most would kill for. But it wasn't enough. Not for her. And now I realize, not for me either."

"What do you mean?"

"I mean I wanted more. She wanted more. But what we wanted were two different things. I wanted a family. A wife and partner. Love. Peace. A happy home and the ability to raise our children in privacy. Veronica wanted fame, attention, fun, flying by the seat of her pants. And I don't know what I was thinking. That was exactly who she was when I met her. She never changed. I just wanted her to. I guess I was thinking that since I had grown up, she would too. But what did surprise me was her change in feelings toward me. I don't think she liked me anymore. I had grown up. I was a mommy. A homemaker. I no longer partied or 'had fun.' She grew bored. She sought others."

"You're very insightful," Kennedy said.

Shawn looked at her in confusion.

"Most people wouldn't be able or willing to analyze their relationship so honestly. Most want the blame solely on the other."

"It doesn't work like that," Shawn said. "At least not in my case. Besides, how can I ever learn from it if I just blame it all on her?"

"You're very brave."

Shawn scoffed. "Not really. I'm just terrified of it all happening again with someone else."

"That's understandable."

"Do you think it will?"

Kennedy thought hard, Shawn's pleading gaze penetrating her. "It could. If you follow your pattern and choose another like her. Then again, you could follow your insights and fall for someone more like yourself."

"That was a nice neutral answer." Shawn laughed. "Way to cover your bases, Scott."

Kennedy's skin burned at the sound of her name. They both grew quiet. Finally Kennedy couldn't take the silence any longer.

"It's difficult to change behavior."

"For most people," Shawn added.

"Yes."

"Well, here's hoping I'm not like most people."

Kennedy had trouble swallowing. She forced down some coffee. *Oh, you're not like other people.*

Needing a distraction, she turned to her laptop and the printouts. After rifling through the copies of the photos, she chose one from the security cameras at the Ryan property in New York.

She held one up for Shawn. "Ever seen this car before? Maybe outside your gate?"

Shawn set down her mug and leaned forward. "No."

Kennedy pulled out another one. "Ever seen anyone like this?" The grainy black-and-white photo showed a hooded figure in sunglasses approaching the call box.

"No. Is that—" Her eyes went wide. "Do you think that's the person doing all this?"

Kennedy thumbed through more pages. "Yes, I do. I think she's been watching your house for quite some time."

Shawn took the last photo and studied it. "It's hard to tell if it's a man or woman."

"Look at the hands. I know you can't see them well, but they appear to be smaller boned than a man's. Also," she pointed at the figure in another photo, "there seems to be a slight swelling on the chest in this shot."

"A breast?"

"Could be."

"It's difficult to tell with the baggy clothing. But here also you can see the high cheekbones."

"I never would've picked up on these things."

Kennedy thumbed through more pages and showed Shawn the latest magazine letter. She covered her mouth with a trembling hand as she read the simple sentence.

*I won't miss again.*

Then Kennedy showed her the picture that was sent along with the letter. It showed the Ryan family in a sunny room, sitting on a flower-patterned sofa. Veronica and Shawn sat holding the girls, who were laughing. The photo looked professionally done, only now the eyes had been crossed out with what appeared to be a black marker.

Shawn couldn't look at it for more than a second. The blood drained from her face and her breathing changed.

"Are you okay?"

"No."

Kennedy placed the stack of papers on the coffee table. "Do you want to lie down?"

"No. I just need a glass of water or something."

Kennedy headed for the kitchen. "How about some juice? You look weak."

"Okay."

She returned with a glass of orange juice and studied her. Shawn sat staring into space, her face pale, her body drawn in, knees into her chest and injured arm, which she still wore in a sling. She looked very different from the photograph. She had lost weight and her cheeks seemed more sunken in.

Maybe Kennedy should've waited until morning to show her. She'd just needed to steer their conversation back to the case so badly. Not just because she needed answers, but because she'd had so many more questions. And they weren't about the case.

"Can I talk you into some toast too?"

Shawn didn't look at her. "I'll try."

"Good enough." Kennedy prepared some lightly buttered toast, then took it out to Shawn and sat down beside her on the sofa.

Shawn spoke. "That photo was taken for a magazine article. About two years ago. We showed up and they had this little room all ready."

"It looks like it was taken in a home."

"Yes, it does. But it wasn't. It was at this studio, a loft in SoHo."

"And it ran in the one magazine?"

"Yes. A magazine for the GBLT community. Called *Family*."

"I'm sure the Bureau has already found the issue and are looking into it fully." She'd also requested that copies of Veronica's fan mail be sent to her at once. She wanted to go through them all to search for the handwritten letters from the UNSUB. Ones she was sure were there.

"Funnily enough, that was my favorite public photo of us."

"I can see why."

Shawn nibbled the toast. "It's funny how good the media can make your life appear to be."

"There wasn't anything good about your life?"

"Aside from the girls? Not much."

Kennedy was a little surprised at her bluntness.

"The girls were great. They've always been great. But our family life—mine and V's relationship—weren't good. It hasn't been for some time. It was all a carefully orchestrated façade."

"I'm sorry to hear that."

"Don't be. It's the truth." Her face grew sad. "I've been unhappy for some time. I'm just now finally admitting it to myself."

"Forgive my personal question, but why did you stay?"

Shawn lowered the toast. "I don't know. I guess that's something I'll have to work out within myself. Obviously I was just as sick for staying, for agreeing to put on the happy face, and for agreeing to exaggerate on our lives. I think I wanted to buy into it too. I wanted the happiness and the ideal life."

"I don't think there's any fault in wanting those things."

"No, there isn't. But I was living a lie. And I knew I was living a lie. Yet I stayed and I fed into the lie. I watched it grow and grow and I did nothing."

"Like I said, sometimes it's hard to step back and change."

Shawn teared up. "Yeah, I guess it is."

Kennedy had the urge to reach out and touch her cheek. To wipe away the falling tears. But her phone rang before any more could be said.

She answered by the second ring. "Scott."

"Kennedy, it's Allen." She at once knew that something was wrong.

"What is it?"

"It's Veronica Ryan. We had an incident with her this evening."

"Incident?"

"She's okay. But we've got a problem. She went out to a club this evening, despite her security's warnings not to. We were busy tailing Sloan Savage, who showed up at the same place. There was an altercation in the restroom. A woman saw it all. And we've got word that two major tabloids are going to run the story."

Kennedy looked at Shawn, who was watching her intently.

"Not only is the private conversation between Veronica and Sloan going to be published, but so is the fact that we're looking into Sloan for the shooting."

Kennedy tapped her eyebrow with the pad of her finger. "This isn't good."

"No, it's not. Having the press around now will only hinder our investigation. And they are going to be everywhere."

"Where's Ms. Ryan now?"

"She's at home. But she leaves for her movie shoot soon."

"Where is that going to be?"

"Upstate."

"So not far."

"No. Listen, Kennedy. You better prepare Shawn. Some of the things this lady heard Sloan and Veronica say—it's ugly. It could possibly ruin Veronica's career and her marriage. I thought you might want the heads up."

"Thanks, Allen. Any word on the gate rammer?"

"Not yet. We've put out a search for all early model Honda Civics with front-end damage. We're also canvassing the neighborhood for any eyewitnesses. I'll let you know when we know something."

Kennedy signed off and looked at Shawn. Her throat grew tight as she searched for the words.

"You're scaring me," Shawn whispered. "Just say it."

"I'm not sure how." She cleared her throat. "Apparently, Veronica went out tonight to a club where she encountered Sloan Savage. There was an altercation in the restroom and a woman overheard everything. Allen called to tell me that some tabloids have gotten a hold of the story and they are going to run it. He said the content was personal and potentially damaging for Veronica's career and…marriage."

Shawn stared at her. She looked like a young bird, frail and afraid.

"What does potentially damaging mean?" Her voice was weak, her pulse jumping in her neck. "It means they talked about their affair, doesn't it? And now it's going to be all over the world." She stood. "Why did I do this, Kennedy? Why did I stay when I knew?" She began to cry and then shouted, "Now my family, my little girls…everyone who loves us and cares…they will all know the dirty details and I just sat back and allowed it to happen! What's wrong with me? And why in the *hell* was V out tonight after someone just tried to fucking kill us? What's wrong with *her*? She can't keep it in her pants for a few nights? Oh my God. Oh my God." She slammed the toast down on the coffee table and ran through the living room. Kennedy followed and watched as she hurried up the stairs, crossed the hall, and slammed her bedroom door.

# CHAPTER FIVE

*Yonkers, New York*

The supermarket was bright and shiny and it smelled of fruit and detergent. Up the last aisle she went, basket heavy in her hand. She stared at her dirty sneakers as she followed the worn path on the white floor past the soda and popcorn, beyond the candy and chewing gum.

She hated being here and she only came after sunset. It was less crowded and she didn't have to worry about anyone looking at her. She didn't like people looking at her.

She preferred having her world under perfect control with little human interaction. She didn't like big open places and she didn't like crowds. She liked the dark, but only outside. In her apartment she always had a light on. Even when she slept.

She preferred to be either in her apartment or in her car. But she'd had to abandon her car recently. The front of it was terribly damaged from Veronica's gate and she couldn't risk someone recognizing it. So she'd cleaned it from top to bottom, knowing her prints were on file, and left it behind an old gas station, buried in the woods and covered with weeds and branches.

She thought she'd be more upset with herself, having run into the gate and damaging her car, but she found that she didn't regret it one bit. In fact, she wished she'd done more damage to the gate. She could easily steal another car. She knew how to cut the wires on older models and start up the engine. She'd learned how from a magazine. She learned a lot from magazines.

They were her world. And as she neared them at the check-out lanes, she forced herself to remain calm. Magazines were her main reason for coming to the supermarket. It was time for the new issues. But she must be patient. She glanced at her watch. Yes. It was time.

Now she just had to wait and remember to breathe.

She approached one of the five check-out lanes and stood behind a middle-aged woman wearing stretch pants and a bright pink shirt. Her reading glasses, which were also pink, were perched on the tip of her nose and she was rifling through her coupon book.

"I've got a coupon for that," the woman said, searching.

She waited for the woman's groceries to edge farther down the belt before placing hers on it. It was her normal assortment of ramen noodles, bananas, canned soup, and milk. Cheap but edible.

"I've got a coupon for that," the woman said again.

"And those were two for a dollar. Not those. Those. And I still want to use the coupon on them."

She looked at the rest of the magazines.

Veronica Ryan was no longer the cover story and hadn't been for two days. It infuriated her. Quickly, she searched through one and found a brief tidbit. Veronica was in hiding with her family and Shawn was healing from her wound. Veronica was soon to start filming on her new movie.

Upset at the little information, she shoved the magazine back on the rack. Where were the new issues? She hoped she wouldn't have to ask. She'd had to do that twice and she hated it. They always stared at her. They always thought bad things about her. That was why she timed her arrival. To avoid having to wait or to ask.

As if on cue, a young man walked up. He had on dirty work pants and he was carrying bundled stacks of brand-new issues.

She avoided him, doing her best to act disinterested. He placed the new copies on the stand and left. Her blood raced as she caught sight of the covers. The copy she held fell to the ground.

Ahead of her, the coupon lady continued to fuss over her items with the cashier.

She fought for breath, still staring at the magazines. Veronica was on the cover of each of the new ones.

AMERICA'S FAVORITE LESBIAN CAUGHT CHEATING WITH ROCK STAR.

VERONICA AND SLOAN: SEX, DRUGS, AND ROCK AND ROLL.

Hurriedly, she flipped through them, hungry for the information.

She scanned the articles, her face reddening as she read about Veronica with yet another woman, as if Shawn weren't bad enough. She'd heard the rumors about Sloan, but this seemed to confirm it. Her hunger for information quickly turned to anger.

"A dollar twenty-nine," the woman ahead of her said again.

She glanced at the woman's groceries. All were scanned but she was arguing over a can of bean soup.

She read further. About Sloan and Veronica having sex, about how Veronica told Sloan she was the best she'd ever had.

*No. No.*

She looked again at the woman. She was still arguing. The can of soup sat in front of the cashier. A can of fucking soup.

*Pay. Pay. Pay. Hurry.*

The woman argued some more.

Suddenly she wanted to tear her head off. Then her thoughts went to beating her relentlessly in the head with the can of soup.

Again and again and again.

She couldn't take any more. She needed these magazines. Needed their words. Needed that info on Veronica. Now.

She walked up and shoved the complaining woman aside. It took all of her strength not to do anything further.

"Wha—what are you doing?" the woman whined.

"Here." She dug in her jeans and threw some wadded-up bills at the cashier. She gathered the magazines, leaving the food. "For these," she said, hugging them to her chest and hurrying away. She ran past the concerned-looking manager out the sliding doors and into the parking lot. Breathing heavily, she sprinted to her right and rounded the supermarket. She ran past the Dumpsters and into the woods, the light from her apartment a beacon through the trees, calling her home.

❖

*Hudson Valley, New York*

"Look, I don't give a fuck who you are, I need to speak to Veronica Ryan," Sloan said with anger, trying to push her way past security. Veronica could see and hear her from her position in the back of the limousine.

"No unauthorized visitors on the set," a security person thundered out. Veronica eased down her window as the car crawled up to the entrance.

"I'm not just anyone. I'm Sloan Savage and I know if you tell V I'm here, she'll see me."

"You're not on the list."

"What the hell do you think she wants?" asked Flo, Veronica's new assistant.

"I have no idea."

"She's going to cause another scene."

"Not if I can help it."

Veronica watched as Sloan drifted back from the security checkpoint. What could she possibly want now? Wasn't it enough that their pictures were all over the tabloids? Was she going to tackle her again in front of all these people? She didn't need this. Not now. Today was the first day of shooting. She needed to concentrate.

Veronica eased back against her seat. Maybe Sloan would go away.

She focused on the beautiful countryside.

The movie set was just beyond the security checkpoint and it encompassed hundreds of acres of thick grassy hills and heavily wooded forests. Extras walked about casually, dressed in costumes of the mid-1800s, the women in tight but billowing dresses, carrying parasols. The men wore Victorian cutaway coats with vests and top hats, strolling with their walking sticks. The higher-paid actors moved in and out of wood-framed houses, talking amongst themselves, waiting for the next scene. Some headed toward their trailers with assistants hurrying along after them.

She couldn't wait to get out and be a part of it all.

"V!" Sloan was back, this time knocking on the window, looking right at her.

The car stopped to check in with the security. Sloan knocked and called out, following it.

"V, it's me, Sloan!"

"Ma'am?" her new security, the one she called RoboCop, called out. He was looking at her over his shoulder. "Do you want me to get rid of her?"

Veronica glanced around, wondering if the FBI still had Sloan in their clutches. She saw no one. Damn.

"Yes."

RoboCop flung open the door and confronted her. "Ma'am, step away from the vehicle, please." He stepped between her and the car.

"I need to talk to her." She looked past him to Veronica. "Now," she emphasized.

"I'm sorry, ma'am, that won't be possible."

"Why?" She maneuvered around him and bent to talk to Veronica. "V, I need to talk to you."

"Ma'am." He cupped her elbow. "Step away from the vehicle." He pulled her back and motioned for them to drive ahead without him. The driver complied and the car pulled forward to just inside the entrance of the set.

"Look," she said, her voice still loud enough to hear. "You can search me or do whatever you want, but I need to talk to her."

Veronica had enough. Sloan wasn't going to be stopped.

"I'll talk to her," Veronica called out.

"V, are you sure? Who knows what she's up to." Flo uncrossed her long, supple-looking legs.

"I don't have a choice. I can't afford another tabloid article right now."

RoboCop told Sloan to spread her arms and legs.

Sloan immediately complied. He searched her and then nodded.

Veronica and Flo climbed from the vehicle.

"Go on ahead," she said to Flo.

"Are you sure?"

Veronica nodded. "I'll be fine." She walked up to Sloan, who looked absolutely horrible, with pale sunken skin and stringy greasy hair. She looked like she hadn't eaten or slept in days. *Why can't she just go away?*

"Sloan," Veronica said with insincere kindness. "To what do I owe the pleasure?"

"Cut the bullshit, V. You know why I'm here."

"Actually I don't. So you need to tell me."

Sloan eyed RoboCop. Veronica waved him off. She began to walk toward her trailer. Sloan fell into step next to her. Veronica could tell she wasn't happy, but Veronica did not want to be seen with her out in the open. She prayed that no one would snap a photo of them together.

"I need you to tell everyone I'm not involved."

"That's the FBI's job, not mine."

"But you know I'm not!"

"I don't know anything, Sloan."

"They're still following me. They're taking my picture, searching my house. Everyone stares at me like I'm some, some killer." She tugged at her hair. "God, I just can't take it." She looked around, paranoia evident on her face. "They're probably here now. Watching from a distance. I can't go anywhere. Do anything." She fingered her eyebrow piercing. Tugged on it in a painful looking way. "I need it to stop. I need this to stop."

She stared at V like a desperate little mouse begging a hawk for its life. She blinked profusely, fingered her hair again.

"What are you on?"

"What?" Sloan narrowed her eyes.

"You're high."

Veronica quickened her pace.

"Fuck you. I'm dying here, V. Going insane."

"Go home and go to bed." Was anyone watching? RoboCop was close behind. It comforted her a little.

"I can't! I won't!" She stopped and held her head. Then spoke softer. "I can't do this. I can't do this." She jerked her head around. "They're watching me. They're in my house planting bugs, looking for drugs. I think they found my crank and switched it out with something else." She blinked again rapidly. "I just, God, I fucking hate you."

"You're still upset. That's what this is all about."

"You think so? I guess being stalked by the FBI does that to a girl. Or maybe it was having my house thoroughly searched that got to me. Oh, no wait. It was that tiny story in every major tabloid. Yes, that was it. That did it. Not to mention the fact that every human being alive looks at me like I'm a killer."

"I'm sorry about that."

"Sorry? Fuck you, V. This has been a nightmare."

"We had to be sure you weren't involved."

"We? What are you, an agent now? How could you even think I was involved? After what we shared—"

"I don't know you that well, Sloan," Veronica interrupted without emotion. "We messed around a little, that's it." She had to make this clear. They weren't going to be all buddy-buddy.

"Messed around?" she whispered angrily. "It was way more than messing around. It was the best goddamned sex I've ever had. And I know you felt the same." She expressed the latter part loudly, causing Veronica to look around hurriedly, hoping no one heard. But thankfully the set was huge and most folks were just doing their own thing.

"I miss you," Sloan said.

Great. Not this again. Veronica sighed with impatience. How had she not seen this coming? Who knew this sassy little punk rocker would've been so goddamned needy? She had to take care of this. But not outside.

They slowed their walk as they approached the trailer.

"I don't have much time," Veronica said quietly. "Come on."

RoboCop spoke up.

"Ms. Ryan, we have been instructed to—"

"No. I want to speak to her alone."

"I'm afraid we can't allow that," he said, almost as if he knew he would regret it.

"Try and stop me." She threw the door open and walked inside. The trailer smelled brand new and there were three vases with fresh flowers arranged inside. The little fridge would contain bottled Fiji water, Diet Sierra Mist, and Perrier, along with plenty of salad and fresh fruit. The bed would be made with 500-count Egyptian cotton sheets and the carpet would feel soft and lush on her bare feet. She suddenly couldn't wait to sit on that bed and just relax.

Sloan was ruining everything.

She told RoboCop to give her five minutes. Then she closed the door and looked to Sloan.

"Now, what do you really want?"

"I want you to tell these guys," she motioned with her hands, "to back the fuck off."

"I can't do that. They're up my ass too. Now, what else? Really?"

Sloan pulled at her hair and glanced nervously out the windows. Her face seemed to quiver, especially her lips.

"I miss you."

"Oh, Jesus."

"I do. I can't help it. God, can't we just go back to like we were?"

"No. It's over, Sloan. Move on."

"How can you say that? How can you be so calm?"

"Sloan. It's over." She walked closer to her. She could smell the strange odor coming off her body. Like weed and something sour. "Go away."

A quick knock came from the door just before it was pulled open. Flo entered.

"I brought you your coffee and blueberry muffin." She set them on the table. "Am I interrupting?" She smiled at Sloan. They knew of each other but had never formally spoken. She played it up. "I'm a huge fan. And that new video of yours is hot."

Sloan smiled slightly and fingered her piercing. "Thanks."

"You're very talented."

"Yes, she is. She was also just leaving."

"Oh. Well, I'll leave you to your good-byes, then." She gave a wave and exited the trailer, leaving the scent of her perfume swirling in the air behind her.

"I see you're busy as always," Sloan said staring after her.

Veronica didn't respond.

"So how long have you had her?"

"Long enough."

Sloan laughed. Everyone knew Veronica couldn't keep assistants. Her moods and fiery temper kept the turnover rate high.

"I give her another week before you either fuck her or scare her off."

"Thanks for the optimism."

"You're never going to change, are you?" She stared at Veronica with contempt. It almost oozed from her pores.

"I'm not your concern."

"No, you aren't anyone's concern, are you? You just do what you want when you want."

"Did you really come all the way out here to win me back?"

Sloan's entire body shook. "Yes. I mean, now that Shawn knows, why can't we be together?"

"Shawn is my wife, Sloan."

"You don't love me?"

"No."

"Do you love her? Because if you call that love—"

"It's not your business."

"If you love her so much, then why did you cheat? Why do you cheat? You're—"

"You're absolutely right, Sloan. I need to focus more on my family."

A knock came from the door as RoboCop pulled it open.

Sloan laughed again at Veronica's words. But before she walked out she faced her and pulled her in for a deep warm kiss. When Veronica didn't fight it, she lingered just a moment and then pulled away. Her face was flushed and her gaze full of wickedness and pain.

"If it's one thing I know about you, V, it's that you can't give all this up. All this glitz and glamour, all the women. You can't. It's in your blood." She walked down the steps and gave her one last look. "It's who you are. It's who you'll always be. Good luck." And then, without another word, she walked away.

❖

*Hilton Head, South Carolina*

Shawn leaned back in the lounge chair, grateful for the warm sun, even if it was covered in haze. She let it soak into her skin and hoped it would somehow seep into her bones. She felt dead inside. Deader than dead. Like there was nothing left, not even her organs, much less her cells.

She watched her girls splash in the pool. It was heated and they were happy, playing with Monty in the shallow end. Rory had on Swimmies and Kiley had on a life vest. Both were dog-paddling, grins on their faces.

In the distance the sea churned onward, waves collapsing and sweeping up onto shore and then retreating back out. It just kept on and on, despite all the craziness and heartache in the world. Just like the beating of her heart. It continued on, almost as if mocking her.

She closed her eyes behind the protection of her sunglasses. She still felt groggy from her drug-induced sleep the night before. She'd gone forty-eight hours without much sleep or food, and Kennedy had finally insisted on her taking something. Two Xanax later, she'd fallen asleep and hadn't awakened until noon.

Kennedy and Monty had cared for the girls and she was grateful, promising to make them dinner sometime soon. As soon as she felt like it. As soon as she felt like living again.

Her shoulder ached dully as she removed the sling and tossed it aside. She'd promised to let Kennedy look at the wound. She'd also promised to eat something and take better care of herself. She had yet to do either. But she was about to.

From the sliding glass door, Kennedy emerged, carrying a plate and a glass of iced tea. With a smile, she handed both to Shawn and then sat next to her.

Shawn thanked her and noted that Kennedy was back to wearing her dress slacks and a button-down shirt, firearm attached to her belt. Shawn decided she looked striking in anything she wore. She looked at her and decided to be frank.

"I'm filing for divorce."

Kennedy didn't even blink. "Okay."

"I called my lawyer and it's settled. He's drawing up the papers. It will be released to the public the day after tomorrow."

"You're sure, then?"

"After those tabloids? Do you even have to ask?" The articles had been devastating to her. Both in content and presentation.

"Not only did she cheat on me, but she's been abusing drugs too? She told me she gave that up years ago. I can't have that around my kids."

Kennedy rested her elbows on her knees and linked her hands together. "They're tabloid stories, though. You know you can't count on them to be a hundred percent truthful."

"No, but I can count on Agent Douglas. I called him before I spoke to my lawyer. He confirmed it all to me. He also confirmed the other women. The *numerous* other women. She's been cheating since before we wed."

Her voice cracked on the last statement.

"Mommy, are you okay?" Rory asked, climbing from the pool.

"Yes, I'm fine, my love. Come here." She waved her over and kissed her wet cheek and lips.

"Where's your sling?" She stood dripping, arms out wide from the orange Swimmies.

"I don't need it anymore." It was a slight fib, but she didn't want her to worry. "Go swim, sweetie. I'm okay."

Rory smiled and waved at Kennedy. "Look, Kennedy, I'm gonna jump from here!" She curled her toes around the pool deck and bent strongly at the knees. Then she jumped as high as she could into the water.

"Good job," Kennedy said as she surfaced, clapping. Rory coughed and grinned.

"Very good job," Shawn said, proud. Her girls were so happy here. And they adored Kennedy almost as much as they did Monty, if not more.

"I'm sorry you had to hear all that," Kennedy said softly, watching as the girls continued to play.

"I needed to hear it. It was the only thing that would get me to leave. I could and have forgiven her so many other times over many different things. But this—this is too much. I'm just not enough for her. Neither are the girls. *We* aren't enough." She fought back the burning tears and toughened up, as she promised herself she would do. "I always knew and suspected, but actually hearing it from a reliable source, it's, I don't know, life altering. I can honestly say that I'll never ever be the same. I'm changed. I'm different inside. And I know it sounds crazy but I almost want to laugh. At the craziness of it all. At realizing that I have never truly known her. That all of it, all of it was a façade. Just something to amuse her."

"Do you really believe that?"

"Do I have a reason not to?" She paused as she thought. "She said she loved me and maybe in her way she did. Maybe that's all she's capable of. But love means more to me than that. And now I'm going to laugh, because you know what? I'm done. It's done. No more. I'm not going to have to deal with her anymore. No more worrying, second-guessing, questioning her, begging her for her presence. Nothing. And *that* feels good."

"Have you spoken to her?"

Shawn knew Veronica had called the house several times wanting to talk to her. But she had refused. She'd also deleted her e-mails without reading them.

"No."

"Maybe you should. Just to hear her out."

"To forgive her and take her back?"

"No. Just to hear what she has to say about it. I know what she did was wrong. And very nearly unforgivable, but she had her reasons, warped as they may be. People behave the way they do for reasons, whether they be serial killers or liars or cheating spouses. Something drove her."

"What, me?"

"No," Kennedy said softly. "I'd be willing to bet that Veronica had a traumatic childhood, especially in regard to her parents. One was probably neglectful or absent, and the other may have been overbearing and poor at showing affection. She wasn't shown a whole lot of attention, or love. So she seeks it now. And can't seem to control herself in order to get it." Kennedy looked out toward the girls, to make sure they were out of earshot. "I'd also guess that she's probably suffered some sexual abuse, probably at or soon after puberty. And this person probably showered her with attention and material things. She learned early on that sex and being sexy would get her the attention she craved."

Shawn listened quietly and her heart rate began to slow. Kennedy was right on many points. "Maybe so, but lots of us had bad childhoods and went through terrible things. That doesn't give us the right to do whatever the hell we want."

"No, it doesn't. But it does explain a lot. Veronica herself probably can't explain why she is the way she is. It's probably very confusing for her. And she probably does feel some remorse at having hurt you over it."

Shawn sighed. "I don't want to talk about it anymore."

"I'm not trying to upset you."

"You're not. She is. All you're doing is making sense. Which is what you're good at. But I'm just not in the mood for calm logic and sense right now."

Kennedy chuckled softly. She sat back in the chair and squinted up at the sun. "I understand."

"You'd think after all this time of her always being gone and my always questioning her whereabouts…you'd think this would be easier. That I should be able to shrug it away and say, 'Oh well, not much is going to change.'"

"It will get easier. The pain will dull with time."

She thought for a moment and clapped again as Rory did a trick off the steps. "I wish I could believe you, Kennedy Scott."

# CHAPTER SIX

*Lafayette, Louisiana*

"No, I'm fine, just a little tired," Keri said into the phone to her mother-in-law, Miss Norma. "We took the kids to the rodeo today and had a good time. It was the first time we really have gone out as a family for more than an hour. And now I'm making Natalie some bottles. She started on formula yesterday."

She walked into the kitchen and retrieved two bottles from the cupboard.

"Sha, baby. I can't wait to see her tomorrow."

"I know, she misses her grandma too."

The house was quiet with the distant sound of cartoons coming from the living room where Tom and the boys lay sprawled out on the thick shaggy rug and soft sofa. They were all tired and tanned from their earlier adventure.

"How's everything else?" Miss Norma asked her. "You doing okay without Kennedy?"

She dished out the formula with the tiny plastic scooper and tapped it into the water in the bottles.

"For the most part. Everything's been real quiet."

"Good. You know me, I worry. And I get up and check those deadbolts three times a night."

Keri laughed. "I know the feeling. I'm just now starting to sleep the night through." After screwing the lids back on the bottles, she held the nipples tight and shook them, then placed them in the fridge. Natalie was down for a nap but would be up at any moment.

"Tom leaving tomorrow?"

"Yes." She hated it when he had to go, but this year it was especially difficult. "He's missed a lot of the summer training, but the team's been very understanding."

"You gonna be okay?"

"I think so. Kennedy's encouraged me to stay here with the kids. Our new security team will be with me and this house isn't publicly listed. She seems to think we'll be okay here. And hopefully, she'll be home soon."

"Well, if you need anything, you know where we are."

"I do. And thank you."

"No need, sugar." Keri heard her sip from a drink. After swallowing she said, "You heard about Miss Clarice?"

"Miss Mary's friend? No, what?"

There was a click and Miss Norma's voice was clipped. Then she came back.

"Oh shoot, that's her now. Let me call you back later?"

"Sure."

"Okay. Bye, sugar."

"Bye."

Keri ended the call and set the phone down. She ran a hand through her hair, then poured herself a glass of ice water. As she sipped it she saw the stack of mail on the counter and flipped through it. Most were junk and she quickly tossed them in the garbage and placed the obvious bills in their place over the little desk near the corner. Then, grabbing the remaining one, she headed toward the living room with her water. She opened the envelope addressed to Mrs. T. Boudreaux with little bubbly feminine hearts drawn around it. Then she fished out the paper and opened it.

Her breath rushed from her lungs and her glass fell and shattered on the tile. A cry escaped her. Tom sat up and rushed to her. The boys followed but Tom kept them back from the glass.

"What? What is it?"

With her hand shaking, she showed him the paper and sank down, letting out a terrified cry.

She watched as Tom hurriedly read the letter. It was written in red, dark red. Smeared and thick, wrinkling the page. Blood. At once she'd known what it was and who it was from. Words like "gut" and "rip" and "miss you" and "is the baby out of you now?" told her all she needed to know.

In a voice tense with fear, Tom told the boys to go to their rooms. He searched for the phone and returned to her. Helping her to stand, he helped her to the couch, where they sat and clenched one another's hands. With the room beginning to spin, she eased back and heard Tom dial and speak to Kennedy.

❖

*Hilton Head, South Carolina*

"What is it? What's wrong?" Shawn was looking at her with wide, fearful eyes. "Is it Veronica?"

Kennedy fought to steady her hands as she paced. "No."

"Then what is it?"

Kennedy was blunt. "I have to leave."

Shawn sank into a kitchen chair. "Why?"

"My sister. She's received a threat."

"Oh, no."

Kennedy stopped. Her heart fluttered in her chest. Tunnel vision threatened. "It's not good. It means he knows where she's at. And Tom has to leave tonight because the season's starting up again."

"So you have to go. I understand."

"I don't know what else to do."

Just then her phone rang. "Scott."

"Kennedy, it's Allen."

She sank into the chair next to Shawn. "Did you get anything?" They'd had the letter sent to headquarters for forensic evaluation.

"Nothing helpful. The blood was human. Type O. We're sending it to the lab for DNA testing, maybe we'll get lucky and have the DNA on file. The letter was mailed from Virginia. That's all we know."

"He knows where she is."

"Yes, it seems so. But honestly, Kennedy, it wouldn't be hard to find out. Ask anyone in Lafayette where Tom Boudreaux lives and eventually you'll get the right answer. It doesn't mean he was even physically there."

"It's too much. And now she'll be alone with the kids."

"She has security."

"I've got to go, Allen. I can't leave her there."

He sighed. "I know you're concerned. And I've thought about it. You going there isn't really going to help anything, is it? He'll still send the letters to harass her. He'll still know where you are."

"So what do you suggest?" She bit at her cuticles, unconcerned that Shawn was watching.

"Fly her to you. There in Hilton Head."

"Have them all here?"

"Why not? It's secure and you're already protecting the Ryans."

Kennedy looked at Shawn. "I don't know."

"I know Shawn will understand. Kennedy, it's the best solution. Get Keri and the kids out of there."

"There isn't enough room in this house."

Shawn scooted forward, obviously catching on to the conversation. "The house next door is up for rent."

Kennedy covered the phone. "Really?"

She nodded.

"Kennedy? You there? I've had it checked into and we can get her into the house next door."

She ran her hand through her hair. Her body went limp with temporarily relief. "Okay."

"Great. We'll make the arrangements."

"Thanks, Allen."

"Don't mention it."

❖

Shawn tucked the covers in around her oldest daughter.

"Mama?" Rory said.

"Yes, sweetie?"

"Is Kennedy here so you don't get shot again?"

Shawn smiled weakly, trying not to show her immediate reaction at Kennedy's name. A reaction she was starting to worry about. She swept the hair from Rory's forehead.

"Yes." She was wary about discussing the shooting at great length with her daughters for fear of scaring them. She and Veronica had told them the truth, that someone had shot at them but that they were okay and there was nothing for them to worry about.

"Will she always be here?"

"No, only for a short while." She paused. She didn't like that statement. She didn't like to think of their lives without Kennedy. They were growing so comfortable with her, and her presence was so calm and reassuring.

"How come?"

"We won't always need her to protect us."

Rory thought for a moment, her tiny brow creased with questions. "What if she wants to?"

Shawn sighed and kissed her warm forehead, inhaling the clean scent of the baby shampoo she had washed her hair with minutes before.

"Because it's just her job, sweetie."

"But I like Kennedy. And I want her to stay with us always."

"Me too, Mommy," Kiley chimed in from her bed.

Shawn thought back to earlier that day. They'd been on the beach playing and Kiley had gotten her clothes wet. She'd come up to Shawn crying, holding her arms up in the air, wanting to be carried.

"I can't carry you, honey. You'll have to walk," Shawn explained, her arm too sore.

"I can't walk," Kiley wailed, moving stiffly in the wet jeans.

"I got her," Kennedy had said, holding out her hand. But Kiley had shaken her head at Kennedy and cried up at her mother. Insistent.

"Kiley Marie," Shawn had said. "I can't carry you. Mommy's hurt, remember?"

Kennedy had knelt down in front of the girls, giving a quick wink to Rory.

"Who wants a piggyback ride?"

"Me!" Rory said, instantly latching on. Kennedy stood, held her tight, and ran off in a circle, swinging Rory through the air. "Whee! Look, Kiley, I'm riding a horsey!" Rory cried out with glee.

Kiley had immediately stopped crying and came bounding after them, holding her little arms up in the air, beckoning Kennedy to return to her.

"My turn!" she had declared, wanting desperately to take her older sister's place. Kennedy had stopped and set Rory down, giving her another wink and high five.

Then she'd said, "Okay, Kiley, climb on."

Shawn had watched in amusement as Kennedy carried Kiley all the way back to the house, at one point even managing to carry both girls.

Shawn thought about that now as she tucked in her girls. Kennedy had handled that situation well. Her situation. Once again showing how kind and considerate she was. Shawn refocused on Kiley.

"We'll talk about this later, okay?" She rose to place a kiss on Kiley's forehead. She knew she was fighting a losing battle—the girls were too young to understand, so it was easier to just leave the topic for now.

"Good night," she whispered, flicking off the light.

"Night, Mommy," they both said, the peach and pink butterfly night-light glowing from the corner.

Her heart ached at the fragile innocence of her children. She pulled the door halfway and headed for her bedroom. She couldn't help but replay Rory and Kiley's words. Truth be told, she liked Kennedy too, probably too much. And she wondered what it would be like to spend more time with her. More personal time, under different circumstances.

She stepped into her dimly lit room and undressed, carefully minding her sore shoulder, readying herself for a nice, hot bath. She'd been longing for the claw-foot tub since she'd arrived. The water tumbled out and pooled quickly, a haze of steam rising into the air.

As she waited, she turned and caught a glimpse of herself in the mirror. The body reflected was thirty-five, pale and soft from her time spent recuperating from her injury. Normally she was fit and strong, her muscles lightly defined, her body curvy and feminine. She and Veronica were about the same size, but Veronica was thinner with less muscle development. She brushed her hand over the angry red scar on her shoulder. Was she still attractive? Or was she now a used-up mother? What about Kennedy? Did she think she was attractive?

She quickly shook the thought from her mind. It was silly and useless and she didn't have time to wonder about Kennedy Scott and what she thought. She had a divorce to think about. A life to salvage and rebuild. Or did she? The dull pain returned to her insides as she thought of Veronica and their crumbled lives lying in ruin. The sting of betrayal made its way back up her throat, threatening more tears. She swallowed with difficulty, refusing to let them return. Clearing her mind, she turned off the faucet and stepped into the tub. As she leaned back and soaked, she rid her mind of all thoughts. For the moment, she was content with just being.

❖

"Well, what do you think?" Kennedy asked Allen, referring to their one and only suspect, Sloan Savage. They had just ended a conference call and Kennedy was disappointed to learn just how few leads they had. Nothing was going as she'd hoped. Things were just getting worse. Keri's situation was escalating, the Ryan situation also seemed to be escalating. What else could they do? There had to be something.

"She's clean," Allen replied, disappointment thick on his voice. "In the Ryan case, anyway. She does enough recreational drugs to easily kill any human, but that's it."

"Can you give me details?" Kennedy's mind raced and she, for the first time since she left, wished she was back in the Bureau heading up this investigation. The waiting was killing her and she wanted her hands in it, making sure everything was being done right. Every rock unturned.

She bit at her cuticle, frustrated, yet accepting that she was needed here with Shawn and the girls. They needed her and so did Keri and the boys, who were due to arrive the next morning.

"Her polygraph was inconclusive, all over the map. But we did search her place. Nothing there, excluding the drugs. We could charge her but it's not up to me."

"Nothing there that ties her to our UNSUB?"

"She had some personal photos of Ms. Ryan and some personal journal entries she'd written about her, but nothing else. Nothing out of the ordinary."

"Do you think she's had time to get rid of anything?"

"She tried before we got the warrant. But we watched her and retrieved the trash bag. Most of it was drug paraphernalia. And there were a couple of pornographic movies and some sex toys."

"I'm surprised she kept the drugs."

"She had them hidden and there wasn't very much. So my guess is she flushed most of it."

"So you're sure she's out, then?"

"I'd say so. I know our surveillance has taken its toll. She's looking haggard and she's quite paranoid. She's not faring well. She went to Veronica's movie set and insisted on talking to her. Veronica told her to get lost. Sloan left hurt but okay. I think she got the message this time."

Kennedy still didn't feel comfortable. Not after the confrontation at the nightclub. Sloan had gone there with intent. She'd hunted Veronica down and held her captive. Even if she wasn't the UNSUB, her behavior was escalating and she needed to be watched.

"Are you going to keep surveillance on her?"

"Not for much longer."

"Unless you get something else," she stated, knowing the routine.

"Yes."

"What about Veronica's fan mail, you had any luck on your end?"

"We're still looking." He sighed heavily. "For one woman, she gets a hell of a lot of mail."

"They're there, I know it."

Silence filled the phone line as Allen thought. "How are things going with Shawn and the kids?"

"So far everything's been relatively quiet." She was grateful for that and she failed to mention how quickly the trio were growing on her. The brief time she had spent with them had been special and meaningful, warming her insides in a way that only her own family had ever done.

"Yeah, well, be thankful. Veronica's giving her new guys one hell of a hard time."

"How so?"

"She's difficult, uncooperative."

"I was worried she might be. But I was hoping she'd come around and try to help us out a little." Veronica seemed worried about her family's safety but more than willing to disregard her own.

"Well, she's not," Allen continued. "Apparently she's angry and depressed and raising all kinds of hell with the new team."

"Maybe I should call and talk to her." Someone had to make her listen—her life depended on it.

"I wouldn't. She's upset at the separation and the tabloid circus, and you calling to talk to her will just drive that nail right home."

"You're right."

They rang off and she sat staring in thought down at her leather Rockports. Yawning, she bent and pulled them off, ready for a good night's sleep. Monty was once again keeping the night watch downstairs. Knowing that allowed her to sleep soundly upstairs with Shawn and the girls.

She set her shoes aside and stood to unbutton her slacks. But just before she could, she heard something. Ears alert, she looked up and stilled her movements. The sound came again, a woman's voice calling out for help. At once she retrieved her gun off the night table and bolted out the door.

It was Shawn and she was crying out from her bedroom. With her heart surging at a maddening pace, Kennedy sprinted past the girls' room to the master bedroom, where she flung open the door and swung her gun from side to side, ready to fire.

"Shawn!" she called out, seeking and clearing every corner.

"In here!" She was in the bathroom.

Kennedy approached slowly, her breathing quick, her mind flying, not sure what to expect.

"Are you okay?"

"I'm fine." Her voice was lower. "I just need a little help."

Kennedy lowered her gun and looked behind her as Monty entered the room. He stared at Kennedy with intensity, his massive chest rising and falling with adrenaline.

"Stand down," she said, tucking her weapon into the waistband of her slacks. Monty relaxed and bent to catch his breath from his fast run up the stairs. Kennedy gave a little knock on the bathroom door before easing it open.

The room was heavy with steam and dew and it smelled of lavender and shampoo. Kennedy squinted, her eyes adjusting to the candlelight. Her heart rate kicked back up as she caught sight of Shawn, lying back in the large tub, consumed by bubbles, the soft golden candlelight caressing her face and glistening shoulders.

"I can't get out," Shawn said softly. She looked down in obvious embarrassment.

Kennedy stood very still, her legs heavy yet weak.

"Everything okay?" Monty asked from behind.

"I'm fine, Monty!" Shawn called out and then laughed. "I'm just stuck in the bathtub! I can't believe this," Shawn continued in a softer voice, looking at Kennedy. "I tried to stand up and I slipped and fell. Now my shoulder is killing me. What was I thinking getting in here?" She gave another nervous laugh. "I'm so embarrassed."

Kennedy took a careful step in, knowing she had to help, but scared to death to do so. Her cheeks flushed with heat as she reached for a towel.

"It's okay," she said softly, handing it to Shawn.

Shawn took it hesitantly. "Kennedy, I only have one good arm. And I need to use it to grab on to you."

"Oh, right."

Shawn set the towel on the edge of the tub and reached up to grab Kennedy's hand. Kennedy hoisted her up easily, her gaze focused on the floor. Shawn stood in the bath, dripping with soft white suds, completely naked. Kennedy cursed her peripheral vision but she could not help herself. Shawn was smooth and glistening, curvy and beautiful. A golden angel in the candlelight. The sight would, no doubt, keep her up for nights on end.

Shawn reached down and clutched the towel to her wet body. "It's okay. I'm covered now."

"Do you need help to step out?" Kennedy asked, turning her head slightly to look at her. She cleared her throat nervously, wishing the towel would cover up more. If she had questioned her attraction to Shawn before, there was little doubt now. Shawn stirred her in ways she never thought possible.

"Yes, if you don't mind." Shawn flung the towel over her shoulder and reached out to grip Kennedy's shoulder. Kennedy eyed her at the contact, her eyes quickly taking in the exposed, wet flesh. More heat rushed to her face and she felt suddenly light-headed as her body awakened. She looked away again, the vision too much.

"Thank you." She had stepped out of the tub safely and wrapped the towel around her as best she could.

"You're okay, then?" Kennedy asked, looking only into the blue-green irises.

She could feel her own heartbeat in her ears, she was so moved. And something else.

Aroused.

"Yes."

"Okay, well, good night, then."

"Good night, Kennedy," Shawn voiced from behind.

Kennedy reentered her room in a daze and sat on the bed. She rubbed at her cheeks, embarrassed at the hot blood that stirred just beneath her skin.

The image of Shawn nude and wet came into her mind again and again. Glistening skin, the sharp dip above her collarbone, the delicate swell of her small breasts, the pink of her nipples, the indentation of her abdominal muscles, the dark blond hair between her legs…

With her heart still racing, she stood and stripped out of her clothes. She pulled out a pair of shorts and a T-shirt. Quickly, she put on both and then stepped into her sneakers. As she laced them up, she willed her mind and her heart to slow, to somehow make peace with what she had just witnessed.

But she knew it was no use. She knew she would be up most of the night, excited and moved in a new and foreign way. Closing her bedroom door behind her, she stepped out into the hall, needing to escape. The house felt warm, the upstairs air thick with the heat of a soaking and wet Shawn Ryan.

She ran down the stairs and waved at Monty, who gave her a nod. She stepped outside and wound her way beyond the pool, through the small gate, and onto the thick sand. She hit the beach at a trot, which soon increased quickly to a full-out sprint. The salty air and the cool sea breeze did wonders for her aching soul and she pushed herself harder and faster, desperately trying to outrun her growing feelings and emotions.

She ran until her legs ached and her lungs screamed out for mercy, wet sand flying up behind her as she blazed a trail along the dark beach. She ran until she could no longer breathe, until a stabbing in her side insisted she stop. Nearly tripping, she slowed and rested her hands on her knees. Then, looking back toward the distant house, she sucked in powerful gusts of salty air and nearly collapsed as she realized one thing.

No matter how fast or far she ran, Shawn Ryan would forever be in her mind.

❖

*Yonkers, New York*

Veronica had cheated.

Cheated.

Cheated on her! With Sloan fucking Savage.

The slut.

Slut Savage.

She downed some more burning whiskey and then tossed the bottle aside, hearing it thud as it hit the carpet.

She needed him now. More than ever. That voice. His eyes. The tender love. Yes yes, the tender love. Tender love no one else had given her. But he had.

Now she was alone. And she was hurting. *Why did you do it, Veronica?* Why didn't she call her so they could be together? And then they would have the tender love.

Oh, how she longed for it. Veronica, Veronica.

Her love.

Her tender love.

She closed her eyes and curled up into a ball.

She imagined being back at the house when she was young. She could smell its musty scent, remembered the moldy walls and the dim light, the warmth of her breath as it came back to her when she slept in the small space.

Slowly, she began to relax. She was safe there. So quiet. Cave-like. Cocooned. Hot. Soft. Silent.

Until the crying. The crying and crying. She hated the crying and she tugged her pillow over her ears. She rocked. And rocked. Until the cries grew muffled and finally disappeared.

Then she was safe again.

In the home on the hill.

Where Veronica awaited her with open arms.

With the sun shining bright. So bright she had to squint. Yes, she was there. Waiting. She could smell her. See the tiny beads of sweat on her neck.

She hopped up from the bed and slid her feet into her shoes. Veronica. She was there. With her.

Yes.

She snapped on a surgical glove and retrieved the letter from the table. Her sunglasses felt cool against her skin as she pushed them on and stepped out into the bright sunshine.

She floated as if on a cloud to the mailbox. Veronica, Veronica. She deposited the envelope and stared down at the sidewalk as she walked. People were all around her now and she was extremely anxious and uncomfortable. She just kept thinking of her love. Of the home. On the hill.

Looking down, she walked briskly, weaving in and out of people, careful not to look at their faces. It didn't matter that she wore sunglasses. They could see. They could see her thoughts and her fears. They would know what she thought of herself. But most important, they would judge.

She shoved her hands inside her big jacket and pulled off the latex glove she had used to deposit the envelope. While she was careful to leave no prints, she made it a point to leave her DNA on the stamp. DNA wouldn't identify her right away like a fingerprint would. For DNA comparison they would have to catch her first. Something she was not worried about. So she left her mark purposely, secretly letting the world know that it was her, that she held the power.

She walked on, still thinking of Veronica and the waiting and the sunshine. She clung to the vision, held it tightly against her heart. But every beat brought Veronica's image, her scent, her sweat.

She had to get control. Get her head where it needed to be. She had things to take care of, but she had to take her time and do it right.

She needed to get a grip. Something to ease her insides. The whiskey was dangerous. It stirred her fears and her anger, stirred them up inside.

Cars whizzed by as she crossed the busy street and ducked into a used bookstore. She relaxed a little as she stepped inside. The place was familiar and quiet and generally uncrowded. She felt safe here, wandering down the aisles, the smell of the books filling her nose. She didn't have much money, but it was just as well.

She reached out and ran her hand across the spines. What would it be today? Fiction or nonfiction? She generally chose nonfiction, choosing to read about people that really existed, relishing their tragedies as well as their triumphs. She could live vicariously through them, something she loved to do since she was so afraid of the world.

He had brought her books. Worn paperbacks. Presents. She would always get lost in them. First in their smell, which she inhaled when she first got them, and then in their words. She loved them.

A brightly covered book caught her eye and she stopped to examine it. It was science fiction, her other great love. She flipped through the pages and inhaled deeply. Yes, she loved this genre as well. Loved the adventure, the idealism, the morals. She wished she could exist in a world different than her own, wished she could interact with brave and noble people, content in the ideal worlds in which they lived.

She smiled and held on to the book. Yes, she would get two today. One science fiction and one true crime. She made her way over to the nonfiction section and found a book about the Green River Killer. Six dollars total for both. She could live with that. She held them carefully and went to check out.

In her mind Veronica still stood in the sunshine, in front of the house on the hill, arms open wide.

# CHAPTER SEVEN

*Hilton Head, South Carolina*

Kennedy awoke from her light slumber on the recliner downstairs. Fan mail was strewn at her feet, most of it useless. She'd gone through two boxes before the words had started running together. She glanced at her watch. It was after eight a.m. and she had been asleep for a couple of hours. Sitting up, she listened intently to the sounds of the house. Monty sat at the kitchen table reading a newspaper, and she mentally chided herself for falling asleep in front of him. She didn't want him to think of her as weak.

Slowly, she stood and stretched. She had been up most of the night, unable to get Shawn from her mind. The image of her standing in that bathtub nude and dripping wet had assaulted her all night long. Nothing, it seemed, could shake Shawn from her mind. Not even the stacks of fan mail she'd been going through. She approached the kitchen counter and poured herself a mug of steaming coffee.

"Good morning," she said as she made herself comfortable at the table.

"Morning," he grumbled, not sounding all that rested himself. She suspected he didn't sleep well, the shooting no doubt replaying in his mind, not letting him rest.

"Did you get any sleep?"

"Some."

"It'll get better," she said softly, taking another sip of her coffee.

"I'll believe it when it happens." He met her eyes briefly. He wasn't convinced.

"If you ever want to talk about it…I'm here." She felt for him. Could see the pain and anguish nestled in the wrinkles on his face.

"I don't think it'll help."

"Couldn't hurt." She offered a weak smile.

Monty looked at her for a moment as if examining her true motives. Then, deciding she was truly offering her ear, he smiled back and flipped a section of the paper, angling it better to see.

"I saw the bastard," he said softly looking at the paper as he spoke. "I saw the bastard that shot her."

Kennedy repositioned herself in the chair, sitting up straighter. She'd seen the useless artist's sketch, had heard Monty's story through her colleagues and the written reports. But she wanted to hear this for herself.

"Tell me about it," she said.

"He—"

"He?"

"Yeah, looked like a man."

"How so?"

"Big coat, you know, had an NFL logo on it. Ball cap, short hair."

"Was there facial hair?"

"A mustache."

"Monty," she started softly. "Is there any way it could've been a woman in disguise?"

He thought for a moment, looking out the kitchen window to the sea beyond.

"I suppose it's possible. He wasn't a big guy. The coat nearly swallowed him whole."

Kennedy breathed deep. "When did you first notice this person?"

"After the shot went off. I turned toward the noise and jumped on Veronica. As we were falling to the ground I saw him. He was shoving the gun into his coat. I could see and smell the smoke and my ears were ringing. Veronica and I hit the ground and that's when I saw Shawn. The hole in her shoulder, the blood…" His voice trembled as he thought about the horrible scene, replaying it in his mind. "I tried…" He coughed as his throat tightened with raw emotion.

"It's okay." She reached out to cover his hand with her own. She didn't usually touch people but she understood his attachment to this family, beginning to feel greatly for them herself.

As his emotion continued to pour out, she stood to get him a tissue.

"Thanks," he said taking it and wiping his nose.

"Anytime."

"You know, no offense," he said. "But I never thought you would be the type to be so nice." He chuckled a little as he spoke. "You came off as sort of a…"

"Bitch?"

"Yeah."

"It comes with the job."

"So why are you being so nice now?"

"Because I understand your pain. I understand how you can love this family so much." As she said the words she thought of Rory and Kiley. She smiled as she thought of their joy, their love, their innocence. Her smile vanished as she thought of Shawn. Instead, her heart rate picked up and a wave of dizziness washed over her. Warmth spread from her stomach to her chest. All of that just from thinking of Shawn's smile. She stared into her coffee as she thought about the affection Shawn showed her daughters. Loving them, playing with them, tucking them in at night. Yes, she could understand how Monty could care so much about this family.

"They're easy people to love," he said, his voice regaining its strength.

"Who is?" Shawn asked lightly as she walked into the kitchen. She was freshly scrubbed from a morning shower and Kennedy could smell the fresh scent of shampoo on her as she walked past her to the fridge.

"You are," Monty clarified.

Shawn stared at them in front of the open fridge. "Me?"

"You and Veronica and the girls," Monty added.

Kennedy looked away from her as Veronica's name was spoken. While she didn't out-and-out dislike Veronica, she certainly had no positive feelings toward her. Her fondness was for Shawn and the girls.

"Oh," Shawn said, smiling at them both. "Thank you, Monty. We love you too."

"Did you get any sleep?" Kennedy asked, still concerned. Shawn was still weak and somewhat pale.

"Some, thank you." She placed the heavy-looking gallon of milk on the counter. "You two didn't sleep?"

"Some," Monty answered.

"Morning, Mommy!" the girls shrieked happily, bounding down the stairs. They were already dressed in shorts and sweatshirts, ready to go claim the beach as their own.

"Good morning," Shawn said, hugging them both.

"Morning, Kennedy, morning, Monty," Rory said as she went to hug them both with Kiley close on her heels. Kennedy stiffened a little, surprised at the easy affection. She watched as Monty smiled, hugging the girls back.

She looked up after her hugs and saw Shawn watching her.

"Sorry," Shawn offered. "They really like you."

"It's okay," Kennedy said, her heart warming at the gentle affection. She watched as Shawn retrieved bowls from the cabinet. Then she watched as she filled each bowl with Fruity Pebbles and then tried to lift the large gallon of milk to pour it into the cereal bowls. Unable to hold the milk with her injured arm, she shrieked with pain and dropped it. Kennedy moved quickly, grabbing the milk and setting it upright.

"Are you okay?" she asked, worried about the sudden flash of pain that had come over Shawn's face.

Shawn nodded as she grabbed at her shoulder. "I should've known better than to try it with the bad arm."

"Let me see." Kennedy stepped up to her, wanting to see the wound, but she stopped herself short, realizing Shawn would have to remove her shirt.

"I think I'm okay." Shawn continued to hold her shoulder, massaging it gently. Suddenly feeling awkward, Kennedy moved to the sink to get a rag to wipe up the milk. As she cleaned she watched Shawn, truly worried about her.

"Why don't you sit down and rest?" Kennedy suggested, not liking the ashen look on her face. It was more than obvious that she was in terrible pain. So much so that she looked like she was about to faint. Kennedy cleaned up the mess and then she gently led Shawn to the couch where she sat for some rest.

"I'll give the girls their cereal."

"Mommy, are you okay?" Rory asked with fear in her little voice.

"I'm fine, sweetie. I shouldn't have tried to lift the milk is all."

Kennedy brought the cereal to the girls at the table. They ate happily, every once in a while looking at their mother to make sure she was really okay. Kennedy busied herself pouring Shawn some coffee and making her some toast. She figured the pain had probably nauseated her and the toast would go down easier than eggs or sugary cereal.

"Thank you," Shawn said, looking up at her.

"You're welcome." There was a softness there. An understanding. It shot right through Kennedy. "You should see a doctor about that shoulder."

Shawn glanced away. "I think I'm okay. It was just the lifting that did it."

"I still think you should. Just to be safe. I can call one."

"No, please don't. I'll think about it, okay?" She offered a smile and Kennedy didn't argue.

Monty got up from the table and stretched, breaking the intensity. "I'm gonna go out and do my rounds." With a wave, he disappeared out the back door.

"Mommy, are you going to play pirates with us today?" Kiley asked in-between bites of cereal.

"Oh, I don't know, sweetie." She winced as she tried to move her arm.

"Oh." The girls moaned their disappointment in unison. "You promised."

"I know and I'm sorry, but my shoulder…"

"I'll play with you," Kennedy said quickly. She knew how badly Shawn needed to rest. And she would do anything to make sure that she did.

"You will?" Rory asked with surprise.

"Sure."

"Cool!"

"Yeah, big cool!" Kiley added.

"But only if you finish all your cereal," Kennedy added. The girls grinned and happily dug back in, anxious to go play.

Shawn relaxed against the couch and finished her toast. She felt warm and fuzzy and genuinely happy for her girls. Kennedy was kind and attentive and willing to play with them, allowing her to get some rest. She was grateful and truly thankful.

She leaned back against the couch and brought her feet up off the floor. She thought back to how uncomfortable Kennedy had been the night before. How she'd done her best not to look at her in the bathtub. How she'd flushed profusely, her body stiffening.

Her heart surged with heat as she relived that moment. Kennedy was attracted to her. She knew it. Could feel it. Could almost reach out and touch it.

She had tossed and turned all night, trying to examine her own feelings, wondering why Kennedy Scott affected her so. There were many reasons, almost too many to count. But why now? What did it mean? Was it real or was she just so upset over Veronica that she was pushing everything onto Kennedy, wanting her to be some sort of savior?

She was attracted to Kennedy. She had admitted that much. But the realization only caused more questions and brought on more confusion. It left her feeling guilty, making her think about her own marriage and whether or not she'd made the right decision in going ahead with a divorce. It was the right thing. It was. But it wasn't the easy thing. The betrayal still stung. Facing that and the pending divorce would continue to be difficult. But she couldn't turn the other cheek this time. Her mind clouded with all the negativity as she thought of Veronica. It almost hurt her head, it was so powerful and consuming.

When would it ease up? All the anger and hurt and confusion? She was tired. Too damn tired to think about it at the moment. So she eased back and breathed deep and allowed the fog to consume her, falling fast asleep.

❖

Shawn awoke some time later, the house very still and quiet. She sat up slowly and looked around. Her shoulder screamed at her for the movement and she winced, wishing it would go back to just being uncomfortable. But the fall in the tub had irritated it.

Pushing herself up off the couch, she noted the time. It was after noon. She'd been asleep for hours. A soft blanket was snuggled around her, as if it had been placed with great care. She uncovered herself and stood, trying to wake up, quickly realizing that the sleep had done her good. While she was still in pain, she felt better rested, her mind clear and focused.

"Ms. Ryan," Monty said as he walked into the kitchen.

"Where is everyone?" The house was unusually quiet and she knew her girls must be out somewhere or taking a nap.

"Down on the beach. Ms. Scott's sister arrived."

She walked to the back door and looked out. She'd slept through the arrival. She'd been so tired she'd nearly forgotten they were coming.

She smiled as she saw four little ones playing along the surf, pails slinging from their hands. A red dog ran along with them. Kennedy stood alongside a woman near her same height. The hair color was similar as well. It must be Keri. Opening the door with her good arm, Shawn stepped out into the salty air. She walked beyond the pool and hit the soothing sand with her bare feet. It was cold and soft, giving under her as she walked. She shaded her brow as the wind blew the scent of sea into her face. As she edged closer, her girls caught sight of her and they came bounding up to her with great excitement. She noted the bandannas tied on their heads and the jeans with the rolled-up cuffs to their knees. Both the girls wore large hoop earrings, clipped on. She laughed at the sight.

"Mommy, look!" Kiley exclaimed. "Treasure!" She held up her hand. It was full of tiny shells and chocolate coins.

"Wow," she said, kneeling to greet them both. "Looks like you guys are having fun." She kissed their windblown faces, inhaling the salty scent of their hair. This was a moment she would remember always. She hadn't had many of those recently and it surprised her a little.

"Kiley found the treasure that Captain Kennedy hid," Rory reported.

"Yeah, and now it's ours! We're the good pirates."

Shawn looked up, suddenly curious about Captain Kennedy. As if on cue, Kennedy approached from close to the dunes. The woman Shawn assumed to be her sister walked with her. Both had on jeans that were rolled up just like Rory's and Kiley's. Two little boys sprinted past them, hurrying to a destination unknown. They also wore bandannas and rolled-up pants. One held up a toy sword and swore vengeance on the bad pirates.

Shawn smiled at them as they kicked up sand and bolted by her.

"Please excuse them," the woman next to Kennedy said. "They're focused on treasure." She held out her hand and gave a warm smile. "You must be Shawn. I'm Keri. Keri Boudreaux."

Shawn returned the smile, noting just how similar Keri looked to Kennedy. The boys, too, looked like their aunt. "I'm Shawn Ryan, and I see you've met my two girls."

"Gosh, yes. What cuties. The boys are smitten."

Shawn watched as the four children gathered over something of interest in the sand. "It looks like the girls are too."

"They are," Kennedy said. "They're having a great time."

Shawn studied Kennedy in her jeans and flowing white blouse. It was unbuttoned fairly low on her chest and open at the wrists. She also had on a bandanna and large earrings. Shawn didn't know whether to laugh with amusement or openly drool. She was breathtaking standing there like that, facing the wind and sea, caring for her children so openly. Tears actually formed, her emotions so raw and overwhelming. She was like an open book—all anyone had to do was take the time to read. She forced herself to calm down and thankfully Keri helped.

"Thanks so much for welcoming us. We really appreciate it."

"Oh, it's no problem. Sounds like we all need some time away."

"You mean away from the wackos?"

Shawn laughed. "Yeah."

"They sure seem to be in full force lately." She looked off toward the sea and hugged herself, visibly shaken. The humor had vanished quickly and Shawn knew exactly what was going through her mind.

"Hopefully things will quiet down," Shawn said softly. "For all of us."

Keri seemed to relax a little, the fresh sea air probably helping. "I hope so."

"Are you all settled in the house?" Shawn asked.

Kennedy sank her hands into her jeans pockets. "They're all moved in. It's smaller than the one you're in, but it will do. At this point smaller is better. Easier to watch."

"So you're staying with them, then?" Shawn hoped the disappointment wasn't too evident in her voice. Of course Kennedy would stay with Keri and the boys.

Kennedy watched her closely. She seemed to sense the disappointment.

"I hope you don't mind. Monty and—"

"It's fine. No need to explain. Really."

"We're close together. With all of us on the lookout we should be fine. Two men came with Keri and we've still got Monty and Larry and Phil."

"I'm sure we'll be okay. I trust you." She held Kennedy's gaze for a long moment. She did more than trust her. She wanted to fall into the security of her embrace.

"Auntie Kenny!" The boys came running up, cheeks red, hair blowing in the wind. "You have to come find the treasure." His pirate hat had *Landon* embroidered on the front. He tugged on Kennedy's hand.

"Yeah, we hid it and now you find it!" the other one said, jumping up and down. He pointed back toward where Rory and Kiley stood. The girls bounced on their feet, excited as well. The wind carried their laughter.

"Okay, but I need a shovel. Can I borrow yours?"

"No."

Kennedy bent and grinned. "No?"

The boys started to run. "Uh-uh."

"What do you mean, 'uh-uh'?" She reached out for them and purposely missed. The boys laughed harder as she chased after them.

Shawn and Keri watched, standing in the cool sand.

"She's so good with the kids," Shawn said.

"Yes, she is."

"My girls have really taken to her."

"I'm not surprised. Somedays the boys refer to her as Mommy number two."

Shawn smiled. "I can believe it."

They were silent as the kids helped Kennedy dig in the sand. The ocean churned and hissed, rhythmic, sliding up onto the sand and then slipping back out. She could stare at it endlessly.

"How has she been?" Keri asked, looking at Shawn with concerned eyes. They were golden brown, just like Kennedy's.

"She's been good, I think."

"Quiet?"

"Yes."

"Intense?"

"Yes."

"Lost in thought a lot?"

Shawn blinked. "Come to think of it, yes."

Keri looked at her feet as she kicked at some sand. "I worry about her."

"I think she worries about you too."

"We're quite a pair, aren't we?"

Kennedy called out as she found the treasure. She held it up in the air. It was a toy truck. The boys ran in a circle around her while the girls hopped with excitement.

Shawn couldn't help but smile. There was such joy there at that moment.

"I didn't think she would be like this," Shawn said.

"Like what?"

"So caring. And I don't know, soft? Especially with the kids."

"Why not?"

"I guess because of her job. All of the horrible things she's seen. I expected her to be uptight and detached. You know, one of those by-the-book people."

"I think in some ways she is. But not with children. Children are her soft spot."

"She told me about the missing children case," Shawn said. "Told me some of it."

"That case has nearly killed her. It will forever eat away at her. Until one day, there's nothing left."

"That's so sad."

"It is. She blames herself. I don't think anything will ever make it easier for her. Not even if they found him. The damage has been done. Although I would love to see that bastard get what he deserves."

"Doesn't it scare you? Realizing that there are people in the world like that? It terrifies me. I don't know how Kennedy handles any of it."

"Me neither. What little she would tell me gave me nightmares. And that case…the kids, finding them dead…and then the harassment."

"Harassment?"

"The killer wrote to Kennedy."

Shawn blinked. "You're kidding me."

"No, no. He did it for years. Since the first one turned up missing."

"Oh my God."

"The last letter came about three years ago. She hasn't heard from him since."

"They couldn't get any evidence from the letters?"

"Not much. No prints, no DNA. Just one or two sentences. The same verse that was found on the bodies. 'Seek and ye shall find.'"

Shawn felt dizzy and a bit sick. "What was that supposed to mean?"

"Well, Kennedy thinks it means many things. Me, I just think the guy's a kook. He's a game player and the children were his pawns, Kennedy his opponent."

"What a nightmare."

Keri nodded. "It was. I'm just glad he stopped. Kennedy says he's dead. Because even if he were incarcerated, he wouldn't be able to resist writing her."

"Let's hope she's right."

"Whatever happened to him, I can't help but hope it was horrible."

Shawn closed her eyes, her imagination running wild. She said a silent prayer, thankful for her children and their safety. She prayed their security would last. And finally, she said a prayer for Kennedy and for all those poor souls who never made it home safely.

❖

*Nyack, New York*

She sat in the car rubbing her cold hands together. She had no heat and it felt like it was freezing out. The old car barely ran and she was grateful for that much. Surprisingly, she wasn't as cold as she should be. Her adrenaline warmed her, hot liquid energy running beneath her skin. The house behind the gate fueled that adrenaline.

It was time to claim Veronica as her own once again.

A quick glance at her watch told her she had ten more minutes. Something flickered in her chest. Excitement? Laughter? Nerves? It was so easy, really. Too easy. Sloan was actually expecting her. People were so stupid.

She studied the house and thought of the Ryan mansion. She had been inside it too, many times. She knew almost all there was to know about Veronica Ryan and her home, from the children she had with Shawn to the names of their pets to what side of the bed she slept on.

She smiled as she remembered waking Veronica on that winter afternoon months ago. She had been there to clean the house, a one-time-only job, and Veronica had fought getting up out of bed. Shawn had yelled for her countless times to no avail, and finally she'd given up and told her to go on in. Carefully, she had crept in, carrying her dust cloth and the vacuum cleaner. She could recall every detail, from the way the room smelled, like plumeria, to the color of the cream carpet, to the way the sunlight poured in through the tall windows, tiny particles dancing in the rays. The room was large and open, with vaulted ceilings and thick crown molding. Expensive artwork hung on the walls, but that hadn't interested her. No, what had interested her were the two half-empty bottles of Fiji water on the night table. The bottle of Tylenol PM. A small stack of fashion magazines, a box of Kleenex, and a small plastic container. The other night table held an alarm clock, two paperback books, and a large framed photo of the children.

And then she'd heard it. The groan. The lump on the left side of the bed stirred. Veronica.

There.

In the bed.

"Go ahead," Shawn had encouraged her. "She needs to get up anyway."

"No, I don't need to get up!"

The feather duvet flipped off a head of dark hair. A pinched face appeared. Angry. It was glaring at her.

"Have you no respect?"

She'd nearly jerked. Veronica was speaking to *her*. Addressing *her*.

Shawn spoke, moving around the room, tidying up.

"Get up, V. For God's sake, it's three o'clock."

"I'll get up when I'm damn good and ready." She jerked the covers over her head and flopped back down.

Shawn said again, "Go ahead."

So she had. She turned on the vacuum and began cleaning, much to Veronica's dismay. She wasn't even halfway through the room when Veronica threw back the covers once again and hopped out of bed. The plastic container on the night table was gobbled up by her hands and opened. Then, with her thumb and forefinger, she dug in her mouth and removed a fitted clear mouthpiece. She placed it in the container and snapped it shut. Then she looked at her.

"Who the hell are you?" Her oversized T-shirt barely covered the tops of her thighs.

The sight had left her momentarily speechless and she'd just stood there staring, holding the running vacuum cleaner. Agitated, Veronica had stomped off to the bathroom, stripping out of her T-shirt along the way.

She continued to vacuum, but left it frequently to try to peek in on Veronica. When she saw steam emerge from the open bathroom, she walked to the night table and opened the container. The mouthpiece was fitted almost perfectly to Veronica's teeth, probably to protect them from grinding. Saliva glistened where it rested toward the bottom as she held it up for examination. She smelled it. Caught the lingering scent of Veronica's breath. Then she extended her tongue and tasted. The cold saliva had seemed to shoot right through her, exciting her beyond belief. Veronica. It was Veronica. Her very essence.

She wanted to run her tongue deeply inside the mouthpiece, lick out every last drop of saliva. Move it around in her mouth. Taste it, relish it. Then swallow it down to be hers forever and then place the piece inside her mouth and suck on it. Feel it slide into place over her own teeth. Yes, this was perfect.

Quickly, she'd glanced back toward the bathroom. Then she'd shoved the mouthpiece into her pants pocket and closed the empty container before returning it to the night table.

She glanced at her watch again. Almost time. She thought back to her most prized possession. She wore the mouthpiece every night. Slid her tongue over it again and again until she fell asleep. If she tried real hard she could still smell Veronica, taste her.

Shuddering, she huddled herself in the roomy driver's seat. The car was big and old and she loved it. The vinyl seats were cushy and worn and she liked the way they smelled. She enjoyed digging into the cracks to rub the insides. She'd even found a piece of candy corn.

Yes, this car was special. Hopefully, she'd be able to keep this one for a while.

She stared at herself in the mirror. She wondered what people would think about her if she was ever caught. More than likely they would think she was sick, some pervert who was obsessed with Veronica Ryan. But she wasn't like that at all. She wasn't a man, she wasn't driven by sex. She was driven by love. Couldn't people see that? She would never harm Veronica Ryan. Only those people who were bad for her. Someday Veronica would see what she'd done for her. Someday she would see that they were meant to be together. In the meantime she had to keep doing what was right. She had to rid Veronica of these bad women. And since she couldn't find Shawn, she would have to deal with Sloan.

She looked at her watch again.

It was time.

❖

*Hilton Head, South Carolina*

Kennedy headed into the master bath to check the window locks. She'd already been through the entire house, checking all the locks again upon waking. All was secure. Turning to leave, she caught a glimpse of herself in the mirror. Her cheeks had a redness to them and she rubbed at them, confused. It was as if she were in a state of permanent blush. Her face always felt hot, especially anytime she thought of Shawn.

As she walked away from the mirror she realized that she had never been in a situation like this before. Not just in regard to finding herself attracted to someone on assignment, but in general. No one had ever stirred her inside before. The feeling was as new as it was frightening.

Frustrated, she approached the window in the master bedroom and looked out at the beach. She saw Shawn walking with her girls, making their way through the thick sand. The girls twirled happily around, swinging their sand buckets through the salty air.

Shawn Ryan was a very beautiful woman with wonderful kids. But she was married. Maybe not happily, and it would probably end in divorce, but she was married nonetheless. There was pain evident in Shawn because of that marriage. Both physically and emotionally. Kennedy could see it in her walk, slow and unsure. In her shoulders, the way they slumped. In her eyes, the ache filling them in a heavy fog. There was pain. And Kennedy wasn't about to complicate things further.

She headed downstairs. She could smell toast and she found Keri standing at the kitchen counter making a bottle. Natalie sat strapped into a bouncy chair, cooing and sucking on her fingers. Kennedy kissed her forehead and inhaled her warm baby scent. Natalie smiled.

"Good morning," Keri said.

"Morning."

"Sleep well?" Keri's tone indicated that she knew otherwise. Kennedy decided to answer carefully.

"Off and on."

"Uh-huh."

Keri shook the bottle and took it to Natalie, who clutched it eagerly.

"Did you happen to hear the boys?" Keri asked, smoothing down her terry-cloth robe.

"They're still out. I peeked in on them."

"They were beat."

The boys usually rose around seven. But yesterday had been long, with the flight and then playing on the beach for hours. They needed the sleep.

"What about you? You look beat."

Kennedy stared out at the beach. She could see Shawn hugging herself against what must be a crisp sea breeze. Kennedy gazed to her left and right. Larry and Phil were a hundred or so yards from her, one on either side. It relaxed Kennedy a little.

Shawn hugged herself tighter and bent a little. Then she staggered. At once Kennedy wanted to go to her, to hold her close, to warm her heart and soul. But she fought the urge and Shawn got her bearings and straightened. Kennedy could feel Keri looking at her.

"What's going on, Ken?"

"Hmm?" she continued to watch Shawn, concerned.

"With Shawn Ryan."

Surprised, Kennedy turned to look at her. Keri had her hands on her hips. She was serious.

"How do you mean?"

"How do I mean? I mean are you sleeping with her?"

Kennedy reared back, shocked. Were her feelings that obvious?

"You know me better than that."

Keri's face was overcome with surprise. "Oh my God. You want to."

"What?"

"Yes. You do. You didn't deny it. You didn't tell me I was crazy. You want her."

"Cut it out, Ker. I would never do anything like that."

"I know. But you want to. Oh my God."

"Will you quit saying that?"

"You're in love with her."

"No, I'm not. I'm just doing my job."

She was starting to grow defensive.

"I know you, Kennedy. I know you better than anyone else on this planet. And I can see it in you. And I can see it in her."

Kennedy turned from the window. "There's nothing to see. Shawn's married."

"From what I hear, that's not much of a marriage."

They were interrupted by the sound of the boys rushing into the room, hair tousled, faces slack with sleep. Keri kissed them good morning and then got busy pouring them cereal. Landon turned on the television and settled down on the floor to watch cartoons. Luke followed, rubbing his eyes.

Keri's words burned Kennedy's ears. She could see it in Shawn? Shawn was feeling the same way? No. Impossible. Shawn was just in pain. Kennedy refocused on her and saw her sit carefully in the sand. She was cold. And weak.

Her need to comfort Shawn was becoming powerful and her feelings were quickly overwhelming her. She would care for Shawn, look after her, but from a safe distance. It was the only thing she could do. The right thing to do. And if her feelings of attraction continued, she would swallow them down until her time was up. What else could she do?

She found some hot cocoa and busied herself heating up some water.

"You're going after her, aren't you?" Keri asked, placing the two bowls of cereal on the table. "Boys, breakfast." They trudged to the table and climbed up on the chairs. Natalie shook her bottle in her fists.

"She looks cold," Kennedy said, stirring in the mix.

"She's very pretty. And very nice. I can see why you like her."

"I'm just looking out for her."

Keri studied her. "Just be careful. She's married to a very powerful woman. I don't want to see you get hurt."

Kennedy didn't respond. She just took the mug and headed outside, hoping the fresh air would clear her mind and rid it of Keri's words.

She breathed in deeply, letting the sea air soothe her. A large teal-colored pool sat between the house and the beach, surrounded by the native foliage of palm trees and bushes. Suddenly, a beautiful vision assaulted her mind, of Shawn climbing out of the pool, running her hands through her wet blond hair, the ocean crashing behind her in the distance.

It nearly caused her knees to buckle and her chest ached as if someone had socked her in the ribs. She had to stop for a few seconds and catch her breath. The image kept on. Shawn with glistening wet skin, water dripping from her hair. It was no longer Shawn at the pool. It was Shawn in the bath. She could smell the suds, see the candlelight flickering over her body.

Kennedy's own body churned with fire, heating her skin, shaking her up. She walked a ways out onto the beach, but she didn't walk down to the water. Instead, she sat on a thick dune a good ways from Shawn and Phil and Larry. When Larry caught sight of her, she waved. Then she stared out at the sea and sipped the hot cocoa.

What was she going to do about Shawn Ryan?

Shawn turned over and awoke clutching the bed covers to her chest. She blinked back the hot tears. She had been having another nightmare. This one about Veronica and Sloan Savage. Sitting up slowly, she swallowed back more tears as the dream's harsh reality hit home.

It was real. It had happened. Veronica had cheated. She'd driven the fact home that their marriage was over.

The nightmare kept on. And on. And on.

Shawn threw back the covers and went to rinse her face. Her injured shoulder screamed out at her as she bent to splash the cold water upon her skin. She looked in the mirror, noting the wound's redness. She must've strained it in her sleep. Cringing once again at the horrible nightmare, she finished rinsing her face and filled a glass with water.

As she studied herself in the mirror she wondered if she would ever be able to get over the affair. True, Veronica had apologized, and she had seemed devastated herself, with all the guilt that accompanied the affair. But was Veronica sorry for the affair, or sorry for getting caught and having to tell?

She would like to think that Veronica was truly sorry for the affair, that it was a one-time thing. In Veronica's words, "a serious and stupid mistake." But she knew about all the others. It was just taking her mind and heart time to accept it all. She wasn't sure if she'd ever be able to really do it.

It just felt easier to cut and run. To pretend it never happened, that she and Veronica had never even been together.

Feeling nauseous, she patted her face dry and walked back into the bedroom. The phone rang as she sat on the bed.

"Hello." Her voice was heavy with sleep.

"Hi." It was Veronica, and Shawn could hear people talking and moving around in the background.

"Hi." What did she want? She wished she'd at least have the courtesy to call her in private.

"What's wrong? Did I wake you?"

"No, I'm up. I was having a nightmare."

"Oh, I'm sorry."

"Yeah, it was a bad one."

"About what?"

"You and Sloan."

"Jesus," Veronica whispered, as if offended.

"Sorry, but it's what's going on with me. It eats at me night and day." She grew angry. "No. You know what? I'm not sorry."

Veronica bit right back. "What do you want from me?"

"How about the truth?" She hated this. Their bickering back and forth. It had been nice not to have to deal with it.

"I've told you the truth, Shawn. And I can't really talk about this right now."

"Then why did you call?"

"I called to see how you were doing."

"I'm fine."

Veronica sighed, frustrated. "No, you're not."

"You're right, I'm not. But everything else is off-limits."

She was mad and she was hurt, but more than that she was betrayed because she'd lost faith. She'd lost her best friend, the person with whom she shared her life.

"Don't do this, Shawn. You know I can't discuss this in front of everyone."

"I can do it. I finally *can* do it. If you can't, then that's your problem. If you don't want to hear it, then don't call."

There was silence. Shawn could hear the background noise. Then Veronica spoke. "How are the kids?"

"Fine."

"They enjoying the new place?"

"Yes, very much so. They really like Kennedy too." Right away she realized what she'd done. And she didn't care. It was the truth.

"Kennedy?" She sounded surprised and a little annoyed.

"Yes, she plays with them and they really enjoy having her here."

"What about you?" Veronica eventually asked. "Are you enjoying her?"

Shawn laughed. She knew where this was headed and she was enjoying the jealousy dripping from Veronica's voice. It was nice to have the tables turned, however wrong it was.

"She's nice."

"Don't give me that," Veronica whispered with anger. "You know damn well what I mean."

"No, I don't."

"Do you want to fuck her?" she asked loudly, getting right to the point. Shawn heard the numerous voices around her silence.

"I'm going to go now, V. I've had quite enough." She lay back in bed, staring at the ceiling. Veronica was getting carried away now, just like she always did when something got to her.

"The way she looks at you, I should've known. Now she's probably fucking you right under my nose. I wanted her to protect you and I bet she's doing a hell of a job!"

"Enough!" Shawn said loudly. "You have no right to behave this way. We are no longer together. Or have you forgotten that I've filed for divorce?"

"I haven't forgotten. Hardly. I'm just trying to be nice."

"Well, don't bother. It's a little late to play kind, caring Veronica."

"I want to work it out."

Shawn was shocked. "What?"

"I'm sorry. We can work this out. I know we can."

"I don't believe what I'm hearing." She wanted to throw the phone across the room. Veronica still hadn't admitted to the other women, to the drug use, to the lies. And she wanted to work it out? Was she out of her fucking mind?

She clenched her jaw, so angry her chest hurt and her throat burned with barely harbored harsh words.

"Good-bye, Veronica."

Veronica tried to speak again but Shawn ended the call, unable to take any more. She lay on the bed in silence, examining their brief conversation and her swirling emotions. She was so confused and so hurt it was a miracle she could think rationally at all. The images of Veronica and Sloan making love kept flashing in her mind like a torturous movie played over and over again. Even when she slept she couldn't escape the hurtful scenes of the two of them grinding against one another. But why did it hurt? She examined her feelings. She was expecting jealousy but none came. Instead, she realized she was more upset because of what the image truly relayed. The marriage was over and had been for some time. Sloan and Veronica making love just confirmed what she had already known deep in her heart.

Shuddering, she sat up and replaced the phone on its charger. Her stomach growled, protesting the lack of food it had endured lately. Her thoughts had been consumed with the whole affair thing, and on top of that there was the shooting and the threats. Oftentimes she wondered what else she could take. One tiny thing more and she might slip off the edge of sanity.

Right now that edge was crumbling. V. Sloan. The shooting. The UNSUB, to use the FBI term. Kennedy. All of it again and again.

She went to the dresser and retrieved a comfortable pair of sweats. As she dressed she thought about Kennedy and went over Veronica's jealousy. Kennedy was attractive, very much so, but Veronica knew

Shawn. She knew she'd never consider the idea. Shawn was too devoted. Too serious and usually way too caught up in her marriage. Usually. So it must be the fact that everyone had taken to Kennedy so well. The girls adored her, and she was finding Kennedy's presence more and more enjoyable. Kennedy was intelligent and kind, a very warm person.

Yes, she supposed there was good reason for Veronica to be jealous. Because the truth was, she was losing her children and Shawn to her. And Veronica *had* to be number one. Always.

Rubbing her temples, she crossed to the bedroom door, ready to put Veronica from her mind for the time being. It flung open just as she was reaching for it.

"Mommy!" the girls cried out with glee, attaching themselves to her lower body.

An instant grin came along with the warming of her heart. The girls could always bring a smile. "Good morning, my little princesses," she said, tousling their hair. The princess dresses they had on were pulled over pajamas, so they hadn't been awake for very long.

"Yes, we're princesses, and that makes you the queen!" Rory exclaimed.

"Yeah, and Kennedy is the king!" Kiley said with excitement.

Shawn blushed at the innocent comment and tried not to respond. She didn't know what to say.

"No, dummy, Kennedy can't be the king 'cuz she's a woman," Rory said.

"Yes, she can! She can be a girl king."

"Nuh-uh. Mommy, tell Kiley that Kennedy can't be a king 'cuz she's a girl."

"Kiley, kings are men," Shawn said, a part of her wishing they would drop it.

"But what about Kennedy?" Kiley asked, pushing out her lower lip. "Kennedy has to be something."

"Come on, let's go downstairs and I'll fix you breakfast." She led the girls from the bedroom.

"Kennedy's cooking breakfast already," Rory reported, holding Shawn's hand.

"She is?" Shawn was pleasantly surprised. They usually didn't see Kennedy until after breakfast when she and Keri and the kids came by to play.

"Yeah, she's making pancakes!" Kiley said. She grabbed Shawn's other hand and they all three walked down the stairs.

"Mommy?" Kiley asked softly.

"Yes?"

"Do knights have to be boys?"

"I'm not sure, honey."

"'Cuz Landon and Luke are knights and I think Kennedy could be a knight too."

"Yeah!" Rory proclaimed.

They hit the bottom of the stairs and Shawn could immediately smell the warm scent of a homemade breakfast. The girls released her hands and ran into the kitchen ahead of her, calling out to Kennedy. The boys were there too, running around with fake swords in the air. Keri sat on the sofa bouncing Natalie on her lap. She greeted Shawn with a smile.

"Good morning. Hope we didn't wake you. The boys were anxious to see the girls. You're lucky we weren't here at six."

Shawn laughed. "Wow, yeah, thanks for holding off for a while."

Kennedy turned from the stove top and smiled, a spatula in hand. She had on khaki cargo capris and a plain white V-neck tee. A simple gold cross rested on her olive skin just below the base of her throat, her hair swept back into a loosely twisted bun. Her eyes shone as Luke bounded up to her requesting some orange juice.

"Give me a kiss first," she requested, bending. Luke wrapped his arms around her neck and kissed her and then hung on for a brief spin around the kitchen. Shawn rested her cheek against her hand, pleasantly amused.

Kennedy poured the juice into a sippy cup and Luke disappeared, cup shoved in his mouth, pinky finger extended.

"Good morning," Kennedy said, focusing on Shawn.

"Morning." Shawn straddled a stool and continued to watch her as she cooked.

Kennedy flipped the pancakes and then turned off the stove. She placed the plate of fresh flapjacks on the kitchen island in front of Shawn. The kids were running up and down the stairs with excitement, retrieving more toys before they were called to breakfast.

"These look great," Shawn said, eyeing the pancakes. More

than anything she wanted to look up at Kennedy, but she was sure her attraction would be written all over her face.

"Thanks." Kennedy smiled once again. "You look like you could use a good meal."

"I look that bad, huh?"

"No." Kennedy's face fell.

"It's okay, I can take it." Shawn held up her hand, knowing she probably looked worse than she felt.

"You haven't been eating much. And from what Monty says, your sleeping hasn't improved much either."

"You're very perceptive." And so kind and thoughtful. Shawn stared at her, longing to get lost in the tenderness of her eyes. God, she could really just fall right into her.

"It's my job," Kennedy replied with a half grin.

"Kennedy, look!" Kiley exclaimed suddenly, holding up a plastic sword. "You're a knight!"

"I'm a knight?"

"No, she's not a knight yet," Rory said, Landon standing by her side.

"Yeah. Antie Kenny, first the queen has to knight you."

They looked to Shawn. "Yeah, Mommy. You're the queen, you have to make Kennedy a knight." Kiley walked over to Shawn and held out the sword. Shawn took it, though reluctantly.

"I don't know, girls. Maybe Kennedy doesn't want to be a knight." Shawn felt unusually embarrassed, so much so that she couldn't bring herself to look back at Kennedy.

"Sure she does!" Rory exclaimed, looking up at Kennedy. "Don't ya?"

Kennedy stood straighter and held her hand over her heart. "I would be honored."

Shawn wanted to laugh. And then collapse. She felt so out of control.

"Okay then. You have to go kneel before Mommy…I mean the queen." Rory took Kennedy's hand and led her around the kitchen island.

Once in front of Shawn, Kennedy hesitated slightly, glancing at her, waiting for someone to object. But the kids acted quickly.

"Okay, Mommy, now you stand up," Rory directed her. Shawn gave Kennedy an "I'm sorry" look as she stood and took the sword. Kennedy smiled warmly in return, letting her know it was okay.

"Now, Kennedy, you kneel before Mommy," Rory said with Kiley jumping up and down in excitement next to her. Landon just grinned from ear to ear.

"But you have to pretend she's a queen." Rory giggled, clapping her hands in anticipation.

"Okay," Kennedy said, unable to hide her smile. She knelt on one knee and bowed her head before Shawn. The kids giggled hysterically, so excited they could hardly contain themselves. But Rory kept the ball rolling.

"Mommy, touch her shoulders with the sword and say, 'I knight thee Madame Kennedy.'"

Shawn swayed a little with embarrassment and adrenaline. There was a beautiful woman down on her knee in front of her. She cleared her tight throat and touched Kennedy on the shoulders, praying she wouldn't look up at her.

"Say it, say it!" Landon said.

"I knight thee Madame Kennedy," she said in a whisper. Kennedy raised her head slowly and locked eyes with her. Shawn took an unsteady step back as the fiery golden brown blazed.

The kids didn't seem to notice.

"Now Madame Kennedy has to kiss the queen's hand," Rory said, making sure the deed was done properly.

"Yeah, yeah!" Kiley said loudly, clapping once again.

Kennedy hesitated slightly and then reached out and took Shawn's hand. She brought it slowly up to her mouth and Shawn shuddered as she felt her warm breath against her skin.

"Your majesty," Kennedy said softly just before placing a lingering warm kiss on the back of her hand.

The kids cheered loudly and hopped around as Shawn pulled her hand back and looked away, her skin hot and hungry from the feel of Kennedy's lips. Powerfully stirred, she gave Kennedy a quick smile and then excused herself. She walked quickly into the nearest restroom to get hold of herself. She stared at herself in the mirror and willed her heart to slow.

*What's wrong with me? Am I crazy? I can't be attracted to Kennedy Scott.* But as she thought over the reasons why, she realized that the main reason was growing ever dimmer. No longer did her marriage ring out loud and true. It had been forever tainted. It was gone.

She rinsed her face with cold water and reminded herself that there were still several other reasons why she couldn't risk being attracted to Kennedy. And two of them were out in the kitchen most likely chowing down happily on pancakes.

It was too soon and they would only be confused.

Sucking in a big breath of air, she rubbed her cheeks and walked back into the kitchen. The girls were just as she pictured them, happily eating their homemade breakfast, the smell of syrup dark and rich and sweet in the air.

"I made you a plate," Kennedy said, placing it on the table.

"It's good, Mommy," Kiley said with a happy smile.

"Yeah, Kennedy's a good chef."

"Yes, it looks as though she is," Shawn said sitting down to eat. "But you certainly don't have to serve us." She met the hot golden gaze with her own and nearly swooned once again.

"Cooking is a treat in my line of work. It's a great escape."

"Besides, you'll never get her to stop," Keri said from the couch. "Trust me on that one. She's just like our grandmother. Always feeding everyone."

"Sounds good to me," Shawn said, meaning it. She took a warm soft bite and chewed. It was good. Damn good. She ate slowly, watching as Kennedy stood at the kitchen island sipping her coffee. Monty came in and poured himself a cup. Kennedy made sure to tell him there was plenty. He thanked her and made a hearty plate for himself. He gave Shawn a wink and joked with the kids.

When Shawn looked back at Kennedy she caught her watching her.

Looking away, she wondered what Kennedy had been thinking.

Was it possible that in their crazy, chaotic world where spouses cheated and unstable people shot at them, was it possible that something pure and honest and passionate could be happening? Was that really how the world worked?

# CHAPTER EIGHT

*Yonkers, New York*

She had done it. She had finally killed. She paced her little apartment in an excited gait, too keyed up to sit. She had underestimated the thrill, and she was still feeling it, nearly paralyzing, coursing through her veins as if she were still there. She could still hear the pop of the gun, smell the smoke, see the enormous splat and spray of blood.

It had been hours now and she still couldn't sit still. Her mind kept replaying the sequence of events over and over again. She leaned against the wall and allowed the image of Sloan's house to fill her mind.

*She rang the doorbell at the oversized front door. Sloan answered looking like she had just awakened. Looking like certifiable hell.*

*"Come in." Sloan sounded agitated.*

*She followed her inside, trying not to gape at the enormity of the house. She'd been there before, but this house always took her breath away. Opening up just beyond the entrance, three large rooms merged into one and at its center stood a grandiose staircase. It would've been perfect if it weren't for the smell of cigarette smoke.*

*"Where's the other girl?" Sloan asked, shuffling ahead of her. Her feet were covered in white sweat socks and she had on flannel sleep pants and a worn tank. Her tattoos seemed to jump from her arms. "They usually send two of you."*

*"She should be here any time," she lied.*

*Sloan led her into the kitchen where she opened a drawer and dug out a lighter. She plucked a cigarette from a box in the giant stainless* steel freezer and stuck it between her lips. After lighting it, she inhaled deeply.

"You can start in here. Clean all the appliances and countertops and don't forget the sink."

She nodded in compliance. Sloan always gave directions for some reason. As if she had no clue what it was she was doing. This time the place didn't look too messy. Mostly dirty dishes and empty beer bottles. Sloan wasn't there for long periods of time.

"You've been here before, right?" Sloan studied her from across the counter. Yes, she had been there before and Sloan had been in a mood. High as a kite and willing to share details about her crush on Veronica Ryan.

Again she nodded.

"Yeah, I recognize you." Sloan tapped her temple and some ash fell from the cigarette. Her pupils looked large and her movements were off. She was high.

When she didn't say anything Sloan pushed off from the counter.

"I'm going to go take a bath. Help yourself to a drink. You can show yourself out when you're done." She walked a little ways and then stopped. "Oh." She snapped her fingers. Turning sharply, she disappeared from the room. When she returned she lazily tossed a stack of twenties on the counter. "Two fifty, right?"

Another nod.

Sloan sucked on her cigarette. "All right, then." She left, leaving a trail of smoke behind.

Watching her go, she set down her carrying case full of disinfectants, rags, and sponges. The yellow gloves smelled rubbery and stuck to her skin as she got to work scrubbing Sloan's kitchen. As she worked, she listened to the bath water being run overhead. The sound was strong and loud as if the water were truly cascading downward through the ceiling. After a while, it stopped and then a new sound came. Water jets.

It was all going to play out so perfectly. She smiled and rinsed out the bleach cleaner from the white porcelain sink. It gleamed.

Wiping her brow, she walked into the living room, through the posh furniture, to a showcase room. She referred to it as Sloan's "ego room." Frames housing gold and platinum records hung along *the walls, trophies of a famous rock star. Cases stood in the corners, showing off signed guitars and clothing that had been worn on stage. She walked along the back wall and looked at the photos of Sloan taken with some of the biggest names in the business. Sloan had quite a little collection.*

*It was impressive. Anyone would think so. But she wasn't like everyone else. The room and what it contained and what it represented repulsed her.*

*She halted in front of another glass case. A large picture of Sloan and Veronica Ryan stood staring at her. The two were side by side, arms behind one another. Their grins said it all. She had seen the photo before but now it held new meaning.*

*Clenching her fist, she straightened her back and went to the stairs. She stood still for a moment, enjoying the feel of her blood hammering angrily throughout her body. The water jets called to her. Telling her now.*

*Walking slowly, she ascended the stairs, rubber-gloved hands gripping the banister. She moved silently until she stood outside the master bedroom. The double doors were open and she could smell the stink of marijuana. She entered, knowing the large bathroom was deep within the room on her left. She glanced to her right and stared at the giant four-post bed. Her anger and jealousy flared again as she imagined Sloan making love to Veronica in it. Taking an angry breath, she turned toward the bathroom and reached into the pocket of her apron for her weapon.*

*She pulled it out slowly and took soft steps into the bathroom. The stench of the weed was strong and she nearly coughed as she entered. The room was warm and muggy, the steam from the water mixing with the weed. She blinked and wiped the sweat from her brow as she focused on Sloan. The bathtub sat ten feet ahead and on her left. She was expecting Sloan's back to be to her, but it wasn't. After stepping back quickly, she hid behind the corner and watched. Sloan glistened and moaned, her hands holding fast to the side of the tub. Her knees were bent over the wall of the tub, legs splayed. She clung to the tub tighter, thrusting herself against the flow of the water jet.*

*She watched in silence as Sloan made love to the water. Her fury grew as she imagined her making the same noises with Veronica Ryan.*

*Fury built as the moans of pleasure came louder and quicker, Sloan throwing her head back in a powerful orgasm. Sloan shuddered and strained, riding the climax out.*

*She was disgusted. Almost nauseous. The moans, the groans...now she knew what sex with Veronica had sounded like. It stabbed at her in ways she never could've imagined. How could Veronica do that? With this woman? Someone who got her kicks from her bathtub? She wiped more sweat away as Sloan swung her legs around and eased back into the water. Sloan took deep breaths and relaxed, submerging her entire body. Sloan reached for the joint, wanting another toke. Pinching it in her fingers, she took a long, deep drag.*

*The water jets continued to surge, creating noisy bubbles and waves in the water. She approached slowly and stealthily, knowing Sloan couldn't hear her. She flipped off the safety on her gun. She took another step and aimed, both hands gripping it tightly. Her arms shook as the jealous thoughts plagued her mind, pitting her insides with angry burning holes. Sloan was pathetic, a loser, not nearly good enough for her true love, smoking weed and getting off in her bathtub, too good for the help. What did Veronica see in her? She bit her lower lip and shook her head, knowing she had to do it. She took one last step and stood beside Sloan. Sloan started to turn her head, startled and confused.*

*The gunshot was deafening and her ears rang as she watched the bullet tear through Sloan's temple and exit her skull, blood and tissue splattering the tub and the wall.*

*Sloan's wide eyes went blank and then her head slumped, her chin against her chest. Her body began to slide farther into the tub, the bubbles and waves consuming it.*

*Carefully, she placed the gun in Sloan's right hand, curling her fingers around the weapon and then allowing her hand to fall into the water gripping the gun. The water began to turn pink from the heavy amount of blood. There was a sharp smell in the air, overpowering the weed. Spent gunpowder. And then the emerging metallic scent of blood.*

*She stepped back and stared. Sloan's head slid all the way into the water. Her knees and feet bobbed at the surface. The water boiled, the pink darkening. Blood and brain tissue oozed down the wall.*

*She walked away slowly, her mind in a numb sort of shock, her*

*body on autopilot. She reached into her apron and pulled out the letter.*
*Carefully, she placed it on Sloan's dresser for all to see.*

*Then she walked to the head of the stairs and stopped. She shook*
*with adrenaline as she realized what she had done. And then she smiled.*
*There was no more Sloan.*

She smiled again as she resumed her pacing in her tiny apartment.
She had done what was needed to rid Veronica of the people who didn't
love her like she did. Now there was the most important one left to take
care of. All she had to do now was find her.

❖

*Hilton Head, South Carolina*

Kennedy put down the letter and sighed. She was sitting on the floor
going through the boxes of mail Allen had brought her. She glanced at
her watch. It was after eleven. She stood and stretched, unable to sleep
but frustrated with the task at hand. She knew the letters were there.
She was willing to bet her life on it. But simple, unassuming fan letters
were a dime a dozen and her head hurt from the strain of reading each
one, analyzing every word.

She kicked the latest box, nudging it with frustration. She had
gone through two boxes, and three more remained, but she needed
some sleep.

Letters.

They seemed to be her worst nightmare. First they came with the
child murders, then they came to harass Keri. Now she was looking for
more in regard to Shawn and Veronica. For a brief moment, she wished
she could just toss out the boxes and lie on the beach and truly relax. No
more letters. No more jumbled words. No more taunting Bible scripture.
Just nothing. Nothing but the sound and the smell of the sea.

How nice that would be.

But it came again. That gnawing. It usually came late at night.
And she knew it was no use fighting it. Rising, she walked to her laptop
and switched it on. Sinking back into an oversized chair, she called up
the case file and started reading. Then she brought up each letter and
studied the words.

*Seek and Ye Shall Find.*

Simple block letters. Written in black marker, the kind anyone could buy at a local drugstore. Same with the paper. Sometimes it was white copy paper, sometimes it was lined notebook paper. The only thing they'd ever found on the letters was a tiny hair. Canine. Brown. A terrier mix. Nothing else.

The letters had been postmarked from the southern United States. Sent from hotels, mainly. The UNSUB would mail out the letter to various hotels. The large envelope would contain a smaller one. He would politely ask that the smaller one be placed in their outgoing mail. He always included a twenty-dollar bill for their trouble. The concierges obliged.

He seemed to favor Texas. Houston, Dallas, Austin, Corpus Christi. Only one had come from a different state. St. Louis, Missouri. No rhyme or reason. Not one she could figure out.

She studied one of the letters.

> *Scott,*
> *Seek and ye Shall find.*
> *Time's a wasting.*

She cringed. *Time's a wasting.* He toyed with her, taunted her. And he enjoyed it. She studied the words, the block lettering. What was she missing?

She closed out the letters and called up the photos. She knew every one by heart. The environment, the position of the bodies, exactly where the note was pinned or taped. She lined them up on her screen. Twelve little bodies.

She scanned them all, noting similarities.

They were all blond. Caucasian. Six to nine years of age. All from small towns. Most from the Midwest but two from New York state. The bodies were always found hundreds of miles from where they were taken. Most of the time in New York state, leading them to believe that's where he resided.

They found canine hairs matching the one from the letter on six of the bodies. Lead-based paint was found under all of their fingernails where they'd tried to claw their way out of something. Each had the same stomach contents. Kentucky Fried Chicken and biscuits. Their last meal.

She looked harder. The bodies were relatively clean, leaving them to believe they had been clothed up until he dumped them. They all had marks on their wrists and ankles where duct tape had been used. Some had the sticky remnants along their mouth and cheeks as well, where he had gagged them. Each child had been manually strangled and sexually assaulted. The UNSUB had carefully cleaned the pubic regions with bleach, yet he left semen on their abdomens, masturbating shortly after killing them.

She studied the way they were positioned. All of them had been placed face down, arms up, palms down. One knee was always raised. Almost as if they were sleeping. He'd cared for them. In his own sick way. He wasn't able to bring himself to leave them face up. He couldn't look at them like that. He knew what he was doing was wrong and yet he couldn't seem to stop himself.

She studied further. Each child held something in its hand. Something the UNSUB used to pacify them with. A balloon, a toy car, a toy baby bottle, a tiny toy soldier. Many of the toys were too old to find in stores. Some dated back to the 1960s.

The UNSUB was clever. Very clever. He was organized. Had elaborately planned each kidnapping. He had a house where he lived alone, somewhere he could take the children and hold them for days. He had old toys. Probably lived in an older house, maybe the one he grew up in. He had a job that allowed him to travel. Blue-collar work. Something that would be easy for him to make money at without putting in a lot of thought or effort, because his main goal was molesting and murdering children. It consumed him night and day. He was always moving toward that goal. The abductions gave him an adrenaline rush, the molesting and holding captive excited him, but the killing gave him the ultimate high.

She rubbed her eyes. The bodies started to run together. They would come to her in her dreams that night. She was sure of it.

Rising, she decided to get some fresh air. She waved at one of Keri's new security men, who sat reading a magazine on the couch. He nodded. She silenced the alarm and went out the back door and headed for the beach. The night was cool and crisp and the sea sounded calm and it seemed to whisper as it rushed onto the shore.

Her feet sank into the thick sand as she climbed a dune. The moon hung small but bright, showing her the way. A figure startled her when she reached the top.

"Hi."

It was Shawn. And about a hundred feet back stood Larry or Phil, she couldn't tell who.

"Hi."

"Couldn't sleep?" She was sitting with her knees pulled to her chest, sandals resting in the sand next to her. The moonlight kissed her shoulders. She was wearing a tank and sweatpants. She shivered.

"No." Kennedy sank into the sand next to her. She peeled off her button-down shirt and draped it over Shawn's shoulder.

"Thanks." She looked sad and tears glistened.

Kennedy nodded. "You okay?"

Shawn dug her hand into the sand. "Oh sure. Probably about as good as you are."

"That good, huh?"

Shawn laughed. "What a pair we are."

Kennedy was silent.

"It's funny, isn't it? Here we are in this beautiful place, where people play golf and tennis, swim in the sea, ride bikes down endless green trails, soak up the warm sun, watch gators crawl into ponds, and we're sitting here near midnight wrapped up in our own misery. We're pathetic. We should be enjoying this."

"We have a lot going on."

"Yes, we do. But still. We should be making the most of this. For the kids' sake at least."

"They're happy, aren't they? They seem happy."

"They're having fun but they aren't naïve. Rory knows something is wrong. She's asking. She can see it in my face."

"Have you told her?"

"About what? V and me?"

Kennedy nodded.

"I told her we need to be apart because we aren't getting along. She asked for how long. I told her I didn't know." Shawn wiped away a tear. "She took it well. She didn't cry. I did. She just took my hand and told me it would be okay." Shawn laughed. "She actually comforted me."

"That sounds like Rory."

"She's a strong little girl, my daughter."

"Yes, she is."

"What about Landon and Luke? Do they know what's going on?"

"No. They think they're on vacation. So they're having a ball."

"That's good. What about you, Kennedy? Do you ever have fun?"

Kennedy stared out at the sea.

"I'll take that as a no."

"I don't feel I have the right to."

"Why not?"

She decided to tell her the truth. The reason she didn't sleep, rest, relax or have fun. "Because there are thirteen families missing their children right now. Twelve of them grieving over their deaths. Thirteen little kids who didn't come home. So how can I have fun knowing that?"

"But it isn't your fault, Kennedy. You're still alive. You need to live."

"I can't. It isn't fair. And part of it is my fault. I should've found them. I should've stopped him."

"You're only one person. You did all you could."

"It wasn't enough."

Kennedy swallowed down the burning pain. She fought back the tears. Shawn's warm hand came to rest on hers. It shot right through her and she almost pulled away. Shawn noticed and retreated, lowering her head.

"I'm sorry."

"No, don't be."

"I shouldn't have done that."

Kennedy reacted quickly and took Shawn's hand. She squeezed. It felt nice. The world felt better. Warm.

Shawn looked into her eyes. She returned the squeeze. Then she slowly brought Kennedy's hand up to her mouth, where she kissed it.

A hiss escaped Kennedy and Shawn placed another kiss along her palm. And then another. The sensation bolted through her and pulsed between her legs. Her heels dug into the sand.

"Shawn," she whispered, nearly coming out her skin as she felt her hot, moist lips skim along her skin.

Shawn lowered her hand and reached out to cup her jaw. Ran a thumb over her cheek. She leaned in. Close. So close. The sea whispered. Her eyes sparkled in the moonlight.

"Kennedy," she said, barely touching her lips to hers.

Kennedy's heart jumped from her chest. The lips, so soft, so hot.

And then a ringing started. From her pocket. Shawn pulled back. Kennedy plucked out her phone. It was Allen.

"I'm sorry, I have to take this."

Shawn nodded and fingered her lips. The look of disappointment was not lost on Kennedy.

"Scott," she said, having trouble finding her voice.

"Kennedy, sorry to wake you."

"No problem. What's going on?"

"I'm afraid I have bad news."

"Oh?"

He told her as Shawn watched. When Allen finished, she hung up.

"What is it now?"

Kennedy cleared her throat. Shawn looked so frail. It was hard to believe that just seconds ago she was brimming with heat and passion, with tender, confident kisses.

"It's Sloan Savage."

A look of anger crossed her face. "And?"

"She's dead."

❖

*Nyack, New York*

Kennedy pulled her rental car to a screeching halt outside Sloan's mansion. Throwing it in park, she yanked out the key and shoved open her door. Several uniformed personnel eyed her warily as she slammed the door shut and slipped into her navy blue FBI windbreaker.

Even though she was no longer FBI, Allen wanted her to wear it so no one would give her any trouble.

"Kennedy," he called from the entryway where several people stood dressed in crime scene garb, snapping photos.

"Allen, what the hell happened?" She jogged up to him, her face feeling stiff with discontent.

"They're saying suicide."

"How?" She fell into stride next to him as they entered the large house.

"Shot once in the head, close range."

"Temple?"

"Yes."

"No forced entry?" They reached the stairs and began to climb.

"Nothing yet."

"You still think she's clean as far as the Ryan case?"

"Until now."

They entered the master bedroom. Clothes were strewn on the floor, along with shoes and belts. The bed was large and unmade, sheets loose and comforter bunched. Two full ashtrays were on the night table. The smell of marijuana lingered in the air.

Technicians worked the room, vacuuming the carpet, folding the clothes and placing them in paper bags. A young man was sweeping the bed with fluorescent light. Kennedy and Allen slipped on shoe covers.

"I talked to the county medical examiner. They're letting us take lead on the investigation for the time being. In here." Allen led her into the bathroom. More people milled. Two of them lifted the body from the tub. They placed her on a white sheet on the bathroom floor for an initial evaluation. A body bag was ready nearby. Allen excused them.

Kennedy could smell the clotted blood. The water in the tub was red.

"We get a time of death yet?"

"She's been dead over twenty-four hours."

"Who found her?"

"Cleaning lady."

"Cleaning lady?"

"Yeah, she showed up to clean and nearly finished the house before coming upon her in here."

"Must've been quite a shock."

"She's a mess over it. We've got our translators working with her. Her English is poor, she's from somewhere over in Eastern Europe."

Kennedy studied the body. The skin was pale and slick looking, slightly bloated. Her eyes were wide and staring up at the ceiling. There was a small hole on her right temple and a large exit wound on the left side of her head. Significant blood and brain matter stuck to the wall and the edge of the tub.

"There was a joint right here," Allen said. "It was nearly finished."

Burn marks scarred the marble. She must've smoked quite often in the tub and didn't bother with an ashtray.

"What do you think? She was working up the nerve and needed a little help?"

"Could be. But knowing her drug history, she would've probably gone for something stronger. Weed alone wouldn't cut it."

She knew that almost all suicides were accompanied by drugs or alcohol. The victims were almost always inebriated in some way to help them accomplish their deadly task.

"We'll have to wait for labs."

Kennedy looked at her hands. The fingernails were a little dirty. "We might want to bag these. See what we can get." She glanced over the rest of her. There were no marks or abrasions. She looked to Allen. "Anything else?"

"There was a letter. Found next to the joint on the bathtub."

They went back into the bedroom.

"Over here." He snapped on gloves and tossed her a pair. He opened a sealed bag and pulled out the letter. She took it.

"It's typed." Red flags shot up. "We can't do a handwriting analysis." She skimmed the contents.

*I'm sorry. My love for Veronica overtook me. I wanted her for myself. Tell Shawn I'm sorry I hurt her.*

She nearly scoffed as she returned the letter to Allen. He had that look. He knew too.

"There won't be any prints on it," she said, pretty sure.

"Probably not."

She removed the gloves. "It wasn't a suicide."

Allen agreed. "I don't think so."

"We won't find any conclusive evidence of a suicide but we won't find anything conclusive saying it wasn't either. Not right away anyway. But I do have my suspicions. There won't be any fingerprints on the letter and the wound won't be self-inflicted. The cleaning lady probably washed away any evidence downstairs."

She tapped her eyebrow.

"Where is this cleaning lady? I want to talk to her."

"She's downstairs." He looked concerned. "You sure you want to do this? We can handle it." He'd been surprised when she insisted on coming.

"I want back in. On everything."

"Why the change of heart?"

She wanted to tell him the truth. That it was Shawn. But she didn't. "I want this UNSUB. Now."

"What about Veronica Ryan? She's counting on you to watch after her wife and kids."

"And that's exactly what I'm going to do by solving this case."

"Glad to have you back. For however short a time."

They walked down the stairs.

"I need to speak with Veronica Ryan as well."

"Okay."

"I want all the info you got on her background check. I need to know about each and every woman. You've ran the checks on them?"

"Yes."

"Nothing?"

"Nada."

"I want to go over them." She thought about the boxes of letters and her need to examine them all. "Along with every last letter she's ever received."

# CHAPTER NINE

*Hudson Valley, New York*

She sat in her car, watching once again, all alone and in silence. Sprinkles of rain dotted the windshield, distorting her view. Outside, people scurried about with umbrellas or newspapers held over their camera-perfect hair. Filming had been briefly stopped due to the rain and she sat perched in her car, clenching the steering wheel while she scanned the movie set, searching, looking, for the one.

Desperate to see her, she repositioned and leaned forward a little. Her blood pumped with purpose as her mind focused intently on her love. She squinted through the windshield, unable to make out anyone familiar. She looked so hard she missed the security guard who had walked up to her driver's side window.

A firm knock came and she nearly jumped out of her skin. Startled, she rolled the window down and forced a smile, the courage to get close to Veronica Ryan driving her.

"Ma'am, you can't park here." He was big, over six foot and husky. Rain pelted off his navy ball cap.

"Oh, well maybe you can help me. I'm due on the set and I don't know where to go." She spoke lightly and looked at him with wide eyes.

"You have a pass?" He eyed the car, searching the seats.

"Um, well, I…" She dug around in her back pack and pulled out a business envelope she had typed up herself. She knew there were horses on the set and she had typed up a letter explaining her necessity on the set. She even knew the name of the company who provided the horses. She used their letterhead.

"Pop your trunk."

She did so. He closed it when he finished searching. When he returned to her window, she gave him the letter.

"What's this?" He opened it and read.

"I'm cleanup. I tend to the horses." She held her breath, wondering if he would buy it.

"I don't know. Nobody said anything to me about it."

"That's probably because I'm the last one to arrive. I'm late. I was caught up at another location." She watched as he continued to read the letter, weighing his decision. "Look, you can call Marty and ask him."

"Marty?" He looked at her over the papers.

"Yes, he's the one in charge." She swallowed hard. Marty owned the company. "But I really wish you wouldn't. He's already upset with me." She sighed. "I screwed up and a horse got sick. I've been busy trying to make that right. Now I'm here, but I should've been here two days ago. You can call and check, but my name is probably the last one he wants to hear right now."

The security guard stared at her for a moment and then walked back to his post where he grabbed his clipboard. He eyed the list. She knew Marty's name would be on there. He turned away as he spoke into his walkie-talkie.

She sank lower in her seat and thought of other ways to get inside. There weren't many options.

She fought off panic as he returned. "You're lucky. Marty is busy but I got the go-ahead from somebody named Tom. He said to go straight to the stable." To her surprise he handed over two passes. "This one's for your windshield and this one you clip to your shirt. You have to wear it at all times."

She took them and smiled. "Thank you."

"Just go straight through and turn right. The stable is all the way back. If you hit the craft services tables, you've gone too far." He returned her paperwork and pointed her through to the entrance. She started her car and drove slowly.

She was in. Now it was time for the real fun to begin.

She parked her car where instructed and got out to open the passenger door. She pulled on her raincoat, slid on her shades, and pulled up her hood. Then she retrieved the enormous bouquet of flowers she'd had hidden under the coat. Ready, she shut the door and walked onto the set. She moved casually and was careful not to stare. People hurried around her, paying her no mind, too busy dodging the rain.

Tarps were being unrolled, covering equipment and large areas of grass.

The flowers were her ticket anywhere. She had a million different stories that went along with them. She also had different cards in her pocket, one with the name of every big actor on set. The pass now clipped to her shirt helped as well. She felt confident. And what nerves she did have only excited her.

A man trotted up toward her, the rain having misted his long hair.

"Excuse me?"

He stopped.

"I have a delivery here for Ms. Ryan."

"Oh." He caught his breath. A lanyard hanging from his chest said he worked for a special effects company. "Go back to the trailers. Hers is the first one on your left. Hard to miss. It has purple curtains. But be careful. She doesn't like just anyone walking up to her door."

She thanked him and he continued on his run.

She headed toward the trailers and the influx of people seemed to thin out. Most were indoors by now or under some sort of cover. Veronica's trailer was set off on its own, away from the others. She'd read many articles and she knew it was probably at Veronica's insistence. She demanded privacy when she was resting on set.

The curtains were open and when she reached the trailer she stood on her toes to look inside. She couldn't see much but she was pretty confident Veronica wasn't inside. She knocked on the door just to be sure. No answer. No response.

She opened the door, surprised to find it unlocked. She entered hurriedly and swiftly placed the flowers on the table, inhaling deeply. Her mind buzzed as the scent of Veronica's perfume filled her head.

Thunder rolled in the distance. Dishes were in the sink. She sank a dirty fork into her coat pocket, then checked out the window to make sure she was still alone. To her dismay she saw that a small group of people was headed her way. She had two minutes, tops.

She went to the bed and sat. She ran her fingers over the duvet, feeling where Veronica Ryan lay down to rest. She stood again and pulled the pillowcase from the pillow. She fought the urge to bury her face in it and inhale. That would have to wait. That would be her reward.

Shoving it down into her coat, she moved to the built-in dresser and retrieved the small spy camera from her jeans pocket. It was the size of a Ping-Pong ball and it was motion activated. She made sure it was on and placed it inside a silk plant. Then she hurried from the trailer, flowers in hand. The group was closer, but to her relief, Veronica Ryan wasn't among them. A man rounded the trailer just as she stepped down.

He wasn't happy and he had no neck. Just a massive jaw that led into massive shoulders.

"Can I help you?"

He had on an earpiece and wore a radio on his belt. Veronica's security.

She played dumb, hoping he hadn't seen her exit the trailer. Had he been hiding? Had he really been gone leaving the trailer unlocked? Shit. Thank God she had the flowers. Thank God she planned ahead for this stuff. She started in on her rehearsed line.

"I have a delivery."

He stared.

She glanced at the card. "For a Ms. Ryan? Am I in the right place?"

"Give them to me." He took them from her and searched through them, pulling them back with thick fingers. The he turned them upside down and shook them. When he finished, he swiped the card from her and grunted. "I'll see she gets them."

"Thanks."

The rain came down harder. She ran to her car. Once inside, she started it up and moved it to a spot where she could watch Veronica's trailer. Then she sat back and relaxed.

Now all she had to do was wait. Veronica would enter her trailer. Hopefully with a woman. They would wait out the rain inside. Hopefully for a couple of hours. If not today, then tomorrow. Whenever Veronica decided to bring in a woman. She knew from the rumors that it wouldn't take long. And then when Veronica and the woman emerged, she'd sneak back in to retrieve the camera, through the back window if necessary. She'd break it out if Mr. No-neck was watching from the front. Today, tomorrow, the next day. Whatever it took.

The tabloids were going to kill for the pictures she was sure to get. The camera had a built-in DVR and a good-sized memory. It would give her all she needed to strike out at Veronica Ryan. And more importantly, it was sure to flush Shawn out.

From wherever she was hiding.

❖

*Yonkers, New York*

Kennedy drove in silence to the small bungalow home of Mrs. Olga Valasek. Sloan's cleaning lady. She followed Allen, insisting that she go along, needing to question the woman for herself. Mrs. Valasek had been too upset the day they found the body and she'd been taken home to rest.

They pulled to a stop behind an unmarked Ford. The neighborhood was quaint, with narrow two-story houses lined up like dominos. American flags adorned the windows and hung from staffs mounted on the houses. A siren sounded in the near distance. Someone somewhere was cooking stew. Stiff leaves scratched along the sidewalk in the cool breeze. A handful of boys rode by on bicycles, eyeing them. They whispered something about cops and stopped at the corner to watch.

"They think something's about to go down."

Allen squinted into the sun. "Beats stickball."

Kennedy opened the waist-high gate and followed the narrow walkway, carefully avoiding the well-manicured lawn. The whole drive over she'd thought of the possibilities. What had this woman seen? What did she know? Would she be able to shed some light on Sloan Savage? The Bureau had questioned her and had run the background check. Kennedy knew all about her. A recent immigrant, she'd left the Ukraine two years before and had settled with her husband of twenty years, Viktor, here in New York. He'd come before her and worked as a mechanic, saving money. They'd moved into this rental house nine months earlier. Neither one had any criminal record and they both seemed to be good, upstanding people.

Even so, Kennedy considered the possibility that Olga could've been the one to pull the trigger. But would she have been so careless? To be the one in the house with her? The one who found her? Someone who could've easily planted the suicide note? And what would've been her motive? She didn't seem to have any issues with Sloan, so that left an outside motive. Could she somehow be involved in all of this?

Allen joined her on the front stoop and knocked on the door. As he did so, two other agents emerged.

"What'd ya get, guys?" Kennedy asked as they closed the door behind them.

"Not much." He sounded tired, worn out. She didn't know him but she knew the other man. His name was Hunter. Very appropriate. They'd teased him about it.

"House is clean, no weapons of any sort. Have at it." Hunter nodded her way. "Kennedy."

"How are you, Hunter?"

"Not bad. I hear you're doing well. Got suckered into this Ryan thing." He looked to his partner, who made a face.

"Just trying to help," she said.

"I don't know about you," Hunter said. "But she's driving us crazy. We're definitely going to celebrate when this whole mess is over."

"Drinks on me," the other agent said. They laughed. Hunter waved as they walked away.

Kennedy looked to Allen. "She really that bad?" She was referring to Veronica.

"Oh yeah."

"Wow. Guess I got lucky. Shawn isn't any trouble at all."

Allen smiled. "Wanna trade?"

She laughed. "No thanks."

The screen door creaked as she opened it and knocked again.

Someone called out for them to enter.

"Hello?" She stepped inside. The smell of the stew was very strong and the house was stifling. Her gaze immediately fell upon a small middle-aged woman with red-rimmed eyes. She was sitting on a dark green couch, perched on the edge, tissue in hand.

Another agent rose to greet them. Gale Nickelson. She was slight and well dressed with immaculate skin that always seemed to glow.

Kennedy liked her. She was polite and professional. She was also fluent in five languages.

"Kennedy, how are you?" She shook her hand. "Allen?"

"Good to see you, Gale," Kennedy said.

"Kennedy Scott, this is Mrs. Olga Valasek. Mrs. Valasek, this is Kennedy Scott, former FBI agent, and this is Special Agent Allen Douglas."

They both shook her hand. Olga seemed meek and completely overwhelmed.

Gale was there to translate. She'd been kind enough to wait for their arrival.

Olga motioned with her hand. "Please. You can sit."

Kennedy sat on the couch and angled herself toward Olga. Allen chose a recliner. Gale returned to her position on the remaining recliner.

Kennedy spoke. "We just need to ask you a few questions."

Immediately Olga began to sob. She cried into her tissue. They waited. When she calmed down, her breath hitched in her throat as she spoke. "I sorry. It is bad."

Kennedy touched her shoulder. "I know. And we're sorry for all that you've been through. We appreciate you talking with us."

Allen flipped through his notes.

"You arrived at the Savage house at eleven o'clock a.m.?"

Gale translated the question. Olga answered in English.

"Eleven, yes."

"Can you tell us about it? What was the first thing you did? Did you notice anything odd when you arrived? Like a suspicious car or person?"

"I go and knock on door. I see no one."

"So no one answered the door?"

"No."

"How did you get in?"

"I open door."

"With a key?"

She shook her head and said something in Ukrainian.

"It wasn't locked," Gale said.

"Did you see anyone when you went inside?"

"No."

Kennedy thought for a moment. "You clean that big house by yourself? How often do you go?" If she was only there once a month she might not notice as much as she would have if she was there once a week.

"No."

Olga turned to Gale. The conversation was lengthy and excitable. Gale spoke. "She said she doesn't clean the house alone. Not usually. But the other woman wasn't there."

Kennedy perked up. "Other woman?"

"This is news," Gale said.

Allen wrote quickly in his notebook.

"Do you know her name?" Kennedy asked.

She shook her head. Allen stood, his phone to his ear. He ordered a call to the cleaning agency to find out the other woman's name.

Kennedy continued with the questions. "Mrs. Valasek, did you see anything unusual in the house?"

"Kitchen." She met Kennedy's gaze. "Was clean."

"And it wasn't normally clean?"

Gale spoke. "She means it was clean like professionally clean. She said the sink was shining and smelled like bleach."

"Like someone had been there cleaning before you?"

"Yes."

"When did you find the body?"

Olga stared down at her clasped hands. It took her a while before she could answer.

"I clean downstairs and I go upstairs." Her breath shook. "I clean big bath first. To—" She looked to Gale and asked about a word. "To soak. Soak tub and shower."

Kennedy nodded. "And you saw the body."

"I see red water. Then white." She shuddered. "White skin."

"And you called nine-one-one right away?"

"Yes."

Allen snapped his phone shut. "The Bureau's already contacted the agency. There was no one else assigned to Sloan's house."

"Ever?" Kennedy asked.

"Ever."

"Damn." Kennedy looked to Olga.

"Mrs. Valasek? I'm going to send someone over here to help you identify the other cleaning woman. All you have to do is tell him what she looks like, okay?" She touched her shoulder once again.

Olga wiped her eyes. "I so sorry. Ms. Savage…" She choked up again. "Was nice lady."

"We've got to find this mysterious cleaning lady," Kennedy said to Allen.

He flipped open his phone once again. "Call every cleaning agency in town. I bet she's worked for at least one. I want lists of employees along with photos of all of them. Bring them to Mrs. Valasek."

"This could be our big break," Kennedy whispered, heading out of the house. She stopped on the front stoop and slid on her sunglasses. The boys still stood on the corner, lingering. "I'm going to call Shawn. I bet they used someone to clean their house."

"You think this is it?" he asked.

"Could be."

He slapped her shoulder. "Let's hope so. For God's sake, let's hope so."

"In the meantime, let's go see Veronica. Maybe she can shed some light."

❖

*Hudson Valley, New York*

Veronica Ryan sat very still in her large hotel suite listening to Agent Starling and Special Agent What's-his-name. They were irritating her. The entire Bureau was. They'd been up her butt since the second they found out about Sloan's death, insisting that she stay there instead of her trailer on the set. This meant that she had to be shuttled back and forth, constantly.

"So you think it's someone who was out to get Sloan?" She wiped her cheeks, wishing there were tears, but she couldn't muster any. She was confused by their theory, only paying half attention.

"No." Kennedy sat across from her. "We think it's someone after you. They still are. We still think you're in grave danger."

"Why would you think that?" She didn't like Kennedy Scott very much and she knew it showed in her tone. But she was beginning not to care. Her know-it-all attitude, always speaking so calm and collected. As if she were the most enlightened and intelligent human being to ever live. She really was beginning to hate her.

"I thought Sloan killed herself?" Why were they here? Wasn't this mess taken care of now? Sloan blew her brains out. Confessed to hurting Shawn. No more problem. And thankfully, no more embarrassing tabloids.

"We think someone else shot Sloan," Agent What's-his-name said.

"What? That's not what I've been told." Jesus, they were drawing this out. It was like they didn't want it to be over. Like they had nothing better to do.

"That's what we think," Kennedy said.

Veronica fought off scoffing. Starling. Agent fucking Starling. Kissing ass. Knowing it all. Needing to be perfect. Kennedy had it down pat. She could've beat out Jodie Foster for the part.

"But it's someone after me? That doesn't make sense."

"We think the UNSUB killed Sloan because of you. To get to you."

"But why?"

"Because you and Sloan were lovers."

"Please."

"It makes sense. Those tabloid stories had just run. About you and Sloan. If someone was jealous, controlling, stalking you, it would be enough to send them over. Especially if they think that you are theirs. These people are delusional."

"I'm not buying it."

"We have tests to run, which we hope will help prove our theory. But they may take a while."

"What kind of tests?"

"Tests for gunshot residue, ballistics, DNA we collected from her bedsheets. We also found shoeprints in the bathroom."

"Wait a minute. I thought she was found in the bathtub?"

"She was."

"Wouldn't water wash away the gunshot stuff?" She watched *Cold*

*Case Files* every once in a while when she was to play a detective. She knew her stuff. More than these idiots.

"Maybe, maybe not. The gun was still in her grip and obviously she didn't scrub her hand. If she fired the gun, there may be some chemicals left. We've also collected the bath water. If anything was washed off of her, it will hopefully be in the water."

"What about the bullet thing? The ballistics?"

"We're testing the gun to see if it matches the bullet fired at Shawn."

"And if it is, then you have your man, right? Sloan did it all."

"Not necessarily. We can't even prove that Sloan owned a gun. The one found with her had its identification number removed."

"God." She grabbed her head. "You people. So basically, Agent Starling, you're telling me that Sloan may not have killed herself, may not have been the one to shoot at Shawn, but that you still don't have anything to conclusively prove that?"

Kennedy didn't say anything. Of course not. Because she was an idiot in a smart disguise.

"And in the meantime, I'm supposed to still be on the lookout for someone who may or may not be out to get me? Some mysterious person who shoots Shawn, then breaks into Sloan's house and kills her, planting a suicide note?" She scoffed and stood from the plush couch. "Please. I'm not going to waste any more of my time believing in your ghost stories."

"It's not a ghost story," Kennedy said, her tone showing some irritability.

"What Kennedy means," Agent What's-his-name said, jumping in to douse the rising flames, "is that we don't know anything for certain yet, so you need to be careful."

Veronica stared them down. "Didn't you say you found a letter with Sloan? One that stated she was responsible for all these acts?"

"That's what the letter said, but—" Kennedy started.

"No buts, Agent Starling. I'm tired. I've had just about enough. My life has been torn and shaken, my marriage destroyed, all because of the charades of a jilted lover. And now you want me to continue to be paranoid while you find your answers? No way. I'm through."

"Ms. Ryan," Kennedy started again.

"No, no more. I'm tired and I'm fed up and when I'm done shooting, I'm going home. I'm going home to be with my family. As far as I'm concerned, the shooter just killed herself."

"You could still be in danger," Kennedy said. "Shawn and the girls could still be in danger."

"I think we'll be fine. We will no longer need your services."

Kennedy stood, fists balled at her sides. Veronica had struck a nerve. It pleased her. "You can't do that...Shawn and the girls...Shawn won't allow it...the divorce...it's no longer up to you."

Agent What's-his-name tried to calm her down. She'd hit where it counted and she bit back.

"You're supposed to be personally protecting them, but instead you're running around chasing ghosts! You must not be too worried about them—"

Kennedy clenched her jaw. "It's because I'm worried that I'm here."

"Well, worry no more. We'll be fine without you."

Veronica sat in silence and sipped her hot tea casually, her temper gone as quickly as it had surfaced. She sat still and looked off in silence as if she were completely unaffected by their conversation and their topic.

"I'm still searching for fan mail sent to you before this all started. It's there. I know it's there. Letters from the UNUSB."

"So go find this mysterious letter writer. This make-believe person." She waved off more tea as Flo brought in a tray. She was careful not to look at her long, even though her skirt was high and revealing, and instead tightened the belt on her thick robe.

"We are," Kennedy said, waving off her own mug of tea. "But we need some more information from you first."

Veronica let her continue, curious.

"We need to know about the other women."

Veronica stared. Then felt the beginnings of a smile curl up on her lips. *What are you up to, Agent Starling?* "I don't follow."

Agent What's-his-name cleared his throat, as if it would give him courage. "Cut the crap, Ms. Ryan. We already know about the others. I'm counting on you to cooperate fully here. Your life and their lives may depend on it."

Veronica repositioned herself. The large hotel suite felt too hot all of a sudden. What were they up to? What was this?

"How do you know?" They couldn't know. Not all of them. Some of them had been years ago. They were bluffing.

"We're the FBI, Ms. Ryan. It wasn't difficult," What's-his-name replied.

She looked to Kennedy. She knew she was loving this. Sitting there all high and mighty.

"What about Shawn?" Kennedy had probably told her. And had loved every minute of it.

"What about her?"

"Does she already know?"

What's-his-name linked his fingers together. "She asked, yes. And she knows."

They'd told her. They'd done this. Ruined her life. She stood. She was livid. "You had no right! No right!" She pointed her finger at Kennedy. "Fuck you, Starling. Seriously, fuck you! Coming into my life and telling my wife my personal business?" She swiped her hand across the tea tray, shoving its contents to the ground. Glass broke. Then she threw the tray across the room. How could they do this? This was her life! No wonder Shawn wanted a divorce. God damn these people.

"I was the one who told her," the man said. The sneaky little FBI man. He probably had a secret hate for gays, loved ruining their lives. He probably went home to his wife at night and laughed about it. "And she asked for the information. She wanted to know. If I didn't give it to her, she was planning on hiring someone who could."

He looked smug. She wanted to smack him.

She looked to Kennedy. Glared. Stuck-up bitch.

"I bet you love this, Starling. I bet you love the fact that I've cheated on Shawn so you can move right in on my family."

Kennedy stood. Red tinged her cheeks. Veronica hoped she would take a step forward. She dared her.

"You're wrong."

"Am I?"

"Yes. You see, unlike you, I put Shawn's feelings before my own. And I would hate to see her hurt any more than she is right now. So even if I wanted to, I wouldn't do anything to cause her any more stress. She's barely holding on as it is. No thanks to you."

"You just think you're so goddamned perfect, don't you?"

"No. But I am considerate. Which is more than I can say for you." With one last heated look, she excused herself and walked from the room. Veronica wanted to run after her, tackle her, punch her in the face until she begged for mercy. She trembled, keeping her rage harbored.

Agent What's-his-name stood. He placed his card on the coffee table.

"If you can think of anything important in regard to your previous lovers, please call. In the meantime, we are going to be in contact with them. So don't be alarmed if they start calling you with questions."

"Just one more way to ruin my life, eh, Detective?"

"That's Special Agent Douglas. And no. You're doing that all on your own."

❖

Kennedy was still upset when she met Allen in the hall where he was waiting for the elevator.

"Can you believe her?" she asked. "She almost had our UNSUB beat as far as narcissism."

Allen placed a comforting hand on her shoulder. "She's something, all right. Don't let her get to you."

"Why *is* she getting to me?" She was incredulous. "Dozens of hardcore criminals have tried, but I've never even blinked an eye. I've never lost my cool. And now in walks Veronica Ryan and I'm ready to tear my hair out."

"You know the answer, Kennedy," he said softly. "You know the reason."

She met his gaze. Yes, she knew. And she knew he did too. She was different around Shawn Ryan. Softer. Open. Protective.

"Does Shawn know?"

She pushed again on the down button.

"You know you can talk to me," he said.

"Yes. I know." She looked up at him. "Thank you."

His phone rang. He flipped it open as they stepped into the elevator. Kennedy could hear the voice on the other end but she couldn't make out the words. He closed his phone as the doors slid open. The lobby was quiet as they headed to the main doors, walking on lush carpet. The bellhop held it open for them.

When they stepped into the sun Kennedy finally asked, "What's going on?" She knew it wasn't good.

He searched for their unmarked Ford. "It's Veronica Ryan."

"Again? Now what?"

"Apparently the tabloids have photos of her in bed with another woman."

"Sloan?"

"No. Her personal assistant. The one named Florence. The one we just saw."

Kennedy just stared, too shocked to speak.

"They appear to be recent. She hasn't had Flo as her assistant for very long."

"I don't believe it. I mean, I know I shouldn't be surprised, but I am. I just can't believe she's doing this. What's it going to take to get her to stop? Just for the time being?"

"Apparently nothing. She doesn't care, Kennedy. Only now someone is showing the world her every move."

They crossed the street and climbed into the car.

"How?" Kennedy snapped on her seat belt as he started the engine.

"A small camera. Hidden in her trailer."

"On the movie set?"

"We think so."

"What about her security?"

"It was breached."

"Jesus, Allen."

"I guess so. Twice, even. Once to place the camera and once to retrieve it. We're interviewing the security team now. In the meantime, you better get back to Shawn."

"How am I going to tell her?"

"You won't have to. She already knows."

Kennedy closed her eyes.

# CHAPTER TEN

*Hilton Head, South Carolina*

Shawn ran as hard as she could down the cool beach, her bare feet pounding the dark wet sand, her throat burning with raw emotion as she pushed herself harder and harder. The photographs were seared into her mind, fueling her rage, fueling her fire. Damn her. Damn her, damn her. How could she? How the fuck could she? And right now, no less? What the hell was wrong with her? The assistant? That piece-of-shit-blonde with the fake tits? The one who oohed and ahhed over Veronica's every little move?

She slowed from her sprint, ready to heave. She gripped her knees and struggled for breath. From behind, she heard Phil stop his run too. She wished he would let her go. She needed to be alone. And if someone was going to kill her, then let them. Anything had to be better than this.

She retched. Once, twice. Nothing came up. She sucked in more air, her lungs burning. She went down on all fours. She held up a hand to Phil, who asked if she was okay.

"Leave me," she said, head bowed. Cold water swept in around her, tugging at her knees and hands as it went back out. She wished it would take her.

"You know I can't." He was breathless as well.

"I need to be alone."

"Are you sure you're okay? Can you stand?"

"I'm fine. Just give me some space, okay?"

He placed his hands behind his head and sucked in some air. "Yeah, okay. I'll be back a ways. If you need me just say the word."

"Thanks."

He walked away, leaving her on the sand. Sobs shook her body as the water crashed in around her, enveloping her in her despair. She cried and cried. Despair turned to anger and then pain. She pounded her fists against the sand, splashing up dark mud and cold salt water. She hit it as hard as she could. So hard her shoulder began to scream out for mercy. But she chose to ignore it, welcoming the pain. Wanting it. Letting it face off with the pain of Veronica.

Veronica. Her love. The one she'd given everything to and for.

Veronica was still doing it. Still servicing her own needs. Even now. Even now while telling Shawn that she wanted her back. It was almost laughable.

And now the world knew. The photos said it all. Veronica was fucking her assistant. In her trailer. Everyone would know. Would see.

Her family members had already called, shocked and appalled. They wanted answers. Answers she didn't have.

God, it was awful. A nightmare. She wished the divorce would hurry and wake her up. She couldn't wait to walk away from this horrible dream.

Pushing herself into a stand, she straightened and looked out at the sea. How could she shelter her girls from this? One day they would find out. They would see. Didn't Veronica think of that? Even consider it?

Maybe it was her own fault. She should've never married Veronica. She was too wild. Too selfish. She should've never tried to tie her down. Now her daughters would pay the price.

Her girls. They were all that mattered now.

Squaring her shoulders and wincing in pain, she turned away from the sea and walked back toward the house. She needed to see them. Needed to hold them and feel them next to her.

Her angels.

❖

*Yonkers, New York*

She sat and stared at the tabloid magazines. Veronica Ryan's infidelity was out now, completely out, the photos printed for the public. Courtesy of her, of course.

Veronica and Shawn were plastered all over the covers with captions like CHEATING RYAN GETS CAUGHT IN THE ACT. And even better were the ones that suggested a sick love triangle was to blame for Shawn's shooting. But her favorite, her absolute favorite, was the one that suggested that Veronica wanted Shawn killed in order to continue the affair.

That would be a dream come true. Then all she'd have to do was off the busty assistant. But that wouldn't be a problem. She might not even have to kill her.

And then there was Sloan. Now everyone believed that she and Veronica had had an affair. It was everywhere.

Sloan, the drug-using rocker, was unstable and she was stalking Veronica. Some articles were hinting that she was the one who had done it all. That she'd tried to kill Shawn. That she'd found out about the busty assistant and killed herself.

It was all working out so perfectly. She was almost giddy. Almost.

But there was still business to attend to. She switched off the television. *Entertainment Tonight* had moved on from Veronica. She rose to look out the window. If only Veronica would accept her love and welcome her with open arms. If only she'd love her back. Then this madness would stop. Then she wouldn't have to cause her any more pain. But until she could see that, she had to keep going. She would do anything to show Veronica that they were meant to be together. Anything.

And now she needed Shawn. Sloan had been but a morsel to whet her appetite. She wished she still had her gun. She longed to hold it in her hand, reminisce about the way it kicked when fired. The screams, the stench of gunpowder. The way it had smelled for a long while afterward. Then she thought of Sloan and remembered the spray of blood and brains. The way her eyes just stared. Like some little baby doll.

How foolish she'd looked slumped in that water. One side of her head nearly hollow. That blank look on her face. So stupid. She'd looked so stupid. What had Veronica ever seen in her?

She walked over to the shelves she had hung in her living room. She kept her items there. The ones that were treasured and worth more than anything. She handled them softly, carefully, as if they were alive and needed tender care. Each item had been worn or touched by Veronica Ryan. She breathed in deeply, trying to inhale the aura that each piece brought with it.

She fingered a drinking glass, the rim smudged with Veronica's lipstick. She tried to taste it by oh so delicately running the tip of her tongue along the smudge. She could just grasp the waxy taste of the lipstick. Satisfied, she returned it. Next she reached for the pen. It had been used to sign autographs. There was also a napkin and a signed photo. She retrieved the fork she'd taken and slipped it into her mouth. She allowed it to rest carefully on her tongue. She could feel the roughness of the stuck-on food. When a tiny bit of it dissolved and she tasted it, she removed it. The taste was odd, almost like curry. Veronica loved Indian food. She imagined that's what it was.

And then of course there was her favorite. The pillowcase. She kept it in a sealed bag and only opened it once a day. She never pulled it out, but rather shoved her head inside to inhale. The scent of Veronica's perfume mixed with the scent of her hair and skin caused her head to reel. Oftentimes she had to lie down as she did it, unable to stand. And then she'd slip her hand into her pants for the tender love. And she'd love herself while inhaling Veronica. And she would reach God. Sometimes as many as three times.

She loved it. Loved it so much. She had risked so much in obtaining these items. But it had been well worth it.

*Veronica. Where are you, Veronica? Are you ready yet?* She kept breathing in the scent from the pillowcase. *Are you ready to run to me yet? Or is your life not yet damaged enough?*

Her excitement growing, she quickly resealed the bag and returned it to the shelf. She had to focus. She crossed her room to her computer and checked on the status of several items. The first was a large order of lingerie to be sent to Veronica Ryan, courtesy of Sloan Savage. The credit card was stolen, of course, and it was simple enough to add a greeting to the gift. It was a small, petty act, but she knew it would cause trouble. And the more trouble the better. That gift, though, was nothing compared to what she had purchased for Shawn. Both the bulletproof vest and the lingerie were due to arrive today. She almost smiled.

Her mind went to Shawn and one of her favorite movies, *Cape Fear.* The one she'd watched almost every day for the past two years.

As she called up a photo of Shawn on her computer screen, she could hear Robert De Niro's voice in her head:

"Come out, come out, wherever you are."

❖

*Hilton Head, South Carolina*

Kennedy answered the door and welcomed Allen inside. He looked bone weary and could hardly muster a smile. His presence was serious and the air was thick. All were gathered at the Ryans' beach house to hear the latest news. Kennedy breathed deeply, wishing she knew ahead of time what the news was. Maybe she could've better prepared Shawn. As it was, Shawn was hardly speaking. Or eating. Or sleeping. She just took her girls to the beach and sat and stared.

"You found the letters?" Kennedy whispered, hoping.

"No. But I brought you two more boxes. These date back to over a year ago. One of Veronica's former assistants had them and had forgotten about them until she saw the recent news. Thankfully, she turned them in."

"I'll go through them tonight." She'd finished with the others, frustrated.

"Where's Ms. Ryan?" He looked at her hard, his voice low and serious.

"In the kitchen."

"Get her."

Kennedy looked to Monty, who rose to go after her.

Keri excused herself to go upstairs to check on the kids. The situation with her stalker had been quiet and uneventful. Thank God.

Shawn entered the room looking pale and frail. She moved funny, her shoulder in obvious pain.

Allen greeted her.

"Hello, Agent Douglas. Nice to see you."

He took her hand. "You too, Ms. Ryan."

"Please, call me Shawn. I no longer go by Ryan."

He nodded and they all sat.

"I assume the news is bad?" Shawn asked.

"It is."

They waited.

"Several things. The first of which is a new letter."

"Another one?" Kennedy's heart fluttered, then sank.

"Yes."

Monty mumbled something unpleasant.

Shawn rubbed her hand on her jeans, looking from Kennedy to Allen, searching their faces for clues. Then she hugged herself, wincing slightly at the pain.

Allen opened his briefcase and retrieved the letter. It was covered in plastic and he passed it first to Shawn.

"As you can see, it doesn't reveal much. Not very much at all."

Shawn studied the letter in silence and then passed it on to Kennedy.

*Veronica Ryan. Ry-guy.*

*All that glitters is not gold. You fool the world but you don't fool me. Soon you will see. Soon you will pay.*

Kennedy read in silence before speaking. "She's pissed. And she knows about the affairs."

"Everyone knows," Shawn said. "My eighty-nine-year-old grandmother knows."

"But the letter was postmarked the day before the latest tabloids even got wind of the story."

"And you're just now finding it?" Shawn sounded tired and irritated.

"Veronica's been bombarded with mail. And so have you. We have two agents on it eight hours a day. And we're still barely keeping up. Also, as you can see, this one was typed. She's getting bolder."

"More rash," Kennedy said. "She's going to act out now. Do things she wouldn't normally risk doing. She knows more than we'd like to think. She makes it a point to know."

"You know all that by reading a typed letter?" Shawn asked.

"Yes. A typed letter is more risky. We can get evidence from it. Run tests on the ink, on the font type, on the paper. She's getting sloppy."

Kennedy looked at Allen. He'd flown all the way to Hilton Head to see them. There had to be more.

He caught her look and continued.

"These arrived today." He handed the pictures to Shawn, who made a strangled noise and then covered her mouth with the trembling hand of her injured arm. Her good hand also shook as she held the pictures.

Kennedy rose and glanced over her shoulder. Each picture was of Veronica Ryan in a compromising position with the blond assistant. These were photos the tabloids didn't have or couldn't run. They were highly explicit.

Shawn lowered her hand and the pictures. Her expression hardened as she handed them over to Kennedy. Allen filled them in.

"What we know as of today is this. The assistant passed a polygraph. It's safe to assume that this was their first intimate encounter. It's also safe to assume that she had nothing to do with planting a camera or anything to do with the photos. She's clean."

Kennedy returned to her seat. "Go on."

"Someone delivered a bouquet of flowers to Veronica's trailer a few days ago. Our man caught her at the door after returning from the restroom. He thought he caught her at the door. But she could've already been inside."

Monty whispered more curse words.

"What's the description?" Kennedy asked.

Allen retrieved another sheet from his briefcase. It was a composite. A hush fell over the room as he handed out a copy of a young woman's face to all.

"This is her?" Shawn asked.

"We think so."

"Did you show it to Mrs. Valasek?" Kennedy asked.

"Yes. She confirmed it. We think this is our UNSUB."

"She looks like a baby. She's so young."

Kennedy was a little surprised as well. She was expecting someone older, in her thirties. Someone who'd had more time in life to develop this kind of cunning and cleverness.

"Do we know how she got on set? Is she still there?"

"She's not on set. We've checked and we have her photo up

everywhere. We did question a security guard who admitted to allowing a woman fitting this description on set the same day as the flower delivery. He said she had a paper proving she worked for the company who provided the horses."

"I should've gone with Veronica," Monty said. "This is ridiculous."

"No, Monty. I'm glad you're with us," Shawn said. "We need you. Now more than ever."

"Does Veronica know about these?" Kennedy asked, referring to the photographs.

"Yes. But she didn't have much to say."

"That surprises me," Shawn said coldly. "She always has something to say."

The room fell silent for a moment before Allen continued.

"We also received something else today."

Shawn laughed. It was eerie.

"Using Sloan's credit card, our UNSUB sent you a bulletproof vest and Veronica five boxes full of lingerie."

"Is that all?" Shawn snapped. "Is there anything else?"

"That's all."

She stood. "I can't take this anymore."

Kennedy stood as she walked quickly from the room. She heard the back door open and slam close and Phil rose to scramble after her.

She looked to Allen. "There's got to be something I can do."

His face said it all. "There's only one thing you can do to help her right now, Kennedy. And that's catch this bitch."

❖

*Hudson Valley, New York*

Veronica sat on the couch in her lush hotel suite. The FBI had been in and out all day, asking questions, searching again through her room to make sure no other cameras were hidden there. They were watching her like a hawk, barely allowing visitors. And those who had made it inside had been questioned and searched thoroughly. It was embarrassing. And a huge pain in the ass. And then there was the composite sketch of the supposed UNSUB. She'd stared at it for a long while before shaking her head. The face looked slightly familiar, but she couldn't place it. And honestly, it looked like a lot of young girls do. She could've been a fan. One out of a thousand. Did they really expect her to believe this was the person who'd shot Shawn and killed Sloan? They were way more stupid than she'd thought.

She rubbed her temples and sipped at her hot tea. Her face was puffy from crying. They hadn't been able to shoot today because of it. Her state had caused quite a stir and everyone was acting weird. People either stared or completely avoided her. As if she were some sort of contagious disease. "Don't go near Veronica Ryan or she'll rub off on you. Your life will turn to ruins."

Everyone knew now that she cheated on Shawn. And it was like she'd killed the president or something. She couldn't shake this one off. Everyone saw. What was she going to do? How could she recover?

Get back with Shawn. That's what her team was telling her. Make nice. A public apology would be great for starters. But she wasn't up to it. For once she needed to do something right. She needed to say it to Shawn. To her face. She needed to admit that she'd seduced her assistant. That she'd done it because she'd been upset over her and Shawn. That she'd been selfish and stupid. And what happened from there, she didn't know. Would Shawn even believe her? Probably not.

Maybe she should mention the flirtation on her assistant's part. How she'd nearly begged for it and straddled her lap in the trailer.

No. It wouldn't matter. But wait a minute… Shawn no longer wanted her. She'd told her so. She'd filed for divorce, for fuck's sake. So what had she done wrong? Really?

It was the FBI. Goddamned Starling and Agent What's-his-name. Acting like saints. Turning Shawn against her. And the public? One minute they worshipped you and the next they were ready to hang you. Well, fuck them. She still had her hardcore fans. Hundreds of them. They were still writing and e-mailing and posting on her MySpace and Facebook. They still loved her. And wanted her.

*Just lay low.* That's what her publicist said. *Just fly below the radar for a while. Work hard, keep your head low and your mouth shut. It'll all blow over.*

And as for Shawn…well, nothing she ever did there was right.

She was always in the wrong in Shawn's eyes. She'd tried to call her an hour earlier but Monty had said she didn't want to speak to her. A part of her couldn't blame her, but it wouldn't matter anyway.

She was bad. Bad, bad V.

She lay down and curled up on her side. Maybe Starling was right. Maybe she was selfish.

She'd hurt Shawn, she knew that much. But she wished Shawn could just understand that it wasn't some big plot against her. It was just sex. Just attention. Straight-up seducing and fucking. A game. Just a fun little game. It didn't mean anything. Not like Shawn and the girls. They meant something to her.

Why couldn't anyone understand her?

The dial tone hummed in her ear as she reached for the receiver. She dialed the number to the beach house and listened as it went unanswered. She hung up and tried Shawn's cell. It went straight to voicemail.

A tear fell. Then another.

She needed understanding. Love. Support. She needed somebody. Anybody. She couldn't get through this alone. Was anyone out there?

❖

*Yonkers, New York*

Evanescence played and she turned up the volume. Louder. Bigger. It had to work. It had to take her away. Dark mixed with light. The offspring of the two. Evanescence. Just like her.

His voice was coming more and more often. At first it had been soothing, comforting, reassuring. Like it had been in the beginning. When the tender love was happening every day. But lately, when his voice came, it had a hard edge to it. Sharp, demanding, degrading. Like it had been when the others had come.

She hated the others. Resented them. He loved them more.

The whiskey bottle was nearly empty. She'd have to buy more. It was the only thing that helped. The only thing that drowned out his voice.

She needed something. Veronica. She needed her.

Her eyes tried to close on her, heavy and burning. It hurt. She couldn't hold them open. Couldn't.

A smell came. Vinegar. She was back at the house, jarring cucumbers and beets. Canning green beans. The garden was singing under the sun. The air was thick and hot. The old boombox was playing. Metal bands. Ones she'd never heard of. Old ones. But she got to know them quickly and enjoyed them, working in the sun with them. Getting down on her knees in the warm soil, picking and digging and planting. She'd look up when the cassette tape was switched out. She'd smile for Faith No More. And she'd keep picking until her basket was full.

It made him happy. And she'd be happy. They'd grill then. Bunches of ground beef so thick they remained pink in the middle. And ears of corn. She loved that. The juicy meat, hot as it ran down her chin, the browned kernels of corn, tough but smoky. Summer was the best. So much better than winter, when the house was shut up and the heat barely ran. How she'd long for that summer sun. To be able to stand out in the garden in nothing but a pair of shorts, allowing the rays to massage her shoulders.

She hadn't done that in years. He'd started making her wear a shirt. Started grimacing when he caught sight of her.

His voice came. Deep and demanding. The screams too. Horrible. Never ending. What could she do? She would help. Make it better. And she did. She helped. She knew what to do. Kept things quiet. Worked in the garden. Cleaned. Cooked. Washed herself. Scrubbed until she was red. Shaved. Every day. Everywhere. But the tender love stopped. The grimaces continued.

She could do no right. She thought about leaving but couldn't. The house was home. All she knew. She was safe there. Protected. Comfortable. Where she saw God. The only place she could see God.

Her head felt heavy. The darkness was coming, brought by the whiskey. She wanted to go home. She would soon. And she would stand in the sun. Listen to the radio. To one of the cassettes. She would dig her hands in the soil, lie down in her space.

And she would see God.

She would see God with Veronica.

It was time to go home.

# CHAPTER ELEVEN

*Hilton Head, South Carolina*

Shawn had been in her room for almost twenty-four hours. Kennedy and Monty had cared for the girls, who knew their mother didn't feel well. They seemed to take it in stride, knowing her shoulder had been bothering her. They ate lunch upstairs and Kennedy heard Shawn reading them a story as they snuggled in with her for their afternoon nap. After that they returned to play, leaving Shawn alone in bed.

Her food went untouched. She refused all phone calls.

Now it was after eleven and Kennedy hadn't heard any movement from her room in hours. No lights, no running water. She was worried and so she'd stayed at the Ryan house most of the day. Keri understood, insisting that she go.

Quietly, she headed up the stairs and then down the hallway. Shawn's door was partway open but the room was dark. Kennedy peeked inside and saw no one. Concerned, she gave a soft knock. There was no answer.

Walking farther inside, she flipped on the light and noticed a slew of photos strewn across the large bed. The pictures were scattered everywhere and most of them, she noticed, had Veronica's image cut out of them. A thick photo album lay on the floor, gutted.

Her gaze went to the night table. A bottle of whiskey was open and nearly empty. A glass tumbler was turned over next to it. So she'd been drinking. Drowning away her pain and then sleeping it off.

Her heart ached for her. She wished there was some way she could help her, could take away the pain. But there was nothing. She knew that. All she could do was help with the girls and lend a kind ear. Shawn had to work through the rest.

Movement came from the bathroom and Kennedy turned to find Shawn watching her.

"Hi."

Kennedy swallowed hard, silenced by Shawn's appearance. She still had on the clothes that had been soaked through the day before. She'd gone running on the beach after she'd heard the news from Allen. It had rained. She'd come home soaked to the core.

The clothes were dry now, but they looked stiff and were caked in sand. Her face was red and streaked with dirt and tears.

She looked beaten. And her gaze seemed…empty.

She walked unsteadily, obviously impaired. She wobbled slightly and reached out to steady herself, wincing in pain as her shoulder wound cried out for mercy.

"What are you doing in here?" she slurred.

"I was just checking on you." She wanted to hold her, allow her to just fall into her embrace. But she knew Shawn would fight it. She could sense it. This was a different Shawn. A difficult Shawn. A dying Shawn.

"I'm fine. Don't I look fine?" She waved her arms dramatically.

"Please tell me you haven't let the girls see you like this."

Shawn blinked. Slowly.

"No, missy. I only drink after they're gone. You think I'd do that?"

"No, no, I didn't. I just had to be sure."

"I love my kids." She grew angry. "I love them. Don't you tell me I don't."

"I didn't. I'm not saying that." She sighed. "You need to rest." Kennedy tried to hold her gaze but Shawn wouldn't look at her. She kept looking to the bed where the cut-up photos lay.

"I need a match." She turned toward the fireplace. Searching.

"For what?"

"I need to burn those pictures."

"No, no, no. You don't need to do that. I'll get rid of the photos. Right now you just need to rest."

Shawn looked at her square in the eye for the first time.

"What I need is a good woman." She laughed. She tried to take a step but then thought better of it. "I just want to love and be loved. Is that so much to ask?" Her normally blue-green eyes were more of a gray from the storm brewing within.

"No, not at all," Kennedy said. "Everyone wants that."

"What about you, Special Agent Scott? Do you want that?"

Shawn was staring her down and Kennedy felt the weight of it. It was hot and thick and tainted with lust.

She'd been in many precarious positions in her life, but never one like this. She had no idea what to say. But she knew she couldn't think about herself and her own feelings.

"I-I don't know…"

"Of course not!" Shawn threw up her hands and then grimaced at the pain in her shoulder. "That's why you don't have anyone." She swayed and her face hardened. Her voice took on an edgy tone and she glared at Kennedy as she spoke. "You're just like Veronica. You think you don't need anyone. You think you can just do what you want, and no one else matters."

"That's not true." The words were out before she could stop them. Her voice rang with hurt and surprise. She resented being paired with Veronica, someone, who in her opinion, valued other people's feelings very lightly in comparison to her own needs, wants, and desires.

"Do you cheat on your lovers, Special Agent Scott?"

"No, I never…"

"Oh, that's right. You've never had a lover. Never?"

"I… There's been no one." She shook her head, unable to understand why she kept answering. Why she didn't just walk away and allow Shawn to sleep it off.

Shawn scoffed and then staggered to the bed where she plopped herself down. "You expect me to believe that?" She winced again as she tried to move her arm.

"You can believe what you want." *She's hurting. She's hurting so bad.*

"Never had a lover?" The questions were becoming louder and meaner, Shawn's face a twisted expression of hurt and anger.

Kennedy moved toward the door. "No." It was time to go.

Shawn looked at her with wounded eyes. The depth of the pain was breathtaking. "I—you're. Don't go."

Kennedy stopped. The anger was gone from Shawn's face.

"You need to rest." Kennedy approached the bed and took her hand. Tears slid down Shawn's face.

"Come on," Kennedy said softly. "Let's get you tucked in."

With a gentleness and a patience she'd only ever used with her nephews, Kennedy slowly and carefully helped Shawn from her clothes. The jeans could nearly stand on their own and she tossed them, along with her long-sleeved shirt, to the floor. Then she watched as Shawn stood and peeled off her underwear. Then she hugged herself, cold, embarrassed, exposed. Kennedy saw the red slash on her shoulder. It looked harsh and painful.

She reached out for it, but Shawn took her hand.

"No."

"It looks bad."

"Not now. Let it fall off. I don't care."

Kennedy stared into her eyes, too moved to look anywhere else. Though she thought her beautiful, her attraction had to give way to the concern and caring brimming just underneath. She had to focus on that now.

She led her into the bathroom and turned on the shower. After helping her inside, she returned to the bedroom and pulled the sandy sheets from the bed. As she tucked in the fresh sheets, she thought of how small and almost atrophied Shawn's body looked. It pained her to think of Shawn sleeping in dirty clothes and sheets. Not to mention the girls, napping with her.

She finished with the bed and then rummaged through the dresser drawers. She found a pair of sweats and a T-shirt. She also grabbed a pair of panties and some socks. She laid the pile neatly on the bed.

The water stopped and Kennedy went to make sure she had a towel. As Shawn dried, Kennedy found some Tylenol in the medicine cabinet and filled a glass with water. When Shawn had wrapped herself in her robe, Kennedy handed them to her. Her hand still trembled as she took them.

Kennedy encouraged her to finish off the water.

They went back to the bed. Kennedy helped her dress. Her synapses fired rapidly as she inhaled the fresh soapy scent of her. She tried to fight them off but knew it was useless.

She pulled the covers back and helped her into bed. Shawn held her hand as she tucked in the duvet around her.

"Thank you."

Kennedy smiled. "You're welcome."

"Please—don't go."

Kennedy hesitated. Shawn's look was pleading.

"Okay." She switched off the light and settled into bed next to her. Shawn turned into her and held her. Then, as the black of night enveloped them, Shawn cried herself to sleep.

❖

*"The mother is hysterical," Allen said, hands on the wheel. The night engulfed them, dawn close. She'd heard something somewhere, that the darkest part of the night came right before dawn. She could feel that now as she breathed it in, felt that blackness flow through her body and seep into her bones.*

*"How long now?" she asked, glancing at her watch.*

*"Four hours."*

*"What do we know?" She adjusted the vehicle's a/c and cracked her window. The scent of jet fuel still lingered.*

*"Same M.O. as the previous two. He waited until the house was asleep, then approached and slit the screen to the boy's bedroom. He slipped inside, probably used a Taser on the boy, picked him up, and carried him out the front door. The mother rose to check on the kids around midnight. We got the call soon after."*

*Taser.*

*Taze-er.*

*It played around in her mind. The previous two had marks on them. Taser marks.*

*"The footprint outside the window matches," she said, knowing it was their same UNSUB.*

*"Yes."*

*They pulled into a lower-class neighborhood on the outskirts of Cleveland. The houses were small but spaced well apart. Cop cars surrounded the house on the end, floodlights illuminated the front and back of the house. Allen pulled the car to a screeching stop and they seemed to float through the crime scene tape.*

*Officers stared. Someone greeted them. Took them inside away from the humid night. The house was lit up but felt dark. The lamps were too small, they didn't produce enough light. Yelling was coming from the living room. It was the mother. When she saw them she stopped. Someone introduced them. Her eyes were wild, her face drooping in pain and torment.*

*"You have to find him," she said. "You have to find my baby. He's only seven—"*

*A boy sat hunched on the couch. He looked young. He hugged his knees and covered his ears. He rocked.*

*"You have to find him—"*

*Another agent entered the room.*

*Gale.*

*She sat next to the boy. He wouldn't talk.*

*"You have to find my baby. He—"*

*"We'll do all we can," Allen said.*

*"All you can? You mean like the other cases?" She started to cry and then yell. "Is it true he keeps them alive for a week?"*

*No one spoke.*

*"Is it true he does things to them? Sexual things. That he hurts them and keeps them tied up? That he starves them until the last day, when he feeds them—is all of that true? That you'll find my boy but it will be too late? You'll find his body. His naked, hurt body—" Her yelling ceased, overcome by sobs.*

*Family comforted her.*

*They turned away.*

*Allen led her down the dim hall to the bedroom. Police were still taking photos. The floor was wooden and bare. A rug had rested there but they had bagged it for evidence. The bunk beds were also bare, the mattresses old and thin. The room was covered in fingerprint dust and smelled of bananas. The boy and his brother always ate one before bed. The peels were still on the dresser.*

*She looked to the window. It was open, the screen slit vertically and then horizontally. Like a gaping L.*

*She walked to it and stared out.*

*"He watched from over there," she said, pointing to the treeline of the neighboring property. "He watched."*

*Watcher, watcher, watcher.*

*She saw a stuffed dinosaur on the floor. It was near the bed in a toy bin. She scooped it up and smelled it. It smelled like crayons and cookies and Play-Doh. All things kid. They went back to the living room.*

*The mother started in again.*

*"My baby. My baby."*

*She handed the dinosaur to the little boy curled on the sofa. He looked at her for a long moment, then took it. Snuggling up with it, he turned away from his mother and closed his eyes.*

*"My baby. My boy. You better find him. Go find him. God help you if you don't. God help you."*

Kennedy awoke, heart thundering. Next to her, Shawn mumbled in her sleep. Shook up, Kennedy crawled from the bed and headed back downstairs. Shawn's words still played over and over in her mind. The sharpness of them, the pain. The god-awful look upon her face when she compared her to Veronica.

The words stung her down deep. She would have to analyze them, search for their validity. She would rather die than be anything like Veronica Ryan. Shawn had been intoxicated and angry, but even so. She wanted to be sure. Maybe Shawn would talk with her about it sometime soon.

After making herself a fresh pot of coffee, she resumed her position on the floor. She opened the boxes Allen brought and delved back into the letters. She worked until dawn, searching for their UNSUB. She knew the letters had most likely come steadily at first, slightly beckoning Veronica to correspond with her. If this was the case then the letters would have a true return address. It was vital she find them.

As she was filing through letter after letter, sleep weighed heavy on her. She was just about to call it a night when one letter caught her eye. She read it and reread it. Her heart rate sped up. She stood.

*Dear Ms. Ryan,*

*I hope this letter finds you well. I wanted to write and tell you how much I enjoy your work. I think you are an incredible actress. No one is better. I hope others see your talent as I do.*

*Please feel free to write me anytime. It would be great*

*if we could be friends. I'm also enclosing my phone number should you feel the need to call. I believe God has brought you to me for a reason. We need to embrace that. I look forward to hearing from you. Please don't take long.*
   *Sincerely,*
   *Ashley (Ash)*

This was it. She could feel it. The letter was handwritten in black ink. The handwriting looked like the writing of a young girl. She searched for the envelope. The Bureau had been sending her copies of the letters and they'd copied the envelopes as well, attaching them to the letters. This one, though, was missing.

Panicked, she dug through the box. She rifled through all the papers and re-checked the ones she'd been through. Nothing.

She started in on the second box, studying the black ink and feminine handwriting.

"Come on, come on."

She found one. A new one. The copy of the envelope was attached.

"Yes." She hopped up. Looked for the return address. Her heart fell to her feet. There was only a name. And a postmark. It was mailed from Yonkers.

Hurriedly, she searched the letter.

*Dear Veronica,*
   *It's me again. I hope you know who I am. I wrote you before and waited for your answer. I never got one. Maybe it got lost. That happens sometimes. I know you are very busy but we have to do as God says. We have to see God together. I will send you another letter with a time and date. I will check your schedule and arrange a meeting time for us. You will hear from me soon.*
   *If you find my other letter and you want to write me, go ahead.*
   *I am here. I will be here for you. I will come to you when you need me. Always.*
   *Sincerely, Ash*

She searched again for the first envelope. Where the hell was it?

She dumped the boxes, fanned the papers along the carpet, spreading them out.

Damn it.

Looking again at the name on the second envelope, she leaned back against the sofa and dug out her phone. She called Allen and woke him.

"I've got something."

She could hear rustling and imagined him reaching for the light and his eyeglasses.

"Okay."

"I found two letters. They both scream UNSUB. There's no return address but there is a name."

"Go ahead."

"Ashley Williams."

"You think it's real?"

"I think so. I think she really wanted Veronica to contact her at first."

"Then where's the address?"

"The envelope for the first letter is missing. It's on there, I'm sure of it. Have those agents go through everything to see if they can find it."

"Will do. Anything else?"

"The postmark is Yonkers." She crossed the room to the small alcove where a computer and fax machine sat. "I'm faxing it all to you as we speak."

"I'll start the search right now for Ashley Williams in Yonkers and surrounding areas."

"We also need to go over those employee lists from the cleaning agencies."

"Got it."

"This is it, Allen. We're closing in."

"She knows."

"She's eyeing the case. Following Veronica. Be careful."

❖

Shawn stared out at the beach below. Dawn greeted her with blues and grays, the sea a churning tide of the emotions coursing through her veins. She ran her hands through her damp hair. Unable to sleep, she finally gave in and took another shower, allowing the steam to help clear her head and the hot water to massage her aches.

Her head throbbed in a soft, steady way. More of a nuisance than a pain. However, it did not distract her from the memory of the night before. She could recall every moment, every gentle touch, every long stare. And the whiskey bottle on the nightstand reminded her of the other details. The less pleasant ones.

Exhausted and strung out, she carefully dressed in a pair of soft jeans and a T-shirt. Her shoulder was angry and red and terribly sore. She'd done some damage to it, pounding on the sand, acting like a crazed animal, desperate to know why and what for. Answers that had yet to come.

The house was quiet as she walked to the girls' room. They were sound asleep, curled up in their beds. Kiley was snoring. The sight seemed to relax her rib cage, enabling her to breathe easier. Her girls always had that effect on her. She said another prayer of thanks. Where would she be without them?

After she adjusted their covers, she headed downstairs. She walked slowly, unsure of her weak and exhausted legs. The smell of coffee came and she immediately craved some. Maybe it would nurse her soul as well as her head.

Entering the living room, she saw Monty through the back door. He was outside sitting by the pool. He waved. She reminded herself to thank him for helping to care for the girls. She owed him and Kennedy big time.

She returned the wave and walked farther to find Kennedy asleep on the floor, boxes and letters surrounding her. She looked so peaceful, her face so beautiful, partially hidden by her thick brown hair. She was haloed like an angel in the early morning light. Shawn bent to a knee and brushed the hair aside and gently stroked her face. She hated to wake her, but she needed to talk to her.

Kennedy made a small noise. She was beautiful. And vulnerable. Just like everyone else.

"Kennedy," Shawn said softly, placing a gentle hand on her shoulder. "Kennedy?"

She stirred and her eyes fluttered open. Upon seeing Shawn she jerked and sat up, on high alert.

"It's okay," Shawn said with a weak smile. "It's just me. Everything is fine."

Kennedy blinked as reality set in. She exhaled with relief. "I must've dozed off. Everything's okay?"

"Yes."

Kennedy lifted some of the letters and studied them, as if she was willing her mind to catch up.

"Any luck?" Shawn asked.

Kennedy held up a finger as she scanned some papers quickly. "Yes. Yes, I think so. I could hardly stay awake last night, but yes, I think I found something."

She showed them to Shawn.

"They sound almost like regular fan mail."

"They do," Kennedy said. "But they go a bit further. A bit deeper."

"Do we know where she is?" Could this really be over?

"No, not exactly. We have a name, we're running it. And we have a Yonkers postmark."

"What's the name?"

"Ashley Williams."

Shawn mulled the name over. Ashley Williams. Was this her? Their tormenter?

"Do you recognize it?"

"No."

"What about the handwriting? Or the words?"

She shook her head.

Kennedy lowered her head and sighed. Then she picked up all the papers and placed them back in the box. She kept the two important ones, placing them on the coffee table. The wind in her sails had seemed to deplete. Shawn tried to cheer her up.

"That is great, though. Right?"

"Yes."

Shawn smiled. Kennedy stood and nearly lost her balance. Shawn steadied her.

"I think we both need to take it a bit easy."

"No, I'm all right. Just not awake yet." She smiled a little back at Shawn. "How are you this morning? You look better."

"Honestly? I've been better. But I feel okay. Will you walk with me?"

"Sure. Give me ten minutes?"

Shawn agreed and busied herself pouring them both some coffee. When Kennedy returned, her face looked pink with life and her eyes were dancing in the sunlight. She'd changed into a pair of jeans and a light blue sweater. Shawn couldn't help but stare.

Kennedy didn't seem to notice. "Ready?"

They exited to the backyard where Monty sat by the pool. Kennedy told him about the letters and encouraged him to go look at them. The news was like a much-needed shot in the arm and he hurried inside to do so.

"You know," Shawn said as they reached the beach, "she seemed so normal looking in that sketch."

"Yes, she did."

"She doesn't look like a monster."

"No. They rarely do."

"She hates me, doesn't she?"

"She doesn't know you, Shawn. She just knows that you are in the way."

"I never thought that somebody would want me dead. Would actually try to kill me." She hugged herself. "It's—I don't know— horrifying."

"Yes, it is."

"Will I ever get over it?"

"I think you will. You have to remember that this UNSUB, she's caught up in herself. She's lost in her own mind. And right now her mind isn't well. She doesn't know you. It's not personal. I know that sounds weird, but it's true. You're just a barricade. A fly in her perfect soup. An obstacle."

"So I'm not even human?"

Kennedy met her gaze. "To her? No. She doesn't have the capability to empathize with you. She doesn't feel for anyone, really. Just Veronica. And herself. Everything revolves around that."

"But she doesn't even really know Veronica. How can she worship her?"

"Because she's obsessed with the Veronica she's created."

"What would happen if she ever met her?"

"It wouldn't be good."

"She would hurt her?"

"Yes. The second Veronica turned her down, or told her to get lost, it would anger her. The more Veronica spoke, the more danger she'd be in."

"Because it wouldn't be what she's imagined?"

"Exactly. She might beat her or tie her up. Her mind would struggle to realize that this wasn't the Veronica she'd dreamed of."

Shawn thought about the UNSUB. She couldn't seem to get used to the strange word. *UNSUB*. She wondered who she was and what had happened to her to lead her down this path. *How does someone completely lose touch with reality?*

She breathed in the cool sea air, letting it awaken her from the inside out. Her thoughts went to last night.

"I owe you an apology." She looked over at Kennedy. "I was way out of line last night and I'm truly very sorry for the way I spoke to you."

Kennedy walked with her hands behind her back. When she spoke, her voice was soft. "Apology accepted. I understand more than you know, Shawn."

Shawn sighed with relief. "Thank you. After the way I spoke to you I thought for sure you'd be upset. But I didn't mean it. The part about Veronica, I didn't mean it."

"What made you say it?"

Shawn groaned. "Oh God, you had to ask didn't you?"

"You don't have to answer. I'm just curious. Was it something I did?"

"No. It's what you didn't do."

"What I didn't do?"

Shawn wanted to disappear down into the sand. Just completely disintegrate into a million little pieces and be swept up by the sea.

"Last night, I was in a bad, bad state. And more than anything I just wanted you to hold me, to tell me you—"

"Go on."

"I don't think I can." Her heart was going wild. She was sure Kennedy could hear it.

They walked on in silence.

Kennedy let her off the hook. "Rain check?"

"Yes, please."

Kennedy laughed.

Shawn was grateful, still confused over her growing feelings. She moved on to a more somber topic.

"There's something I need you to do for me."

"Yes?"

"I need you to find the truth for me."

"The truth?"

"About Veronica. I need to know…everything."

Kennedy stopped walking. "I thought Allen already had."

"I asked him if there had been others and he told me yes. He didn't give me details."

"Why would you want to know? Why put yourself through that?"

"I need to know the truth. All of it. I want to know how long this"—she motioned with her hands—"all this has been going on."

"But why?"

"If you were me, Kennedy, if you truly understood like you say you do, you would want to know too. I need to know if my whole life the past eight years has been a lie."

They started walking again, Kennedy shaking her head.

"I don't know, Shawn. I can understand wanting to know, to put your life in perspective and all, but can you handle it?"

"I have to. I have no other choice. I have to know so I can move on with a clear head. I don't want lingering demons in my life. I don't want this to ruin my next relationship."

Kennedy glanced at her. "Your next relationship?"

Surprisingly, Shawn felt herself smile. Sort of. "Yes."

"That sounds good. Very positive."

"It does, doesn't it? So will you help me?"

"Yes."

"Thank you."

❖

"So you found the letters?" Keri asked, cutting up spaghetti for the boys.

"I'm pretty sure."

"That's good. Does Shawn know?"

Kennedy nodded, twirling some noodles around her fork. Outside, the waterfall on the pool ran and beyond that the ocean churned, muted. The sunset was beautiful.

"How's she doing? Really." Keri slid the plate over for Landon, who dug in.

"Not too good."

"I didn't think so."

"Mama, I'm thirsty," Luke said, his mouth already stained with marinara.

"Here, baby. Here's your milk." She placed it in front of him and watched as he gulped. "She doesn't look well."

"She's in pain. Shock too. It's just one piece of horrible news after the other."

"If anyone knows how that feels, it's you." She took a hearty bite and stared at Kennedy as she chewed.

"Yes, I do. But still, I feel helpless. She holes up in her room, self-medicates."

"A lot of people react this way."

"I just wish I could soften the pain. I hate that she sits up there in misery."

"Go to her." Keri took another bite. The boys slurped up their noodles and giggled. Natalie played drums on the high-chair tray. "You know you want to."

Kennedy held her gaze. She took a sip of iced tea. "This isn't about what I want."

"No, of course not. Nothing ever is."

"Don't start."

"It's hard to sit back and watch you waste your life, Kennedy."

"I'm not wasting it."

"You have. You've put everyone else first."

"I care."

"Well, maybe you should care about yourself too."

"Mama, I want some bread," Luke said.

"What do you say?"

"Please and thank you."

She handed him a piece of garlic bread. "You say please when you ask and thank you after you receive it."

"Yeah," Landon said.

He took it with a grin but shot his brother a quick look.

Kennedy was glad for the interruption but Keri didn't forget.

"Go to her, Ken. Hold her. Love her. Tell her how you feel."

Kennedy played with her spaghetti. "I can't."

"Why not?"

"Because of her current situation. And because I'm here to help her."

Keri dropped her fork. "Boys, cover your ears."

They did so quickly, giggling. Keri stared her down.

"Pardon my French, but screw Veronica Ryan. Shawn has filed for divorce. And as for you, you aren't doing anything wrong. You're not even working for the Bureau. So you go to her. Go to her before I pull you over there and shove you in her face."

"What if she doesn't feel the same way?"

"Oh my God." She sat back in her chair, incredulous. The boys continued to giggle. Natalie continued to beat on the tray of her high chair. "For someone who can delve deep into the criminal mind, you are mighty naïve."

"You're not helping."

"Yes, I am. Kennedy, she wants you. She feels for you. It's written all over her. All over the both of you. Surely she's said something or done something…"

"She did kiss me."

Keri blinked. Then laughed. "You're unbelievable." She motioned for the boys to lower their hands.

"What did you say, Mama? Something bad?"

"No, I just told Kennedy a secret. That's all."

"What was it?" They looked to Kennedy.

"I can't tell."

"Man!" Landon shoved his arms down to his sides. "I never get to know the good stuff."

Kennedy laughed. "It wasn't anything you would want to know, buddy. I promise."

"Then tell me."

"Landon," Keri said.

Kennedy leaned into him and whispered in his ear. His face lit up and he clapped his hands. Luke demanded to know the same, so she rose and whispered in his ear.

"That's it?" He crossed his arms over his chest. "That's not exciting."

"Excuse me?" Mike, one of Keri's security, approached the table. "We may have an issue."

Kennedy stood. "What is it?" What could it be now? They were so close to catching their UNSUB. So close.

He motioned for her to follow. They entered the living room. He pointed at the television and turned up the volume. A radar image covered the screen, and in the center swirled a large green mass.

A hurricane. Category four.

"It's headed here?"

"Yes."

The green swirl moved closer as the weather man showed its trajectory. It was headed right for them.

"How long?"

"Less than forty-eight hours."

"Not now. No, not now." She turned. Keri looked ashen.

"We have to leave, don't we?"

Mike spoke. "I'm afraid so."

The boys rushed to Keri's side. "What's the matter, Mama?"

Luke saw the TV. "A storm?"

Living in Louisiana, they'd been through three hurricanes already. They knew the routine.

"Another hurricane, baby."

"Again?" They walked closer to the TV.

"Is this one gonna blow away our treehouse?"

"Yeah, and Jaxx's doghouse?"

"Not this time," Kennedy said. "This time the storm is coming here to South Carolina."

Keri retrieved Natalie and sat on the couch, bouncing her lightly.

"Are we gonna cover the windows?"

"We're not going to be here. We're leaving."

"Where are we going to go?" Keri asked softly. "I can't go back to that house. Not without you and Tom."

"I know. We'll figure something out."

"You better go tell Shawn. Better yet, hand me the phone."

Mike did so.

"What for?" Kennedy asked.

"I'm going to call and tell her to send the girls over because you have something to tell her."

"Ker..."

"I'm dialing. Go."

Truth be told, she did have something to tell Shawn. Several things, in fact. So at Keri's insistence she walked next door and greeted the girls and Monty and Phil as they crossed her path, heading to the Boudreaux house.

"We're gonna go play with Luke and Landon," Rory said, skipping.

"Have fun."

"We will. Have fun with Mommy."

Kennedy flushed. It had only been a matter of weeks, and she had already grown so attached to Shawn and the girls. They felt like family. Like she'd known them and cared for them for years. She wanted that feeling to continue.

Entering the house, she waved at Larry, who sat watching TV. She told him to tune in to the Weather Channel. He sat forward, alarmed.

"We'll have to leave soon," she said. "Where's Shawn?"

He thumbed up the volume. "Upstairs."

She approached the banister and stilled. Shawn was waiting. The image of her in the bathtub came. It smacked her ribs, knocking her heart around. She swallowed and ascended. More images came. Shawn on the beach, sun setting in her eyes. Shawn laughing with the girls. Shawn looking at her in the moonlight, touching her lips to hers.

With every step her heart rate increased. Desire and nervousness flooded her body.

She had to do this. For herself. For once.

She stopped outside Shawn's door.

The light was on, a bar glowing at the base of the door. Taking a deep breath, she knocked lightly.

"Come in," Shawn said.

Kennedy opened the door and peeked in.

"Yes?" Shawn was sitting on the bed. The photo album from

before was gone, along with the cut-up photos. She sat reading a small paperback. She still appeared tired but not nearly as tired as before.

"I was hoping we could talk? If not—"

"Sure, come in."

"Okay."

Kennedy entered and gently closed the door behind her. Shawn tugged a wrap onto her shoulders, obviously cold. The room was a little chilly. She winced with pain.

"Your shoulder," Kennedy said.

"Oh, it's nothing. Just taking a while to heal."

"A while?" Kennedy crossed to the bed. "I need to look at it."

"No, no," Shawn said, trying to downplay it. "It's nothing, really."

"I'm not taking no for an answer." Kennedy locked eyes with her, and all the worry she'd ever had in regard to Shawn's well-being now surfaced tenfold. "Not this time. Now, ease out of that shirt."

Shawn didn't speak. It seemed that she didn't know what to say.

"Now," Kennedy said softly.

"It's cold."

"I'll start a fire." Quickly, she moved over to the fireplace and tossed in two logs. Hungry flames started up in no time, warming the room. Behind her, Kennedy could hear Shawn moving.

She turned. Shawn was standing next to the bed in a threadbare tank and sweatpants. Her shoulder looked bony and awkward from the way she carried herself, the injured side higher than the other.

"Do you have that salve I gave you?"

Shawn opened the night table drawer. She held out the round container.

"Have you used it?"

Shawn looked guilty, ashamed. "No."

"I won't ask why. I'll just assume that you've been stubborn."

Shawn laughed softly. "That's probably wise."

Kennedy took the salve and then Shawn's hand. She encouraged her to sit in front of the fire. Then Kennedy sat across from her, both of them settling in lotus style.

"What is it?" Shawn asked, eyeing the jar.

"It's goldenseal salve."

"Seal?"

"It's made from goldenseal root. It helps to heal wounds and infections." She carried it everywhere. It had been her grandmother's creation and they'd used it frequently growing up. Now she was about to use it on someone very special.

The moment was not lost on her.

She swallowed hard as she took in Shawn by the firelight. The orange and yellow flickered across her face and teased with a dance in her eyes.

"I'm going to need you to take off your shirt." Kennedy spoke with a heated whisper and Shawn hesitated but then complied, her gaze never leaving Kennedy's. She winced again as her shoulder protested over the removal of the thin tank top.

Kennedy wavered slightly, doing her best not to stare at the exposed flesh before her. Seeing Shawn nude for the second time sent her head spinning out of control. Her breasts were smooth mounds of milky white flesh, her nipples soft and supple looking, the palest of pinks. Scared and aroused, Kennedy locked eyes with her once again, determined to control herself.

"Should I cover up?" Shawn asked, sensing her discomfort.

"Yes—no," Kennedy answered quickly. "You're fine. I mean, it's fine." She was nervous and her words were coming out jumbled and strange while excited heat rushed to her skin as if it, too, was hungry for Shawn. She wanted to touch her, feel her. Wanted Shawn to touch her and feel her. Never had she wanted anything so much.

"Are you sure you're okay?" Shawn asked, breathless.

Kennedy nodded and forced down more saliva.

Carefully, she removed the small bandage and exposed the wound. The scar appeared tender and red and open slightly. It had healed almost completely before Shawn had done something to aggravate it. A slight swelling around the wound caused some alarm.

"Why haven't you asked to see a doctor? You promised to think about it. I should've just called one myself." The powerful arousal was instantly replaced with worry. She set the bandage down and opened the jar of salve.

"Spite," Shawn replied. "I guess I wanted to feel the pain. If you called, I probably would've refused to see him."

Kennedy didn't respond. She understood. She could imagine

needing to feel the physical pain. Any pain would be better than the emotional pain she was having to endure.

"I understand."

"Do you?"

"Yes. Hold this right here. I need to pour in the peroxide."

Shawn held the thick towel below the wound as Kennedy poured. The liquid almost sizzled with foam. Kennedy took the towel and pressed. Shawn winced.

"It's infected. You'll need to see a doctor as soon as we get back."

"Get back? Why can't one come here?"

"We have to leave tomorrow."

Shawn's eyes grew wide. "Why? Is she here? The UNSUB?"

"No, no. It's not that. There's a hurricane."

"A hurricane?"

"Category four. It's headed right for us."

"Oh."

"We need to leave tomorrow. We have less than forty-eight hours."

"This is what you had to talk to me about."

"Yes."

She looked a little disappointed. Kennedy poured in more peroxide and squeezed the wound.

"Ow, God, it hurts."

"I'm sorry."

"This is what I get for spite."

Kennedy chuckled. "Was it worth it?"

"No."

They both laughed. Kennedy dried the wound and lifted the salve. "This should be a lot less painful."

"No more squeezing?"

"Scout's honor."

"Okay." She breathed deep and relaxed. Kennedy rubbed the salve in gently, working her way from the inside out and then back in again.

"It almost feels good." She winced. "Almost." She set her jaw, fighting the pain. "Can I ask you something?"

"Sure."

"Is it difficult for you to imagine love?"

Kennedy thought for a moment. Her body had already reacted but she fought hard not to show it. "It used to be."

"But now?" Shawn reached up and grabbed hold of her hand, stilling it. Her eyes were burning in the firelight.

"It's not difficult at all," Kennedy whispered.

"What's different about now?"

She breathed deep, watching the heat rise in Shawn's cheeks. "You."

Shawn's face lit up in the dancing, hot firelight. Her breasts swelled and rose with deep, quickening breaths.

Shawn brought Kennedy's hand up to her mouth where she gently kissed the back of it. The heat from her mouth seared into Kennedy and sank into her blood, rushing throughout her body. Burning alive, Kennedy moved in and took Shawn's face in her hands. Then, as if she had been waiting to her whole life, she leaned in and pressed her lips to Shawn's.

The kiss was warm and tender, Shawn's lips like plumps of satin beneath her own.

Shawn moaned into the kiss and wrapped her good arm around Kennedy, pulling her down atop her. They kissed hungrily, their tongues dancing like the flames of the fire. Kennedy's head swam and her body growled as she felt Shawn respond underneath her. Shawn was clinging to her, digging her nails into her back, aching for the closeness.

Needing, wanting, dying to get ever closer to her, Kennedy positioned herself between Shawn's legs and thrust herself against her. Shawn bucked upward, desperate for her heated pressure. Hungry blood surged between Kennedy's legs, demanding, a sensation she'd never had before.

A beast was clawing within her, wanting desperately to remain atop Shawn, to ravish her, to taste and consume every last part of her. She groaned as she gyrated against her. She could feel the meaty heat of Shawn's sex through the thin fabric of her sweatpants and it only fed the fire of the monster. She clenched her jaw as she moved, knowing by Shawn's thrusts and moans that she was dangerously close to orgasm.

"Kennedy. Oh God, Kennedy. Yes."

Shawn looked up at her with fierce need, her teeth pressing into her lower lip. Her hand found the back of Kennedy's neck, nails biting in.

"Yes," she cried out, straining to reach Kennedy. "I've wanted you for so long." She nearly choked out the words as she pulled Kennedy down for another heated, starving kiss. Then she tore her mouth away and whispered, "Take me. Make me feel. Make me feel, please. All those thoughts I've had…about you. All the feelings. Please, Kennedy. Let me have them. Let me have you."

"I—oh God, I want you so bad." Shawn spoke directly into her ear and then extended her tongue to seal the message.

The sensation bolted through Kennedy's body and then sparked to life between her legs.

Rational thought kept fighting for dominance in her mind but the beast raged on, determined. Shawn's mouth found her neck, nearly melting her, nearly causing her eyes to roll back in her head. Shawn groaned in her ear.

"Yes. Kennedy. Yes. Oh, God, baby."

The words were weapons. Wanton weapons of passion and desire. She would remember them always, seek them out always, do anything for them…always.

Shawn bucked up against her, her flesh hungry and wet.

"Touch me. Touch me, Kennedy." She took her hand and led it downward. Kennedy knew if she felt her flesh she would die. All reason would be forever gone. Nothing would ever be the same.

An image flashed in her mind. The letters. Then came an image of the girls. She looked down and caught sight of the red wound.

"Wait," she cried out softly. The beast growled in protest within her and she fought to keep it harbored inside.

"What is it?" Shawn asked breathlessly, her entire being seemingly alive with need.

"I can't do this," Kennedy whispered.

"Why? I want you to." Shawn reached up and tried to pull her down once again.

"It's not right. For so many reasons." Kennedy pushed herself up, her body instantly crying out at the absence of Shawn beneath her. "Not right now."

Shawn sighed and looked away. She closed her legs and sat up, the heat from their encounter still high on her cheeks. She stared into the fire and the fire stared back, caressing her beautifully sad face, her large liquid eyes ready to spill over with tears.

"Hey," Kennedy said softly, moving to her. She reached out and gently touched her face as her own voice threatened to cave from the rush of emotion. "It's me. I need to be sure of some things."

"Like what?"

"I need to be sure I can handle this. You. I've never had anyone and—"

"You don't think you can commit?" She sounded hurt. Angry.

"No, it's not that. I've just had to deal with a lot."

Shawn just stared at her.

"I see. So you think it's too soon. You and I…"

"*You* feel right to me. You *are* right. But the situation we're in isn't. Things need to be sorted out first. I don't want this to be something rash and quick. I want more than that."

Shawn stared into the fire. "I don't know, Kennedy. I don't want to hurt any more. I don't want to give anyone that power. Right now, this. You not being sure. It just scared me."

"I understand."

They sat in silence for a while.

"How's your shoulder?"

Shawn hugged herself. "It feels a little better." She slipped the shirt back on.

"I'm glad." Kennedy knew at once she would not sleep that night. The feel of Shawn underneath her, crying out for her with her body and soul, it would weigh heavily on her mind and in her heart. She tilted Shawn's chin up to her own.

"I—"

"Don't. Don't say it unless you absolutely mean it."

Kennedy stared into her eyes. She saw the world. Her world. Shawn's world. The hurt, betrayal, passion.

"Please. Please just go. I need to be alone."

Kennedy hesitated but then rose. She placed the salve on the night table.

"If you need me, I'm here."

Shawn stared into the fire. "I know. And that means more than you know."

*Shawn turned over and pulled the covers closer to her chest. Knowing hands traced up her arms to her shoulders.*

*"Good morning, beautiful," Kennedy greeted her in a deep, sexy whisper. She'd crawled into bed with her, planting soft kisses on her neck.*

*"Mmm...good morning yourself," she replied with a sheepish grin. "When did you get here?" Shawn couldn't remember why she was gone, just that she'd missed her terribly.*

*"Just a few minutes ago." Her brown eyes were the color of honey, warm and mesmerizing.*

*"I've missed you so much," she said, her emotions threatening to spill over.*

*"I've missed you too."*

*"You make me feel so good. So safe." She held her face.*

*Kennedy moved in slowly, painfully slowly, and kissed her. "I love you, Shawn. I love you."*

*The words came out on a whisper and danced in the air. They tickled her ears and warmed her skin.*

*"I love you, too," she said softly. She found her full lips and kissed her. There was warmth and softness. Hands sought and found. Touching, holding, insisting. "Mmm, make love to me."*

*"I...I've never..."*

*She understood and she silenced her with a gentle finger. "Shh." She kissed her again, this time softly and slowly, carefully exploring and awakening. She eased Kennedy down and placed her full weight atop her. "Just relax," she said as she examined Kennedy in her jeans and soft T-shirt.*

*Slowly, she eased up her shirt and lifted it over her head. Then, sighing breathlessly at the exposed breasts beneath her, she traced her fingers around the small mounds of soft flesh, watching them gather in response. Leaning closer, she breathed upon the dark rose of nipples and felt her own hot blood surge with excitement as Kennedy cried out with pleasure.*

*Not yet.*

*Slowly.*

*She traced her fingers over Kennedy's stomach down to the waistband of her jeans. Once there, she slowly unbuttoned them and eased down the zipper before she slid the jeans down over her hips.*

*Kennedy tried to sit up to speak but Shawn gently pushed her back down, pulling her long legs free one at a time. Then, tossing the jeans on the floor, she breathed upon the naked skin of her legs, moving up toward the small patch of hair.*

*"I'm going to make love to you all morning long," she said huskily, careful to breathe upon the awakening skin of her inner thighs.*

*Kennedy cried out again and lifted her hips.*

*"Not yet, baby," she said, positioning herself over her center. Carefully, and as she looked into the honey eyes, she gently encouraged the long legs to open. "Yes, like that." She bent down and blew gently, watching with delight as the clitoris awakened and grew with hungry blood.*

*"Slowly," she said, gripping Kennedy's excited hips. She bent and blew again, this time inhaling as much as she exhaled, and she became intoxicated with the sweet scent of her. What would she taste like, feel like, respond like? With her impatience growing, she extended her tongue and carefully touched the outside of her satiny folds, purposely avoiding the excited center.*

*Her brain swam in bliss as her mouth registered the sweet tart taste of her. Kennedy moved and thrashed underneath her, gripping the covers in hasty pleasurable excitement.*

*"Please," she groaned, lifting her head off the pillow.*

*"No, baby, not yet," she said, teasing her with long lapping strokes just to the side of her extended clitoris.*

*"Shawn. Shawn, please."*

*The words were keys to her locked-away passion. The prison doors of her soul flew open as she flattened her tongue and eased down, feeling the firm, soft tissue of Kennedy underneath her. Then, with her own excitement building between her legs, she licked and pressed and flicked.*

*"Shawn, oh God, Shawn."*

*She massaged her with her tongue, gathered her in her mouth and sucked—*

"Mommy. Mommy."

Shawn moaned and turned over, still feeling Kennedy beneath her.

"Mommy, Kiley wet the bed," Rory said, tapping her on the shoulder.

Shawn looked around slowly. She had her covers clutched close to her chest and gathered between her shaking legs. Sweat beaded her brow as she sat up and looked at Rory. Blood pounded between her legs and in her ears. God, how she wanted to return to sleep to finish the dream.

"What's wrong, sweetie?" she asked instead, trying to focus on reality.

"Kiley wet the bed." Rory placed her hands on her hips. "She's all wet."

Shawn pushed back her covers. "All right."

The dream quickly took the back burner as she busied herself with the girls. She put Kiley in the shower and rinsed her and then ran a warm bath for the both of them. They crawled in happily and began to play. She busied herself changing Kiley's sheets and remembered that they were leaving today.

Outside the window, storm clouds brewed in the distance, looming over the gray, churning sea, promising a large hurricane.

Veronica had called the night before. She'd heard about the hurricane and had insisted they come back to New York. Shawn had argued, not wanting Veronica to think they were leaving just because she wanted them to. They were leaving because they had to. And they weren't going back to the house.

She stood by the bed and hugged herself as she looked outside. Sadness settled in as she realized they would be leaving behind not only the house, but maybe Kennedy as well. How much longer could they keep her?

She headed into the bathroom to help the girls with their bath. She wasn't about to give Veronica another chance, but she knew she had to face her, to talk through the horror and betrayal. Even though she knew she wouldn't be graced with an answer, she at least had to ask Veronica why. Why had she done it?

Would any answer satisfy her? No. But she still had to try her best to find out why. So she could put the whole thing to rest.

She dried the girls off after their bath and walked with them out to the beach for one last pirate adventure. She sat in the soft sand and relaxed a little as the strong sea breeze ran its cool hands through her hair and across her face. She squinted into the wind and watched her girls. The sea crawled hurriedly toward shore, like a million tiny little crabs running for the sand. Thunder rolled deeply, causing the girls to shriek with delight. The clouds rolled as well, blowing inward in one smooth, quick motion, as if the wind never stopped to take a breath.

A drop of rain pelted the envelope in her hand. The manila envelope was full and unopened. She'd found it outside her bedroom door. She knew what it was, what it held.

Tearing it open, the thunder spoke of her pain, voicing her fears. She slid out the contents and found a handwritten note from Kennedy.

*Shawn,*

> *Here is the information you asked for. It goes back nine years. I'm sorry. If you need to talk, I'm here. Anytime.*

*Kennedy*

She leafed through the pages, one at a time. The names and dates came before the photos. All ten of them attractive, well-known women, excluding the most recent assistant. She sat staring, eyeing each woman, one at a time. Eight of them came after they'd exchanged wedding vows. Four of them had been good friends at the time. Thunder boomed again and she shuddered in the wind as the tears warmed her cold cheeks. She looked up and bit back her sobs, smiling through the pain at her girls, who danced happily in the wind's strong arms.

And there was one now. Right now.

Marion Grace.

But now she knew. And now she could heal.

# CHAPTER TWELVE

*Scarsdale, New York*

The knock came and Larry answered, allowing Veronica inside. Shawn was nervous and edgy, not really wanting to see her, but she'd shown up uninvited at their hotel, insisting on seeing her. Veronica had wanted them back at the house but Shawn had refused, too scared and too upset.

Veronica stepped into view and smiled. Larry closed the door, locked it, and left them.

"Hi," Veronica said, crossing the room to embrace her. Shawn stiffened in her arms. Her perfume set Shawn's neurons firing and all of it came rushing through her. The betrayal, the lies, the hurt. A sob threatened and she pulled away.

"What's wrong?" Veronica asked. Her silky dark hair was full and beautiful, hanging just below her shoulders. Her black eyes beckoned.

How could she stand there and look at her like that?

Shawn couldn't do it. It was too much. She couldn't pretend like it was all okay.

"Girls," Shawn called out, turning away.

Rory and Kiley flew into the room and then stopped cold when they saw Veronica.

"Hi, guys," Veronica said, bending to embrace them.

"Hi," they both responded, going to her, but shyly.

"Why so shy?" Veronica asked, running her hands through their long hair.

"They're tired," Shawn said, knowing her girls were exhausted and confused. They had witnessed her crying upon leaving the beach house. They didn't understand why they weren't at home. "Why don't you girls go get ready for bed? I'll be in to tuck you in soon."

"But I haven't seen them in weeks!" Veronica looked at Shawn with surprise and hurt, just like a child. "I thought maybe we could stay up, maybe play some games like we used to do." She eyed the girls, baiting them.

"You'll have plenty of time to see them tomorrow."

"Yeah! Yeah! Let's play!" Kiley exclaimed, bouncing up and down. "Can we, Mom, please?" She clutched her hands together in front of her, begging with an excited toothy grin.

"Not tonight, girls." Silence filled the room as the answer set in. Shawn gave Veronica a stern look, letting her know not to push it.

"Okay, Mommy," Rory said softly, walking over to hug her leg. Kiley was close on her heels doing the same.

"I'll be in in a few." She kissed them both, giving Rory a wink of gratitude for following her directions.

Veronica stalked off to the suite's living room, so upset that she didn't tell the girls good night. Shawn wanted desperately to ignore her, but more than that, she wanted her gone. She found her sitting on the couch.

"What the hell was that?" she asked, angry.

"What the hell was that?" Shawn repeated. "What about what the hell is this? What are you doing here?"

"I came to see you guys. You've been gone for weeks."

"You're not supposed to be here, V. We're divorcing."

"Those are my kids."

"I had them."

"They're mine."

"They're ours. Even though you have yet to officially adopt them."

Veronica opened her mouth to bite back, but she seemed stymied.

"Why aren't you at the house?"

"For many reasons."

"Such as?"

"Well, there's a psycho out there trying to kill me, I'm divorcing you and don't want to be around you, and oh yes, you said on the phone that the house was yours."

"It is."

Shawn wanted to scream, but she held back and said, "We are legally married. I am entitled to half."

"Half?" She laughed. "Is that what this is about? You wanting half?"

"No. I'm saying that the house isn't solely yours. But never mind. The girls and I will look for another one soon."

"With what money?"

"With my money."

"Your money?"

"Yes." She had savings and she had made damn good investments over the years. It wasn't millions, but it would buy them a decent home.

"You're cracking me up, Shawn."

"I want you to leave."

"And I want to see the girls."

"It's not about what you want. It's about them. They've had a long day. We all have."

"So let me guess, you're too tired to talk?"

Shawn started to say something in her own defense but then changed her mind. How soon she had forgotten that she would be fighting a losing battle. One never won an argument with Veronica. But thankfully, the war was finally over—she had nothing to defend. There was no more relationship. Relief washed through her and she almost smiled at how good it felt. She had always hated fighting with Veronica, and now it seemed she would no longer have to.

"We'll have plenty of time to talk."

"Yeah? When? Tomorrow, when I'm scheduled for a magazine shoot?"

The question was rhetorical and meant to upset her, but this time it didn't. It was amazing how freeing apathy felt. "Whenever you have the time." She said the words softly and sat on the love seat across from her. Her voice was calm and almost soothing, something that would no doubt surprise Veronica, who had always been good at pushing her buttons.

"How about now?"

"What did you want to discuss? I think our attorneys should handle the majority of it."

Veronica squirmed, looking intensely at Shawn's face. Fire brimmed just below her surface, Shawn could feel it.

"We need to talk about us."

"What about us?"

"Are we over?"

"I've filed for divorce, V."

"That can be stopped."

"No, it can't. It won't."

"You're serious about this."

"Yes."

"Just like that?" She lurched forward as she said the words, her emotions ready to fly high.

"No, not just like that. It was over the first time you cheated on me. But unfortunately I just found out the details today."

"What are you talking about?"

"It wasn't just Sloan or this new assistant. It was eight others. At least eight others. One right now."

She stared at her hard, disbelief on her porcelain face. "You're crazy."

"Am I? Because I have the proof right over there in my bag." She pointed to her luggage.

"You're out of your mind." She paced the room, walking forcefully and quickly, like a mad dog. "What, did you pay some ungodly amount to some sleazy, lying private eye?"

"No."

"Then who? Who told you these lies?"

"The FBI." Was Veronica really this stupid? She had to know that the FBI would look into her background thoroughly. No, she wasn't stupid. She was just convinced that she could talk and act her way out of anything.

"What?"

"I said, it was the FBI." She spoke louder, her anger fueling her confidence. No longer did she have to listen to Veronica's ranting and raving. No longer did she have to listen to her drama. "I don't think they're known for making up extramarital affairs for money."

Veronica stopped pacing and stood still, her chest rising and falling. "Well, that's just fucking great. Kennedy. Just like I suspected. She's been moving in on my family from the start."

"It wasn't Kennedy who did the investigating on you. They had already run a check on you soon after the shooting. It was standard procedure. All I had to do was ask for the information." She knew

Veronica was just looking for a scapegoat. She always did like to blame others rather than herself.

"Who gave you the information?" she asked with her hands on her hips.

"It doesn't matter who—"

"It was Kennedy. That self-serving bitch." She grabbed at her head, then slammed her fists down to her side. "She's after you. Trying to ruin me. I knew it!" She grabbed a statue off a table hurled it against the wall, shattering it into a million pieces.

The noise was deafening, like a shotgun blast, and Shawn instinctively covered her ears. "V, stop! The girls."

"The girls? You won't even let me see the girls!" She glared at her and threw two other statues, smashing them into pieces.

Shawn ran from the room. The girls were out of bed, scared.

"Mommy!" Tears sat like crystals in the corners of their eyes.

Shawn hurried them into their bedroom.

"Mommy, what was that?"

"Shh. It's nothing."

They heard more commotion as Larry confronted Veronica in the other room. Yelling. Cursing. Veronica talking about the girls.

"Is Mommy gonna be okay?" Rory asked.

Shawn closed the door and locked it. She urged the girls to crawl back into bed.

"Yeah, why is she mad?" Kiley asked.

Shawn smoothed her hair.

"Sometimes, when people get real mad, they do crazy things."

"Like throw things?" Rory asked.

Oh God, they knew what was happening. "Yes."

"So is it okay to throw things when you get mad?"

"Not always. Because sometimes you break things that mean a lot to you."

"Oh. So what do you do then?"

"Well, it's best to hit your pillow or throw your pillow. But only if you absolutely have to."

"Oh," they said in unison.

There was more yelling but then a door slammed. They listened intently to the silence.

"Does Mommy know that?" Kiley asked.

"She's not thinking about it right now."

"But she will later, huh? She'll be mad she broke such neat stuff."

"Yes. But let's not worry about that. It's over. Everything is fine." She smiled and snuggled between them, kissing their foreheads. "Who's ready for a story?"

The girls clapped and Rory ran from the bed to her book bag. She climbed back in with three books.

As Shawn read to Rory and Kiley, she thought of Kennedy. Even though she and Keri were in the suite across the hall, she wished for her presence more than she'd ever wished for anything.

❖

*FBI Field Office, New York City*

Kennedy entered the building and checked in. She glanced at her watch. She was five minutes early.

Allen had called requesting her presence. They had something and he knew she wanted in on it. So she'd flown to New York, bringing Keri and the boys with her. They were back at the hotel, swimming in the indoor pool, security still with them.

"Kennedy."

She turned. Allen greeted her with a handshake and led her farther into the building.

"How are things?" he asked.

"Okay."

"You don't sound convinced."

"I'm worried about everyone. Shawn and the girls, my sister, this case."

"Well, I've got good news as far as the case."

"I was hoping you would say that."

He chuckled as they waited for the elevator. "As you know, we have a composite and a name."

They stepped inside.

"We ran the name through our database and got zilch. The numerous A. Williamses we found were not our UNSUB, based on name, age, sex, or location. The two Ashley Williamses that were close were both under twenty and enrolled at community college. They still lived at home, both dated regularly, and both had no idea what we were after. Their main concerns were school, boys, and partying. Nationwide, the search is ongoing. So far the results are more of the same."

The elevator doors opened and they exited and headed toward a conference room. Even though it was after hours, several agents were still working. She nodded to the ones she recognized, and they nodded back. Allen held the door for her and showed her inside to the long table. It was just the two of them in the room. He offered her a seat but she declined.

He leafed through some files and pulled out a page.

"What we did find was this." He handed it over. It was a list of employees from a place called Courtesy Cleaners. The name Ashley Williams was highlighted.

Kennedy grew excited and Allen smiled, pleased.

"Did you show them the composite?" she asked.

"Yes. They identified her just like Mrs. Valasek."

"What do we know?"

Allen switched on his laptop. The screen behind him came to life on the wall as he moved his mouse. A page came up. A profile.

"We went to the address she provided to Courtesy Cleaners. It was an apartment, a cheap one, one of those rent by the month. The residence was vacant. As if she'd just walked out one day and didn't come back."

Kennedy listened intently.

"We found old, used furniture." He brought up photos of the apartment on the screen. Kennedy could see the small golden striped couch, the broken kitchen chair and worn kitchen table. The carpet was the color of rust, the linoleum a deep green. An older-model television sat on a small table. It was bolted down, along with the table. It belonged to the rental property.

"Aside from the furniture, we found magazines. Hundreds of them. Some with missing words, some with missing pages. They date back to the early eighties. Dozens of them had writeups on Veronica Ryan. But the articles were missing."

Kennedy arched a brow. Allen brought up another photo. It was the bedroom.

"We found most of those missing articles and photos here."

The walls of the bedroom were covered.

"My God." Kennedy approached the screen. Each wall was covered in photos and articles, all of them of or about Veronica Ryan.

"The ceiling too," Allen said, showing yet another photo. "And the bathroom. Even in the shower. Especially in the shower. They were hung on the shower walls, up away from the water. Even on the ceiling. Some were literally falling apart, wet pieces of them caught in the drain."

Kennedy stared at the screen.

"But there were none in the living room?"

He changed the photo again. Brought her back to the living room.

"Not anything like the other rooms, no. There were marks on the wall from where thumbtacks had been used. But there's no way to know what hung there. There were also empty shelves. You can see the dust marks here, where something has been removed."

"Anything else?"

"We're locating copies of the all the magazines, to see just what is missing. We might be able to prove that she used words from them to create the threatening letters."

"What about her past?"

"That's just it." He moved his mouse so the original page came up on the screen, listing everything from Ashley's possible behavior to the known facts. "There were no bills, no mail. We ran a background check and it's like she doesn't even exist."

"What about prints?"

"The place was wiped clean."

"Entirely?"

"Yes. I'm telling you, this woman is like a ghost. No school records, no utility records, no bank accounts, no driver's license, nada."

"What about the job? Didn't they ask for ID?"

"She had fakes. Courtesy Cleaners still has the copies. They weren't good fakes but they enabled her to get work."

"What else?"

"She worked for Courtesy Cleaners for less than a year. She was quiet and did her work well. She showed up on time and rarely spoke. Then one day she just didn't show. When they tried to call, they found the number to be out of use."

"Strange."

"Yes, and get this. They still have her paychecks. She never took them."

"Ever?"

"No."

"So she didn't need the money. Even though her apartment screams otherwise."

She tapped her eyebrow. "Money wasn't important. She scraped by and didn't seem to mind. No, she wouldn't mind. Because *her* life wasn't her focus. Veronica Ryan's was."

"There's something else. Guess who had used Courtesy Cleaners in the past?"

"Sloan Savage."

He nodded. "And Veronica Ryan."

Kennedy sank into a chair.

Allen called up another screen. "We found that envelope. The one that came with the first Ryan letter."

She sat up straighter, recalling the letter she'd found.

"You were right. She listed a return address."

"The apartment?"

"Yes."

She looked at the screen where a photo of the envelope glowed. She noted the black ink and the longhand script. She saw Veronica's name and address.

Allen spoke. "They're dusting it for prints as we speak."

Kennedy blinked. Something in her mind clicked. Her thoughts raced. She studied the handwriting. Veronica's name. She stood.

"Oh my God."

Allen looked at her. "What is it?"

"There." She pointed. "At the end of Veronica's name."

"The heart?"

Kennedy's heart nearly jumped out of her chest.

She looked at him.

"It's the same. The same handwriting."

"Same as what?"

Kennedy swallowed. "As the letter sent to Keri."

❖

*Hudson Valley, New York*

"Drive her straight to the shoot," Monty said, talking to Phil. Veronica, unfortunately, was having to overhear it. "I would take her myself, but I'm worried about Shawn. I want to stay with her and the girls."

"It'll be fine," Phil said as if he'd done this hundreds of times.

Monty chuckled. "Uh-huh. You know she's a pistol, right?"

Veronica wanted to scoff but she remained silent, listening.

"You've only told me around fifty times."

"Well, here's fifty-one. She's a pistol. Stubborn. Rude. Bossy."

"I thought you liked her."

"I do."

"And you talk like this about her?"

Monty laughed again. "I'm being nice."

*Fuck you, Monty.* It was bad enough he was sending her off with this musclehead.

Phil pulled on his navy blazer and she forced herself to look outside rather than react. It was cold and damp outside, the sky furrowing with dark clouds, as if preparing for the weather from the broken-up hurricane. It had been three days since the crew had returned from South Carolina and the bad weather had followed them like an impending doom, promising at the very least a severe thunderstorm.

Monty spoke again. "Johnson wants a break. Care to take a guess why?"

"Because she's a pistol."

"Yup. So you're it today. Larry's in town and will meet you later. As for the other one who was with her, Botkin? He quit."

"When?"

"An hour ago."

"That makes, what, three?"

He nodded.

Botkin? She could think of several other more appropriate names for him.

"More of her charm, I take it?"

Monty grinned. "Now you're catching on." He patted him on the back. "I put a call into that FBI guy. They're working on getting replacements. In the meantime, you and Larry take Veronica, and Johnson and I will stay with Shawn."

He rubbed his hands together in a gesture that suggested he wasn't cold, but nervous.

A mental chill swept through Veronica and it wasn't just the less than favorable things the guys were saying about her. It was something else. Something strange. Like those gut feelings you sometimes get, convinced something is going to go wrong.

Veronica swept into the room. She knew she looked nice in expensive jeans and a purple cashmere sweater. It made her feel a little better about herself considering what she'd just heard. She tried to relax as she slipped into her worn leather jacket.

"You both taking me?"

Phil was staring at her. She knew he was looking at the shadows under her eyes and the lifelessness of her gaze. The mirror hadn't lied to her. Monty was right to be worried. And she knew they'd all heard the yelling and the fighting the night before at Shawn's hotel.

"Phil's going," Monty explained. "He's driving you to the shoot and Larry will meet up with you there."

"Larry?" She rolled on lip gloss, pretending she didn't have a clue.

"The other security—"

"Right." She stared at them both. "Where's the Terminator? RoboCop?"

Monty cleared his throat. "Johnson is still with us, but Botkin has left."

"Which one's which?" She pocketed the lip gloss and waved her hand. "Never mind. They're all the same. I can't keep up. Except for you, Monty." She kissed his cheek and looked at Phil. "Let's go then."

They rode the elevator down. Veronica walked quickly, slipping on sunglasses despite the rain. She breezed through the hotel doors.

She saw Phil give Monty one last look before he hurried outside after her, anxious to open the door for her. She slid into the waiting Mercedes sedan without a word. She did not buckle her seat belt.

He climbed behind the wheel and they drove in silence for a while, heading into the New York countryside.

"Looks like we're going to be a little early," he said. She was staring out the back window in silence. The windshield wipers whined a few times before she decided to speak.

"I know. That's why I wanted to leave right away. There's somewhere I need to go."

He didn't say anything in response but she could feel the car slow.

"Slowing down won't help."

He stared straight ahead.

"I think maybe we should just head toward the shoot."

"No," she said, drawing the word out. "There's somewhere I need to go."

She leaned forward.

"Make a left at the next light." She spoke sternly and removed her sunglasses to eye him in the mirror. He clenched the steering wheel.

"I'm sorry, Ms. Ryan, but I have my orders."

"I'm giving you the orders."

She could see his skin redden. "Monty said to drive you straight to the shoot."

"Do it or you're fired." She stared at him hard. Waiting for him to argue. When he didn't she eased back and crossed her arms over her chest.

"Monty's my boss."

"No, you idiot, I'm your boss. I'm Monty's boss, I'm everybody's boss. I pay your salary and you'll do as I say."

He didn't reply and he acted like he couldn't bear to look in the rearview mirror. He fumbled with the cell phone.

"Turn here," she said again. "Now. Then you can call Monty and complain."

He released the phone and gripped the steering wheel. The turn signal flashed as he switched it on and slowed.

"Turn right again up here. The gravel road."

He did as he was told and drove the car over the crunching gravel. The road led into the trees, and beyond them stood a beautiful stone house, large but single story.

"I'll be right back," Veronica said as she quickly exited the car. He stepped out after her.

"No, you stay."

"I have to come with—"

"Wait in the car." She shot daggers at him. "I mean it. I'll be fine.

I'm not staying long. Just wait out here and do your thing. Watch for bad guys or goblins or whatever it is you do."

She felt him watching her as she trotted up to the door. Before she could even knock. Marion stepped out and embraced her. They kissed softly and she fought just collapsing in her arms. She heard the car door close and knew he would be calling Monty now but she didn't care. All she cared about at that moment was Marion Grace. She hurriedly followed her inside.

❖

Ashley Williams knocked on his window. He visibly jumped in surprise.

She stood looking right at him, large sunglasses covering her eyes, her head covered by the dark green hood of her raincoat. She could feel the rain pelt it. She motioned for him to roll down his window.

He seemed cautious and only lowered it a little.

"I need to see some ID, sir." She spoke confidently and looked into the interior of the car, searching.

"Sorry?" He looked carefully at her, trying to see her face.

"Identification. I need to see some." She eyed him sternly. "Who are you with?"

"Veronica Ryan."

"Did she have an appointment with Ms. Grace?"

"I'm sorry, who?"

"Marion Grace. You're on her property."

He fished out his ID. "An appointment? I don't know."

She saw a flicker of recognition just as he reached for his cell phone. Before he could hit speed dial, she pushed into him with the Taser, then opened the car door. He fell to all fours and tried to speak, but she Tasered him again. He fell to his back and she knelt to deliver another shock to his ribs. Strange gasping sounds came from him as his large body contorted. She knew the pain was excruciating but he wasn't out yet. Once more to his neck did the job and he stilled. Hurriedly, she removed his blazer and tossed it on the driver's seat.

Then she studied him. His eyes had rolled back in his head and he was curled up on his side. He would be tough to move. Glancing around, she bent and grabbed the man under the armpits.

"Heavy motherfucker," she said, dragging him into the woods.

His shoes were shiny and they wobbled as she dragged him over pine needles and brush. When she was about fifty yards in, she released him and tried to catch her breath. His head was turned and he looked as if he were asleep. She knew that look.

He was sleeping the sweet sleep. Seeing God required that sometimes.

Regaining her strength, she yanked off his blazer and then pulled out the roll of duct tape she had hidden in her coat. She busied herself binding his hands and feet, rolling him over to hog-tie him. Then she gagged him.

Satisfied, she returned to the car and slid into his blazer, her raincoat still on underneath. The rain pelted her hood and her breath came out in white wisps.

She left the engine running as she waited for Veronica Ryan. Her heart raced but it also hurt. She could only imagine what the two women were doing inside. Veronica had been seeing Marion Grace for a short while now, and it angered her. It seemed that Veronica had a handful of women she could choose from at any given time. It wasn't just Sloan Savage, it wasn't just Shawn. She gripped the steering wheel tighter as she thought of how many women she would have to kill in order to win Veronica for herself. It was too many. She could do it, but it would take too much time. So she had decided to simply take Veronica. To kidnap her and take her away. Then and only then would she be hers. Solely hers. She glanced in the rearview mirror once again. This time she smiled at her reflection.

Veronica Ryan was almost hers.

Movement came from the house. The front door opened and Veronica and Marion stepped out and embraced. Heat angered her skin as she watched Veronica kiss Marion Grace passionately.

She squeezed the steering wheel.

Maybe she would come back for the Grace bitch. And Shawn. Yes, she would get Veronica settled and come after them. Maybe then her heart could rest.

Veronica Ryan approached the car and she sat straighter and tried to make herself appear taller. Veronica hurried, trying to avoid the rain, and opened the door herself. She climbed in and Ashley immediately locked the doors and drove away from the house.

She drove quickly, desperately wanting to look back at Veronica, at her love, but she wanted to hide her identity as long as she could. She heard Veronica sigh and fidget in the back seat.

"Was that so bad?" she asked and then laughed. "Guess Monty's pretty pissed at me, huh? I'm surprised he didn't drive down here."

Ashley drove on in silence.

"Figures. He's always pissed at me about something. But let me tell you, that trip was well worth it." She let out a long breath. "That's quite a woman."

Ashley kept driving, wringing her hands on the steering wheel. Eventually, the silence got to Veronica.

"Now you're pissed at me." She laughed. "So you're not going to talk to me. You think I jeopardized your job. That's fine. Whatever."

Ashley could feel her eyes on the back of her head. After a few more moments of silence, Veronica leaned forward.

"Hand me the fucking phone and I'll call Monty and tell him it was all my fault."

Ashley didn't move.

"Um, hello?"

Silence.

"Rambo. Give me the phone. That's your new name now. Rambo. Like it?" Veronica sighed dramatically. "Fine. I don't need to call him. You both can kiss my ass."

The phone next to Ashley rang. She looked at it but didn't answer.

"Would you please get that?" Veronica demanded.

It stopped after a few rings but then started up again.

Veronica complained, "Jesus, answer the phone, it's driving me crazy."

The ringing was getting to Ashley too. She couldn't take it. Veronica leaned forward and tried to reach over the seat. Ashley acted quickly and grabbed the phone. She lowered the window and tossed it out. Veronica called out, shocked.

More silence filled the car.

Veronica spoke. "Pull your hood down."

Ashley didn't move.

"I don't remember you having a hood." Her voice cracked.

Ashley kept driving, making a turn to go deeper into the country.

Veronica opened her own cell phone. Ashley heard it.

Immediately, she pulled off the road and slammed the car to a screeching halt. Excitement filled her belly as Veronica shrieked.

Ashley opened her door and sprang from the car. She yanked open Veronica's door and reached in. Veronica retracted and shrieked again.

"Get away, get away from me!"

Ashley grabbed the phone and pried it from her hand. She studied the screen. No call had been made. She chucked it over her shoulder.

Then she stooped to look at the woman she'd long been after. She tossed her shades aside.

"Hello, Veronica." She slipped out of the navy blazer and lowered the hood of her raincoat.

Veronica stared at her, hunched against the other side of the car. She reached down and fumbled with the door handle.

"I wouldn't do that if I were you." Ashley reached in her back pocket and pulled out a handgun. She aimed it at Veronica and watched as she stilled, her big brown eyes trained on the weapon.

"Wha-What do you want?" Her voice was strong at first, but then trembled.

"What I've always wanted. You."

Tears formed but didn't fall. She seemed at a loss for words.

"Don't cry. I love you."

Veronica sucked in a sudden shaky breath. "You don't know what you're saying."

"Yes, I do. I've always loved you, Veronica. And now it's time I show you." She leaned into the car, taking Veronica's hand.

Veronica jerked and tried to pull away.

"Come on, now. Come sit in the front with me." She waived the gun at her and backed up. Veronica slowly complied and crawled out of the car. She tried to stand her ground, but her hands gave her away. They shook.

Ashley motioned for her to climb into the front and slide over. Veronica did so and clung to the passenger door, one hand on the handle.

Ashley eased in behind the wheel and closed the door. She started the car and looked over at her.

"Now." She sighed with a smile. "We're ready to go." She put the car in drive and accelerated slowly. "I wouldn't think about jumping out if I were you. The road sure would mess up your pretty face. And not to mention what would happen after that." She held up her gun. "Understand?"

Veronica nodded. She began to cry softly.

"Good."

"Where's Phil?" She sounded meek now.

Ashley smiled at her.

"Phil? Oh, you mean Rambo? Is that what you called him?"

"My driver."

"He's back at Marion's, sleeping off a bad case of shock." She laughed. "Rambo. I never did see that movie."

"You didn't kill him?" For someone who had a reputation for being a bitch, she sure was timid.

"I don't think so."

Veronica looked out the window. Her breathing changed. She was truly afraid.

Ashley slid the gun into her coat pocket and reached down to take Veronica's hand. Veronica pulled it away quickly.

"It's okay, baby." She laughed and tucked a loose strand of Veronica's hair behind her ear. "Hold my hand." She reached out again and held her hand tightly. "I love you."

Veronica cringed and squirmed.

"But I don't love you!" she yelled, ripping her hand away. Ashley laughed heartily.

"Finally," she said. "There's my girl. For a minute there I thought you were a coward. And I would've been very disappointed indeed."

"Let me go. You're crazy. Crazy bitch!" She tried the door handle but found it locked. Ashley laughed again and accelerated.

"Go ahead, I dare you." She unlocked the doors. "Go ahead."

She knew she wouldn't. Veronica watched the road and toyed with the handle. She remained in her seat.

"That's what I thought," Ashley said, locking the doors again. "You know, I know you pretty well. And it doesn't bother me that you don't love me. Because you don't love anybody."

Veronica straightened. "You're wrong." She stared straight ahead. "I love Shawn."

Ashley scoffed. "No, you don't."

"Yes, I do. And nothing you can think, say, or do will change that."

Ashley wasn't fazed. "If you love her, then why cheat on her with all those women? With Sloan Savage and Marion Grace. With—"

"Because I'm selfish! Because I fuck up all the time!" she yelled between her angry tears. "I hurt her, but I love her."

Ashley didn't like hearing her say that. Didn't like it at all. Veronica was selfish. She was famous. She was rich and beautiful. But she wasn't in love with Shawn. She couldn't be.

"You'll love me."

"No."

"Yes. You have no choice, it's destiny."

"Fuck you."

"We'll do that too."

"No. No!"

Ashley clenched her jaw. Veronica kept on.

"I said no. Do you hear me? I said no!"

Ashley retrieved her gun. She aimed it at her and spoke slowly. "I hear you. And now you will shut up."

"I love her," Veronica said.

"You love yourself."

Veronica closed her mouth.

"It pains me to say it, but it's what I've found. Still, you can change. You will love me. It is God's will."

"Fuck you!" she screamed again.

Ashley swung her arm and brought the butt of the gun down hard on her head. Veronica yelped and tried to fend off the blow. Ashley swung again and connected and Veronica went limp, chin resting on her chest.

She set the gun on the dash. The words kept replaying in her mind and she rubbed her temple.

Veronica was selfish and stubborn. But still, she was so beautiful. So perfect.

But she loved Shawn.

Ha.

She loved no one.

But soon, she would love her. And soon they would see God together.

# Chapter Thirteen

*FBI Field Office, New York City*

"I don't know what it means," Kennedy said, meeting Allen's gaze. They were going over all the letters sent to Keri. The handwriting on the latest threatening letter was a match to the very first letter to Veronica Ryan. Her head spun.

"She was after your sister," Allen said.

"The labs on the blood are in," Gale said, sliding into a seat next to Kennedy. The testing on the letter Keri last received was finished. Kennedy refused the lab work, encouraging Gale to read it.

"Human blood. Type O positive."

"So we have nothing."

"We have her DNA."

"Which is useless." She stood and paced. Her mind wouldn't stop and neither would her body. "Why Keri? She doesn't look like Veronica Ryan, she's not famous…"

"She could be after your brother-in-law," Allen said.

"No. You saw her place. She wasn't into football. She's not into anything other than Veronica Ryan."

"What does Keri say?" Gale asked.

"She's clueless. She's never seen any woman like the composite."

"What about her assailant?"

Kennedy ran a hand through her hair. "Keri said it was possible that it could've been a woman. But she's not sure."

"Williams would've had to travel to Seattle," Allen said.

"Yes. But it doesn't make sense. The handwriting has to be a fluke. There are no connections between my sister and Veronica Ryan. There's nothing."

Allen's phone rang. He excused himself and answered. Kennedy studied Ashley's photo on the large screen. It was one she'd used on her fake ID for her job, and it was a good match to the composite. Her hair was heavy and thick and it hung over the sides of her face. There was no smile. Just a detached look.

"Who are you, Ashley Williams, and are you after my sister?"

"Kennedy." Allen returned, he could hardly breathe.

"What's wrong?"

"It's Ms. Ryan. She's gone."

Kennedy's stomach dropped. "Shawn?"

"Veronica. She left for a photo shoot and never made it."

Panic rushed through her. Possibilities and scenarios did as well. None of them good. "Wasn't anyone with her?"

"Phil."

"Just Phil?"

"Yes. Larry was meeting them at the shoot."

"What happened?"

"They may have detoured. We don't know. We just know they didn't show for the shoot. And neither one are answering their phones." He looked to several other agents who had come over to hear the news.

"Check with her contacts, her friends and colleagues." He pointed at Gale. "Call Marion Grace." Gale rose and went to a nearby desk.

Kennedy closed her eyes. Where would she have gone? Why?

Allen continued. "Monty said they left for the shoot early. So she may have had Phil stop somewhere else first. My bet's Marion Grace. She's renting a house close to the movie shoot."

"Her security should know better," another agent said.

"Phil hasn't worked with her before. She probably sank her teeth into him," Kennedy said.

"And we all know how difficult she is," Allen added.

Kennedy felt on edge. She felt sick. Just like she felt every time those calls came in about the missing children. The calls reporting a body. They made her want to scream, to rage, to pull her hair out. They made her want to sink to her knees and cry.

"God," she said, voice quaking. "Let's just hope she's at Marion's."

❖

Ashley remained crouched in front of Veronica's chair. Her love was strapped to it tightly, with lots of duct tape. The chair was bolted securely to the cement floor. Veronica would be safe there for a long while.

She rose and rounded the chair, running her hand lightly through Veronica's hair. The room was tiny and dank, nearly dark save for the lantern. The smell of the deep earth comforted her. This was her home. The only place she felt safe. Water dripped from one of the overhead pipes behind her. She found it without the light of the lantern, by scent and hearing alone. She stuck her tongue out and tasted the drops. There was a slight metal taste and the drops were cold and heavy. She loved them. Her water drops.

Veronica stirred, gaining her attention. She was trying to shake the chair. She moaned against her gag.

"If you stay quiet, I'll untie you," Ashley said, coming to stand in front of her. "But only if you're good." She stroked her face. It was wet from where she'd been crying. "Shh. Now, now. You have to calm down. It's the only way out of the chair."

Veronica made another muffled noise and tried to move. She angled her head toward the ceiling.

"No one will hear you. No one knows about this place or this basement. They have no idea where you are. You're mine now."

Veronica shook her head.

"Yes. I've waited so long, Veronica. So very long." She knelt and kissed her forehead, then her brow, then her cheeks.

Veronica sat with her head slumped, tears softly making their way down her face. Her chest shook with sobs.

"Are you sad?"

Veronica glared at her.

"I was sad too, at first. But it gets better. You learn your purpose and you accept it. But you have to be calm." She rose. "I bet you're wondering what your purpose is. That's understandable." She stood before her and started unbuttoning her shirt. "It's simple, really. It's about seeing God. You and me." She slipped the shirt from her arms and let it fall to the ground. Then she removed her under tank. Her hands skimmed over her small breasts. "Yes," she hissed. "I can already sense him near."

Veronica started jerking again, trying to cry out. Ashley frowned. "Stop it."

Veronica jerked some more, shook her head violently.

"I said stop!" Ashley took a step and smacked her hard across the face. Veronica stilled and her head went limp. Ashley raised her chin.

"You must watch me. You need to learn how."

Veronica blinked, slowly. When Ashley saw her focus, she continued.

"Now, where were we?" She moved her hands down to her jeans. She undid the button and lowered the zipper. Then she slid her hands inside the waist and eased the jeans down, underwear too. She tossed them to the side.

Veronica was looking at her in a hazy way. Her head was limp and her eyes were glassed over.

"Are you watching me?" Ashley wanted to be sure. She'd dreamed of this moment. "Veronica? You must tell me you are watching."

Veronica nodded.

"Good." She lowered her hand to her center, her sacred place. It was clean shaven and ready; she was already wet and eager. "This is how we do it," she whispered, touching herself. "Yes, we do it like this. It feels so good. It's the love. The tender love." She relished knowing that Veronica was watching her. "I'm going to see him now. I'm going to see him now with you watching. Oh God, I'm here. I'm ready. God. God." She trembled and tensed, her body convulsing in sheer pleasure. "God, God! I see God, oh God." Her hand flew in a fury of passion and then stilled at once as the moment passed. Breathless, she walked to Veronica and straddled her, collapsing against her. She held her head to her breasts and hummed.

"Oh, Veronica. It was so beautiful. So blissful." She kissed her hair. "Soon it will be your turn. God is waiting. But right now, I have to take care of something. Something I thought I wouldn't have to do after all. But you've changed all that." She held her tighter. "I have to go find Shawn and take care of her." Veronica tensed and shook her head. Ashley stilled her, holding her tighter. "Shh. It has to be done. It's the only way. You must be free to love me."

Veronica moaned through the binds. Jerked in the chair.

"Shh, it's okay. It will be okay." She stood. "Come, you can lie on the bed and think about me and God." She retrieved a knife from a dark corner and cut Veronica free from the chair. Then she cut the tape around her legs so she could walk.

Leading the way with the lantern, she tugged Veronica into a small room with a thin wooden door.

Inside, the musty dank smell was worse, mixed with the stench of urine and human excrement. Ashley didn't mind; she was used to it. Perhaps having Veronica down there would help to air it out a little.

She led her to the blue flower–patterned mattress that sat against the wall. It had a blanket and her yellowish pillow on top. She eased her down and then lifted her ankles onto the bed. Then she showed her the ceiling with the light from the lantern. She'd taped magazine photos of Veronica everywhere. She still had stacks of them against the walls.

"See how much I love you?"

More tears fell down Veronica's face.

"I told you I did. Now do you believe me?"

Veronica turned her head, refusing to look at her.

Ashley crawled atop her, rested her weight on her. "Oh, Veronica. So, so beautiful." She kissed her neck, sucked on her skin. God, it was glorious, perfume mixed with nervous sweat. She could lick her from head to toe and never tire.

"My desire for you is so great. It's all consuming, and only God understands. He wants this, Veronica. You and me. In this bed. Giving the tender love, in his name." She traced her hand down to Veronica's blue jeans. She unfastened them and then lowered herself to pull them down. Veronica cried.

"Shh." Ashley tugged her half boots off and removed the jeans. She folded them and placed them on the dirt floor. Then she inhaled the flesh of Veronica's thighs up to her panties, where she stuck out her tongue and pressed it against her covered flesh.

"Oh, yes. Veronica. Heavenly." She pulled away and looked at her. "I cannot wait to discover you and take you to God. It will be so good. So very, very good." She licked her lips. "I can already taste you, smell you." She squeezed Veronica's hips. "I can hardly wait."

She pushed herself up on the bed. "Tonight. It will be heaven tonight." She pointed to the bucket in the corner. "If you have to go, use the bucket. I'll be back in a few hours."

Veronica sat up and moaned furiously. She tried to stand.

Ashley came up on her and smacked her once again. Veronica fell back to the bed, but shook her head. Ashley hit her again, this time a backhand.

"You will stay here and be quiet."

She hit her again and again.

Veronica lay back, head lolling to the side. Blood trickled from her nose.

"Look what you made me do to your pretty face." Ashley made a tsking noise. "It's okay, though. You'll learn in time."

She left the room and pulled the wooden door closed. As she stepped into her clothes, her thoughts went to Shawn.

❖

Kennedy sprang from the vehicle and hurried up the steps to the home of Marion Grace. Allen followed closely behind. Veronica had been missing for three hours, and they finally had a lead.

Soft thunder rolled in the distance, grumbling from a gray sky. Cool rain dripped down, wetting the grass and trees, giving an earthy scent to the crisp air.

Kennedy caught her breath as she and Allen hit the cover of the front porch. Three agents came out from the house and got them up to speed.

"We found Mr. Phillip Frye over here." He pointed across the gravel drive and walked down to the steps back into the rain. Kennedy and Allen followed as he led them into the woods. The rain pricked their skin as they maneuvered through the trees.

"He'd been shocked with a stun gun. Several times. And bound with duct tape."

"Is he going to be okay?" she asked, wiping the rain from her brow.

"Looks that way. He's a little weak and maybe a little hypothermic.

His blazer was taken and he was left out here in the rain. We found him thirty minutes ago."

"Is he talking?"

They stopped outside the yellow crime scene tape. She eyed the ground and noticed the fresh drag marks.

"Not yet."

An indentation in the pine needles showed where he had been tied and dumped. There were button prints in a small area of mud where he'd been lying on his stomach.

She followed the drag marks back to where the Ryans' car had been parked. She saw the tire tracks and stated her theory. "She zapped him over here next to the car and then dragged him into the woods."

"Ashley Williams?"

"I believe so."

"You think she could've moved Phil on her own?"

She examined the footprints in moist earth. She matched them up to the footprints they'd found in Sloan's bathroom. They were boot prints. Military style.

"It wasn't that far. Sure, if she's determined." She continued to search the area. "Anything missing?"

"The Ryan vehicle. And, well, Veronica Ryan."

"What's Miss Grace have to say?" They began their walk back to the house. The place was crawling with FBI.

"She says Veronica showed up, stayed for about thirty minutes, and then left. She didn't notice anything suspicious, other than the fact that Veronica got in the car to leave without assistance. But she said when she'd arrived she got out on her own as well. She assumed it was because of her security. Veronica was unhappy with her driver and she complained to Marion."

Kennedy sighed. She had a headache coming on. A bad one. "Any news on Ashley Williams?"

Allen held up a hand as he answered his cell phone. Kennedy glanced over at Marion Grace, who was being questioned by two agents. She was a tall woman with thin, graceful, elegant beauty. Her dark hair and green eyes were a striking combination. She'd just divorced.

And now she was seeing Veronica.

Kennedy watched as Marion shook her head and wiped her tears. What a mess.

Allen snapped his cell phone shut.

"We got her. Williams."

Kennedy nearly jumped.

"Where?"

"Her father owned a home about thirty miles east of here. He's dead but the house still stands."

"How did we find the house?"

"We checked her mail at the apartment complex. A letter came in regard to the house. We ran the address, and boom. Howard Williams. Daughter Ashley."

"And there's movement on the house?"

"We're not sure. Agents haven't arrived yet."

Kennedy moved with him, quickly jogging to his vehicle. Once inside he started the car and peeled out of the gravel drive. They were on their way in a flash and Kennedy hoped they wouldn't be too late. She knew Williams was highly unstable and prone to extreme violence. She'd shot to kill Shawn and most likely had killed Sloan as well. She gripped the armrest as Allen sped down the highway.

He had his phone glued to his ear, calling for backup. He asked that all responding units wait before entering. He wanted to be there.

She imagined Veronica, tied up, beaten, or worse. She imagined Ashley Williams in a hooded mask, just like she'd worn to break into Keri's. She imagined her holding a knife to Veronica's throat.

She prayed.

*Please let us get there in time.*

She'd seen far too much death for one lifetime.

Allen slowed as they neared the address. Like the home of Marion Grace, the Williams house was far back from the road, nestled near the woods. They approached slowly, through the grass that had grown over a dirt driveway. They parked before the house came into view and motioned other arriving agents to do the same. Four agents were already there, running along the tree line, weapons drawn.

Three more cars pulled in, along with a SWAT vehicle.

Kennedy strapped into a bulletproof vest and tried to breathe deeply. Hot adrenaline spilled into her blood, accelerating her heart and mind. She pulled out her weapon and made sure it was loaded and ready, the safety off. She looked to Allen, who stood looking a lot like her, vest on, weapon ready. Rain speckled his graying hair and forehead. She gave him a nod and they motioned for the SWAT team to move ahead of them.

The small team descended on the house. The yard was overgrown with weeds and trees. A red brick base led up to worn steps and a small porch. The posts were red brick as well. Four windows stared out at them, all of them covered by some sort of blind. One window, the front left, had a crack in it. Many more cracks veined throughout the front of the house, the pale green paint old and peeling.

Kennedy crept quickly, slightly bent, holding her gun in both hands, pointed toward the ground. She hurried up the overgrown drive and noted no vehicle. A milk crate of old Coca-Cola cans sat nudged up against the porch, most of them rusted.

The SWAT team spread out, three men going up the porch steps and three men rounding to contain the perimeter. They shouldered against the wall and gave hand signals.

They called out. "FBI. Open the door."

Kennedy's heart thumped. *Come on, come on. Be here.*

The SWAT team called out again but there was no answer.

They gave more hand signals and then they kicked open the door.

Kennedy and Allen followed up the porch. They waited as the SWAT team searched and called out from inside.

"Clear."

Twenty seconds later.

"Clear."

"All clear."

"Clear."

Two minutes later a SWAT member poked his head out. "We're clear."

Kennedy lowered her weapon and walked inside. Allen followed, along with the other agents. The floor creaked and the house smelled musty and sour. It crawled to the back of her throat and stayed there. She wanted to gag. Obscured light filtered in. The SWAT team moved about with powerful flashlights.

Someone began opening blinds. It didn't help much.

"Kennedy, look at this," Allen said, having switched on his own Maglite.

The walls were covered in papers. Pages. She stepped closer. Bible pages.

Something in her gut turned. She started to sweat.

Allen shone his light around the room. Each wall was covered, from the floor up. And then the beam hit the ceiling. More pages. Completely covered with them. It was as if the room were wallpapered in Bible pages, like some sort of religious papier mâché. The beam fell above the worn couch. Two large velvet paintings of Christ hung: one was Christ on the cross, the other Christ in prayer. Both were surrounded by pages.

A roach scurried across the floor. Cobwebs glinted in the hazy light. Dust mushroomed into the air as Allen tried to turn on a lamp. She tried a wall switch. Nothing. There was no electricity.

Another agent called from the kitchen. She stood pointing at the table. There were smudge marks in the dust and an open bag of bread with peanut butter. Somebody had been there recently.

"We'll put a watch on the house," Allen said.

Kennedy looked at a SWAT member. "Is there a basement?"

He shook his head. "Just the three rooms."

"Are you sure?"

"If there is, there's no door."

She walked to the kitchen window and stared out into the backyard. What had once been a good-sized garden was now dead and overgrown. But a small shed stood out back. More SWAT guys moved in and out of it.

"What's out there?"

He followed her line of sight.

"Canned vegetables. Cases of them."

"Anything else?"

"Yeah. A chair."

"A chair?"

He wiped the sweat from his brow. "Covered in duct tape."

Veronica drifted in and out of consciousness. The smell of piss was old yet strong, the light dim yet piercing. She stared up at herself. Photos. Some of them over ten years old.

Where was she?

A house. An old house.

Why? Her head swam as she struggled for answers.

A woman. A woman had taken her.

Why?

To hold captive. To… She saw that her legs were bare, her jeans on the floor. She remembered the woman's touch, the way she tried to kiss her, the way she smelled…like Veronica's signature perfume. The perfume she'd never cared for. Now the lingering scent of it made her want to vomit.

Struggling for breath, she rolled off the bed and then struggled to stand. Her face throbbed; her nose was surely busted. Pain shot throughout her head and blood oozed down the back of her throat. Because of her gag, she was forced to swallow it—hot, thick, and metallic, choking her.

She couldn't breathe. Couldn't breathe.

The air was stuffy and the gag was too tight. The room spun.

*Help. Help.*

She slammed her shoulder into the door. It gave a little. She tried again. It didn't budge.

She struggled with her binds. Her wrists were taped together. She looked around the small room, searching. Her gaze fell on the bucket. It was large and plastic, like a paint bucket. She focused in on the rim. It was worn and tattered. Staggering, she went to it, and then brought it to the bed and sat down. Legs straddling the bucket, she held it between her ankles and rubbed her bound wrists against the worn rim.

As some of the tape began to give, a dark tunnel threatened her vision.

❖

Kennedy walked the Williams property, refusing to leave. They'd searched the house high and low and found nothing leading them to Veronica. They had no other leads, but she just knew they were missing something.

"Tell me again about Howard Williams," she called out to Allen, who was walking a few yards away.

"He died two years ago. Heart attack. He was driving his big rig when it happened. Lucky he didn't kill somebody."

"And what about Ashley?"

"Nothing on her, really. One of the neighbors remembers seeing her in the summertime, working in the garden. She said she thought them strange, though."

"How's that?"

"She said the girl was always outside without her shirt on. But once she got a little older and she started to develop, she was covered completely. She said she thought she was even wrapped to make herself smaller."

"In the summer?"

"Yes."

Another haunting rush of familiarity came. Allen continued.

"But other than that, no one really saw her. And they only saw him when he was leaving in his rig."

"What about her mother?"

Allen shook his head. "Nothing. No one knows who she is. We can't locate a birth certificate."

"Strange. You think Williams was an alias?"

"We're checking. But I don't think so. His family has owned this house for years."

"Why would he keep his daughter out of school? Did he home school her?"

"That's what he claimed. On a medical form. She broke her arm a few years back and he took her to the emergency room."

"Something's not right." She stared at the ground, willing clues to emerge from the earth. "What aren't we seeing?"

Allen looked up into the gently leaking sky. "I don't know. Williams was a bit odd, obsessed with religion, a bit of a recluse, kept his daughter home, away from the outside world. Even when he worked, he was shelled away from the world."

"But why? I guess that's the question."

They headed back into the small shed behind the house. Cases of jarred vegetables lined the walls.

"He liked to garden."

"Yes, he did." Allen held one up. "Wonder if they're still good."

She looked around. The cases were stacked to the roofline on three walls.

The chair was sitting in the center all on its own, as if it were waiting for them. Kennedy knelt to examine it. Her heart slammed behind her ribs as she focused on the loosely hanging duct tape that wrapped around the arms and the top and bottom of the legs. The back was also covered. She examined the back of the tape, touching it with a pen as Allen shined the flashlight.

"It's old," she said. "Looks like it's no longer sticky."

"Check out the legs, the bottoms."

A square of metal had been welded to the bottom of each leg. The squares each contained one hole.

Allen knelt along side her. "This chair was fastened to something."

"There weren't any marks in the house."

"No."

Kennedy rose. The hair stood up on her skin. "Where, then?"

They emerged from the shed and Kennedy winced as the rain once again hit her skin. It no longer felt cool and penetrating. Now it was hot and insistent, telling her again and again that something wasn't right.

She stared out at the yard, walked the property line, stepped farther into the woods. They needed more men. She wanted search and rescue, dogs, the works.

Something wasn't right.

"She left that bread and peanut butter," she said to Allen, walking through the trees. "She's coming back. She was planning on coming back."

"What are you thinking?"

She stopped. "Veronica's here. She's hidden."

"Do we call in SAR or do we sit and wait for her?" He flipped open his phone and dialed.

"We may not have time to waste." When children were taken in non-family abductions, they were almost always killed within the first few hours. That fact played inside her mind…a lost lullaby…singing to her now…why?

"Veronica's not a child." She said this aloud and Allen covered the phone.

"Kennedy?"

She stared through the woods, scanned the ground. Something red stuck out from beneath the brush. Bending, she retrieved her pen and pushed at the leaves and vine. A toy car was buried halfway in the ground, its back end sticking up. The toy was old and nearly faded. Her heart skipped.

And then she heard it. A far off-cry. Almost like an animal's moan.

"Kennedy—"

"Shh." She stood and silenced him with her hand. The noise came again, this time stronger. A cry. A plea.

Help.

She took off through the woods, heart pounding blood in her ears.

"Help!"

It was muffled but growing stronger. She ran harder. It was coming from the back woods. She heard it again and again. She slammed to the right, nearly tripped on a vine. She drew her weapon and slowed. She scanned left and right. The cry was coming from right in front of her.

But there was nothing there.

She blinked a few times and wiped the rain from her face.

The cry came again and she inched closer. Allen caught up to her from behind.

"I can't find her," Kennedy said. "She's here, but I can't find her." It was her nightmare. In the flesh. She couldn't get to her. Not in time.

"Allen, help me find her."

"I'm here." He crept alongside her, gun ready. Several of the other lingering agents came rushing up as well.

Kennedy blinked and tried to focus. She was worried about an ambush, a trap of some sort. But they had no choice. They had to find Veronica.

One of the SWAT team jogged ahead. He held up a fist and Kennedy and the others stopped.

"Get down," he whispered.

They dropped to the ground. More SWAT members bled in from the trees, silent ninjas in black gear. They approached what looked like an old pipe sticking up from the ground. In the thickening silence Kennedy could hear a stream nearby. A trickle in the falling rain.

The cry came again.

Her heart leapt. It was Veronica.

The SWAT guys surrounded it. Then they fanned out, weapons

aimed at the ground. The leader looked up suddenly. They had something. He held them at bay as two of his men cleared away some loose brush.

Then they lifted a door. An old, worn wooden door. They tossed it aside, switched on the lights attached to their weapons, and descended. Kennedy waited in the brush, pine needles poking the flesh of her arms. The sky growled overhead, promising more rain.

She tried to steady her breathing as she prayed. And then, after what felt like an eternity, she saw the black helmet of a SWAT member. Then another. Two ran up and out, weapons by their side.

"We got her." He smiled, but only briefly.

Kennedy jumped up.

"She needs a medic," he said.

"Can I go down?"

"I'm not sure how safe that tunnel is. It's tight."

Kennedy sprinted for the hole, unwilling to let him finish. Allen tried to get her attention but she wouldn't be stopped. She stood at the mouth and paused. There was only a small hill of dirt, no steps. She pocketed her weapon and braced herself on the roots and dirt of the thick earth. Then she stumbled down. Allen followed.

He switched on his Maglite.

"Smells like shit," he said.

They had to bend to walk through the tunnel. She'd never been claustrophobic before, but the dirt walls were dark and stifling. Her lungs screamed for air. Her legs screamed for her to turn around. But she kept going. Had to keep going.

"This led back toward the house," Allen said. "A fucking underground passage."

Kennedy moved as quick as she could. She coughed from the lack of fresh air, then gagged as the tunnel opened up into a basement. She straightened and sucked in stale, horrible-smelling air.

Allen knelt and caught his breath.

Three SWAT members were huddled around a figure. In the beams of light Kennedy saw bare, dirty legs. Then she saw a dirty sweater and filthy hands. Loose strands of duct tape hung from reddened, chafed wrists.

"Kennedy." The voice was ragged and tired.

The figure stepped forward. Veronica's face was contorted in pain and covered in blood and bruises. Her body trembled and her eyes welled with tears. She tried to walk but nearly fell.

Kennedy caught her.

"She's close to shock," Kennedy said. "We've got to get her up."

"No," Veronica said, nearly hoarse. "Kennedy."

"What is it?"

She swallowed and grabbed at her throat. She fought for breath.

"She's gone after Shawn."

❖

*Scarsdale, New York*

Shawn smiled at the girls as they jumped into the hotel pool. "Very good!" She clapped, but her heart wasn't in it.

The indoor pool was heated and they had the place to themselves. Keri sat next to her holding the baby, and her security flanked the pool, looking bored.

"The waiting is killing me," she said. "I should be doing something."

"I know. I feel terrible," Keri said. "But they said for you to stay here. You're safer here."

"I'm not worried about me. I'm worried about Veronica. God, I can't imagine what must be happening to her. I feel sick."

She stood. The air was hot and smelled strongly of chlorine. Her head spun.

"I just can't sit here."

Keri looked at her with sympathy. "What else can you do?"

"I don't know. Make phone calls. Go out searching."

"Who would you call?"

Shawn thought. "The press?"

"I wouldn't. I would wait for the FBI to do their best first. The media will obsess and the public would be frantic. The suspect might never show her face again."

Shawn steadied herself on the back of the lounge chair. "I can't just sit in here. I'm going nuts."

"Go get some air. Clear your head. I'm sure Kennedy will call with news soon."

"Mommy, where you going?" Rory asked in the middle of a frenzied dog paddle.

"I'm just going to the restroom." She smiled. Rory returned it. She hadn't told the girls. No sense scaring them. They wouldn't understand anyway. Even she didn't understand.

She passed one of the Boudreaux security. He walked with her to the door.

"Ma'am?"

"I need to use the restroom."

He nodded and held the door for her. Then he followed her. The hallway was cooler and she breathed in the air, grateful for it. It soothed her lungs but it did nothing for her nerves. Her hands shook with fear.

They reached the restrooms and he opened the door and walked in. When he returned he nodded and allowed her to enter. She headed inside and went for the sink, where she splashed her face and tried to calm herself.

It didn't work.

What was she going to do? She had to do something. Should she call Kennedy? Call the Bureau? Ask them what she could do? Should she be out there helping?

A knock came from the bathroom door.

She sighed.

"Coming." She dried her face with a rough paper towel and pulled open the door.

The security man was standing there but he had a strange look on his face.

"What's—"

"Shut up." A woman appeared from behind him. A gun was shoved into his back.

Shawn covered her mouth, horrified.

"Shut up."

The woman shoved them back into the bathroom. She dug in the man's suit jacket for his weapon. After shoving it into the front of her pants, she pushed him into a stall.

"Take off your jacket and shirt." She nudged him with the gun. "Hurry."

He did as instructed and dropped them to the floor.

"Turn around," she said. "Now get on your knees."

She pointed the weapon at Shawn and said, "Don't you move." Then she gathered up the clothing.

Shawn began to cry, and she hated herself for it. She should be strong and brave, but her mind said otherwise. She knew who the woman was. She'd seen the composite sketch and the ID photo.

She looked to the door, thought about sprinting for it. But the woman saw her looking.

"No, no, no. If you do that, I'll do this." She wadded the jacket and shirt into a ball and held it to the back of his head. Then she shoved the muzzle of the gun into it and fired.

The sound was sharp but muffled. Like a low pop. Shawn jerked.

The man slumped forward, a spray of blood running down the wall and toilet. Shawn's hand flew up to her mouth. She cried into it.

*No, no, no, no, no.*

*God, no.*

The woman turned. "Come on." She waved Shawn toward her with the gun. "Hurry up."

She forced the gun against Shawn's back and they left the bathroom and walked down the hall. Shawn hoped that maybe she hadn't seen where they'd come from and she tried to walk past the door to the pool.

"In here. Take me to the pool."

Shawn stopped. "No."

"Do it."

"No."

There was silence. "I could shoot you right here. Just like I did him. Or better yet, I'll just go in there and shoot your kids."

"No!" Shawn turned. She met her hard blue eyes. Saw the chaos churning in their depths.

The woman slapped her. Shawn cried out.

"Then don't fuck with me." She grabbed Shawn by the hair and flung her toward the door. "Got it?"

Shawn nodded, the tears coming quicker. Her world slowed as she was forced to pull open the door, gun rammed into her back.

The heat of the pool caved in around them as they stepped inside. The other man, Keri's security, saw Shawn's face and ran up to her. The woman turned Shawn a little so he could see her.

"Stop right there."

He slid to a stop on the wet cement. His face registered the danger and then went slack. The splashes from the pool stopped. Monty grabbed the girls and carried them to the steps. He hid them behind Larry and then did the same with the boys. He looked as terrified as Shawn felt.

Keri began to gasp for air, shielding herself and the baby behind the lounge chair. The kids all cried out.

"Shut up!" the woman yelled.

The room went silent.

The woman stepped out from Shawn and fired her weapon. The gunshot was loud and echoed throughout the tiled room. Another security man fell to the ground, blood oozing from his shoulder. Shawn winced, and her ears rang. Sobs shook her body. The woman urged her forward, yelling at Monty and Larry.

"Don't move! Don't you dare move."

The man on the ground stirred a little but then stopped. Shawn wanted to help him but she was pushed into the lounge chair where Keri hid.

The woman smiled.

"I've got you all right here." She looked at Keri. "What? You don't remember me?" She held up the gun. "Are you sure?" She leaned forward. "I'm your sick, twisted fuck."

Keri made a small noise. Like a mouse caught in a trap.

"That's right. And now I've got you all right here." A sinister grin spread on her face. "Welcome to the jungle."

❖

"Kennedy, will you wait?" Allen was once again on her heels, trying to slow her down. She'd ridden with Gale and three other agents. They'd flown to a small airport a few miles from Shawn's hotel.

"I can't, Allen. Shawn didn't answer her phone. Neither did Monty. Or Keri. Hotel security says they're not in their room." She hurried across the parking lot. "I'm scared shitless."

He caught up to her and touched her shoulder. "Kennedy."

"What?" She stopped and glared at him, breathless. Gale and the others turned as well.

Allen looked strange. Almost—sorry?

"Kennedy, I have to tell you something."

"Can it wait?"

"No." He looked to Gale. She looked at the ground.

"Will someone tell me what the hell's going on?"

Allen squeezed her shoulder. "The prints we ran from that envelope? They matched the prints on the table at the Williams house."

"Okay, so?"

"We got a hit."

She waited. "They were Ashley's."

"Yes and no."

"Allen, what—"

"Kennedy, her name isn't Ashley. Her name is Abigail Perry."

"What—" And then it hit her. Her hearing completely left her. Allen spoke but he sounded far away. "Kennedy?"

Then suddenly she was back and everything was on high speed.

"She's Abigail, Kennedy."

"No."

"Yes."

"It can't be."

"It is."

"This isn't funny."

"No it's not."

"She—it can't be. She—"

"Was never found. The only one never found. It's her, Kennedy. Abigail Perry. Missing eleven years. Blond hair, blue eyes. Type O positive. Taken from her own front yard."

"I—"

"You need to sit down. Let us go in. I'm sure Shawn is fine. No one knows she's here."

Kennedy refused. She shook her head. "I'm okay." She walked ahead. Gale studied her.

Kennedy kept going. "We have to find Shawn and Keri."

"She's after you too, Kennedy. Why else would she be after Keri?"

But Kennedy pressed on. They entered the hotel and drew their weapons. People saw them and hurried out of their way.

Allen headed for the elevator.

"Hotel security says they might have gone for a swim," Kennedy said, turning toward the indoor pool. As they jogged down the hall, a woman emerged from the distant bathroom. She was screaming.

"We're too late," Allen said. "She's here."

Two agents flanked the door to the pool. They nodded. One kicked and the other covered. They caught a glimpse and retreated.

"Suspect is armed," one said. "Standing directly at twelve o'clock."

"Is there a back way in?" Allen asked. "We're on it."

"They're all in there," Kennedy said to no one in particular. "Everyone I love and care about is in there right now."

She looked to Allen. "I have to go in."

"Not without cover you're not."

"Yes, I am."

He tried to stop her but she went anyway. Gun in her right hand, she opened the door and stepped inside. She flinched slightly when she saw Abigail, expecting a barrage of bullets. But the woman had moved and she now held Shawn, gun trained at her head.

"You're more clever than I gave you credit for, Agent Scott. For years you had your head up your ass but now all of a sudden, you're on to me." She grinned. "Took you long enough."

Kennedy stood very still. Monty and Larry stood in the pool, faces ashen but set in stone. The kids were on the pool steps behind them. They were crying, but very softly.

"You outsmarted me, Abigail," she said, studying Shawn, wanting to run to her and take her in her arms. Then she saw Keri holding Natalie tightly. Tears were streaming down her face.

"What did you say?"

"I said, you outsmarted me." She held out her hands, a peace offering. "Abigail."

"My name's not Abigail."

"What is your name, then?"

Behind her, Kennedy heard more agents enter the room. Abigail backed up, frantic.

"Stop! Hold it right there! I'll kill her. I'll kill her just like I did your other man."

Kennedy saw a man down to Shawn's right. He wasn't moving.

"Your so-called security is a laugh."

"What do you want, Abigail? Tell me what you want. You've got our attention."

Agents surrounded the pool. The SWAT team came in through the back door.

Abigail began to panic, walking backward with Shawn.

It was too much. Kennedy wanted to tell them all to back off.

"I'll kill her. I'll kill her!"

Kennedy stepped forward. She dropped her gun. "Slow down, just slow down."

"No. No. You back off, you all back off."

She tightened her arm around Shawn's neck. She pushed the gun into the side of her head. Shawn tried to speak but couldn't. She stared at Kennedy, mouthed the words *I love you*, and then a shot rang out.

Agents dropped to the ground. Kennedy did as well. She dove for her gun. SWAT guys ran for Shawn, who lay on the ground along with Abigail. There was blood.

"No." Kennedy stood and ran to her. The men surrounded Abigail. Shawn was pulled up. She was bleeding. She fell into Kennedy's arms.

"I'm okay, I'm okay."

"You're shot." Kennedy searched desperately for the wound.

"It's not mine. I'm not hurt." She hugged Kennedy tighter. Then she pulled away and ran to her girls.

Abigail was disarmed and rolled onto her stomach. The wound was in her back but she was alive. SWAT members held her down. And the man who had been shot and lay motionless on the floor got up. He stared at his gun and dropped it.

He was the one who'd fired.

Agents ran to him and helped him out. Sirens wailed in the distance. Kennedy hurried to Keri and hugged her tight. They both cried. They kissed Natalie. The boys ran up from the pool. Kennedy squeezed them so hard they protested.

Then she caught Shawn's gaze. "Veronica?" she asked.

Kennedy nodded. "She's going to be okay."

❖

*FBI Field Office, New York City*

"Allen, I love you, but I hope like hell I don't have to see you again anytime soon," Kennedy said, leaning back in a chair. She linked her fingers behind her head as he laughed.

"I understand."

They sat at the same conference room table, files and notebooks neatly stacked. The lights buzzed overhead. Nearby agents laughed. Kennedy smiled. She actually felt like laughing herself.

"You going to be okay?"

"I think so. I really think so."

"What are you going to do?"

She pressed her lips together in thought. "You know, I have no idea."

He chuckled. "Ever think you'll come back?"

"To the Bureau or to the job?"

"Either."

"I might…if a case calls. But I need to heal. And I need to heal properly."

"It's been a lot to take."

"Yes, it has."

"But you know none of it was your fault. You know that, right? I know we've been trying to beat that into your head, but will you ever accept it?"

She contemplated her answer. "I don't know." She dropped her hands and sat forward. "You saw her. Heard her. Jesus Christ, Allen, he kept her for years. Molested her. Filled her head with nonsense. Kept her in a damn hole in the ground."

"Yes."

"He brought new ones home, made her take care of them when he was gone. Made her tend to them and pacify them. Tied them to that chair down there where she slept."

"It was horrible, Kennedy. There's no denying that. But it's not your fault."

"Isn't it, though? If we'd found her—"

"We didn't."

"But if we—"

"We can't play what-if, Kennedy. I mean, what if he'd killed her? He killed the others."

"That's another thing," she said softly. "She would've almost been better off dead."

Allen cleared his throat. "What happened, happened. We can't change it."

Kennedy felt like crying. "She sat down there. Sat down there and looked at the magazines he bought for her. She lived through them. Lived for Veronica. For years."

"She can get help now," he said. "Real help."

"And then the obsession with me. He told her I was a demon. I was out to destroy what they had and what they did. That I was against God. She believed him. Tried to kill my family, for God's sake." She shook her head.

"She was completely brainwashed. She didn't even know that he had killed the others. She thought he just took them home."

"I'm not sure she knows now. We've told her, but her mental state... It will take years to get her thinking straight. Years. Maybe never at all."

Kennedy blew out a long exhale. "She doesn't understand. She doesn't see how she was hurt."

Allen rose. "It's over, Kennedy, finally over."

She nodded. The DNA from the letters matched up. Abigail had confessed to it all.

"But she still hates me," Kennedy said.

"She hates us all."

Kennedy stood to follow him out.

# EPILOGUE

*One month later,*
*Hilton Head, South Carolina*

Shawn pedaled leisurely down the winding bike path through the pine forest. The girls followed close behind, Rory on her purple bike with white wheels and Kiley on her pink one with training wheels.

The wind blew and she inhaled deeply. The path led them past one of the island's numerous posh golf courses. The day was pleasantly cool and beautiful and the trees thinned out as they continued along, the path leading to the thick dunes and eventually to the ocean. She stopped her bike and the girls fell in behind her, walking their bikes through the sand.

"This sand's hard to ride in," Kiley said. She grunted as she pushed on her bike. "Look how strong I am, Mommy. I'm pushing it all by myself."

"Yes, I see that. It must be all that milk you drink."

Once they hit the firmer, wet sand, the girls climbed back on and resumed their afternoon biking adventure, this time riding near the lip of the water. Shawn smiled after them, enjoying the sea breeze. She thought back to the last few weeks.

Upon Veronica's release from the hospital, they'd sat up all night long at the house in Scarsdale talking and crying. Veronica had been shook up and surprisingly honest, telling Shawn she loved her but she couldn't love her like she needed. She'd faced death and she knew the right thing to do. She wanted to do right and she wanted to do right by Shawn. So they'd decided to go their separate ways, and while Veronica hated that, she also confessed that she needed for Shawn to find happiness.

The separation had happened slowly, mainly so the girls could gradually adjust. She had taken her time packing and she'd thought hard about where she wanted to live. Veronica had helped. She'd come to her quietly one evening, handing her a large envelope full of legal forms. She had given Shawn and the girls several million dollars. Through tears, she'd smiled and urged Shawn to find the home of her dreams. She'd also promised to always look after the girls financially. Shawn agreed to let Veronica have visitation. She could see the girls whenever her busy schedule allowed it. Veronica had thanked her.

Out of all the years she had known Veronica, she'd never seen her so humbled, so sincere, and so devastated. The kidnapping had changed her. Truly changed her.

Shawn offered to be there for her, but Veronica politely declined. She'd said Shawn had suffered enough. She found her solace in the arms of Marion Grace. The two were seriously seeing each other. Shawn liked her. She seemed down to earth and understanding. Just what Veronica needed.

She walked on, content with hearing her girls giggle as they rode their bikes through the dunes. She loved this island, and she had purchased a house on the beach three weeks ago, winning shrieks of joy from the girls. She felt at home here, and relaxed. But as she walked into the breeze she glanced at the sea, knowing that something was missing. The island brought her warmth and security and comfort, but it didn't bring her what she longed for. Love.

The sea churned gently, sending its waves of greeting gliding toward shore. She stopped and stared, almost wishing that the water would bring her what she truly wanted. It had been a few days since she had last spoken to Kennedy. They spoke frequently, but Kennedy had been busy, closing up the investigation, making sure it was tied up from every angle. While Shawn had missed her, she had failed to tell her how she truly felt. After the shoot-out with Abigail, she'd retreated a little, a little uncertain about bringing it up with all that Kennedy had to face.

She was in love with her, of that she had no doubt. But was Kennedy in love with her? Would she want a life with her and the girls? She longed for her presence. Wanted her. Needed her. Ached for her.

And now they were free to be together. Truly free. So what was she waiting for?

She lifted her head in surprise as she heard the girls shriek up ahead, hidden by the dunes. Picking up her pace, she called out. The girls sounded excited. One little head bobbed above the sand dune, followed closely by another. The girls were on foot and running toward her with huge grins and giggles.

"Mommy! Mommy!"

"What, what is it?" They collapsed into her legs, bouncing up and down.

"Pirates! Let's play pirates!" Rory exclaimed.

"Yeah!" Kiley joined in.

"Oh, girls. Maybe tomorrow, okay?" She rubbed their heads, hoping they would understand. She felt lonely and her soul cried out for Kennedy. She needed to call her. To tell her the truth. To explain her feelings.

"But—" Rory started.

Shawn glanced up, seeing movement beyond the dunes. She swallowed the lump in her throat as a figure stepped into view. Kennedy moved with confident grace as the wind blew back her thick brown hair. Her jeans were rolled up and her blouse was billowing in the breeze.

Shawn stared in amazement, all but convinced it was a mirage. The woman approached her slowly and the girls continued to jump in excitement. Shawn's blood pumped with heat, awakening her entire body. Her eyes met the golden brown ones before her and she tried to speak but her voice faltered.

"Hi," Kennedy said, a slow grin spreading across her face.

Shawn leaned into her bike, completely captivated by her beauty. She found her voice. "Hi."

"I wasn't sure about coming. I hope it's okay." Kennedy stared into her, slow and steady. She was different. She was confident. Her voice was deep and smooth. Sexy.

"Yes, yes, it's fine."

"We missed you, Kennedy!" Rory declared as she and Kiley moved to hug Kennedy's legs.

"I missed you too." She tousled their hair but her gaze never left Shawn's. "Why don't you guys go see if you can find the treasure?"

The girls jumped up and down and bolted back to the dunes.

"I'll race you, Kiley," Rory said.

Their little legs carried them to where a little flag stuck out of the sand. There they dropped to their knees and began digging.

"Well, you certainly got them going." Shawn said, clinging tightly to her bicycle.

"I needed to be alone with you for a minute."

Shawn swooned a little as the heat continued to rush through her body. "Okay."

Kennedy took a step toward her. "I need to tell you something."

"There's something I need to tell you too."

They both stood in silence for a moment, the wind playing with their hair. Kennedy took another step, and one at a time, she peeled Shawn's fingers from the bike. It fell to the sand. Kennedy licked her lips.

"What is—" Shawn tried.

Kennedy wrapped a strong arm around her waist and pulled her close.

"This," she said, bringing her in for a long, hot kiss.

Shawn fell into her, nearly limp with longing. Her lips were soft and deliciously hot. When her tongue came, the sensation went straight down her spine to pulse between her legs.

She groaned.

The tongue came again. Seeking. Shawn let it, her toes curling in the sand. Her hands tangled in the hair at the base of Kennedy's head. She kissed back, easing her tongue in, playing with Kennedy's.

A groan came. This one from Kennedy. She grabbed Shawn's head, held it as she kissed her harder, deeper.

Shawn responded at once by sucking on her tongue.

"Jesus," Kennedy whispered, finally pulling away. Her eyes danced like the sun off the water. Her cheeks were burning with red desire.

Shawn was melting. Right there. In the sand. "I love you," she said, the words spilling from her mouth.

Kennedy skimmed her thumb over Shawn's lips. She smiled. "I love you."

"You do?" She was breathless and so painfully vulnerable.

Kennedy searched her face. "Of course."

"Of course?"

"I mean, yes. Yes. Couldn't you tell? Keri said it was written all over me."

"No, I couldn't tell. Not for sure."

She stared at her mouth. Longed again for her lips. "You really do?"

Kennedy caressed her face. "Yes, I really do. I'm crazy about you."

Their lips met again. Soft. Hungry. Hot.

The girls ran up from behind.

The women pulled apart, but Shawn couldn't tear her eyes from Kennedy.

"Mommy, we found the treasure!" Kiley said.

"Yeah, yeah, and we got lots of gold." Their little hands were full of chocolate coins.

Shawn finally looked directly at Rory and Kiley. "Okay, good job! How 'bout we go inside and count them?"

"Okay! I bet I got the mostest," Rory said, leading the way.

Kennedy retrieved their bikes and hitched them over her shoulders and Shawn pushed hers.

They walked toward the setting sun.

"Care to come count the bounty?" Shawn asked, her face flushing.

Kennedy smiled. "Wouldn't miss it for the world."

"What about counting your blessings? I plan on doing that a little later on. Want to join me?"

Kennedy fired her a heated, passionate look. "Oh, absolutely."

Shawn laughed, a bit nervous and giddy. Her skin burned from Kennedy's embrace and every cell ached oh so pleasurably as the wind blew against her.

The walk back to the house was dreamlike and she blinked several times, convinced Kennedy would disappear. But to her amazement Kennedy remained and she found herself staring at her muscular calves, the slight sashay of her hips, the tendons in her wrists. The sea breeze carried her scent to Shawn and it was something new. Something tingling and masculine, and she knew it was on her neck and jawline where Kennedy had held her and kissed her. She wanted that scent all over her. She wanted it in her bed and all over her sheets. She wanted it in her mouth. How long would she have to wait to get it?

Kennedy slowed as they reached the two-story beach house. They had just gone inside when the doorbell chimed and Rory and Kiley sprinted, anxious to see who it was. Shawn was calling out for Monty, who was still her main security.

"He took the night off," Kennedy said with a grin. Shawn still seemed confused as Kennedy answered the front door and found Keri and the boys waiting on the landing. Keri waved at Shawn and Kennedy explained, "I thought the girls might want to stay the night at Keri's."

Shawn's face showed genuine surprise and Rory and Kiley began jumping up and down.

Shawn touched their heads in a failed attempt at calming them. She chuckled a little as she said, "Sure."

"Yay!"

Landon and Luke cheered as well and Keri had to speak over them. "Why don't they come now and you can drop their clothes and toothbrushes by later? The pizza is on its way."

There was more jumping and cheering.

"Okay, okay. Go have fun," Shawn said with a smile.

The girls ran out the door and the kids all held hands as they headed down the stone path. Kennedy knew they'd be safe with Keri's security and new nanny.

Silence engulfed the house as Kennedy closed the door.

"You planned all this," Shawn said, looking at her like she was prey.

"Yes."

Shawn stepped toward her. "For how long?"

"A few days."

"Monty knows?" She took another step.

"Yes. He seemed quite happy. And a little relieved."

"Well, you've grown on him. You've grown on us all." She tilted her head and bit her lip in a playful manner.

"Have I?"

"Oh yes."

"Even you?"

"Especially me." She took Kennedy's hand and placed it on her chest. "Right here."

Kennedy felt her heart beating, and her own heart rate kicked up. She swallowed and inhaled deeply.

Shawn touched her face. "Have you missed me?"

"Yes."

There was a brief silence as they stared into one another.

Finally, Shawn asked in a whisper, "Do you want me to kiss you?"

Kennedy could hardly speak. "More than anything." She inhaled again, this time quickly, as Shawn pressed her lips to hers.

Softly. Gently. Tentatively tasting and feeling. Her mouth was so incredibly warm and when her tongue came it felt hot and slick, sending a bolt of fire throughout her entire being. In and out it came, just rimming her lips and then vanishing once again.

Something was building inside Kennedy. A wildfire spreading into every cell.

"I want you," Kennedy said, breathless. Yes, that was it. It was desire. For Shawn. She didn't know how else to say it. She only knew what she wanted to do.

"I—"

But Kennedy silenced her with a deep, probing kiss, moving quickly to pin her against the wall. Her tongue filled Shawn and she was lost in an erotic dance, tongues gliding and seeking.

She felt Shawn heat beneath her touch. Heard her moan with desire. Felt her tongue respond with wild abandon.

And then all rational thought was gone.

There was only need.

To take. To give. To worship. To love.

She leaned into her and attacked her neck, sucking and licking and nibbling.

"Kennedy," Shawn rasped.

"You feel so good," Kennedy said, breathing into her ear. "Better than I ever could've imagined. God, and your skin. I could inhale it for a lifetime."

Shawn's nails dug into her back. She groaned at the sensation, wanting them scratching her bare skin. Her head spun as her superheated blood slammed through her. This was all so new. So crazy. So primal. So damn good.

"Now," she said, sinking her teeth into her neck for a long suck.

Shawn laughed wickedly and inhaled sharply.

"You feel so good too. I can't wait to taste you. Thought about it—oh God—for so long."

The words sent Kennedy into a frenzy. She bit and sucked Shawn's neck and lifted her up so she straddled her waist.

Shawn called out softly in surprise. "Where are we going?"

"I don't know." She hurried across the living room and growled with need as she headed up the stairs. Shawn was laughing softly and licking her ear.

"Don't hurt yourself, Agent Scott."

Kennedy's skin had erupted in goose bumps and her center screamed for mercy. Unable to go any farther, she knelt and set Shawn down at the top of the stairs.

"We didn't quite make it," Shawn said, stroking her cheek.

"Yes, we did." And Kennedy was on her again, crawling up to kiss her and ease her back on the landing. Then she tore open her blouse and assaulted her with hot, hungry kisses leading all the way down to her loose jeans.

"Kennedy," Shawn said, raising her head to look down at her.

But Kennedy kept on, driven. She unbuttoned her jeans and pulled them off quickly. Shawn still had her head raised and Kennedy stared at her for a few long seconds before she lifted her hips and moved her forward, placing her at the lip of the stairs. Then, without missing a beat, she peeled off her panties and tossed them aside. Kennedy bent Shawn's knees and gently set her feet flat on the top step. They were both breathing heavily as Kennedy ran her fingertips softly across the tops of her legs.

"Kennedy," Shawn said again. "I—"

Kennedy waited.

And then, "Hurry."

Kennedy flushed with an insanely hot heat and she lowered herself to lick along Shawn's inner thighs to her center. Once there, her heart hammered in her ears and she gave into that animalistic yearning and forced her tongue inside the smoothly shaved lips until she felt a firm knob of flesh beneath her. Shawn at once came up off the floor with her hips. Her nails clawed at Kennedy's scalp.

"I—Kennedy—"

Kennedy pressed herself harder into her, moving her tongue

heavily in an up and down motion, focused on her clitoris. Her taste was light but stirring, like a distant sea breeze. She couldn't get enough of it. She groaned into her, wanting more.

She eased Shawn's legs farther apart and then used her thumbs to open her up more. She found her clitoris red and waiting, a tiny vein racing with blood just next to it.

Shawn cried out as Kennedy returned her tongue to it, flicking and massaging it, listening to Shawn's cries for direction. She pressed more firmly, causing her to groan deeply, and then she teased it in a hurried motion, causing Shawn to lift her head up and plead for more.

Kennedy kept on, flicking madly, wrapping her arms around Shawn's legs to hold fast to her as she began bucking.

"Kennedy—God, I—oh my God—I—it's coming so fast—I've wanted you so—long—I—"

And then Shawn groaned, madly, deeply, like a creature of the night, tearing at Kennedy's head while her own thrashed back and forth.

She was climaxing. Calling out to the rising moon. Insane with pleasure. Pleasure Kennedy had given her.

Nothing had ever moved Kennedy more.

The moment seemed to last a lifetime. Everything in Kennedy's world froze. Shawn fell still and silent, her flesh throbbing against Kennedy's cheek.

When Shawn raised her head to look at her, her face was scarlet and her eyes were sparkling like crystals. She had a new look to her. One Kennedy hoped to see for all eternity. Like a woman at her most primal and elemental level. A woman pleased but yearning for more. Much more.

"Come on." Shawn stood on shaky legs and led Kennedy to the bedroom. She switched on the gas fireplace and headed for the bed. She looked incredibly sexy in nothing but a long, torn blouse.

"God, you are an unbelievably good lover," Shawn said as she turned and unbuttoned Kennedy's blouse.

"I could've done that forever," Kennedy said, wanting more, a raw new addiction already taking hold of her.

"I know. But now it's my turn."

Shawn helped her step out of her pants and slipped her fingers under her panties to push them down. Then she pushed Kennedy back onto the bed and seared her with a long, hot kiss. "Mmm. Thank God we've got all night." She tugged on Kennedy's lower lip and then dropped to her knees.

Kennedy watched as she opened her up a bit and licked. Kennedy tensed with surprise and then with need as a mad wave of pleasure washed over her. Shawn moved closer, held on to her thighs, and buried her face in her. Her tongue moved wildly and expertly, assaulting Kennedy with slick, firm thrusts.

Nothing had ever felt so good. It was pure primal pleasure.

Truly overcome, Kennedy gripped Shawn's head and tightened her fingers in her short hair. Shawn moaned at this, and stopped to gaze up at her.

"I'm going to do this first. Make you come in my mouth right here on the edge of the bed. Then we're going to crawl into the bed and I'm going to lay you down and ravish you. Act out every fantasy and dream I've had about you."

Kennedy struggled for words. "I need to have you." She didn't know how long she'd be able to wait to taste her again. To feel her writhe beneath her with pleasure again.

Shawn grinned. "We've got all night." She rose and kissed her, once again tugging on her bottom lip. Then she looked deep into her eyes. "Even better, though, we've got eternity."

"We do?"

"Yes, we do."

Kennedy could feel Shawn's breath on her inner thigh. She shuddered with lust and fought the urge to yank her up on the bed, hold her down, and lick her from head to toe. Her desire was powerful and intense—so much so that she couldn't ever imagine stopping.

"I'm afraid eternity won't be enough." She could hardly speak as she cupped Shawn's face.

Shawn smiled and kissed her thighs. She groaned as she edged closer to Kennedy's flesh. "I know what you mean." She looked up at her. "I will never get enough of you, Kennedy Scott."

Kennedy swallowed, her heart melting at the fire in Shawn's eyes. "Nor I you."

"So what do we do?"

Kennedy licked her lips, aching for Shawn's skin, aching for Shawn's mouth to be on her.

"Try," she let out on a whisper. "To get enough." It would be impossible. But oh so worth it.

Shawn stood and eased Kennedy back onto the bed. She stared into her eyes as she crawled alongside her, running her hand down Kennedy's body to her center where she teased at the hairs and slid her fingers into the folds to frame her clitoris.

Kennedy tensed and cried out at the sweet pleasure. Her hips moved.

Shawn's face flushed and she kissed Kennedy hard, tongue swirling. When she pulled away she trailed kisses along her neck and whispered in her ear.

"Okay, baby. Let's try, then."

# About the Author

Ronica Black spends her free time writing works that move her, with the hope that they will move others as well. She is a firm believer that "what does not kill you makes you stronger." Each step she takes in life is a journey meant to be experienced, whether it be a smooth step paved with green grass, or a rocky one marred with boulders. She keeps stepping, keeps writing, and keeps believing that women are far stronger than they think they are. She's an award-winning author with six books currently published by Bold Strokes Books: *In Too Deep*, *Deeper*, *Wild Abandon*, *Hearts Aflame*, *Flesh and Bone*, and *The Seeker*. Several of her short stories appear in the Bold Strokes Books Erotic Interludes series: *Stolen Moments*, *Lessons in Love*, and *Road Games*. She was also published in *Ultimate Lesbian Erotica 2005*.

# Books Available From Bold Strokes Books

**Battle Scars** by Meghan O'Brien. Returning Iraq war veteran Ray McKenna struggles with the battle scars that can only be healed by love. (978-1-60282-129-3)

**Chaps** by Jove Belle. Eden Metcalf wants nothing more than to flee from her troubled past and travel the open road—until she runs into rancher Brandi Cornwell. (978-1-60282-127-9)

**Lightbearer** by John Caruso. Lucifer dares to question the premise of creation itself and reveals that sin may be all that stands between us and living hell. (978-1-60282-130-9)

**The Seeker** by Ronica Black. FBI profiler Kennedy Scott battles ghosts from her past, deadly obsession, and the evil that haunts her. (978-1-60282-128-6)

**Power Play** by Julie Cannon. Businesswomen Tate Monroe and Victoria Sosa are at odds in the boardroom, but not in the bedroom. (978-1-60282-125-5)

**The Remarkable Journey of Miss Tranby Quirke** by Elizabeth Ridley. When love enters Tranby's life in the form of a beautiful nineteen-year-old student, Lysette McDonald, she embarks on the most remarkable journey of all. (978-1-60282-126-2)

**Returning Tides** by Radclyffe. Insurance investigator Ashley Walker faces more than a dangerous opponent when she returns to the town, and the woman, she left behind. (978-1-60282-123-1)

**Veritas** by Anne Laughlin. When the hallowed halls of academia become the stage for murder, newly appointed Dean Beth Ellis's search for the truth leads her to unexpected discoveries about her own heart. (978-1-60282-124-8)

**The Pleasure Planner** by Larkin Rose. Pleasure purveyor Bree Hendricks treats love like a commodity until Logan Delaney makes Bree the client in her own game. (978-1-60282-121-7)

**everafter** by Nell Stark and Trinity Tam. Valentine Darrow is bitten by a vampire on her way to propose to her lover Alexa Newland, and their lives and love are placed in mortal jeopardy. (978-1-60282-119-4)

**Summer Winds** by Andrews & Austin. When Maggie Turner hires a ranch hand to help work her thousand acres, she never expects to be attracted to the very young, very female Cash Tate. (978-1-60282-120-0)

**Beggar of Love** by Lee Lynch. Jefferson is the lover every woman wants to be—or to have. A revealing saga of lesbian sexuality. (978-1-60282-122-4)

**The Seduction of Moxie** by Colette Moody. When 1930s Broadway actress Violet London meets speakeasy singer Moxie Valette, she is instantly attracted and her Hollywood trip takes an unexpected turn. (978-1-60282-114-9)

**Goldenseal** by Gill McKnight. When Amy Fortune returns to her childhood home, she discovers something sinister in the air—but is former lover Leone Garoul stalking her or protecting her? (978-1-60282-115-6)

**Romantic Interludes 2: Secrets** edited by Radclyffe and Stacia Seaman. An anthology of sensual lesbian love stories: passion, surprises, and secret desires. (978-1-60282-116-3)

**Femme Noir** by Clara Nipper. Nora Delaney meets her match in Max Abbott, a sex-crazed dame who may or may not have the information Nora needs to solve a murder—but can she contain her lust for Max long enough to find out? (978-1-60282-117-0)

**The Reluctant Daughter** by Lesléa Newman. Heartwarming, heartbreaking, and ultimately triumphant—the story every daughter recognizes of the lifelong struggle for our mothers to really see us. (978-1-60282-118-7)

**Erosistible** by Gill McKnight. When Win Martin arrives at a luxurious Greek hotel for a much-anticipated week of sun and sex with her new girlfriend, she is stunned to find her ex-girlfriend, Benny, is the proprietor. Aeros Ebook. (978-1-60282-134-7)

**Looking Glass Lives** by Felice Picano. Cousins Roger and Alistair become lifelong friends and discover their sexuality amidst the backdrop of twentieth-century gay culture. (978-1-60282-089-0)

**Breaking the Ice** by Kim Baldwin. Nothing is easy about life above the Arctic Circle—except, perhaps, falling in love. At least that's what pilot Bryson Faulkner hopes when she meets Karla Edwards. (978-1-60282-087-6)

**It Should Be a Crime** by Carsen Taite. Two women fulfill their mutual desire with a night of passion, neither expecting more until law professor Morgan Bradley and student Parker Casey meet again…in the classroom. (978-1-60282-086-9)

**Rough Trade** edited by Todd Gregory. Top male erotica writers pen their own hot, sexy versions of the term "rough trade," producing some of the hottest, nastiest, and most dangerous fiction ever published. (978-1-60282-092-0)

**The High Priest and the Idol** by Jane Fletcher. Jemeryl and Tevi's relationship is put to the test when the Guardian sends Jemeryl on a mission that puts her not only in harm's way, but back into the sights of a previous lover. (978-1-60282-085-2)

**Point of Ignition** by Erin Dutton. Amid a blaze that threatens to consume them both, firefighter Kate Chambers and property owner Alexi Clark redefine love and trust. (978-1-60282-084-5)

**Secrets in the Stone** by Radclyffe. Reclusive sculptor Rooke Tyler suddenly finds herself the object of two very different women's affections, and choosing between them will change her life forever. (978-1-60282-083-8)

**Dark Garden** by Jennifer Fulton. Vienna Blake and Mason Cavender are sworn enemies—who can't resist each other. Something has to give. (978-1-60282-036-4)

**Late in the Season** by Felice Picano. Set on Fire Island, this is the story of an unlikely pair of friends—a gay composer in his late thirties and an eighteen-year-old schoolgirl. (978-1-60282-082-1)

**Punishment with Kisses** by Diane Anderson-Minshall. Will Megan find the answers she seeks about her sister Ashley's murder or will her growing relationship with one of Ash's exes blind her to the real truth? (978-1-60282-081-4)

**September Canvas** by Gun Brooke. When Deanna Moore meets TV personality Faythe she is reluctantly attracted to her, but will Faythe side with the people spreading rumors about Deanna? (978-1-60282-080-7)

**No Leavin' Love** by Larkin Rose. Beautiful, successful Mercedes Miller thinks she can resume her affair with ranch foreman Sydney Campbell, but the rules have changed. (978-1-60282-079-1)

**Between the Lines** by Bobbi Marolt. When romance writer Gail Prescott meets actress Tannen Albright, she develops feelings that she usually only experiences through her characters. (978-1-60282-078-4)

**Blue Skies** by Ali Vali. Commander Berkley Levine leads an elite group of pilots on missions ordered by her ex-lover Captain Aidan Sullivan and everything is on the line—including love. (978-1-60282-077-7)

**The Lure** by Felice Picano. When Noel Cummings is recruited by the police to go undercover to find a killer, his life will never be the same. (978-1-60282-076-0)

**Death of a Dying Man** by J.M. Redmann. Mickey Knight, Private Eye and partner of Dr. Cordelia James, doesn't need a drop-dead gorgeous assistant—not until nature steps in. (978-1-60282-075-3)

**Justice for All** by Radclyffe. Dell Mitchell goes undercover to expose a human traffic ring and ends up in the middle of an even deadlier conspiracy. (978-1-60282-074-6)

**Sanctuary** by I. Beacham. Cate Canton faces one major obstacle to her goal of crushing her business rival, Dita Newton—her uncontrollable attraction to Dita. (978-1-60282-055-5)

**The Sublime and Spirited Voyage of Original Sin** by Colette Moody. Pirate Gayle Malvern finds the presence of an abducted seamstress, Celia Pierce, a welcome distraction until the captive comes to mean more to her than is wise. (978-1-60282-054-8)